Kan Ya Ma Kan
Folktales and Recipes of Syria and Its Ethnic Groups

Kan Ya Ma Kan
Folktales and Recipes of Syria and Its Ethnic Groups

Muna Imady

Edited by

Elaine Imady & Susan Imady

DAYBREAK PRESS

2018

Kan Ya Ma Kan: Folktales and Recipes of Syria and Its Ethnic Groups, was first published in 2019 by:

Daybreak Press | 720 Washington Avenue SE | Minneapolis, MN 55414 | USA
Online: rabata.org/daybreakpress | Email: daybreakpress@rabata.org

Library of Congress Control Number: 2018939996

ISBN: 978-0-9992990-2-9

Illustrations by Alexander Mitchell
Cover design by Sammy Zarka
Book design & typesetting by Neville Blakemore, Jr. & Muhammad Hozien

Printed in USA

CONTENTS

Part I

Folktales from Ethnic Groups in Syria

INTRODUCTION

This introduction is a joint effort written by Muna's mother and sister. We two are the "we" in this piece. In the book, however, all the comments and personal pieces are Muna's alone unless otherwise noted.

We never expected to work on this book. This was Muna's project and we, including Muna herself, expected she would finish it and see it published. Sadly, this did not happen. Muna died twelve days after open heart surgery in an operation that has a low fatality rate of 3 percent. She was working on this book up to days before she died, and we only hope the book is all that she dreamed it would be.

Muna (far left), Susan and Elaine Imady, Damascus, Syria

Muna Imady was born in Damascus in the year 1962 and began writing at a very young age. As a little girl, Muna always wanted to be Queen in the games of make believe with her sister. When Suad, our housekeeper, would playfully call Muna *Malikay bil Tanakay,* Muna would reply, "No, I am *not* the Queen of the Tin Can, I am Muna Imady, a writer and a poet." And indeed, she was. When she first uttered these words, she was perhaps seven years old and we would laugh. But she kept on saying it and, as a teenager, she would post her short poems on the door of her closet. Even then, her imagery was original and striking.

Muna's attachment to her country started early, like her love for writing. As a little child, she observed and remembered everything around her and stored it away: her grandmother's folktales, Damascene sayings, superstitions, habits, and customs. She spent a lot of time with her Syrian grandmother and thus, early on, Muna became aware of the richness of Syrian culture. Perhaps it was at this time that the seeds were planted that made Muna blossom into a dedicated culture preserver.

When she was seventeen, we moved to Kuwait for six years, but Muna preferred to remain in her beloved Damascus with her two aunts and attend Damascus University. Although she would later move to France with her husband Nizar, her homeland continued to take hold of her heart.

The first years of her marriage were spent in France, during which time she had her daughter Nour and her first son, Sammy. She showered us with letters and continued to write stories and poems. When Muna and Nizar came back to Damascus, Muna began writing and publishing Arabic stories for several popular children's magazines.

Around this time, someone suggested to Muna that she consider teaching English. It was a reasonable suggestion since she came from a family of teachers: her parents, her brother, four paternal aunts, and one maternal aunt had all been teachers at one time or another. Her sister, her daughter and three American cousins are presently teachers. It is not surprising Muna turned out to be a born teacher.

She began teaching English to Syrian children at Amideast* and ended up teaching there for ten years until it closed when the American Embassy left. She then taught another five years at a private language teaching center. Muna was a gifted teacher who designed her own curricula and textbooks. As teaching aids, she used hand puppets, games, and skits she created herself. Her classes became renowned for teaching young Syrian children English in an enjoyable and successful way. As busy as she was teaching and raising her three children – her son Kareem was born in 1998 – she never stopped writing.

When the war closed down the language center where Muna taught, she suddenly had time on her hands. She had always been interested in folktales and while teaching at Amideast had gathered folktales and recipes from the parents of her students. Now, Muna conceived the idea of translating these collected folktales and recipes into English, and the result was her first book, *Syrian Folktales*, which was published in 2011.

Muna was a prolific writer and had the astounding drive needed to follow up on her stories - asking her nieces and nephews for feedback, writing the magazine editors who accepted her stories to ask when her stories would be published, and later on requesting family and friends to like and share the stories she wrote on Facebook.

Muna took to the internet and Facebook as though it all been created just for her. She tirelessly promoted her book and made friends with people in different countries who were interested in folktales. Some of her folktales were published in an English

---

* Amideast is a U.S. non-profit organization that works to strengthen mutual understanding and cooperation between the peoples of America and the Middle East.

folktale magazine called *Storylines* in August, 2015 and many of her folktales and other stories were published in the prestigious online magazine, *Wild River Review.*

Her next research project was for a book that would include more folktales from Syria and also folktales from the different ethnic groups in Syria: the Armenians, the Assyrians, the Kurds, the Albanians, the Circassians and other people from the Caucasus, the Turkmens, and the Uzbeks. In Muna's words, these people made up "the patchwork quilt" of Syria.

The idea of including these ethnic groups in her new book was very dear to Muna's heart. Once the war started, she saw her beloved country spiral into sectarianism. She began to look back nostalgically to a time when, as she saw it, Syria had warmly welcomed refugees from different countries and had appreciated the rich diversity they added to the country; a time when Syrians of different backgrounds could be friends. She wanted to celebrate this happier time and make sure it was remembered.

The ethnic section of this book was the most difficult to edit, and at first we thought completing it would be an insurmountable task. Muna had prepared a table of contents so it was clear what she had in mind, but some sections were in the planning stage, many stories and recipes were missing, and some pages were still in Arabic. And yet, since it was so important to Muna, we decided to take up the challenge and keep her book intact as she had intended it.

Muna became fascinated with how folktales travelled - around Syria, to different Arab countries, and also to far-flung countries. In her research, she read hundreds of folktales from many different countries and was always delighted to point out similarities between a Syrian tale and, for example, a Serbian, an Iraqi or an English tale. She wrote, "This is how folktales progress, traveling from one place to another, adding and losing aspects as they move along." The similar themes and archetypes in folktales worldwide demonstrated to Muna how connected we all are.

Muna's original title for this book, the title she chose, was Preserving Syrian Folktales Amid the War. It is noteworthy that the folktales in Muna's first book are on the whole gentle tales where good prevails and all ends well. In sharp contrast, more of the tales she was given for this book "amid the war" are darker and crueler tales, perhaps reflecting the violence of the civil war raging in the country.

Finishing Muna's book has been a positive yet painful project for us this last year. Reading her notes, trying to collect documents from the various computers she worked on, and collecting and translating her Arabic notes made the pain of losing her all the more vivid as we longed to ask her what she meant, how she planned to organize her notes, and where the missing stories or endings or recipes were. On the other hand, harnessing the shock of her loss into finishing a project that meant so much to her gave us purpose and direction, and we can see that working on this book has been a healing experience for us.

It is with bittersweet pride that we present this work of our Muna. So much has been lost in this war, and Muna wanted to save what she could. As the horrific and heart-rending circumstances continue around us, it pleases us to know that Muna's book is proof of and a contribution to the idea of the common human family to which we all belong.

Elaine Imady
Susan Imady
Damascus, Syria
February 2017

A Note About the War

Muna lived on the slopes of the mountain overlooking Damascus. From her home, she had a panoramic view of the city below which, starting in 2012, began to give her a frightening overview of the war. Shells were fired from the top of the mountain behind her home to the outskirts of the city below. Planes roared overhead and she would see the fiery aftermath and smoke. We lived down below in the city, and the constant barrage of bombing and shelling that we heard, Muna not only heard but saw. We are convinced the war aggravated her weak heart and contributed to her death.

The brief notes she wrote on the war in the different muhafazat date from around 2014, and probably none are more recent than 2015. Since the war has continued, her "war bulletins" are frozen in the past. We have not attempted to update them because they offer a glimpse into the world Muna lived in while writing this book.

Publisher's Note

In the magical pages of this book, you will find many passages that employ atypical usages of English. This was done to retain the flavor of the folktales in their original, colloquial Arabic and to facilitate their being read aloud.

In Memory of

Muna with her children, Beirut, September 2015

Muna Imady

February 18, 1962 – April 23, 2016

May God have mercy on her and shower her with His choicest blessings

Part I
FOLKTALES FROM THE MUHAFAZAT

1

DAMASCUS

With the war in Syria entering its fifth year, people's lives in Damascus have changed drastically. There are checkpoints which make it hard to get around. Prices have risen drastically because the Syrian pound is losing its value. Many families have become fractured as relatives leave the country to escape the draft, the shelling, and the instability. The long electricity cut-offs make winter evenings dark, cold, and lonely, and summer days stiflingly hot.

I recently ran into the mother of one of my old students, and she was glad to tell me that my wish to revive folktales in people's lives is coming true in her family, at least. Her children, she said, are no longer able to watch their favorite TV programs or recharge their electronic games and mobiles, so they now begin to spend their evenings with their Tete, grandmother, and actually enjoy her stories, riddles, and games.

She let out a nervous laugh and said that being unable to watch violent films and play violent electronic games had made them less aggressive with each other and more loving and respectful with older people.

FOUR FOLKTALES FROM DAMASCUS

"Once upon a time" is the familiar phrase that begins all English folktales. In Arabic, this magical phrase is, "Kan ya ma kan, fi adeem ez zaman" which literally means, "There was when there was, in an olden time." All the following folktales will begin with the Arabic words, "Kan ya ma kan" to give a little of the flavor of their origin.

THE ROOSTER AND THE FOX

I can still close my eyes and see Tete sitting on her bed in her white nightgown, which matched her wavy white hair, telling this story in her soft but animated voice. Perhaps it was the way Tete told the story that made it so special for me. Perhaps it was the catchy tunes or rhymes in the story, so typical of many Syrian folktales, that mesmerized me as they were repeated over and over. I can see her blue eyes twinkle as she told me this story. Even though many, many years have passed, our giggles still ring in my ears as she imitated the crowing rooster in this folktale.

Kan ya ma kan, a long time ago, a Hen and a vain Rooster lived in a small chicken coop. The Rooster was proud of his voice and loved to crow whenever he was happy. The Hen had many friends and loved to get together with them. One beautiful spring day, the Hen looked outside the chicken coop and saw the Rooster standing on the fence crowing happily. The Hen said to herself, "This is no day to stay home in this small chicken coop. I am going to go on a picnic on this beautiful day."

She prepared some delicious food and drinks for the picnic and put it all in a cloth bundle. Then she hung the bundle on a long stick, jumped astraddle the stick, and headed for the fields, dragging the stick behind her.

The Duck was the first to see the Hen. "Quack, quack, quack," said the Duck as she clapped her wings happily "Where are you going my dear friend?"

"I am going on a picnic," answered the Hen happily.

"A picnic!" said the Duck "Oh, it has been such long time since I went on a picnic."

"Come along then," said the Hen. "Hop on the stick." The Duck quacked with joy and hopped on the stick. Next they passed by the Goose who was busy cleaning her soft, white feathers.

"Honk, honk, honk," honked the Goose. "Where are you going?"

"We are going to the fields to have a picnic," they both said at once.

"Oh, a picnic!" exclaimed the Goose. "I would love to go with you."

"Then hurry up and hop on the stick," said the Hen. The Goose quickly hopped on the stick behind the Duck and they went along until they met a Sheep standing under a tree.

"Baa baa, baa," bleated the Sheep. "Where are you going, dear friends?"

"We are going to the fields to celebrate this beautiful spring day with a picnic," said the Goose. "Come along with us!" The Sheep happily waggled his fat tail and trailed behind them.

All of a sudden, the Rooster came running up to them crowing loudly. "Cock a doodle doo," crowed the Rooster. "Where are you heading on this beautiful spring day?"

"We are going on a picnic," they all answered at once.

"A picnic!" said the Rooster. "What a good idea! I am going to come with you."

"No, no," said the Hen, "You cannot come with us. You will crow and crow as you always do and the sly Fox, Abu Hossain, will hear you and eat us all up."

The Rooster retorted, "I am coming with you, and don't worry, I won't crow."

"You must give us your promise not to crow," said the Hen.

"Yes, yes, I promise." said the Rooster.

"Very well then, come along," said the Hen.

So they kept going until they reached a beautiful field with a river running through it. The Hen placed her cloth bundle on the grass, then unwrapped it and arranged the food and drinks on the cloth. They all sat down and ate and drank until they were full.

Soon the vain Rooster said, "Oh, I'm so happy I feel like crowing!"

The Hen said, "But you promised to be quiet!" The animals were horrified by his suggestion and all said:

No please, oh please, don't crow dear Bird!
Your crowing I fear will soon be heard
By the hungry Fox called Abu Hossain
Who will eat us all - not one will remain!

But the Rooster ignored them all and insisted on crowing. "Cock a doodle doo," he crowed loudly, and sure enough, the sly Fox, Abu Hossain, suddenly appeared! He smacked his lips and then seized first the Hen, then the Duck, and then the Goose with his sharp fangs and swallowed them one by one. Then he gobbled up the poor Sheep.

The moment the Fox appeared, the Rooster flew towards a tree and perched on a branch, still crowing. The Fox longed to eat the Rooster as well, so he decided to trick the Rooster down with sweet talk:

> Come down from the tree
> Come closer to me,
> With diamonds I'll dress you,
> With pomegranates feed you,
> If you'll come to me.

The Rooster strutted happily on the branch and said:

> No, no, I won't come down!
> No, no, I won't come down!

The sly Fox, Abu Hossain, tried his luck again:

> Come down, come down my dearest one
> I'll spoil you and treat you like my son.

But the Rooster kept flapping from one branch to another and sang over and over:

> Burst, burst, Abu Hossain
> My meat is full of fat.
> Burst, burst, Abu Hossain
> And you'll never eat any of that!
>
> Burst, burst, Abu Hossain
> My meat is full of fat.
> Burst, burst, Abu Hossain
> And you'll never eat any of that!

Abu Hossain was very frustrated by the Rooster, who kept teasing him and flapping from branch to branch as he sang. In fact, the Fox became so frustrated that all at once – he really did burst! His stomach popped open and out came the fowls one by one, followed by the Sheep, looking very frightened. "How dark it was inside the stomach of the Fox!" said the Duck.

Then the Hen turned on the vain Rooster and scolded him furiously for crowing and not keeping his promise and not listening to them. The Hen said, "See what happened to us as a result of your crowing! I will never, ever take you with me on a picnic again!"

My sister Susan always said she would never forget Tete telling how the hen scolded the rooster and told him she would never take him on a picnic again. Tete would say that solemnly with laughing eyes, and Susan loved this ending. She thought it was a nice twist that the vain rooster was told off by the hen.

His Mother was Well Pleased with Him

In the early twentieth century, one of the well-known prayers Damascene mothers would offer for their children was, "If you pick up a handful of earth, may it turn to gold." Among these mothers was my Tete. Every time she was pleased with my father she would raise the palms of her hands to the heavens and pray that the earth would turn into gold as soon as my father touched it.

Three years after the death of Tete, my father became the Minister of Economy and, one year later, new bills were issued for the Syrian currency. He and the governor of the Central Bank were asked to add their signatures to the paper bills, in accordance with the law. As my father signed the bills, he remembered his mother's prayer. Worthless paper was turning into money at the stroke of his pen. Although it has been fifteen years since my father left the cabinet, the bills that he signed are still valid.

The wrinkled old woman was thrilled when my son, Kareem, gave her his seat on the bus. She looked me in the eye and softly said, "May Allah be pleased with your son. There aren't many good-hearted boys these days." Then she said in her sweet Damascene accent, "Always be pleased with your son. It will open up closed doors for him wherever he goes." She tied a knot in her small scarf and looked up at my son who was standing near us and said to him, "I'll tell you a story of a man whose mother was always pleased with him and how it made him the most successful young Merchant in Damascus."

Kan ya ma kan, in the olden days, a group of Damascene Merchants were sitting together amusing themselves by bragging about their successful business ventures. Then one of them sighed and said, "Every business I tackle is successful because my mother was always well pleased with me. Yet, somehow, I wish I could experience failure just once in my life!"

His friends all laughed at this strange wish and one of them said, "If you really want to fail, you should buy a lot of dates and go to Iraq where there are plenty of cheap dates. No one will buy any dates from you and you will lose for sure."

The Merchant took his friend's advice. He bought all the dates in the market and traveled to Iraq. When he arrived in Baghdad, the whole city seemed in a state of confusion. The town criers of the King roamed the streets announcing, "He who finds the lost ring of the Princess will marry the Princess!"

All the Merchants locked their shops to search for the ring in the outskirts of Baghdad. They were in such a hurry that they forgot to take food with them. The Damascene Merchant curiously followed them.

As the hours passed, the Merchants got hungry and there was nothing for them to buy but the dates from the Damascene

Merchant's caravan. Every date he had was sold. Again, this Damascene Merchant proved to be successful.

The King of Iraq heard about the successful Damascene Merchant and was curious. He wanted to meet him and asked to be taken to him.

"What is the secret of your success?" asked the king.

The Merchant smiled, bent down to the ground, and picked up a handful of earth. He said, "My mother was so well pleased with me that she prayed the earth would turn into gold as soon as I touched it."

The King looked at the hand of the Merchant and couldn't believe his eyes. There was the golden ring of the Princess, glittering in the sun!

"You have found the Princess's ring!" said the king. "Your reward, my son, will be the hand of my daughter in marriage."

The Merchant smiled and thanked God that his mother had always been well pleased with him.

THE FOOLISH WOMAN

This story is from my daughter's friend, Yesra. As she remembered her Tete acting out every one of the silly actions of the foolish woman in this story, she said, "How peaceful and pleasant were those days."

Kan ya ma kan, in a time long past, a woman and her husband lived in a very small house in a poor neighborhood. This woman was so naïve and foolish that everyone forgot her real name and just called her 'Foolish.'

One day, Foolish visited her rich cousin and was taken by the shiny gold bracelets encircling her cousin's chubby arms. When her husband came home, she told him about the visit to her cousin and said, "I want you to buy me gold bracelets like my cousin has."

"Tomorrow, I will buy you two gold bracelets," said her husband.

She was overjoyed and it didn't occur to her foolish mind that her husband didn't have enough money to buy her even brass bracelets.

The next day, she looked at her thin, bony arms, bit her lower lip, and said, "I need plump arms like my cousin to wear my gold bracelets." Just then, she heard a bee flying near the fig tree.

"I have a great idea!" Foolish thought. "I can get chubby arms by letting the bees sting my arms!" So she climbed up the fig tree and reached out to the beehive. Once she put her hands inside of it, swarms of angry bees attacked and stung her. The tree branch broke and she fell to the ground. Although she was hurt, she was happy since at last she had chubby, swollen arms ready for the gold bracelets.

To her great disappointment, her husband returned home without the gold bracelets.

"Don't worry, dear wife," he said. "Tomorrow I will buy you gold earrings!"

"Aha," she thought, as she remembered her neighbor's big flat earlobes with the gold earrings hanging from them. "Gold earrings are much nicer than bracelets!"

The next morning, Foolish passed by her neighbor who was grinding grain with mill stones. She touched her narrow ear lobes and thought how nice if she only could stretch them so that the gold earrings would show to the best advantage.

"Good morning, my dear neighbor," she said. "Could you please help me stretch my narrow earlobes?"

"What do you mean by that?" asked the neighbor.

"I mean, I need your help in stretching my earlobes with your mill stones," said Foolish.

The neighbor thought it was a crazy idea, but she felt sorry for Foolish and pressed each of her ear lobes with the mill stones. As a result, Foolish wound up with swollen red earlobes that were ready to receive the gold earrings.

That night, her husband came back home without the promised gold earrings. This time, Foolish was very hurt. "I'm leaving the house!" she shouted. "I will not return until you apologize!"

She ran to the cemetery and sat down between the graves of her mother and father and told them what had happened as tears streamed down her face.

Suddenly, a big cat came to her and mewed. She thought her husband had sent the cat to apologize to her.

"Go away," said Foolish, as she chased the cat away. "Tell my husband he must send me a more distinguished animal to win my heart again!"

Next a dog came to her and barked, but she pushed it away, too.

Then a big camel appeared, decorated with beautiful beads and loaded with sacks. Foolish was taken by it. "Now I'll accept your apology, my dear husband," she cried out happily, as she led the camel back to her house.

When she arrived home, her husband was very pleased to see the camel and knew right away that the stray camel belonged to the Sultan. To his delight, the sacks were full of gold coins and jewelry. The husband decided to keep the treasure and hid the camel and the sacks in his storage room for the night.

The next morning, before he left the house, he said to his wife, "Keep your eye on the outside door and guard it with your life. I have heard that black crows are plucking out the eyes of women!"

Foolish stayed home until she heard the Sultan's drummers beating their drums as they marched in the street. She was so excited that she wanted to leave the house and see the drummers, but she remembered that her husband had warned her to guard the door and not leave it. Again, the sounds of drums filled the air and now she heard the Sultan's herald calling out in the street.

She didn't want to disobey her husband's words, so she undid the front door, carried it on her head, and followed the drummers.

The neighbors all laughed to see Foolish carrying her front door, but she didn't seem to care.

"What is going on?" asked Foolish. "What is the Sultan's herald announcing?"

The neighbors said to her, "The Sultan's camel, which was loaded with gold, strayed from the royal caravan yesterday. Whoever finds it will be rewarded."

Foolish threw the door to the ground and ran towards the herald and cried out, "Follow me! Follow me! I have the Sultan's camel!"

The Sultan's men followed her, took the camel, and rewarded her with one of the gold sacks.

When the husband came home, he was a little disappointed that the camel had been returned to the Sultan, but was very happy with the sack of gold.

He bought a new house, a shop for himself, and gold bracelets and earrings for his wife. Then they lived happily ever after.

Hanna and Manna

Several of the old women who visited my Khaleh (Auntie) Kowthar on her monthly reception day loved to smother me with kisses and pinch my round cheeks. How I disliked this! I would rush past the reception room so they couldn't pull me in.

However, I have nice memories of some of the old women who would sit gossiping and telling interesting stories at these receptions. One story which left an impression on me was about a man with two wives; a cautionary tale. How the old women in the reception room would gloat over the man's misfortune!

Kan ya ma kan, a long time ago, lived a certain old man who had two wives. Hanna, his first wife, was fifty years old and Manna, his second wife, was twenty years old. Despite their great jealousy of each other, he tried his best to treat them equally, but it was not easy. Whenever the old man visited his older wife Hanna, she would pluck the black hairs of his beard and say, "Oh dear husband, you look so wise with a grey beard!"

On the other hand, when he visited his younger wife Manna, she would pluck the grey hairs of his beard and say, "Oh dear husband, you look so handsome with a black beard!"

One day, the old man looked in the mirror and found out that he had no beard left at all!

He cried out in despair saying, "Between Hanna and Manna, my beard has vanished!"

This has become a saying meaning if you take conflicting advice, you will get lost.

MEMORIES OF BYGONE DAYS

THE SONG OF THE *NAOURA*

Back in the early twentieth century, Tete was a young mother living with her in-laws in a big house in the Damascene area called Afif. On the nearby river Tora, there was an old waterwheel, a *naoura,* which filled the night with its mournful groans and moans.

I was told by my aunt, Khaleh Lamat, that Tete sang this song in the late evenings to the tune of the sounds from the groaning waterwheel while she sewed for her young children:

> I heard the groaning of the *naoura,*
> Its groans captured my mind.
> The *naoura* groans against the water,
> While I groan for my precious love.

THURSDAY RITUALS

When I was a very little girl, every Thursday I had what we called an Arabic Bath. The bathroom contained an *azan*, a water heater that operated on kerosene, a stone basin and a small low wooden bench just a few inches above the floor. It had no toilet. My aunt, Khaleh Riad, would sit me on this wooden bench and lather my hair with a green cake of soap made of olive oil and bay leaf. Three times she would rub my head with it until it produced a rich lather and then rinse it out. Squeaky, to my aunt, meant clean. "Hear how it squeaks? Now that's what I call clean." At this point my oldest aunt, Khaleh Kowthar, would bring me a tangy sandwich of *zatar*

13

and ma'ood (thyme and apricot jam) to eat in the bathroom while my Aunt Riad scrubbed me with a *kees aswad* (a rough black mitt used as a washcloth) which peeled away the dermis and left my skin smooth and rosy. Meanwhile, the hot and cold faucets in front of us filled the *jirin* (the stone basin), overflowed onto the stone tile floor and down the drain. The bathroom would be filled with a dense steam that made it all seem dreamlike. Next, my aunt would lather soap on a *leefay* (sponge) and go over my body with it. Last, she would fill a *taseh* (copper bowl) from the stone basin, rinse away the soap suds and wrap me in a towel. I greatly enjoyed this weekly ritual, so different from my daily western bubble baths in a tub.

After the bath, I would retire to Tete's bedroom where I'd sit on her lap while she patiently dried and combed my hair with a black, wide-toothed comb. As Tete combed my hair, she sang a traditional hair combing song:

> Aw ha, oh hair of Muna like snippets of gold
> Aw ha, oh hair of (any cousin) with bird droppings on it
> La la la la la la leesh

Then bathed, dressed, and combed, it was finally story time.

EVERY FAMILY HAS A STORY

Passing down stories from one generation to the next has long been a family tradition in the Arab World. Tete, my Syrian grandmother, not only spun folktales from the dark shadows of the night, but she also knitted together memories of the family into wonderful stories. Regardless of how many times they were told by her, they never failed to fascinate us. One favorite of mine was about my father and the "notable Christian doctor."

Tete always began the story by reminding us that Muslims an Christians had lived peacefully together in Damascus for many centuries.

But first, to give the background to this story, here is an adapted version of what my mother wrote about it in her book *Road to Damascus*.

In the 19th century, economic friction first arose between Muslims and Christians in Damascus with the arrival of the European powers. European Merchants preferred to trade with local Christians and Muslims felt the reform policies of 1839 benefitted only the Christians. In addition, the government granted privileges to some European countries and gradually, these European countries conferred honorary citizenship on Christian Merchants so they also benefitted from such privileges. The Christians became richer and the Muslims poorer, and their relationship deteriorated. Also, imported goods put some local factories out of business. Unemployed workers and hungry citizens turned against the rich elite class, which they perceived to be mostly Christian and, as a result, mob violence broke out.

The massacre of 1860 began in May with an attack on the Christians within the walls of Damascus. Christians outside the walls, where they held no economic advantage over the Muslims, were not attacked, so it seems the motives behind the mob's rage were economic, not religious.

Of course, this does not justify the terrible bloodshed and destruction that took place. If the Turkish Governor had acted quickly, he might have stopped the people who took advantage of the absence of any authorities to begin looting, burning and killing.

Many Damascene notables tried to rescue Christian

families and among them were ancestors of the Imadys: Mohammed Effendi Imady and his cousin Abdullah Effendi Imady, who both opened their households and offered shelter, food, and protection to the Christians.

It is against this background that Tete's story of the notable Christian doctor should be understood.

As we all gather around Tete's bed, her sweet face glows and her light blue eyes twinkle as her wavy white hair blows across her face. She straightens her back, sits cross-legged, and begins telling us the story:

> I was married in the year 1912 at the age of 14 and, due to the wide-spread famine and disease during World War I, we had only one child, Saddadeen. He was blond, blue eyed, intelligent, and kind hearted. Every time he saw I was tired, he promised to build me a castle when he grew up, and get me servants and whatever I wanted. It was a terrible blow for me when he caught scarlet fever and died at the age of seven." Tete pauses as she wipes the tears running down her cheeks. "It really broke my heart. Then I had another little boy who only lived a few months.
>
> After that, I had six girls, one every year until, at last, your father Mohammed was born. All the family rejoiced on this happy day, and we vowed to take good care of this child.
>
> Unfortunately, when Mohammed was two, one of his sisters tried to carry Mohammed and he slipped from her arms and broke his leg. I took him to the best doctor in town, a very well-known Christian doctor, to set the bone. When the doctor finished putting Mohammed's leg in a cast, I took out some money to pay him and was shocked that he refused to take it.

When I asked him why, the doctor told me it was because of a promise he'd made to his father when he first became a doctor. Again, I asked him why.

He said, "My grandparents took refuge in the Imady family home during the massacre of 1860. Grandmother was pregnant at the time, and my father was actually born in the Imady house. Because of their merciful hospitality, when I became a doctor my father made me promise to never take money for medical treatment from any member of the Imady family for as long as I practiced medicine."

Tete added, "The doctor was so clever that your father's leg healed perfectly and never caused him any problem in the future."

Tete would shake her head every time she ended the story and say, "This is the real spirit of our city Damascus, and this is how we were brought up - to care for one another."

IN SEARCH OF A *HAKAWATI* (STORYTELLER)

The old city of Damascus never fails to enchant me with the sweet scent of jasmine lingering in its ancient streets and its buildings soaked in antiquity. As I pass by the Umayyad Mosque, the muezzin's voice drifts across the air, calling the Noon Prayer. People crowd at the mosque's door and I manage to slip through them and into the twisting alleyways toward al Nofara, one of the oldest cafes in Damascus, with the mission of investigating whether a storyteller still exists.

The café is empty of the lively tourists that once filled the place with laughter. Now, only older men and women sit and smoke *nargilehs* and sip tea.

Sadly, I find that the famous storyteller, Rashid Hallak, died the year before. He was replaced by another storyteller named Ahmad Laham in the year 2012. It is lunchtime and the only ones in the café are the waiters, who are not able to answer the questions I ask. So I move around the empty chairs, remembering the last time I visited the place with my late aunt. I was not able to stay for a long time then because my little son was getting into everything and imitating the *hakawati*.

That was the first and last time I saw the *hakawati*, Rashid Hallak. He was sitting on a raised platform dressed in his traditional Damascene striped shirt, baggy pants, and red fez. In his hand he held an old book as he eloquently described scenes from the tale of the pre-Islamic hero, Antar, the son of a black slave woman. Antar was famed as a poet and a courageous fighter who fought for his beloved, the beautiful Abla.

On my way out of the café, I suddenly hear someone call me. Looking around, I see a middle aged woman sitting with an elderly man and woman.

"Muna!" she says. "You still look the same as you did in your teens!" I bite my lower lip and feel it is awkward to ask her name. Unfortunately, I don't remember her and am embarrassed to ask who she is. I assume she is an old schoolmate.

"I heard you asking for information about the *hakawati*," she says cheerfully. "My father once lived in this neighborhood and used to come with his father to hear the storyteller. If you want, he can share his memories with you."

My face brightens and I can hardly believe my good luck. "That would be so kind of you," I say, addressing her father as I pull out a chair and sit at their table.

Her father smiles and introduces himself, then says, "Two centuries ago, the *hakawatis* were found in every Syrian coffee shop. Then, when television invaded the coffee shops in the 1960s, the *hakawatis* began to disappear.

Only men went to hear the hakawati's stories after the evening prayers, while women might gather at home and listen to stories told by the elderly women among them.

The *hakawati's* chair was on a high platform and he would be surrounded by men drinking coffee and tea as he told a story, a *hikaya*, a word which, like *hakawati*, is derived from the verb *haka* meaning "to narrate" or "to tell."

The stories he told were the romances of the chivalrous Antar, the heroic warrior-poet and nomad of pre-Islamic times, and the epic adventures of Baybars, a Mamluk Sultan who ruled Egypt and Syria in the thirteenth century. He also told of the fierce battles and adventures of the Banu Hilal, an ancient tribe of North Arabia.

Syrians adored the story of Antar because he represented the ideal Arab hero with pure Arab characteristics.

My friend's father takes a sip of his dark tea and says, "The *hakawati* began his story with the usual phrase, 'My dear gentlemen, pray for our generous Prophet.'"

The audience would respond, "Peace be upon our Prophet Mohammed. May he be embraced with grace and peace."

Then, the *hakawati* would hold his old, worn-out book and start reading the poetic and stylish words, raising and lowering his voice according to the events taking place in the story and the heroic act he was describing. Eventually, the café echoed with joyful cheers.

The *hakawati* had a great ability to both narrate and act. He told his story in an expressive way, using his sword and cane to act out the story and reciting beautiful poetry to charm his audience.

He was also a plotter who knew how to draw his audience into the story from beginning to end. Both the *hakawati* and the audience were interactive parties in the events of the story.

The old man came to a stop and took a long puff of his *nargileh,* then grinned as he remembered the long-ago events that took place in the café.

As the story was told, the audience in the coffee shop divided into two parties, each supporting a main character in the story. They would get into verbal fights which sometimes escalated into physical fights, especially when the story was about Antar.

The *hakawati* devised ways to end his story at an event in which the hero was in trouble. If the chapter of the story ended with Antar locked behind bars, the café would turn upside down and sometimes the two parties would break the chairs and tables. Others might go and knock on the *hakwati's* door, demanding he read the next chapter so as to free Antar. People who supported Antar would decorate the neighborhood when the *hakawati* reached the part of the story where Antar got married.

Suddenly, the ground violently shakes. I look around and wonder whether the café customers of the past have come back to life and are taking revenge for their hero by destroying the place.

My friend laughs nervously at the explosion and says, "And the 'music' continues to play."

I hear the siren of an ambulance from a distance and return to reality.

"I guess I must leave," I say as I thank my friend and her parents. My friend gives me a warm goodbye and I leave feeling guilty and still wondering about her name.

Three Damascene Recipes

Fatoush bil Baitanjan — Eggplant Salad

Ingredients

    4 medium tomatoes

    1 bunch parsley

    1 loaf of pita bread cut into small pieces

    3 to 4 cloves garlic

    4 small eggplants

    Salt and pepper to taste

Method

    Dice tomatoes and chop parsley

    Peel and slice eggplants

    Fry bread in 3 tbsp olive oil and drain on paper towels

    Fry sliced eggplants

    Mash eggplants with garlic in mortar

    Place eggplant mixture, diced tomatoes, and parsley in large salad bowl

ɔsp lemon juice

ɔlive oil

Salt and pepper to taste

Add dressing to salad and toss

Top with fried pita bread

Kusa Mahshi — Stuffed Zucchini

Ingredients

1 ½ kilo zucchini (kusa), cored

Ingredients for stuffing

½ to 1 cup rice

½ kilo minced lamb

1 tbsp *usfor* (safflower)

1 tsp salt, ¼ tsp pepper

2 tbsp melted butter

Method

Mix ingredients well and stuff kusa loosely. Shake stuffing down lightly and leave room for rice to expand

Ingredients for sauce

½ kilo tomatoes, peeled and cut

2 bouillion cubes

1 tbsp butter

½ cup tomato paste

Salt and pepper to taste

Water to cover

Method

> Bring sauce to a boil. Add stuffed kusa and enough water to just cover them.
>
> Stir occasionally and simmer covered about 1 hour.

SLEEKA — A PORRIDGE

Sleeka is traditionally made to celebrate the appearance of a baby's first tooth. The porridge is passed out to relatives, friends, and neighbors.

Ingredients

> 1 cup whole wheat grain/berries
>
> 4 cups water
>
> ¾ cup sugar (or to taste)
>
> Dash salt
>
> 1 tsp anise (optional)

Method

> For less cooking time, soak wheat berries overnight
>
> Discard any stones or straw, then wash berries well
>
> Bring berries, salt, and water to a boil
>
> Simmer until the berries are tender
>
> Add sugar (and anise)
>
> Simmer until berries are well done and liquid has slightly thickened
>
> Adjust sweetness to taste
>
> Serve hot in small individual bowls

JOBAR

Jobar is a municipality of the Syrian capital, Damascus. It was historically a village on the outskirts of Damascus, and now is a suburb of the city. We used to buy *tannour* bread from a bakery in Jobar that was just across the lane from an ancient synagogue. This bakery was hardly a five minute drive from our house. When fierce battles started in Jobar in 2011, the citizens fled for their lives, including neighbors who now live in my parents' building. Battles are still being fought there, and the town has been reduced to rubble.

TWO FOLKTALES FROM JOBAR

THE BAD TEMPERED FARMER

The following stories were given to me by neighbors in my parents' building – two sisters from Jobar, Khuloud and Rama. Khuloud's face glowed as she told me the following folktale from her beloved village, a place she can see from her balcony but can only visit in her dreams.

As Khuloud told the following folktale, I remembered an American folksong my mother used to sing to us when we were children called "The Old Man in the Wood." There is a striking resemblance between the Syrian folktale and the American folksong my mother used to sing to us; yet another example to me of how similar people are despite their geographical, historical, and cultural differences.

Kan ya ma kan, in a time long past, there lived a farmer named Abu Sayah and his wife Umm Sayah in a little village named Jobar.

24

They might have been very happy if only the farmer hadn't been very bad tempered. Abu Sayah complained about everything his wife did.

Whenever he returned home from his farm, he would criticize the food and the house and would say, "You women can't do anything right! You spend your day visiting neighbors and gossiping while we men have to work so hard."

One evening, while Abu Sayah was complaining, Umm Sayah smiled and said, "I have a great idea! I'll go out tomorrow and work in the farm, and you can clean the house, milk the cow, feed the chickens, and cook the food."

Abu Sayah loved the idea and agreed right away, assuming he would have a nice vacation.

The next day, Umm Sayah woke up in the early morning to work in the fields and left her husband to do the housework.

Abu Sayah grinned as he watched Umm Sayah walk towards the fields, and happily carried the bag of grain to the chicken coop. The chickens flapped their wings in delight, hopped out of their coop, and scurried out into the yard as Abu Sayah threw them some grain.

Suddenly, the large rooster flew down from the fence, eyed Abu Sayah suspiciously, and ran at his back and pecked him, ripping his *sherwal* (trousers). Abu Sayah gasped out loud and ran into the house to change his clothes.

Dressed in another *sherwal*, Abu Sayah decided to bake some bread. He lit the *tannour* in the backyard, took a ball of dough that his wife had prepared in the early morning, patted it and laid it on a small pillow. Then, holding the pillow, he slapped the dough on the inside wall of the mud brick oven. In a few minutes, he lifted it out. Abu Sayah was very pleased with himself, but as he was slapping the next piece of dough in the *tannour*, the cow

25

came galloping towards him, mooing. While Abu Sayah tried to push it away, the bread got burned. He grabbed a pail and ran after the cow to milk it, but the cow kicked him and the pail fell on top of his head.

"I'll take care of the bread and the milk afterwards," said Abu Sayah to himself. "Now I must think of lunch."

So he took the pail off his head to draw water from the well and filled the cooking pot. As he bent down to light the kitchen stove, he found there was no firewood.

By now the poor man was exhausted, but he didn't want to admit failure. He climbed up the ladder to get some wood from the storage room, but the cat followed him. He lost his balance as the cat jumped near him, and he fell off the ladder.

At that moment, Umm Sayah came into the kitchen and saw Abu Sayah lying on the floor crying out desperately, "Help! I can't move!"

Umm Sayah ran to her husband and helped him walk to his bed. "What on earth were you trying to do?" she asked.

"I couldn't do anything right!" he said. "I swear, I'll never criticize you again."

Ever since that day, Abu Sayah works happily in his fields while Umm Sayah takes care of the housework, and Abu Sayah is no longer bad-tempered.

As the American folksong puts it, "He swore by all the leaves on the trees/ And all the stars in the heavens/ His wife could do more work in a day/ Than he could do in seven!"

The Two Brothers

This tale is from Khuloud's sister Rama.

Kan ya ma kan, in days gone by, there were two brothers who lived in a village; one was very rich and one was very poor. One day, the pregnant wife of the rich brother went to visit her sister-in-law, the wife of the poor brother. The rich family had four girls and the poor family had four boys.

The poor brother's wife told her sister-in-law that she would pray to God to bless her with a boy this time, and the wife of the rich brother said, "If I have a boy, I will slaughter a lamb, cook it, and bring it to your home to share it with you and your family. Time passed and the rich brother's wife gave birth to a boy. She kept her promise and slaughtered a lamb, cooked it, and took it to her sister-in-law's family, and they ate the lamb together.

When the rich brother heard about this, he asked the poor brother to return the lamb. His brother replied that it had been eaten. "Then you must pay for it," said the rich brother.

"I have no money to pay for it," said the poor brother.

"Then I will take you to Judge Qaraqosh and file a suit against you," said the rich brother. The two brothers set off to the city to find the Judge and each one brought lunch wrapped in a cloth. When they got to the city, the rich man sat in front of a very nice house and began eating his lunch, which was full of meat and sweets and all good things, while the poor man sat in front of a wall by a simple house. He looked at his brother's food as he ate his bread and olives. A pregnant woman came out of the house with a craving for his simple meal and asked to share it. He shouted loudly at her saying, "You want to eat a poor man's food? Look at my brother's lunch!"

His loud shouts caused the pregnant woman to miscarry. The husband of the woman appeared and he was furious. He shouted, "You caused my wife to lose her baby after ten years of waiting for her to have a child! I am taking you to Judge Qaraqosh to sue you!"

So all three men set off for Judge Qaraqosh. On the way, the poor man got tired and upset. He asked himself, "How can I face the Judge with two people against me and one is even my brother?" He began to cry and life looked bleak.

The three men arrived at a hotel and the poor man went to sleep on the roof because he had no money for a room. During the night he said to himself, "I don't know what the Judge will do to me. They are all against me and suing, me and I don't have any money to give them." He decided to throw himself from the roof, and this is what he did. However, he didn't die. He landed on someone passing in the street and instead, killed him. The brother of the dead fellow grabbed the poor brother and said, "You killed my brother! I am going to report this to Judge Qaraqosh!"

When they arrived at the court of Judge Qaraqosh, the three men presented their complaints. First, the rich brother said, "My brother owes me the price of a lamb which he ate when my only son was born." The Judge said to the rich brother, "You must give your son to your brother or pay him a fine of 200 golden pieces."

"Give him my only son – never!" said the rich brother, so he paid the fine.

Then the Judge said to the husband of the woman who miscarried, "Leave your wife with this man until she is pregnant or pay him a fine of 200 golden pieces. He paid the fine and left.

To the man whose brother was killed the Judge said, "Go on the roof of the hotel and throw yourself on the man so you may kill him or else pay him a fine of 200 golden pieces. So he paid and left.

The poor man happily pocketed the 600 golden pieces and hurried home to surprise his wife.

There are many Arab folktales about the bizarre sentences of Judge Qaraqosh. In the chapter on the Muhafaza of Deir ez Zor you will find two more stories that feature Judge Qaraqosh, and there you will learn some interesting information about this Judge.

A TRUE STORY: THE HYENA WHO ATE THE HALAWA PEDDLER

Mr. Omar al Ibish, the grandnephew of the famous Syrian Hunter, Hussein al Ibish, generously told me many stories of his great uncle's hunting adventures in both Africa and Syria. This story particularly interested me because I had heard people talk about "the hyena that ate the halawa peddler," but never realized it was a true story.

During the time of the French Mandate, Jobar consisted of orchard groves and farm land. Most of the houses then were traditional mud brick buildings, and most Damascene sweets were prepared in these households and sold to stores in the city. Among the sweets made in Jobar was *halawa*, or halva, a sweet made from sesame oil paste.

One summer day, sometime during World War I, a young man walked the streets of Jobar selling *halawa*. He carried the large tray of *halawa* on his head and, as it was a very hot afternoon, the young man got very tired. He sat down to rest and munch on a bar of *halawa*, and soon fell asleep in the hot sun.

During World War I there were food shortages all over Syria and not only were the people hungry, but wild animals as well. When the young man was sound asleep, a hungry hyena came sniffing around in broad daylight and was overjoyed to see the young man deep asleep. The hyena leaped on the young man and,

29

before he realized what was happening, he was killed and eaten by the hungry hyena.

The shocking story of the hyena that ate the *halawa* peddler spread quickly from Jobar to the city of Damascus. Hussein al Ibish heard the story the same day and decided to help the people of Jobar get rid of the vicious hyena before it attacked someone else. He arrived in Jobar the evening of the attack and, since it still was very hot, he decided to sleep in the open air.

"Oh, but the hyena will be roaming around!" said the people.

Don't worry," said al Ibish. "The hyena has a full stomach today. It will come looking for food tomorrow and then it will be well received!"

The next day, as darkness descended upon Jobar, the hyena came back sniffing for something else to eat. Its claws were as long and as sharp as knives, while its teeth were as strong as steel, but most terrifying of all were its eyes. They were bright brown and gleamed malevolently as it spotted al Ibish standing in the dark. The hyena stared at al Ibish who faced it fearlessly and fired at it point blank. The hyena let out a fearsome howl and fell dead on the ground.

In the morning, when al Ibish was served breakfast, he told the people of Jobar of his theory, which later on was scientifically proven - at least according to his grandnephew.

"Wild beasts can sense if a human being is afraid of them," said al Ibish. "The fear factor produces a special smell originating in the liver that no one can sense but the beast itself. This makes the predator feel superior to the person, and thus it will attack him."

This long ago vicious hyena attack was so shocking that this true story has passed into the folklore of Jobar.

A Recipe from Jobar

Moasal Bil Burghol — Meat and Chickpeas with Burghol

Ingredients
- 1 cup chickpeas, soaked overnight then strained
- 1 lb onions
- 1 lb lamb chunks
- 1 tsp pepper
- 1 tsp cinnamon
- 1 tsp ground ginger
- Salt to taste

Method

Boil meat in 4 cups water

Cut onions and add to meat

Add pepper, cinnamon, and ginger to meat

Cook until meat is half done, then add chickpeas

Continue cooking on low fire until done

Ingredients for Burghol
- 1 ½ cups coarse burghol
- 3 cups of water
- 2 tbsp butter
- Salt and pepper to taste

Method

Melt 2 tbsp of butter, then add burghol and stir until it turns medium brown

Add 3 cups of water to burghol

Add salt and pepper, then stir, cover, and cook on medium fire 15 to 20 minutes until water is absorbed. Serve with the meat and chickpeas.

2

RURAL DAMASCUS

The civil war has had a devastating effect on the villages around Damascus. Many have fled the muhafaza, and the destruction is widespread. Battles continue to be fought there, and a whole way of life is being destroyed in this once green and fertile land.

From the many areas that make up this muhafaza, I have only included the Ghouta, Zabadani, Tell, Halboun, Kara, and Yabrud in this section. Every one of these areas has been greatly affected by the ongoing civil war.

THE GHOUTA

The Ghouta was once a green agricultural belt surrounding the city of Damascus and separating the city from the dry grasslands bordering the Syrian Desert. This green belt was a very popular place for city dwellers to picnic, especially in the spring when the fruit trees were filled with clouds of blossoms. I remember many family picnics we had in the Ghouta during happier days.

Before the war, the Ghouta provided the city of Damascus with cereals like maize, green barley, and green wheat; with vegetables and fruits such as plums, apricots, and peaches. It was also famous for its olive and walnut trees.

Sadly, all this has changed. The Ghouta is now a dangerous war zone where people are killed on a daily basis.

I have included folktales from three villages in the Ghouta: Kisweh in the west, and Hamourya and Saqba in the east. Also included is the traditional story of how the west Ghouta village of Arbeen got its name.

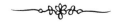

KISWEH

The village of Kisweh is located approximately 8 miles (13 kilometers) south of Damascus, and it used to be one of the most populous towns of the Ghouta. Like the other villages near Damascus, it has suffered greatly in the war.

A FOLKTALE FROM KISWEH

THE ENCHANTED TOAD

Back in the eighties, walking back from the University in the dusk near the Hawakeer – the fields of prickly pears – my friends and I would sometimes hear toads croaking on the river Tora. One day, as we passed this place, my friend, who originally comes from Kisweh, said, "Listen to the toads! It reminds me of a story my Tete told me." And she told us the following story.

Kan ya ma kan, a long time ago, there lived a man and his wife with their only daughter, Laila. It came to pass that the mother fell ill and, after several months, she died.

The father took care of his daughter for awhile, but was soon overwhelmed by the housework and got married.

Unfortunately, Laila's stepmother was a wicked woman who turned her father against her and made her do all the housework.

Years passed and Laila grew into a beautiful young girl. One very cold winter night, Laila heard a strange sound outside. She put her old shawl on her shoulders and went out of the house to find a large toad croaking sadly in the dark and the cold. Laila felt sorry for the toad and carried it into her room.

Her stepmother was horrified by the toad and ordered Laila to get rid of it at once or she would throw her and the toad out of the house in the morning.

Laila didn't listen to her stepmother and left the toad in her room. When her stepmother came into Laila's room in the morning, to her great shock she didn't find the toad but instead, a young and handsome Prince.

"Who is this young man?" screamed the stepmother as she woke up Laila.

Laila opened her eyes and was speechless to see the handsomest young Prince in the world standing by her.

The young Prince approached Laila and gently said, "I am the toad you saved with your kindness. A Ghouleh transformed me into a toad and swore I would never recover my natural shape until a beautiful young girl showered me with kindness. You have broken the evil spell of the Ghouleh by your kindness," said the Prince. "Will you agree to be my wedded wife?"

Laila was so happy she couldn't answer.

Then they both went to the King who gave them his blessing, and they were married and lived many years in great happiness.

HAMOURYA

A FOLKTALE FROM HAMOURYA

THE MYRTLE

Kan ya ma kan, a long time ago, there lived a woman who had no children. She cried all the time and prayed to God to bless her with a girl, even if she were just a myrtle plant.

God answered her prayers and she became pregnant and soon went into labor and gave birth to a small myrtle seed!

The woman was very disappointed, but didn't get rid of the myrtle seed. She planted it in a small pot and watered it daily until it sprouted.

One day she came home from shopping and, to her great surprise, found the laundry washed and the house cleaned.

"Who could have washed the clothes and cleaned the house?" she wondered.

The next day, she left the dishes unwashed and the clothes scattered on the floor and left the house. When she came back, the dishes were washed and the clothes picked up.

The woman suddenly saw the myrtle move left and right and she called out, "Whether you are a human being or a Jinni, appear!"

Suddenly, the most beautiful girl came out of the myrtle and said: "I am your daughter, but I can't always live with you!" The mother was very happy with her daughter, even though she was not human.

One day, while the girl was helping her mother on the roof, the Prince caught a glimpse of her and fell in love with her.

"Go ask for the hand of our neighbor's daughter," he asked his mother. "I shall not marry anyone but her!"

The Prince asked his mother this every day, and his mother's answer always was, "Our neighbor has no children."

Finally, the Queen was fed up with her son's entreaties and went with him to visit the neighbor.

"We have come to ask for your daughter's hand," said the Queen.

"It is a great honor," said the neighbor, "but I am childless!"

The Queen shook her head and said, "My son insists that he has seen your daughter on the roof, hanging clothes."

The neighbor shook her head and said, "I have no child but a myrtle," and she pointed to the pot.

The Prince begged her to sell him the myrtle and offered the neighbor such a high price that she accepted.

Back in the castle, the Prince locked himself in his room with the myrtle and begged the girl to appear.

At last the girl agreed to come out and they were wed. They lived happily together until one day the Prince had to travel abroad.

When the Prince's seven female cousins heard that he had traveled abroad, they decided to take revenge on his wife. They paid a visit to the castle and sat around the myrtle pot and pleaded with her to come out. "We love you, dear Princess," they said. "Come out so we can have fun together."

When the girl was finally convinced by their sweet words and came out of the myrtle, they beat her and scratched her and threw her out in the garden of the castle. The kindhearted gardener found her and took care of her wounds and treated her like his own daughter.

When the Prince came back home, he ran to his room to find the myrtle had withered. "Who came into my room in my absence?" he asked his mother.

"No one!" said the Queen. "It seems that the girl who used to come out of the myrtle is a Jinni."

The Prince was very sad and mourned her absence by wandering around the garden of the castle in silence.

One day, he heard a beautiful voice singing, a voice similar to his wife's voice, and he followed the direction it came from. To his surprise, he saw a woman who resembled his wife disappearing into the gardener's house.

The Prince went to his mother and threatened her. "If you don't tell me what really happened to my wife, I will leave this palace and never return!"

The Queen was afraid to lose her son and told him what had happened. "Your seven cousins were very jealous because you didn't choose one of them to be your wife, so they took their revenge. They beat your wife and threw her out in the garden."

The Prince remembered the young girl who resembled his wife and ran to the gardener, "Who is the young girl who lives with you and your wife?" he asked.

"She is our daughter," said the gardener.

"You are not telling the truth," said the Prince as he drew his sword.

The gardener was scared to death and said, "Yes, she is your wife. I found her bleeding in the garden after your cousins attacked her."

The Prince reassured his wife that no one would attack her again and accompanied her into the castle. Then he sent for his seven cousins, starved his dogs seven days, and set them free to eat his cousins.

And the Prince and his wife lived happily ever after.

This is a shocking ending; perhaps reflecting that jealousy is viewed in the Middle East as the cause of much evil in the world.

Saqba

Saqba is about seven kilometers from Damascus and has about 50,000 inhabitants. It is said that it was named Saqba after one of its camels won a race named Sabak, a name which in time evolved into Saqba. In the past it was known for its furniture industry which was considered among the finest in the Arab World, but the war has put an end to that and the village is in ruins.

A Folktale from Saqba

The Fisherman

Kan ya ma kan, in a long-ago time, a fisherman lived with his wife and his only son Ahmad in a small cottage. The fisherman was very poor, and he and his son could hardly make a living from fishing. They didn't have good luck and usually all they caught with their net was small fish and lots of seaweed.

One day, the fisherman cast his net in the ocean and, to his great surprise, he couldn't pull it in. He called Ahmad to help him, and together they pulled up the net and found that they had caught a whale!

"Go fetch a cart so we can carry it back home," said the fisherman to Ahmad.

Ahmad was about to run and fetch a cart when he heard someone speak to him. He looked right and left but didn't see anyone. Suddenly he heard the voice again and realized it was the

41

whale, speaking like a real human being. "Put me back into the ocean," said the whale. "I have little ones waiting for me!"

Ahmad was astonished, for he had never heard of a talking whale. He freed the whale from the net and pushed it into the ocean, saying, "Swim back to your little ones."

After a couple of minutes the whale reappeared with a thorn plant in its mouth and said, "This is for you, dear Ahmad. Burn it whenever you need me and I'll come to your rescue!"

Ahmad was enchanted with the whale's gift and decided to go on a journey without taking his father's permission.

In the evening, the fisherman called Ahmad but couldn't find him. Then he went back home broken-hearted and grieving for his missing son.

Meanwhile, Ahmad was wandering happily in the wild forests, feeling free. Suddenly, he heard baby birds cry out for help. He looked around and on his right he saw a large snake attacking a nest in a tree.

Ahmad picked up a large rock and threw it at the snake's head, knocking it dead at once. Then he went to sleep under the tree. Soon, he was awakened by the shrill cheeping of many birds swooping over his head. The mother bird had heard from her chicks how he had saved them, and she'd come to thank him with all her friends.

"Thank you so much for saving my baby birds," said the mother bird. "Take this feather and burn it whenever you need help and I'll come to your rescue!"

Ahmad thanked the bird and continued on his journey. Soon, he reached a large field where soldier ants were marching. Ahmad stood still until they passed by.

"Why did you stand still?" the King of the Ants asked him.

"I was afraid I would accidentally crush the ants," said Ahmad.

The King of the Ants was very pleased with Ahmad's answer and plucked a hair from his whiskers and said, "Take this hair and whenever you are in need of me, burn it and I will come to your rescue."

Ahmad thanked him and continued his journey until he reached a fabulous castle surrounded by a great wall decorated with human heads. Ahmad was horrified and asked the guards of the castle for an explanation for the severed heads.

"This land is ruled by a beautiful Queen whom everyone wishes to marry," said the guard. "Unfortunately, she sets three tasks that must be carried out by those who want to marry her. Those who fail are beheaded and their heads are set on the castle wall!"

Ahmad was excited by the challenge and decided to take the risk. He knocked on the door of the castle and introduced himself as the new suitor. The servant led him into the castle where he was introduced to the Queen.

The Queen was the most beautiful young woman he had ever seen. She laughed when she saw him and said, "Go back home, for you are too young to die!"

"Try me!" said Ahmad. "You might be surprised at the things I can achieve."

The Queen nervously tossed her head and said, "Very well." Then she called one of her servants and said, "Lead him to the storage room."

The servant led Ahmad to the storage room where large heaps of different grains were mixed together.

"This will be your first mission," said the servant. "You must separate the rice, the lentils and the burghol into three different piles in a matter of five hours!"

Ahmad sat on the floor and started to separate the grains, but he soon lost patience and took out the bird's feather and burned it. Once the feather was burned, the mother bird flew into the open window, followed by a flock of birds.

No sooner had Ahmad explained his task to the mother bird, than the birds began to separate the grains. In no time, there were three large, neat heaps of lentils, rice and burghol. Ahmad thanked the birds for their help and they flew away out the window.

When the Queen entered the storage room, she couldn't believe her eyes and kept grabbing handfuls of each heap to make sure they were all the same kind.

"Very well, you have achieved your first task," said the Queen. "Now let's move on to the second task. Before sunset, you must find the four thousand pearls which my guards have buried in the sand in the desert."

Then the Queen ordered her guards to take Ahmad out to the desert where the four thousand pearls were hidden under the sand. It was a very hot day, and Ahmad felt exhausted as he dug in the hot sand. Then he remembered the King of the Ants and his promise to come to his rescue when he was in need. So he took out the hair and burned it.

At once, the King of the Ants appeared, followed by his soldier ants marching in formation toward Ahmad.

Ahmad explained his mission to the King of the Ants, and the ants immediately started digging up the pearls with their feet. At the same time, the Ant King and Ahmad counted the pearls and put them in bags. In less than an hour the four thousand pearls were found and packed in bags, ready to be carried to the Queen.

Ahmad thanked the King of the Ants and his soldiers for their kind help and called for the Queen's guards to come help him carry the bags of pearls.

The Queen was again shocked to see that Ahmad had successfully completed his second task before the time she had set, but she was sure he would fail in his third task.

"Very well, my dear young man," said the Queen. "We will go on a sea trip tomorrow, and I will explain your last mission to you. If you can successfully complete it, you may marry me!"

The next morning, Ahmad accompanied the Queen to a large ship, which they boarded. As soon as the ship was in the middle of the sea, the Queen slipped her diamond ring off her finger and waved it in front of Ahmad and said, "This diamond ring has no match in the whole world." Then she threw it into the deep sea and said, "You have five minutes to bring it back to me or you will lose your chance to marry me - and your head!"

"Very well," said Ahmad, "Turn your head and shut your eyes, dear Queen."

Then Ahmad took out the thorn plant the whale had given him and burned it.

Soon the ship was rocked roughly as the whale came swimming towards him.

"I need your help, dear whale," whispered Ahmad. "I need to find a diamond ring which was thrown into the sea in this area."

"Your wish is my command," said the whale, as it dove into the depths of the deep water.

It was only a matter of seconds before the whale reappeared on the surface of the water and spit the diamond ring into Ahmad's hand. Before Ahmad was able to thank the whale, it disappeared into the water.

"You can open your eyes now!" said Ahmad, as he held out the diamond ring. "Make sure this is your diamond ring – the one that has no match in the whole world!"

The Queen took the ring with a trembling hand and was astonished to find it was her very own diamond ring!

"You have proved to be worthy of me," said the Queen. "We shall get married in a few days and you shall become King of this Kingdom!"

Ahmad called for his father the fisherman and his mother to attend the grand royal wedding. Then he built them a beautiful house near the castle and they all lived happily ever after.

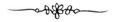

HOW THE VILLAGE OF ARBEEN GOT ITS NAME

The old people here tell a story passed down for generations about how their village got its name. They claim that their village was named "Arbeen" because once upon a time, a long time ago, two Bedouins set up their tent and settled there. As time passed, these two Bedouins generously offered food and water to all the travelers who passed by. Travelers would refer to the place as the place of the Arabieen, meaning the place of the two Bedouins. With time, the name evolved into "Arbeen."

After independence, "Arbeen" was designated as the official name for the city. Arbeen was famous for its fruit trees, especially the apricot trees. From the apricots were produced jam, juice and Kamar al Din, an apricot paste made from dried apricots. From the days of the Ottoman rule until the recent war, Turkish Merchants used to point at good apricots and say, "There is nothing better than these except the Damascene apricot!"

Arbeen, like all the villages of the Ghouta, is now in a war zone.

ZABADANI

Zabadani is a town about forty-five kilometers northwest of Damascus, 1,175 meters above sea level. It is nestled in the center of a green valley and is surrounded by high mountains. It overlooks the plain of Zabadani, a fertile land with thousands of fruit trees bearing delicious apples, cherries, plums, peaches, and pears.

Zabadani was formerly a popular summer resort for tourists, famous for its natural mineral water spring, cool climate, green orchards, and tasty fruits - especially apples. Now, battles are being fought on its mountains and in its valleys.

A FOLKTALE FROM ZABADANI

THE GOLDEN BIRD

Kan ya ma kan, a long time ago, there lived a Woodcutter who had seven daughters, and he wished very badly for a son. When his wife became pregnant again, he said, "I swear by Allah that if you give birth to a baby boy, I will give you five coins of gold."

The months passed until one day, while he was cutting wood in the forest, his eldest daughter rushed up to him calling out, "Mother has just given birth to a baby boy!"

The Woodcutter was very happy to hear the great news. He picked up his little daughter and kissed her, but then remembered his oath to his wife. He didn't have five gold coins. He didn't even have one gold coin. He asked his daughter to return home and congratulate her mother and tell her he would be coming home soon.

Then he wandered in the fields and called out, "Ya Allah, You know my critical situation, for You are the All-Knowing."

Suddenly, out of the blue, a beautiful bird flew over his head and said, "Allah has sent me to help you keep your vow, so listen very carefully!" The bird perched on his arm and said, "I am the Golden Bird. Take me to the market, to the chief Merchant, and sell me to him for five coins of gold. He will agree right away. Then ask him to give you an extra coin so you can buy food and sweets for your family."

The Woodcutter followed the bird's instructions and returned home loaded with food and the five gold coins. When his wife heard his footsteps outside the door she said, "O Dear Husband, do not come into the house! Otherwise, you will break your vow!"

The Woodcutter happily replied, "I have the five coins of gold with me!"

His wife was overjoyed with the gold coins and the food, while the Woodcutter proudly held his newborn son.

In the meantime, the chief Merchant put the Golden Bird in a beautiful cage and took it home. "O, what a lovely present!" exclaimed his wife.

As time passed, the chief Merchant and his wife became very fond of the Golden Bird. It became the child they'd always wished they had. It would tell them beautiful stories and it filled their hearts with happiness.

One day, the Merchant decided to make his pilgrimage to Mecca. He said to his wife, "I have become an old man and I want to fulfill the duty of pilgrimage."

The Golden Bird nodded his head and said to the Merchant, "Don't worry, I will take care of your household and your wife, but I want to ask you for a favor."

"I will do anything you want," said the Merchant.

"On your way to Mecca," said the bird, "you will come across a bird that looks exactly like me. Please ask him how he gained his freedom."

The Merchant promised to do so and, after making his wife promise not to leave the house, set out on his journey to Mecca.

Weeks passed and spring arrived, so the Merchant's wife went out on the balcony to enjoy the good weather. Her wicked neighbor, Saeed, saw her and was taken by her beauty and decided to find a way to approach her.

Soon afterwards, Saeed found a sly old woman with a big crooked nose and said to her, "I will pay you a hundred gold coins if you help me befriend the chief Merchant's wife."

The old woman went to the chief Merchant's house and knocked on the door. "Who are you?" asked the Merchant's wife.

"Open the door," said the old woman. "It is time to pray and I need to pray in your house." The Merchant's wife felt sorry for the old woman and let her in to pray.

After the woman prayed she said, "Today is my daughter's wedding and I wish you could come to the party."

"I am sorry, I can't," said the Merchant's wife. "I promised my husband that I would not leave the house while he is on pilgrimage."

The old woman begged the Merchant's wife, and just as she was about to give in and accept the invitation, the Golden Bird warned her. "If you leave the house, you will regret it, but by that time, regrets will be useless. You will become like the Hunter who regretted killing his hawk."

As the old woman was still trying to convince her, the Golden Bird started telling a story, "*Kan ya ma kan*, in the olden days, a skillful Hunter had a hawk which he took good care of. One day, he went out into the desert to hunt. It seems he took a different path and lost his way. It was a very hot day and he was very thirsty, but there was no water in sight. He reached a big rock and sat under it to rest. Suddenly, he noticed water dripping from the rock. The Hunter by now was so thirsty that he was overjoyed to see the drops of water, so he took out a cup to fill it, but the hawk flew over it and knocked it over with its wing. The Hunter refilled the cup, but the hawk spilled it again. The Hunter lost his temper and threw the hawk against the rock, killing it on the spot. Then the Hunter climbed up to the top of the rock to fetch the water and, to his great surprise, found out that what he thought were drops of water were actually drops of poison dripping from the mouth of a big snake. The Hunter killed the snake and felt terrible that he had killed his loyal hawk." The Golden Bird shook its feathers violently and warned the Merchant's wife, "You will feel the same regret as the Hunter if you don't listen to me!"

The Merchant's wife took the advice of the Golden Bird and refused the old woman's invitation, and the old woman left.

Three days later, the chief Merchant returned from Mecca. The Golden Bird said, "I looked after your wife and house, so did you fulfill your promise? Did you see a bird like me and ask him how he became a free bird?"

"Yes," said the Merchant.

"What did the bird say?" asked the Golden Bird, anxiously.

The Merchant sadly said, "I regret that as soon as I asked him your question, he flapped his wings and dropped dead."

At hearing that, the Golden Bird fluttered its wings and seemed to fall dead inside the cage. The Merchant and his wife cried over the Golden Bird and dug a hole in their garden to bury it. Once they took it out of the cage, however, it shook itself and flew to a tree and said, "Farewell, dear friends, I must go now. The message you brought from the bird made it clear I could only be free by feigning death because you love me too much to part with me. Now, I must go."

"Please stay with us," they both called out.

"No, I cannot. I was only sent by Allah to help the Woodcutter keep his vow and for you to perform your pilgrimage. Farewell, farewell," said the Golden Bird and flew away, rising high in the sky.

PROVERBS

- Like locusts, they eat the green grass and the withered grass.
- Freedom exists in the open air.
- Sadness is never forgotten.

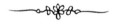

A Recipe from Zabadani

Kaek — Sesame and Aniseed Bread Rings

Ingredients

8 cups flour	½ cup butter
1 cup sugar	1 ½ cups milk
1 tsp aniseed	1 envelope yeast
1 tsp salt	2 eggs

For seasoning

1 beaten egg

2 tbsp water

1 cup sesame seed

Method

Sift flour into mixing bowl

Mix in sugar, aniseed, and salt

Heat butter with warm milk, then dissolve yeast in milk and add to dry mixture

Add eggs and knead, then cover and set aside for an hour until dough rises

Cut into small, walnut-sized pieces, cover with a cloth and let rise 30 more minutes

Take a piece of dough and shape it into thin rolls; bring ends together to make the shape of a bracelet and press ends together

Brush each circle lightly with a mixture of beaten egg and 2 tbsp water, then dip it in sesame seeds

Put kaek on an oiled tray and let them puff a little before baking

Bake in preheated oven at 300 degrees for 20 minutes

Lower temperature and bake another 20 minutes or until they are a golden color

Let them cool

HALBOUN

Halboun is a beautiful mountain village in the Tell District of the Muhafaza of Rural Damascus. It is about 19 kilometers north of Damascus and has a population of about 6,521. Halboun is known for grains, grapes, walnut trees, fig trees, and other fruit trees.

A long time ago, before refrigerators existed in Syria, the people of Halboun used to store ice in their caves. They would cut the ice into rectangular pieces with a saw, wrap them up well, and then carry the pieces of ice to Damascus to sell them.

My interest in Halboun and its bears started when I heard stories from my husband's Aunt Hadia in the village of Tell about hungry bears coming down from the mountain in the winter during snowstorms and invading the fields and farms of Halboun and Tell, searching for food. So began my long quest to track down information about the Syrian bear.

Fortunately, one day I met a young man who smiled and introduced himself saying, "I come from Halboun, where bears once roamed and ate from our grape vines and enjoyed eating our figs and walnuts."

Nodding his head, he continued, "We used to sit around the fireplace on cold winter nights and my great grandfather would tell us the story of the bear of Halboun."

"Do you remember the story?" I asked him.

"Oh yes, just like I remember my name," he said. Before I could say another word, he was telling me the story.

A Folktale of Halboun

The Bear of Halboun

Kan ya ma kan, a long time ago, a fine young man who was very shy lived in the town of Halboun. Back in those days, people considered him a coward.

When it was time for the man to choose a wife, he asked for the hand of his cousin whom he had loved silently for many years. His cousin really loved him too, but since she had heard so many family stories about his cowardice, she asked him to bring her the head of a bear as her dowry.

The poor young man didn't know what to do. If he refused to kill a bear, he would not only lose his beloved cousin, but also prove to all the villagers that he really was a coward. So he decided to go to the valley of Halboun, climb a walnut tree, and wait until the morning to return and claim he had not encountered any bears.

The next day, he carried his knife and went to the valley of Halboun, where he climbed a high walnut tree and passed the time picking walnuts and eating them. But as it grew dusk, he heard a rustle not far off. Then there was another, closer rustle below the branches of the walnut tree. The young man looked down and there appeared below him a bear, climbing up the same tree he was hiding in! The bear sat down on a strong branch and began picking walnuts and eating them. The young man's heart almost stopped beating and he felt that he was going to die once and for all.

There was a full moon that night, and the young man could clearly see the bear take each walnut with his paw and break its shell with his strong claws. Then he would raise the walnut to the moonlight to make sure there was no trace of shells and finally, he would throw it into his mouth.

The walnuts were so good that the bear did not notice the young man snuggled behind the leaves of the tree. From time to time, the young man's teeth chattered with fear, making a slight clicking noise, but the bear took no notice.

Time passed and the young man began to lose his fear. He decided the bear wasn't as frightening as he had thought. When the young man noticed that the bear repeatedly held out the walnuts for inspection, he mistakenly thought that the bear was offering him the walnuts. In fact, the young man began to feel he should thank the bear for its kind gesture.

So the next time the bear raised his paw holding out a walnut, the young man, without warning, shouted loudly, "Thank you, but I don't want any walnuts! I'm not hungry!"

This loud shout took the bear by surprise. He howled with fear and instantly lost his balance. He fell straight down, hit his head on the ground and broke his skull.

The young man was terrified that the bear would get up and take revenge on him, but time passed and the bear didn't move from the ground.

At sunrise, the young man sat up, rubbed the sleep from his eyes as, with the other eye, he stared at the ground where the bear lay. He threw a handful of walnuts at the bear, but it didn't move. Finally, he was convinced that the bear was really dead. He climbed down the tree and cut off the bear's head with his knife. Then, he joyfully carried the bear's head back to the village as he sang:

I am the young man from Halboun

Ma sha Allah aleya[*]
I killed the bear of Halboun
In the valley of Halboun
By the light of a bright full moon
I killed the bear in Halboun!

When the young man arrived in the village, he showed off the bear's head to the amazement of all the villagers. His cousin was delighted that he had proved his courage and was worthy of her. They had a big wedding and lived happily ever after.

---

[*] May God protect me

TELL

Tell is a city near Damascus and is the capital of the Tell District. It is situated in the middle of the Anti-Lebanon Mountains and has an elevation of roughly 1,000 meters above sea level. The city's name means "high hill." The city is built on limestone bedrock, and the inhabitants use the limestone for building.

In the past, the inhabitants of Tell were farmers, but after the severe drought of 1920, they turned away from agriculture and began to work with their native limestone. They would carve stones and design and construct buildings. Many moved to the city of Damascus or emigrated to the Gulf countries to work.

The city of Tell has a history of resistance. During the French Mandate, the city was besieged because leaders of the rebels were sheltered in the city. Today's civil war has also brought hardship to Tell. Because opposition groups are in Tell, the city has been under siege at different times and is now under restrictions.

I hesitated before I decided to include Tell in this book because I couldn't find any folktales from this city. I searched high and low and asked relatives of my husband – whose family is from Tell – to help in my quest, but in vain. Lama al Rifaie, the daughter of my husband's cousin, helped me search for folktales, but gave up. She finally admitted that the inhabitants of Tell are people of few words and thatis why they have no folktales of their own.

However, family tales of the courageous women of Tell who took care of their families during the absence of their husbands, fathers, and brothers began to interest me. My husband's Aunt Hadia proudly told me how she raised her ten children all by herself. Her husband left her the second week of their marriage and traveled to the Gulf, where he and most of the men from Tell worked as builders, self-made designers, and architects – as they liked to call themselves. Aunt Hadia's husband, like all the men of Tell of his time, came back only for short visits every two years. Thus, the women of Tell were bound to become strong and independent.

TRUE STORIES

THE WOMAN WORTH ONE HUNDRED MEN

Years ago, during the time of the French Mandate in Syria, many cities were besieged. Among these cities was the city of Tell, which was accused of aiding the revolutionary leaders. The French officials forbid anyone to bring wheat flour, bread, and other food supplies into the city for many months. As a result, children and old people were starved and weakened with famine. Anyone who tried to smuggle food into the city was shot by the French soldiers.

One day, a middle-aged woman who was known for her great courage decided to venture out of Tell, go to Damascus, and bring back some bread.

"I'm going to Damascus to get some bread," she confessed to her husband. "I can no longer bear to see my people suffer!"

"What!" exclaimed her husband "Many men have been killed trying to smuggle food into the city!"

"I am not an ordinary woman," she said. "I am worth a hundred men!"

The woman hired a truck and a driver and went through several French checkpoints.

When she arrived in Damascus, she went to many bakeries and bought all the bread they had, spreading it in the back of the truck. Then she covered the bread in bed sheets and piled firewood on top of it.

On her way back, every time she was stopped the woman sweetly greeted the soldiers and pointed at the firewood saying, "Winter will soon arrive, and you know how cold it is in Tell." The French solders nodded their heads and let her through.

When the woman finally drove into the city, her husband was waiting for her, along with all the inhabitants of Tell. There, she was welcomed with happy cheers and *zalageet*.

As she took out the loaves of bread from the truck, the smell of bread wafted in the air and the people crowded around her as she generously distributed the bread to everyone in the town.

Among the happy cheers her husband proudly said, "My wife is not an ordinary woman - she is worth one hundred men!"

THE PROJECT OF THE FIVE PIASTERS

Up until fairly recently, there were only elementary schools in Tell for its children to attend. All high schools were located in the city of Damascus, which is about 14 kilometers from Tell. On cold, snowy winter days, it was impossible to reach the capital. Therefore, most well-off families in Tell sent their children to Damascene boarding homes in order to attend high school.

Another problem encountered by the people of Tell was the lack of a hospital. Therefore, the inhabitants of Tell, who consider themselves a big family, decided to collect money to build their own high school and hospital.

All residents were to be included in this project. To raise the necessary money, everyone in Tell paid five extra piasters each time they needed to ride a bus or do some government paperwork. By the seventies, they were finally able to build their very own high school and hospital, which are considered two of the great achievements of the people of Tell in the 20th century.

GAMES

When I first started to collect games, I was stunned by the memories they stirred in people as they remembered them. It was as if they were describing a beautiful painting from the past; a past that they are not able to hand to their children and have thus lost forever. Where, they asked, are the young boys running in the neighborhood playing hide and seek or enjoying their ball games and marbles? Where are the young girls throwing a stone and hopping on chalked and numbered squares next to their houses? New electronic and mobile games have occupied the hearts of our children and erased all traces of the old games.

My husband's Aunt Hadia sighed when I asked her what games she played as a child in Tell with her friends.

"The children in our neighborhood played marbles, ball, and hide and seek," she said "But the most popular game was five stones." Her granddaughter Lama kindly explained the five stages of the elaborate game to me.

FIVE STONES

Five stones is a traditional game that has been played in Syria for centuries. In Tell, they still play this game. All you need to play is five small stones. This game is played sitting on the ground and can be played alone or with a partner.

The game consists of five stages:

First Stage: Throw the five stones on the ground. Then pick a stone and throw it in the air and pick up another while catching the first stone before it hits the ground. Repeat until all stones are picked up.

Second Stage: Throw all stones on the ground. Then pick a stone and toss it in the air. Pick up two stones while catching the first stone before it hits the ground. Repeat until all stones are picked up.

Third Stage: Throw all stones on the ground. Then pick a stone and toss it in the air. This time pick up only one stone. On the second throw, pick a stone and toss it in the air pick up three stones together from the ground and catch the one tossed in the air.

Fourth Stage: Throw all stones on the ground. Then throw one in the air and pick up the four stones at once and catch the first stone before it hits the ground.

Fifth Stage: All five stones are in your hand. Toss one stone in the air and drop the other four on the ground. Then pick up the four on the ground and try to catch the falling stone with one hand without allowing any stone to fall. In the final throw, toss the five stones into the air with one hand and try to catch as many as possible on the back of the same hand. The stones that are caught are then thrown up again into the air and caught in the palm of the hand. If one catches all five, it equals 500 points. Every stone equals 100 points. The player who scores the most points wins!

A PROVERB

- Rice is cooked on a low flame and is presented to kings, while burghol is cooked on a higher flame and is fed to chickens.

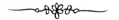

A Recipe from Tell

Burghol with Chick Peas

This is a very old recipe cooked for wedding feasts. A wedding in Tell lasts two days; the first day all the relatives and friends are invited to a feast. The next day, the wedding party is celebrated. This recipe was given to me by Lama al Refaie, who lives in Tell and is a cousin of my husband.

Ingredients
> 2 cups drained chick peas
>
> 3 cups coarse burghol
> ½ cup olive oil
> 5 cups water
> 2 bouillon cubes
> 1 tsp *usfor* (safflower)
> Salt and pepper to taste

Method
> Wash and soak chick peas in water for about 1 ½ hours.
> Strain soaked chick peas into a pot, add 5 cups water and cook.
> Bring water to a boil and skim off white foam.
> Add *usfor*, salt and pepper.
> Lower flame and cover until done.
> Drain chick peas and reserve water. Then dissolve 2 bouillon cubes in 4 cups of reserved water and set aside.
> In another pot, heat olive oil and add burghol after washing it. Stir until it turns medium brown.
> Add chick peas and 4 cups of the reserved water and cook on high flame until holes form on surface of burghol. Cover pot and cook on low heat until done.
> If burghol isn't done, add a little more water.

Yabrud

The name 'Yabrud' is an Aramaic word which means cold. The city of Yabrud rests upon the Qalamun Mountain slopes at a height of 1,550 meters and is about 80 kilometers north of Damascus. It is known for its ancient caves, especially the Iskafta cave, and the Konstantin Helena Cathedral. The parents of the former President of Argentina, Carlos Menem, were both born in Yabrud; they immigrated to Argentina before the end of World War I.

In March 2014, the city was the center of the battle of Yabrud, but it is now under Government control.

On a tour bus in Turkey five years ago, I met a group of very pleasant Syrians from Yabrud. An old man gave me this folktale, while the women generously offered me their special traditional recipes. They also gave me some of their traditional proverbs.

A Folktale from Yabrud

Fatoum and the Stranger

Kan ya ma kan, in a bygone time, there lived a widow named Fatoum Haback with her only daughter in a cottage on top of a mountain. There were very few neighbors living near them, yet they felt secure with the protection of their courageous neighbor, Abu Saleh.

The daughter was a spoiled and an irresponsible girl who never helped her mother or listened to her warnings. Despite all the rumors of strangers wandering in the village and breaking into houses, the girl always left the front door open.

One evening, the girl returned from visiting a neighbor and was too lazy to close the door behind her. At once, to her great astonishment, a great, tall man stormed into the cottage, stared at the mother, and said in a foreign accent,

Fatoum Haback Haback, say!
Your face is as big as a tray!

Then he sat down and ordered Fatoum and her daughter to bring him water and lots of food. They were scared to death and ran to the kitchen to fetch all the food they possessed.

The stranger ate and ate until he was satisfied. Then he ordered Fatoum to sing and her daughter to dance for him.

Reluctantly, Fatoum sang while her daughter danced for the frightening stranger. When Fatoum noticed that he was drowsily nodding, she sang a song asking her neighbor to come and save them:

Ya Abu Saleh, our neighbor dear,
We need your help – I hope you hear.
A stranger here is frightening me,
Ya Effendi, come and see!
Can you hear my poor heart beat?
Like blood oranges, you are sweet,
Bring, oh bring, your Indian sword
The stranger sleeps, I think he snored!

Abu Saleh heard Fatoum's song, hurried into the house, swung his sharp Indian sword, and cut off the stranger's head as he slept.

Fatoum and her daughter were greatly relieved and thanked Abu Saleh for saving them.

Fatoum scolded her daughter and said, "If you only had obeyed me, I would not have had to sing and you would not have had to dance!"

Since that day, the daughter no longer left the door open and always obeyed her mother.

PROVERBS

Proverbs distill the thinking and the originality of a people. Most of the following proverbs rhyme in Arabic.

- Don't befriend a negative person.
- Don't eat with a greedy person.
- Spend your money to keep your dignity.
- Take a family's secrets from its children.
- We ran away from the bear and fell into the well.
- Marry a man because he knows how to manage money, not just because he is rich.
- Talk and discuss, and your name will be remembered.
- Follow the owl and it will lead you to a place of destruction.
- Don't say you have fava beans until they are weighed.
- The safety of a person is in his good tongue.
- He's poor and he walks like a Prince.
- People who talk too much get blamed.
- Their beards turned white and still their brains haven't matured.

THREE RECIPES FROM YABRUD

SAFSOUF — SALAD WITH BURGHOL

Ingredients

½ cup fine burghol

A sprinkle of pepper

1 diced tomato

1 cucumber peeled and diced

1 green pepper diced

Lemon juice and oil to taste

Method

Place burghol in a bowl and cover with cold water

Stir and allow grains to settle at the bottom of the bowl

Drain off the water when the grains puff up

Add tomato, green pepper and cucumber and toss together

Combine oil, lemon, and a sprinkle of pepper. Pour into mixture and toss again

KAWERMA — PRESERVED MEAT

Kawerma is a Turkish name meaning fried meat. This is one way meat was preserved in the days before electricity and refrigerators. The farmer used to slaughter two sheep at the end of the summer and the women would cut the meat into very small pieces.

Ingredients

Chunks of lamb cut into small pieces with lots of fat to fry

Salt and pepper to taste

Method

Fry the meat and let it cool

Sprinkle with salt and pepper

Form round balls - the fat of the meat should help the meat stick together

Save in well-closed pots for the winter in a cold room.

The balls also can be put in a basket hanging from the ceiling

MAJAMER — BAKED MEAT PASTIES

Ingredients
- 2 lbs flour
- ½ cup oil
- 1 envelope yeast
- 1 tbsp salt
- 3 cups lukewarm water

Method
- Mix ingredients together and knead well
- Cover with a cloth and set aside in a warm place until dough rises
- Cut into small balls and cover with cloth for half an hour

Filling Ingredients
- 1 lb ground lamb or beef
- 6 diced
- 1 diced
- 4 eggs
- 1 tbsp yogurt
- 1 tbsp pomegranate molasses (*dibbis)*
- 1 tsp vinegar
- Salt and pepper to taste

Method

Blend eggs with meat, onions, yogurt, and seasoning

Fry on medium flame and add tomatoes, pomegranate molasses, and vinegar and stir until done

Set aside until it cools

Take each small ball of dough and press a finger in one end to make a hollow

Place a tbsp of filling in the opening, then close

Continue with all dough balls and brush with butter

Arrange on an oiled baking tray and bake in a moderate oven (350) for 15 minutes or until bottoms are lightly browned, then broil 5 minutes until tops are browned

QARA

Qara is in the Nabek District of the rural Muhafaza of Damascus. It is located between the Qalamoun Mountains and the eastern Lebanon Mountain range, 100 kilometers north of the capital Damascus, on the road to the city of Homs.

Qara is situated on a little hill. The name 'Qara' means 'a little hill' in Arabic. Qara is well-known for its cherry orchards, and cherries are their most important crop. In 2013, there was a battle in Qara which resulted in the government retaking the town.

A FOLKTALE FROM QARA

KIFAYA AND THE NAME PEDDLER

In the past, Syrian families who produced a string of girls and no boys would sometimes name the unfortunate fifth or sixth girl "Kifaya," meaning "Enough!" So you can see why Kifaya wanted a new name. (-S. Imady)

Kan ya ma kan, a long time ago, there was a poor, hardworking farmer who owned only two pairs of shoes. One pair, which he wore every day, was old and worn out, while the other pair was new which he only wore for special occasions. The farmer was married to a very simple-minded woman named Kifaya.

One day, a street peddler passed by their house carrying a big clay jar.

"What are you selling?" asked Kifaya.

"Names," said the peddler in an important tone of voice. Then he shook his head and asked, "What's your name?"

"Kifaya," said the woman bitterly, for she had hated her name all her life.

"Ya Allah, how could a beauty like you have a name like that?"

"How much does a name cost?"

"What do you have in your house?" asked the peddler greedily.

"I have nothing to give you but my husband's new shoes," Kifaya said, and she handed the shoes to him.

The peddler snatched the pair of shoes and slipped them in his bag. Then he reached in his jar and took out a necklace with a copper plate. He pointed at the name printed on the plate and said, "Wear this necklace around your neck. From now on your name shall be "Qamar" (Moon)."

Then he handed her red and white powder and *kehli* (kohl) and said, "Go back in your house, put this makeup on, and sit down like a Princess. Don't answer your husband unless he calls you by your new name."

The woman put on the necklace and the makeup, then walked around the house proudly repeating her new name, "Qamar." It sounded like music to her ears.

At sundown, the woman's husband came back from plowing and called, "Kifaya, come unload the donkey!"

But the woman didn't move. Her husband got worried. He climbed over the wall and jumped into the yard, shouting, "Ya Kifaya, where are you?"

To his great surprise, he found her sitting down like a Princess. "Why aren't you answering me?" he asked.

"Because my name is not Kifaya," she said. "From now on my name is Qamar."

The farmer laughed and asked, "Where did you get such a name?"

"I bought it from the name peddler for your pair of shoes."

The farmer cried out, "You gave the peddler my only good pair of shoes for a silly name!" Then he rushed towards the chest, threw his clothes in a basket, and headed towards the door.

"Where are you going?" she asked.

"I'm leaving the house forever! I will never come back unless I find someone as foolish as you!"

The farmer traveled for many days until he reached a spring where many women were filling their clay jars with water.

"Where did you come from?" asked one of the women.

"From the world of the dead," answered the farmer, sarcastically. "I have come to fetch some water for them!"

"Are you returning back to the world of the dead?" asked the women anxiously.

"Yes, of course," he said.

"O please, could you do me a favor and take this golden bracelet to my father?" said the woman as she took off her bracelet.

"Gladly," said the farmer.

Then all the other village women gathered around him and gave him their golden rings, bracelets, and necklaces to give to their dead parents, brothers, and husbands.

"These women are out of their minds," thought the farmer. "I had better run off before their husbands find out what they have given me." He filled his pockets with the golden rings, necklaces, and bracelets and started down the road.

The farmer had not gone very far when he saw a fat man approaching him on a horse. "O dear," thought the farmer. "I must hide everything before the man catches me," and he quickly hid the jewelry under a big stone.

Soon the fat man on the horse arrived and asked him, "Have you seen a man carrying golden bracelets, necklaces, and rings?"

"Yes, I did. He went that way."

"Can I catch up with him?" asked the fat man.

"Yes, but you'll reach him faster on foot because the road is rocky," said the farmer.

"Will you look after my horse until I return?" asked the fat man.

"All right," said the farmer.

As soon as the fat man left, the farmer cut off the horse's tail, planted it in the ground and then hid behind a sand dune along with the horse.

When the fat man returned, he saw the horse's tail planted in the ground. He shook his head and said, "The man must really be from the world of the dead. I hope he gives my horse to my dead father." Then he returned to the village on foot.

When the fat man was out of sight, the farmer took out the rings, bracelets, and necklaces from under the stone and rode back home on the horse. When he reached home, he cried out, "Kifaya, I'm back! I found the world is full of people more foolish than you!"

Kifaya snapped back right away, "My name is Qamar!"

Two Recipes from Qara

Safeh — Burghol Appetizer

Ingredients

1 cup burghol

1 tbsp butter

2 cups hot water

1 tbsp tomato paste

4 diced tomatoes

3 tbsp finely cut parsley

A few chopped mint leaves

2 cloves mashed garlic

Salt and lemon juice to taste

Cabbage leaves

Method

Melt butter in pan, then add burghol and stir constantly until medium brown

Add salt, hot water, and tomato paste

Cover and cook on medium flame until water is absorbed

Add siced tomato, parsley, mint, and lemon juice

Toss mixture on the stove for a minute

Serve on cabbage leaves

Bakel — Fried Bread Slices with Syrup

Ingredients

A loaf of pita bread

½ cup milk

1 cup water

2 cups sugar

1 tsp vanilla

Method

Cut bread into slices around 3 centimeters wide

Pour ½ cup of milk on the slices of bread and allow it five minutes to absorb

Fry slices of bread with some oil

Set slices of bread on the serving plate

Heat sugar and water together until bubbly

Cook about 10 more minutes and add vanilla

Remove from heat and let cool

Pour syrup on the slices of bread

3

HOMS

The history of Homs, like many Syrian provinces, goes far back, all the way to the 1st millennium BC. During Roman times, it was called "Emesa" and was the birthplace of the famous Roman Empress, Julia Domna of the Severan Dynasty. Homs is the third largest city in Syria, and its location is strategic since it is in the middle of the various Syrian regions; halfway between Damascus and Latakia and halfway between Damascus and Aleppo. Homs also was one of Syria's most important industrial centers, since it has the country's largest oil refinery. Now, the refinery operates at 2% of its former production.

The imposing fortified medieval castle called Qal'aat Al-Hosn or Crac de Chevaliers is in the Muhafaza of Homs. Even more famous is Palmyra, with its amazing remains of the ancient desert capital of Queen Zenobia. However, the ongoing war has caused unimaginable damage to Homs, its people, and its cultural heritage. Thousands have died in the conflict and the widespread destruction of the city is surpassed only in Aleppo. The Crac de Chevaliers has been damaged and much of Palmyra has been reduced to rubble by ISIS.

Four Folktales from Homs

When grandmothers in Homs sat down around the stove in the evening, their grandchildren would surround them and beg for a new story. The grandmothers would often start these evenings by asking the children, "Do want me to tell you the story of the scissors?"

"O yes, please do!" shouted the grandchildren, cheerfully.

"The story of the scissors / Two words, and that's it!" answered the grandmother, and then she was silent. In Arabic this is a rhyme:

Hakayet al im'us
Kilimtane ou bess!

The children usually protested and asked for a real story. The so called "Story of the Scissors" was often the introduction to a long evening and testified to the readiness of the children to hear the stories. It also filled the room with laughter as the grandmother playfully pretended that story time had ended with the story of the scissors.

Lazy Shaban

When I first heard this story, my mind went straight back to my child-hood and a small American storybook I had called "The Boy who Fooled the Giant," which is a shorter version of this same story. The Ifreet has become a Giant, but how did this story travel to America? Perhaps by way of one of the Brothers Grimm stories, "The Valiant Little Tailor," which has many similarities to "Lazy Shaban." It is my belief that the Arab version is the oldest.

Kan ya ma kan, in a bygone time, lived a lazy boy named Shaban. One day, he went to visit his grandmother in the village to pick figs from her fig trees. His grandmother greeted him in her usual way, "A hundred hellos, my dear grandson Shaban! How do you feel today?"

"I feel hungry!" said Shaban, as he ran to the fig trees behind the house. He climbed up the largest one and ate until he could no longer move. Then he fell asleep in the tree with his mouth open. Flies flew over his head and hovered near his mouth, buzzing around.

Shaban woke up and was horrified at the sight of the flies buzzing around him. "Take that...and that!" he yelled as he slapped them with his big hands. He kept hitting them until many fell dead on his lap, while others flew away.

Shaban counted the dead flies that fell on his lap and the flies missing wings or feet and said with great pride, "One hundred dead in one blow! One hundred wounded and one hundred escaped!"

As soon as he climbed down the tree, he wrote down the number of flies he had killed and wounded on a large sign. Then he bid his grandmother goodbye and said, "I am a great hero! I'm off to seek my fortune."

But before he left his grandmother's house, he took a big piece of white cheese and the little brown bird she kept in a cage and put them in a cloth bag.

As Shaban walked down the street, all the people crowded around him to read his sign.

"One hundred dead in one blow.

"One hundred wounded and one hundred escaped!"

No one guessed that Shaban had only killed flies; they thought he meant men. The news soon reached the king, who was very happy to hear that there was a strong man in his Kingdom.

"Call upon Shaban," said the King to his men. "I hope he will be able to get rid of the great Ifreet who has moved into my Kingdom!"

The King's men fetched Shaban and brought him. "We need you to get rid of the great Ifreet who has moved into our kingdom," said the king. "If you succeed, you shall marry my daughter the Princess and rule half of my Kingdom."

Shaban accepted the King's proposal and climbed up the highest mountain in the Kingdom to meet the Iftreet. When he reached the top, he found him.

"A hundred hellos, my dear Ifreet," said Shaban.

The great Ifreet turned around, saw tiny Shaban, and cried out in rage, "What are you doing here?"

Shaban handed the Ifreet his sign and the Ifreet roared with laughter.

Shaban got angry and said, "You must leave the Kingdom at once!"

The Ifreet laughed louder and said, "Are you going to make me, the great Ifreet, leave the kingdom?"

Shaban said, "Since you think you are so strong and clever, let us make an agreement. We will each show our tricks to the other and see who is cleverer. If you win, you will own this Kingdom, but if I win, you will leave this place forever!"

The Ifreet accepted the challenge.

"Let's see who can squeeze water from a stone!" said Shaban as he took the piece of cheese from his cloth bag while the Ifreet picked up a rock from the ground. Shaban squeezed the cheese and water came out of it right away. The Ifreet squeezed and squeezed the stone until, at the end, it crumbled in his hands.

"Who is cleverer?" asked Shaban.

The Ifreet was furious and picked up another rock and threw it so high into the air that it disappeared for a long time before it fell down to the ground.

Shaban laughed and said, "I can throw my stone so high that it won't come back again, ever!"

Then he took the little brown bird out of his bag and threw it into the air so that the bird flew away and never came back.

"I am dishonored!" wailed the Ifreet, gnashing his teeth. "You win! I am leaving this Kingdom forever!"

The King was very happy to get rid of the Ifreet, and he gave his daughter to Shaban in marriage. When the King died, Shaban became ruler over the whole Kingdom and the Ifreet was never heard of again.

THE FOUR GOLDEN APPLES AND THE IFREET

Kan ya ma kan, a long time ago, there lived a Sultan who owned a large palace surrounded by a beautiful garden. In the center of the garden there stood a large apple tree, which bore only four magnificent golden apples every year. One day, the Sultan woke up to find out that one of the apples had disappeared. The Sultan was very upset and ordered his three sons to guard the tree at night.

"You must guard the apple tree with your lives and find out who picked the golden apple or I will punish you all!"

"Don't worry, dear father," said the eldest son. "I'll guard it tonight and find out who stole your golden apple."

So the eldest son stood beneath the apple tree holding his big sword, but around midnight, he fell asleep. The following morning, to the Sultan's great horror, he found that another golden apple had been stolen.

The next night, the second son went out to guard the apple tree but he also fell asleep and another golden apple disappeared.

The Sultan was furious and sent for his third son, Alaa. "You must discover who is stealing my golden apples or I'll punish you all!" he shouted.

That night, Alaa sat down beneath the apple tree with his eyes wide open. When he felt sleepy he got a big water bag and cut a small hole into it, then hung it on a branch of the tree. The water

86

bag dripped water on Alaa and kept him awake. At the stroke of midnight, the ground shook beneath him and he heard the leaves rustle.

Suddenly, in the light of the moon he saw a great Ifreet bending over to pick the last golden apple. At once, Alaa swung his sword as hard as he could and cut off the Ifreet's hand. The Ifreet let out a loud scream and ran away leaving a trail of blood behind him. Alaa followed the trail of blood until he found himself next to an old, dry well.

"The Ifreet must have jumped into the well," said Alaa. "I'll wait until sunrise to follow him." Then he sat down near the well and fell asleep.

In the morning, the Sultan saw the trail of blood on the ground and called his two other sons to follow it and search for Alaa. The two brothers followed the trail of blood until they reached the well. Alaa told his brothers about his night's adventure and suggested that one of them should follow the Ifreet down the well. "Tie me with a rope and let me down the well," said the eldest brother. "I'll slaughter the Ifreet in no time!"

As soon as the two brothers let their eldest brother down the well, they heard him shout, "Get me out of here!" They pulled him up as fast as they could.

Then it was the second brother's turn and he boasted, "I'll cut the Ifreet into small pieces!" However, once they let him down the well, the second brother also screamed out loud, "Oh please get me out of here!" So they pulled him out of the well.

The two brothers looked at their younger brother Alaa and asked him if he still wanted to go down. "Yes, of course," said Alaa. "But do as I say. If I scream, don't pull me out!"

The two older brothers helped Alaa down the well. Down and down went Alaa into the dark, dry, deep well until he fell on the ground. It was so dark that he couldn't see his own hand, so he touched the sides of the well and noticed that there was a small opening through which cold air was coming in. He knelt down and crawled into it and found himself in a long passage which led him to a door. He opened the door and found himself in a beautiful field.

He looked around and saw traces of blood on the ground. As he followed the trail of blood, he came upon two goats fiercely fighting each other. When Alaa was able to make peace between them, the goats thanked him, gave him one of their hairs, and said, "If you need us, just burn the hair and we will appear at once and help you."

Alaa continued following the trail of blood until he saw a large tree on which a big snake was attacking an eagle's nest. He swung his sword and cut off the snake's head. The eagle thanked Alaa, gave him a feather, and said, "If you need me, just burn my feather and I will appear in front of you at once!"

Alaa thanked the eagle and continued following the trail of blood until he found himself standing next to a great palace. He walked through the open gate and saw three beautiful young women. "Who are you?" asked Alaa.

The three young women looked very sad and said, "The Ifreet kidnapped us from our families and imprisoned us in this palace."

"Where is the Ifreet?" asked Alaa.

"He is asleep in his room," said one of the young women. "He came back yesterday with his hand cut off and he is in terrible pain."

The young women took Alaa to the Ifreet's room where he lay asleep. Alaa entered quietly and in one stroke cut off the Ifreet's head. Then the three young women led Alaa to the Ifreet's treasure and they heaped it all into bags to take home.

The bags were too heavy to carry so Alaa burned the goat's hair and the two goats came at once. They carried them and the treasure to the well. Then, Alaa burned the eagle's feather and the eagle carried them one by one out of the well where Alaa found his two brothers anxiously waiting for him.

The three brothers took the three young women and the treasure to the palace, where they were joyfully received by their father.

Later on, the Sultan married his sons to the three beautiful young women and they all lived happily ever after.

The Money Belt

This story is loosely based on a true story. It has passed into the domain of oral folktales and has been somewhat changed in the process.

Kan ya ma kan, in days gone by, there lived a Damascene Merchant who traveled from one city to another to sell his goods. One day, he reached the city of Homs and entered the mosque to pray, but he was so tired that he forgot his money belt in the room where he washed for prayer.

A young boy named Sameer found the money belt and gave it to his uncle, who put it in a closet and said, "Don't give the money belt to anyone without my permission."

When the Merchant left the mosque, he suddenly realized that he was not wearing his money belt. "Oh, my God," he said. "All my fortune is in that belt!"

He hurried back to the mosque and searched for it, but unfortunately it wasn't there. Then, by chance, he met Sameer and told him about his lost money belt. Sameer asked him to describe the belt to him and to tell him the number of gold coins in it. The Merchant answered all the questions correctly and seemed honest and trustworthy to Sameer.

"I'm sure the money belt is yours, but I can't give it to you because I have to get my uncle's permission, and he isn't at home," said Sameer.

"I can't wait until your uncle returns," said the Merchant. "I have to leave in a hurry to meet up with my caravan or they will leave without me!"

Sameer hesitated, but felt sorry for the Merchant and gave him the money belt.

The Merchant tried to reward Sameer, but he refused to take anything. So the Merchant gave him a gold coin as a token of their friendship, and a paper explaining where he lived in Damascus. As he left, he murmured a couple words which Sameer did not quite understand. He wondered what they meant.

When Sameer's uncle came back from work, he was furious that Sameer had given away the money belt without consulting him, so he beat him. Sameer was so hurt that he ran away from home and swore he would never set foot in his uncle's house again.

Sameer wandered from city to city and worked in many places and tried many trades. One day, he reached Damascus and remembered the Merchant who had given him the gold coin which he had managed to keep. He only wished he had kept the Merchant's address, too.

It was too late to look for somewhere to sleep, so he went into a mosque and fell asleep. In the morning, he was welcomed by the Imam of the mosque, who asked him if he was looking for a job.

"I'm growing old," said the Imam. "We need someone who can give the call to prayer and lead the prayers."

Sameer was very happy and accepted the job at once. One day, the Imam noticed that when Sameer climbed up the minaret to give the call to prayer, he always turned his face towards the left.

"Why do you always turn your head towards the left when you climb the minaret?" asked the Imam curiously.

"There is a river on the right, where I have heard that young women often swim," said Sameer. "I'm afraid that I might accidentally glance at one of them."

The Imam embraced Sameer and said, "You are the perfect husband for my daughter Sameera!" Then he asked Sameer, "How much do you have to give her as a dowry?"

Sameer shrugged his shoulders and sadly said, "I'm afraid I have nothing but one gold coin which was given to me a long time ago."

The Imam asked to hear the story of the gold coin, and his eyes widened as he heard Sameer's words. When Sameer finished telling his story, the Imam took him to his house, opened his closet and took out an old money belt. He said, "I am the Merchant you met years ago. I have saved the money belt for you, my honest son."

"I always wondered," said Sameer, "What were those words you murmured when you said goodbye to me?"

"I prayed to God," said the Imam, "That you would get married to my only daughter Sameera and now, God willing, my prayer will be answered."

Later on, Sameer did marry Sameera, and they lived together in peace and comfort.

ABU ADOSE AND UM ADOSE

Fatima, a young student of mine, gave me this story from her Tete who comes from Homs. I was surprised that this story has similarities to two other stories in this book, "The Foolish Woman" and "Kifaya and the Name Peddler." It also has similarities to a story in my first book, "The Sky is Raining Meat." There is even a Serbian folktale with a very similar plot. This shows how folktales travel from one place to another and gain or lose some of their features.

Kan ya ma kan, in days gone by, there was a woman called Um Adose. One day, as she was standing on her balcony watering her plants, a street peddler passed by selling rings and bracelets. Um Adose was fascinated by the glittering rings and bracelets and ran down the stairs to take a look at them. She tried on the bracelets and rings and fell in love with all of them.

"How much do all these bracelets and rings cost?" she asked.

"Oh, they will cost you everything you own, up and down!" said the peddler.

"I have nothing to give you in return but the two bags of burghol and wheat my husband just brought from the farm," said Um Adose.

"That will do nicely," said the greedy peddler.

The peddler gave Um Adose the imitation gold rings and bracelets and took the two bags of burghol and wheat. Then he quickly ran away before her husband returned.

Um Adose put on the rings and bracelets and happily sat down, taken by their glitter.

Later, Abu Adose came back from his farm. "I'm so hungry," he cried. "Prepare us something to eat!"

"We have nothing to eat," said Um Adose as she admired her wrists and fingers. "I gave the two bags of burghol and wheat to the peddler in exchange for these beautiful rings and bracelets!"

The farmer cried out, "You gave the peddler our only food for these fake bracelets and rings? Oh no!"

Um Adose felt very offended and said, "I'm leaving the house forever!" Then she walked out the door and down the road. After a while, she sadly sat down by the side of the road.

All of a sudden, a big cat came to her and rubbed against her and meowed. Um Adose thought Abu Adose had sent the cat to apologize to her. "Go away," said Um Adose, as she pushed the cat away. "Tell my Abu Adose that Um Adose has sworn to never set foot in his house again!"

After a while, a big camel decorated with beautiful beads and loaded with figs and raisins came walking down the road. It stopped by Um Adose and sat near her.

Um Adose was delighted. "Oh, Abu Adose, now I'll accept your apology!" she cried out happily, as she led the camel back to her house.

Abu Adose was very happy to see Um Adose return with a camel loaded with figs and raisins, but he knew right away that the stray camel belonged to a rich Merchant who must be searching for it. Therefore, he decided to quickly slaughter the camel and keep the bags of figs and raisins. Yet he worried that Um Adose would tell the neighbors about the camel and get him in trouble, so he thought of a plan.

That very same day, Abu Adose slaughtered the camel and made *kibbi* with the meat. When Abu Adose finished cooking, he climbed up to the roof of his house and began dropping the *kibbi* on the ground.

Um Adose was overjoyed to see the sky raining kibbi. She ran out and caught it as it fell and filled her skirts with it.

The next day when Abu Adose went to the farm, the rich Merchant and his men went door to door searching for the camel and announcing they would give a reward to whomever led them to it.

When they knocked on Um Adose's door and asked her if she had seen the camel, she laughed and said, "Oh, yes, I did. My husband slaughtered it and hid the bags of figs and raisins in the closet."

"When did your husband slaughter our camel?" asked the rich Merchant.

"My husband slaughtered the camel yesterday afternoon when it rained *kibbi*!" said Um Adose.

The Merchant realized that he was talking to a crazy woman and hurried away. Um Adose ran after him shouting at the top of her voice, "Where is my reward?"

The Merchant never came back for his camel, Abu Adose kept the bags of figs and raisins, and Um Adose never understood why she didn't get a reward.

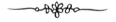

THREE RECIPES FROM HOMS

SHAKRIEH — MEAT IN YOGURT

Ingredients

½ kilo lamb stew meat

1 onion, sliced

Salt and pepper to taste

1 kilo yogurt

1 egg

1 tbsp corn flour, dissolved in cold water

2 cloves garlic, mashed with salt

½ tsp dry mint

Method

Sauté meat with butter until it loses its pink color

Cook meat with onions and add salt and pepper

Cover meat with water, cover pot and simmer until meat is tender

Strain the yogurt, egg, and corn flour into the pan

Stir constantly over high heat until it boils

Reduce heat; simmer for 5 minutes, stirring now and then

Sauté mashed garlic and add to yogurt

Simmer another 5 minutes and sprinkle dry mint on top

Serve with burghol or rice

MUJADARA BIL RIZ — LENTILS WITH RICE

A long time ago, women used to accompany the bride to the local public bath, the Hammam al Souk, where, after their bath, they would eat mujadara. The Arabic hammam was not a place just for bathing. Women would bring food and drinks and have a picnic in the hammam. Older women would always have their eyes open for the beautiful young girls as possible future brides for their sons. Among the songs they used to sing was:

> *We cooked mujadara, and it was full of rice,*
> *Our bride needs no makeup, she looks so nice.*

Rice used to be considered a delicacy because it was imported and much more expensive than burghol, which is why people used to say, 'Rice was esteemed, so burghol hanged itself.'

Ingredients

1 cup lentils

1 cup rice

4 tbsp olive oil

4 onions, sliced

Salt and pepper to taste

Method

Boil 1 cup lentils until done and then drain

Boil 1½ cups water - add salt, pepper, and olive oil

Add lentils and rice

Heat until the level of water gets lower, then cover the pan and simmer 20 minutes or until liquid is absorbed

Fry sliced onions in oil until brown and crispy

Put *mujadara* on a serving plate with fried onions on top

AJJAY — ZUCCHINI FRITTERS

Thrifty Syrian housewives never waste food. When they core out zucchinis to stuff them, they use the cored parts (called "lib al kusa" in Arabic) to make several dishes. This is one. This dish can also be made with zucchini that is chopped up and steamed until tender instead of lib al kusa.

Ingredients

½ kilo *lib* zucchini or chopped, steamed zucchini - squeeze excess moisture out

1 cup flour

2 eggs

1 bunch cleaned and chopped parsley

1 tsp salt and ½ tsp pepper

Oil to fry

Method

Mix all ingredients except the oil until they hold together in a fairly thick batter

Heat oil and drop spoonfuls of batter from a large spoon into the hot oil

Fry until brown on one side, then turn and brown other side

Drain on paper towels and serve hot

4

HAMA

The city of Hama lies 300 kilometers north of Damascus, on the Orontes River. The huge, ancient water wheels on the river are a memorable sight, and the distinctive groan they emit as they turn can be heard all over the city.

Nowadays, there is an ongoing conflict between rebels and the Syrian army for control of the villages in the Muhafaza of Hama.

Two Folktales from Hama

Badra bint al Ghoul - Badra Daughter of the Ghoul

My neighbor Um Hiba frowned as she collected her thoughts and then said, "A long time ago, back in the days of my great-grandmother, there was no electricity in Hama. Children had better things to do in those days than watching TV or playing computer games. Instead, they would spend evenings listening to their Tete's stories. Even my generation enjoyed hearing the old stories. Here is one that I remember."

As Um Hiba begins telling me the story of Badra bint al Ghoul, she undoes her braid, lets down her long blond hair, and then repeats the words of the Ghouleh in the story:

> *Badra bint al Ghoul, so fair,*
> *Let down your long and golden hair*
> *That I may climb it like a stair,*
> *Badra bint al Ghoul, so fair.*

As I watch her hair spill down her back, I feel as if I am drawn into the story.

Kan ya ma kan, in a bygone time, there was a King who had everything anyone could desire in the world. Everything in the world but children. One day, while he was sitting on his balcony looking sad and grim, an old woman passed by and asked him the reason for his sadness.

"I long for a child," said the King.

"Don't worry," said the old woman as she took out an apple from her bag. "I have your remedy. Take this apple and divide it in half. Give one half to your wife, the queen, and eat the other half. Your wife will have a child soon after that!"

TheKing was very happy. "How can I thank you?" he wondered.

"If your wife gives birth to a boy, I want you to give me a river of honey and a river of butter."

The King didn't give a thought to the request of the old woman, but rushed to his wife to offer her half of the apple. After nine months, the Queen gave birth to a beautiful boy, and they named him Aladdin. But the King forgot his promise to the old woman.

Years passed, and Aladdin turned into a young man. One day, as he was sitting with his friends, he saw an old woman carrying a vase. She was the same old woman who had given his father the magic apple. He took out his slingshot and hurled a stone at the old woman's vase, and it shattered.

The old woman was furious and warned him that his father hadn't fulfilled his promise. Then she cursed him and said, "May you fall in love with Badra bint al Ghoul."

Aladdin ran after the old woman and asked her, "Who is Badra bint al Ghoul?"

The old woman said, "She is a beautiful girl who lives in a far-away land." Then she cackled and said, "You will never find her!" At once, she disappeared.

Aladdin thought of Badra bint al Ghoul all night, and in the morning he decided to travel high and low to find her.

"What is the matter, my Son?" asked his mother."

"By Allah, Mother, I have a great yearning to travel abroad."

"You have everything you need here, my Son."

"I want to find a beautiful girl named Badra bint al Ghoul. Give me enough provisions to get me there and back."

So she gave him provisions and he set out on his journey. He rode his horse until he reached a big hut. Next to it sat an ugly Ghoul.

"Peace be upon you, O father Ghoul," said Aladdin.

"Had not your salam (greeting of peace) preceded your words, I would have gobbled you up and munched on your bones."

"Can I ask you a question?" asked Aladdin.

"You must bathe me and cut my nails before anything else," said the Ghoul. So Aladdin bathed the Ghoul, cut his nails, and prepared food for him. The Ghoul sighed with pleasure and asked him what he wanted.

"I am looking for Badra bint al Ghoul."

"Take this spool of thread and unravel it as you follow this road. Once the thread finishes, you will reach the hut of my brother, who is older than me by a day and more knowledgeable than me by a year."

So Aladdin set out on the road, unraveling the spool of thread until he came upon the second Ghoul.

"Peace be upon you, O Father Ghoul," said Aladdin.

"Had not your salam preceded your words, I would have gobbled you up and munched on your bones."

"I was sent by your younger brother who said you are older than him by a day and more knowledgeable than him by a year. Can I ask you a question?"

"You must bathe me and cut my nails before anything else," said the second Ghoul. So Aladdin bathed the second Ghoul, cut his nails, and prepared food for him. The Ghoul sighed with pleasure and asked him what he wanted.

"I am looking for Badra bint al Ghoul."

"Take this spool of thread and unravel it as you follow this road. Once the thread finishes, you will see my brother who is older than me by a day and more knowledgeable than me by a year."

Again, Aladdin set out on the road, unraveling the spool of thread until he came upon the third Ghoul.

"Peace be upon you, O Father Ghoul," said Aladdin.

"Had not your salam preceded your words, I would have gobbled you up and munched on your bones."

"I was sent by your younger brother who said you were older than him by a day and more knowledgeable than him by a year. Can I ask you a question?"

"You must bathe me and cut my nails before anything else," said the third Ghoul.

So Aladdin bathed the third Ghoul, cut his nails, and prepared food for him. The Ghoul sighed with pleasure and asked him what he wanted.

"I am looking for Badra bint al Ghoul."

"Take this spool of thread and unravel it as you follow this road. Once the thread finishes, you will have reached the stone tower where Badra bint al Ghoul lives."

Aladdin thanked the Ghoul and followed his instructions until he found himself next to a beautiful stone tower. Suddenly, he heard footsteps, so he hid behind a tree. To his great surprise, he saw the Ghouleh, Badra's mother, calling her with her hoarse voice:

Badra bint al Ghoul, so fair,
Let down your long and golden hair
That I may climb it like a stair,
Badra bint al Ghoul, so fair.

At once, the most spectacular long golden hair was dropped down to the Ghouleh standing far below. The Ghouleh climbed up the hair and disappeared into the stone tower.

Aladdin was amazed by what he had seen and decided to try his luck and do what the Ghouleh had done. As soon as it turned dark, he stood under the window and called out the same words the Ghouleh had uttered:

Badra bint al Ghoul, so fair,
Let down your long and golden hair
That I may climb it like a stair,

Badra bint al Ghoul, so fair.

Down came the beautiful golden hair and up Aladdin climbed until he reached the window of the tower, where he saw the most beautiful young woman he had ever set his eyes upon.

Badra was shocked to see Aladdin in front of her, but he reassured her and told her his story, recounting his long journey to reach her. By the time he had finished talking, they were both in love.

Soon, they heard the Ghouleh's coarse voice:

Hum, hum, hum,
I smell the red blood of a man so young.
Yum, yum, yum,
I'll drink his blood and give my dog his
    tongue.

"Do you eat human beings too?" asked Aladdin anxiously.

"No! I'm not a Ghouleh!" said Badra. "I'm a human being, just like you. I was kidnapped by the Ghouleh as a baby."

Badra hid Aladdin and helped the Ghouleh prepare dinner, then sang the Ghouleh to sleep with her beautiful songs. While the Ghouleh was snoring, Badra pulled out three long hairs from the Ghouleh's head. Then with the help of Aladdin, she wiped all the furniture, the ceiling, and the floor with honey and butter so they couldn't tell the Ghouleh what had happened.

Aladdin tied a rope from Badra's window, and they descended from the tower together. When the Ghouleh woke up, she was horrified to find that Badra had disappeared. She asked the doors and the windows, the floor and the ceiling - even the furniture: "Where did Badra go?"

They all answered, "She is asleep!"

Unfortunately, Badra and Aladdin had forgotten to wipe the garlic mortar with honey and butter, and it told the Ghouleh that Badra had escaped down the window with a young man.

The Ghouleh was furious; her eyes burned with rage. She cried out, "No one escapes from me!" Then she mounted her giant dog Koko and set out to look for Badra and Aladdin.

As soon as the Ghouleh caught up with them, Aladdin took out one of the stolen hairs, burned it, and threw it behind them. At once, thorns grew everywhere and prevented the Ghouleh from moving forward for a while.

But again, the Ghouleh caught up with them, so Aladdin burned the second hair of the Ghoueh and threw it behind them. Immediately, it set the whole place ablaze. The Ghouleh was paralyzed for a while and couldn't follow them.

Suddenly, they heard a loud shattering scream, and there was the Ghouleh, behind them again! Desperately, Aladdin burned the last hair and threw it at the Ghouleh. This time, water flooded everywhere and the Ghouleh swallowed so much water that she drowned.

Aladdin and Badra were overjoyed and returned to the Kingdom where the King and the Queen happily welcomed them. They soon got married and there was a feast of seven days and seven nights to celebrate their marriage.

THE STORY OF *MASH* (OR NAUGHT)

In the 1930s, there was a great famine in the Muhafaza of Hama due to a severe drought. Women in the villages made up different dishes with what little ingredients they had on hand. Sometimes they boiled water and added a few drops of oil, which would float on the surface and shine like stars. The women named this dish "Al Nujumieh," or "The Starry Dish." Other times, they would boil water and add flour and salt to it and name it "Mash," which means "little or naught" due to the few ingredients in it.

Kan ya ma kan, not so many years ago, there lived a woman called Bahia who had a forgetful husband named Shaheen.

One day, she asked her husband to get her a small bag of flour so she could make some mash. She asked him to repeat the word "mash" so he would not forget what to buy.

Shaheen took his staff and left the house, repeating the word *mash*. He passed by some fishermen on the bank of a river. Each time a fisherman cast his fishing rod into the river, Shaheen would mutter, "*Mash, mash, mash*," and the fishermen caught no fish.

So the fishermen beat him up and told him that he ought to be saying, "*In sha'Allah* (God willing), six or seven big ones and six or seven small ones."

Shaheen continued on his way, but he had forgotten the word *mash* and instead started to repeat, "*In sha'Allah*, six or seven big ones and six or seven small ones."

He passed by an impressive funeral preceded by Judges, jurists, and guards. Shaheen was repeating, "*In sha'Allah*, six or seven big ones and six or seven small ones." The people got angry, especially since it was the funeral of an important Judge, and they began to beat him. One of the mourners said as he beat him, "Are you wishing for six or seven of our relatives to die along with six or seven of our children?"

Shaheen asked, "What should I say?"

"Say, may God have mercy on him; how great he was."

He continued on his way and tripped over the carcass of a dog. He began to shove it with his staff saying, "May God have mercy on him; how great he was." When people heard him asking for mercy for a dead dog and saying how great he was, they attacked him.

"What do you want me to say?" he asked. They answered, "Say: Fie, filthy! Fie, disgusting!"

So he went on his way repeating "Fie, filthy and disgusting," until he reached a house full of guests who were celebrating a wedding. Music played as they happily ate, but Shaheen kept on saying, "Fie filthy, fie disgusting."

The people, who were eating the most delicious dishes, got angry at him and asked him, "Are you disgusted with our wedding and the food we are eating?"

They started beating him from all sides until he begged, "What do you want me to say?"

They said, "Say, oh, how delicious; oh, how tasty!"

So he did and they invited him to eat with them. When he left, he continued to say, "Oh, how delicious, oh, how tasty," until he passed by a group surrounding two men fighting. Each time one would deliver a blow, Shaheen would say, "Oh, how delicious, oh, how tasty." So the two fighting men stopped and decided to teach him a lesson. Each kicked and slapped and beat Shaheen till he was barely able to move. He finally asked, "What should I have said?"

They replied, "Say, come save your Muslim brothers from your Christian brothers. Come save your Christian brothers from your

Muslim brothers." So Shaheen learned his lesson and he continued on his way saying that.

He passed by two dogs attacking each other and said, "Come save your Muslim brothers from your Christian brothers. Come save your Christian brothers from your Muslim brothers."

When the people heard such blasphemous talk, they pounced upon him and beat him soundly, "Are you saying that Christians and Muslims are like dogs, oh infidel?!"

He asked, "What should I have said?"

They said, "Say, hisht, hisht." (Something said to dogs to quiet them down). So Shaheen went on his way saying, "Hisht, hisht," and came across a tanner tanning leather. He was stretching the leather in his two hands and holding the top of it in his teeth. Each time he tried to stretch it with his mouth, Shaheen would say, "Hisht, hisht." When the tanner heard him, he got up and beat him soundly.

Shaheen asked, "What should I say instead?"

The tanner said, "Say, stretch it; expand it so it will be enough for a pair of shoes." So he continued to say this until he passed by a barbershop where the barber was combing the new Judge's very long beard. The beard reached his knees and the barber was praising the Judge as he combed the beard. Shaheen was repeating, "Stretch it and expand it so it will be enough for a pair of shoes." No sooner did the barber hear this than he began to hit Shaheen for his disrespect until he made him bleed.

Shaheen cried, "What shall I say?"

The barber said, "May you live to eat from what is beneath you." (This refers to the way people used to respectfully pay Judges by putting money under the cushion the Judge sat upon.) So Shaheen went on his way, repeating those words.

Shaheen left the village behind him and came upon a man relieving himself, and said, "May you live to eat from what is beneath you." The squatting man was furious and stood up and hit him. Then he admitted that if he had not eaten *mash* that morning, he would not have gotten diarrhea. When he said the word *mash*, Shaheen was shocked and remembered what his wife had asked him to buy that morning. Quickly, he rushed home like a crazy man and he began to whimper and stutter as he apologized to his wife. Bahia took a stick to him and beat him until she felt better. It is not clear whether the family had supper that night or not.

SHADOW FINGER PLAY

Before electricity and TV, the people of Hama used to light the kerosene lamp at night after supper, and the family would gather with the children sitting near their grandmother as she told stories. The old homes had big rooms that were white-washed, and sometimes the stories were accompanied by a finger shadow play on the walls. There would appear on the wall, as if by magic, the head of a deer, or a horse, or a rabbit, or even a person. The stories combined with the shadow play would draw the children into a world of fantasy and often, the children were lulled to sleep in their places.

A LULLABY

Sleep, my child, sleep
That I may slaughter a dove for you
Go, Dove, go. I say this in jest
I'm singing a lullaby for my child to rest.

Sleep, my child, sleep
I don't have diamond earrings
Sleep, my child, sleep
For your father did not buy me.
Sleep, my child, sleep
The Lord of the skies
Indeed will not forsake me.

Sleep, my child, sleep
I'd rock you in a swing
But I fear the eagle may snatch you
Oh, Sharshooha, I plead with you
Rock him till he sleeps.

I wrap you in my abayee
You are as sweet as rock candy
I plead with my sisters and brothers
To serve you oh, so kindly.

I put you to sleep in the uppermost room
But I fear the snake may bite you
I plead with you Subhiyeh
Rock him until he sleeps.

Sleep, O apple of my eye, sleep
O delicious grapes of Zainy
I pray to God that my baby sleeps
That I may hold him in my lap.

Two Recipes from Hama

Shankleesh — Fermented Cheese

Shankleesh is a kind of cheese made by the women of Hama which is served at breakfast and stored to eat all year-round. It is an old recipe known in Syria and Lebanon and its name comes from the Kurdish 'shan', which means a small terracotta pot, and 'qareesh' which is Bedouin fermented milk.

The Kurdish and Arab tribes most probably invented this kind of aged cheese from the necessity to preserve their fresh yogurt cheese. It is said that they either put the cheese in clay jars or buried it in the hot desert sand for a year to mature and age.

Ingredients

    5 lbs cottage cheese

    1 cup melted butter

    1 tbsp powdered red pepper

    2 tbsp thyme (*zaatar*)

    2 tbsp salt

    1 tbsp black cumin seed (black seed or habet baraka)

To coat the balls of cheese

    4 tbsp *zaatar* (thyme)

    4 tbsp powdered red pepper

Method

Put cottage cheese in a clean cloth bag, tie it, press out moisture, and hang it over the sink to drain

When drained, put cottage cheese in a big bowl

Add salt, black cumin seed, thyme, and powdered red pepper

Knead mixture well until smooth and consistent

Form dough into "tennis balls"

Put balls on a cloth and cover for 24 hours until completely dry

Put balls in a jar for 10 days in a dry place until they darken and mold forms

(Some people lay them in the sun for 10 days)

Scrape mold off the balls

Dip balls into melted butter and roll half the balls in thyme, half in red pepper

Put the balls in plastic bags and refrigerate them

They are usually eaten with chopped tomato and olive oil.

BUTRASH OR UMTABAL — EGGPLANT DIP WITH MEAT

Ingredients

1 kilo eggplant

¼ to ½ kilo thick yogurt

1 clove garlic

2 tbsp tahini

½ kilo finely ground lamb or beef

½ cup tomato paste

1 unripe tomato grated

Salt and pepper to taste

Fried almonds and parsley for garnish

Method

Grill eggplant, then pound in mortar with 1 clove garlic (or use blender)

Add yogurt and tahini, mix well and set aside – this is the *umtabal*

Fry meat (set aside a little for topping)

Add a grated, unripe tomato, ¼ cup tomato paste and some water

Cook until it becomes a thick sauce

To serve, put *umtabal* in a serving dish, pour on sauce

Garnish with the meat you set aside, fried almonds and parsley

5

IDLIB

Idlib is 55 kilometers southwest of Aleppo. It is a green land, famous for its fruit, olive, and fig trees. It has many archeological sites, foremost among them is the ancient dead city of Ebla, which goes back to the second and third millennia BC.

However, the city of Idlib is in the opposition's hands, as is most of the province, so it is often subject to bombing as well as attacks from ISIS. Much of the civilian population has been displaced.

THREE FOLKTALES FROM IDLIB

With the news of shells randomly falling, the wedding hall was almost empty. Only close relatives and good friends venture out of their homes for a wedding.

The young girls formed a circle around the bride as she happily danced to the loud music. Having been abandoned by my daughter, who was with the other girls, I sat down alone at my table eating a piece of cake and desperately looking around for someone to talk to. An old woman who seemed lonely, like me, nodded her head, smiled, and asked me to join her.

"Are you from Damascus?" she asked. Then she introduced herself, "I am Um Tofiek from Idlib."

"Idlib!" I exclaimed. The name seemed to have magic. I smiled, introduced myself, and said, "By any chance, do you happen to know some folktales from Idlib? I have been searching for them for so long."

The old woman smiled sweetly and said, "Well of course - I'm a Tete, after all."

I took out my pen and pad to take notes, but soon I was so taken by Um Tofiek's stories that I put them aside and let myself be drawn into the world of make-believe.

Little by little, the sound of shells from outside and the sound of music in the hall disappeared and all I could hear was Um Tofiek's voice telling her stories.

THE RED ROOSTER

Kan ya ma kan, a long time ago, there lived a happy couple in a small house with their son and daughter.

One day, the wife got sick and died. The husband and his two children mourned her for a long time, until things got very difficult to bear. Eventually, the husband was introduced to a pretty woman and asked for her hand in marriage.

"I have one condition" said the husband "My children are as dear to me as my eyes. Starve me, but feed them. Strip the clothes off my back, but dress them!"

"Don't worry, I will treasure them," said the woman. "If the house is not large enough for them, I will put them in my heart."

The man was content with the woman's response and happily went ahead with the wedding plans.

116

The day finally came, and the woman entered her new house. She took one glance at the boy and the girl and felt her heart jump to her throat. She looked at their faces and said to herself, "O Allah! I seek refuge with You from the cursed Satan."* Then she swallowed hard and wondered to herself, *what can I do with these two devils? I gave my word to my husband, but I can't bear to see them.* Then she smiled at them, put the boy on her lap, and put her arm around the girl.

All the neighbors were amazed at her kindness to the two orphans and marveled at her. They wondered what good deeds the man must have done in his life to deserve such a good wife.

Time passed and the woman no longer could bear to have the children near her. She couldn't even bear to see them, so she sent them out to play in the streets every morning after her husband left to work on the farm. The poor orphans didn't dare tell their father and remained outside, rain or shine, until their father returned from the farm.

One day, their father came back with a sheep and said to his wife, "I'll slaughter this sheep for you to cook for my guests who are coming for dinner tomorrow."

The next morning, the man handed his wife the cut pieces of meat. She spiced the meat and began to cook it. As she cleaned the house, the smell of the meat filled the air and she went to the kitchen and took out a piece of meat to taste. The meat tasted so delicious that she couldn't stop herself from dipping her fork in the pot again and again. Before long, she found that she had eaten all the meat.

"Oh, my God," she gasped. "What will my husband's guests have for lunch?"

---

* This appeal to Allah is invoked when one feels horrified or threatened. The new wife strangely reacts as if there is something evil or cursed about the children, "these two devils."

She looked from the window and saw her husband's son playing in the street, and she got an evil idea.

"I must save myself from being scorned by my husband," she thought. "I will slaughter the young boy and cook him for dinner."

She poked her head out the kitchen window and called the boy to come in. The girl looked at her stepmother's face and could sense she was planning something wicked. She ran to her brother and tried to stop him from going in, but he ran to the kitchen as fast as he could - only to be caught by his stepmother and heartlessly slaughtered and cooked.

When her husband arrived with his guests, his wife had prepared a dazzling meal.

Everyone sat down and ate except the brokenhearted little girl. "Where is my son?" asked the father.

"He is playing in the neighborhood with his friends," answered his wife.

Then the father turned to his daughter and asked, "Why aren't you eating?"

The poor girl looked at her plate and all she could think was that this is my brother's hand - that is his leg. She felt nauseous and went to her room and cried.

The guests, the man, and his wife ate all the food and happily retired to the garden to drink coffee.

Meanwhile, the girl sneaked out of her room, went into the kitchen, took her brother's bones, and put them in a bag. Then she left the house to look for a place to put them. She walked and walked until she reached a well. She stood by the well and said:

Oh Father of all Wells, oh Well
If I throw my brother's bones down your well
What will they become? Please tell.

The well answered, "They will turn into a donkey!"

The girl was horrified and said, "Oh no, not a donkey! People will ride it and load it with heavy things."

So the girl picked up the bag of bones and walked and walked until she reached a second well. She stood at the well and said:

Oh Father of all Wells, oh Well
If I throw my brother's bones down your well
What will they become? Please tell.
The well answered, "They will turn into a dog!"

The girl shook her head and said, "Oh no, not a dog! It will bark and children will run after it and throw stones." The girl picked up the bag of bones again and walked and walked until she reached a third well. She stood by the well and said:

Oh Father of all Wells, oh Well
If I throw my brother's bones down your well
What will they become? Please tell.
The well answered, "They will turn into a red rooster!"

The girl liked the thought of her brother turning into a red rooster and threw the bones into the well. Once the bones hit the bottom of the well, a great red rooster flew out of the well and began following the girl wherever she went.

On her way home, the girl met a tall, handsome young man who fell in love with her at first glance. He asked her to marry him and the girl, not wanting to return to her wicked stepmother, accepted right away.

The young man took the girl to his house and introduced her to his mother and announced that he would not marry any girl but her. Unfortunately, his mother disliked the girl from the minute she set eyes on her. Nevertheless, her son married the girl.

Several days later, when the young man went to work, the mother invited all the neighborhood girls, along with her son's wife, to the meadow to enjoy the spring weather. Once they arrived, the girls clapped and danced around the girl and then pushed her into a well. The woman covered the well with vines and returned home.

When the young man arrived, he asked his mother where his wife was. She told him that the girl had walked out of the house and had not come back. The young man looked for her everywhere until he lost hope.

One day, as the young man sat sadly at the window, he saw a red rooster walking to and fro in front of the house. He went outside and followed the red rooster until he reached a well. Then the red rooster stood at the well and sang:

> I'm the red rooster with a story to tell
> My stepmother killed me, my father ate me
> My loving sister threw my bones down the well.

The young man heard the song and guessed that his wife was in the well. He uncovered the well and threw a rope down to pull the girl out. He was furious when he heard that his mother had tried to get rid of her. He took his sword and ran to his house. When his mother opened the door, she saw her son brandishing his sword with a murderous look in his eyes. She screamed and pleaded for mercy. The young man felt sorry for his mother and said, "You almost killed my wife. You must accept and love her if you want to live with us!"

The mother felt guilty and apologized to her son and his wife. The red rooster crowed for joy and they all lived happily ever after.

HUDEDAN AND THE LOAF OF BREAD

Um Tofiek's eyes lit up as she told me this story. She said, "I've been living in Damascus for over forty years, but I never forgot this folktale. It has lived for hundreds of years."

Kan ya ma kan, a long time ago, there lived a kind-hearted Tete with her only grandson Hudedan in a beautiful green village. Tete loved Hudedan dearly and spoiled him thoroughly.

One morning, Tete baked a round loaf of bread in the *tannour* and offered it to Hudedan with a cup of milk and two slices of white cheese. Hudedan yawned and rubbed his eyes and looked at the loaf of bread and said, "What an ugly looking loaf of bread!" He threw it on the ground and protested, "Your loaves of bread are usually beautiful and round!"

His tete was very offended. She picked up the loaf of bread, kissed it and said, "Ugly! I worked so hard to make this loaf of bread for you. I woke up early in the morning and lit the *tannour*, then I kneaded the dough and baked the bread – all to hear you say this!?"

"Oh Tete, the world didn't come to an end. All I said was that it is an ugly looking loaf of bread and then I threw it on the ground," said Hudedan. "Besides, I can make a much better looking loaf of bread than you can!"

Tete looked at Hudedan and said, "Fine. I'll not talk to you until you show me you can make a better loaf of bread than mine."

Hudedan enthusiastically ran to the *tannour* and said:

Oh tannour, you baker of bread

Give me a loaf that is nice and round,
So Tete will forgive me
For throwing one on the ground.

The Tannour opened its large mouth, laughed and said, "How can I bake you a loaf of bread without wood?"

Hudedan looked puzzled and asked, "Where can I find wood?"

"Simple," said the *Tannour*. "Go to the mountain and fetch some wood."

Hudedan climbed the mountain until he reached the top and said:

Oh mountain, so high
Where birds nest and fly,
Would you give me some wood?
The tannour said I should
Bring wood to bake bread
This is just what he said.

The mountain laughed so hard that some of its rocks rolled down. Then it said, "Why should I give you some wood when you don't have an axe?"

"Where can I find an axe?" asked Hudedan.

"You must go and fetch it from the blacksmith."

Hudedan descended the mountain and headed towards the blacksmith's shop. When he finally got there, a strong-looking man greeted him as he was putting charcoal into the furnace and pumping the bellows.

Hudedan said:

Oh Blacksmith, you are big and strong
You pump the bellows all day long.
I need an axe to cut some wood,

Please give me one, I think you could.

The blacksmith wiped his sweat and asked Hudedan if he had money to pay him for the axe.

"No" said Hudedan sadly, as he emptied his pockets. The blacksmith felt sorry for Hudedan and asked to hear his story so he could help him.

"I made my Tete sad by telling her that her loaf of bread was not round and she will not talk to me until I can prove to her that I can make a better loaf than hers. I went to the *tannour* to bake bread and it told me it needed wood, so I climbed the mountain to fetch some wood and it told me I needed an axe! So here I am pleading with you for an axe."

The blacksmith gently patted him on the back and said, "I will give you an axe for free because you want to please your Tete, on the condition that you help me make it."

Hudedan thanked the blacksmith and rolled up his sleeves and hammered the hot iron to change its shape – bam, bam, bam! He hammered so hard his face turned as red as a tomato. When the metal was softened enough to shape it into an axe, the blacksmith finished it and handed the axe to Hudedan.

Hudedan thanked the blacksmith and hurried up the mountain to chop wood.

Back home, he put the wood in the *tannour* and lit it. After that, he kneaded the dough, formed a ball and patted it, and laid it on a small pillow. Then he slapped it on the inside wall of the mud brick oven. In a few minutes, he lifted it out, but it had a big hole in it and it wasn't round. He tried his luck again, but as he was slapping the next piece of dough in the *Tannour*, he thought he heard someone knock on the door. There was no one at the door, but when he returned, the bread had burned.

At that moment, Tete came into the kitchen and found Hudedan crying. He said to her, "I tried, Tete, but I can't bake bread like you. I can't make a beautiful round loaf of bread." Then he looked up at her and said, "I promise I'll never criticize a loaf of your bread again! Please forgive me, dear Tete."

Tete embraced Hudedan lovingly and said, "Oh my dear Hudedan, of course I forgive you! Come my dear, together we will make a beautiful loaf of bread as round as the moon!" And they did.

THE EFFENDI'S THOBE

Kan ya ma kan, a long time ago, a friend of the Effendi held a dinner party and invited him. The Effendi arrived wearing a torn and ragged thobe. When the host saw him dressed like that he got upset and worried about what the other guests would think when they saw his friend in rags. So he asked him to leave.

The Effendi went home and changed his clothes and came back wearing an elegant new *thobe* with his head wrapped in the respectable turban of a sheikh. When he entered his friend's house, the other guests showed him great respect and gathered around him, talking in a deferential manner.

The host was pleased and asked the Effendi to lead the way to the prepared feast and he told him, "My dear friend, please sit down and eat whatever you like.

The Effendi sat down, but he did not eat. Instead, he held his *thobe* and opened it a little bit and said, "Please, my *thobe*, come eat whatever you like."

The host said, "What are you doing?"

The Effendi said, "I am taking care of your guest. You invited the *thobe*, not me."

A True Story: A Syrian Hero, Ibrahim Hanano

Dr. Adel Akel, has been a good friend of my father's since the 1950s, when they both were studying in New York City. He was one of the first Syrians my father met in New York, and for a time they shared an apartment with several other Syrian students. Like my father, Dr. Akel studied economics. He became a Professor in the Faculty of Economics at Aleppo University and later worked for many years as a national income expert for the UNDP. He is such a good family friend, I call him "Amo Adel" – Uncle Adel.

Last year he came with his wife, Fadia Shabarak, to visit us and we had a very good time talking and reminiscing. I asked them both if they could give me a folktale and Fadia told me one from Aleppo, her home town. Amo Adel, who is originally from Idlib, said he really didn't know any folktales. As they got up to leave, the electricity was cut off and we were pleased they didn't want to leave in the dark and decided to spend more time with us.

We all sat back down around a table full of lit candles. The candlelight bounced off the walls, causing shadows to flicker about on the ceiling. Amo Adel leaned towards me over his cane and announced that he did have a story from Idlib for me after all; not a folktale but a true story.

Amo Adel began by saying, "Ibrahim Hanano was a very courageous Syrian leader. He launched a revolt against the French army when it landed on the Syrian coast in 1919, in preparation for taking over Syria. Hanano was responsible for the disarmament of many French troops, the destruction of railroads and telegraph lines, the sabotage of tanks, and the foiling of French attacks on Aleppo. At first, he received military aid from the nationalist Turkish movement of Mustafa Kemal Ataturk. However, once the Turks signed the Franklin-Bouillon Agreement with France in October 1921, Hanano and his men no longer received arms from the Turks, and the struggle collapsed.

"Later on, Hanano was arrested and handed over to the French authorities. The French Attorney General demanded the death penalty, saying, "If Hanano had seven heads, I would cut them all off."

"Hanano was tried by a French military criminal court, but his lawyer argued he was not a criminal, but a political opponent. During the trial, the chief Judge asked Hanano, 'You claim you were a leader of a revolution; who mandated you to defend the Syrian people?'

"'The Syrian people!' affirmed Hanano.

"'Can you prove it?' asked the Judge.

"Silence rang out in the courtroom, and then a man stood up and said, 'I am Saadallah al Jabri, a Muslim Arab Syrian citizen, Your Honor. I declare that I mandated him.'

"Then another man stood up and said, 'I am Mikael Elyan, a Christian Arab Syrian citizen, Your Honor. I declare that I mandated him.'

"Suddenly all the people in the courtroom stood up and shouted in unison, 'We mandated him! We all did!'

"The French military court acquitted Ibrahim Hanano of all charges filed against him. In addition, it acknowledged the right of self-determination for people under occupation. We Syrians consider Hanano's rebellion as the first of many revolts against French occupation, until our independence was finally achieved in 1947."

Amo Adel stopped as the sounds of shells echoed from a distance. Then he looked into our eyes and said, "During that period of time, there was no difference between a Muslim and Christian Syrian. This is a story that reveals the true nature and the spirit of all Syrians. Hopefully these days will come back and the Syrian people will once again be strong and united."

The story of Hanano has passed into folk legend, and here is a popular song about him chanted by Syrian children:

A plane flew in the sky
Full of soldiers, full of light,
With Ibrahim Hanano on board
Riding on his horse.

A Recipe from Idlib
Eggplant Stuffed with Burghol

Ingredients

2 lbs medium-sized eggplants

1 lb (½ kilo) finely ground lamb with some fat

1 tomato, peeled and chopped

1 green pepper, finely chopped

½ cup chick peas

1 ½ tsp salt

¼ tsp black pepper

1 cup coarse burghol, rinsed

1 tbsp butter

1 tbsp pomegranate molasses (*dibbis*)

Sauce

3 cups water

2 tbsp tomato paste

1 ½ tsp salt

1 tsp sugar

The juice of one lemon

1 tsp dry mint

4 cloves garlic, minced

Method

Wash the eggplants, cut tops and reserve

Ream out eggplants with an Arabic vegetable corer (haffara) or peeler

Rinse and drain eggplants

Combine stuffing ingredients and mix thoroughly

Stuff loosely, leaving space for burghol to expand, then replace reserved tops

Combine water, tomato paste, salt, and sugar; bring to a boil

Add eggplants (the water should cover the them)

Simmer covered for about an hour, stirring now and then

Add lemon juice, mint, and mashed garlic and cook 10 minutes more

6

ALEPPO

The Muhafaza of Aleppo is situated in the north of the country on the Turkish border, and before the war was the most
populous governorate in Syria. It is a very fertile land, and some of
its principal crops are olives, plums, figs, pomegranates, and the
famous Aleppo pistachio. Its capital, Aleppo, was once the largest
city in Syria and the industrial and financial center of the country.
Like Damascus, it is one of the oldest continuously inhabited cities
in the world. In the past, its importance stemmed from the fact
it was at one end of the Silk Road, a network of trade routes that
passed from the Far East through central Asia to Mesopotamia.
Now, however, the city of Aleppo is a key battleground in the civil
war. The famous landmarks of the city, including the Citadel, the
12th Century Umayyad Mosque, the Aleppo Museum and the historic covered souk are all damaged or completely destroyed in the
case of the souk. Today the city is a wasteland and the daily death
toll is heartbreaking.

THREE FOLKTALES FROM ALEPPO

*Her eyes sparkled as a wide smile spread across her face "I'm an
optimist and I always have been." She waved her hand as if she were
silencing the sounds of war raging outside and said, "I believe things*

will improve and eventually get better. My Tete used to tell me a story about a Princess named Qamar al Zaman who went through many hardships in her life, but then was rewarded with happiness."

I hurried to take out my pen and pad to write while Fadia Shabarak told the following story.

PRINCESS QAMAR AL ZAMAN – PRINCESS MOON OF TIME (OR "ETERNAL MOON")

Kan ya ma kan, in a bygone time, there lived a King who met once a week with a fortune teller who would tell him what the future held. One day, the fortune teller predicted that the King's twelve-year-old daughter, Qamar al Zaman, would grow up to marry a poor peasant. The King was very upset by this prophecy. Since he dreaded such an unacceptable fate for his daughter, he ordered a palace to be built on an island in the middle of the sea.

When the palace was finished, he commanded that his family be transported there in a stately ship, and said he would follow soon after. When the ship neared the island, a storm suddenly arose; wind tore at the sail, rain came down in sheets, waves tossed the ship around, and finally it capsized, drowning everyone but the Princess. She hung on to a wooden board, and waves pushed her towards the shore.

Qamar al Zaman was so exhausted from her ordeal that she fell asleep on the rocks, where she was found by an old fisherman. He carried her home and asked his wife and only son Kareem to take care of her until she got better.

Many days passed until the Princess regained her strength with the good care of the fisherman's wife and his kindhearted son, Kareem. "What is your name?" asked Kareem. Qamar al Zaman closed her eyes, and images of the giant waves and the sinking ship raced through her mind. She decided that her name should be changed from "Moon of Time" to Gader al Zaman which means "Betrayal of Time," so this is the name she gave.

The fisherman and his wife told her that they had always wished for a daughter and said, "Please consider yourself in your own home."

"Thank you for your kindness," said the Princess, but she chose not to tell them her real identity.

Time passed and the fisherman and his wife treated her as their own daughter. They loved her dearly. The young girl was very helpful to her new family. She was intelligent and resourceful. She not only redecorated the house with a royal touch, but also gave the fisherman new ideas about marketing his fish. After several years passed, Kareem fell in love with her and asked for her hand in marriage. She accepted his proposal and secretly wished her father the King was with her to see her happiness.

One day her father, the King who for years had been struck with grief and guilt, turned to his Wazir and said, "I tried to prevent the predicted fate from happening and, as a result, I lost my wife and daughter." Then he said, "Sometimes I have a strange feeling my daughter is alive. I must go and see the shipwreck myself."

"Your Majesty, you shouldn't feel guilty. You were only trying to protect your daughter," replied the Wazir. "And I agree it is a good idea to search for your daughter."

The very next day, the King and his Wazir set sail for the island where the King had ordered the castle to be built for his daughter. When they reached the island, they walked along the shore for a long time until they came upon shattered pieces of the ship cast on the rocks. The King gently touched a piece of the wreckage, thought of his wife and daughter, and cried bitterly.

"It's getting dark," said the Wazir, "We must find a safe place to spend the night. Our ship is too far away now to reach before night falls."

In the distance they spotted a faint light flickering. Having no other choice, they decided to walk toward the light in hopes of finding shelter.

When they got closer, they found the light coming from a simple mud brick house. They knocked on the door and an old fisherman greeted them and welcomed them into his home.

Gader al Zaman heard the King speaking and instantly recognized the voice of her father. She went into the kitchen and quickly prepared the grape nectar he liked to drink and some of his favorite foods. She also set the table in the way she knew he liked.

The King looked around and said to his Wazir, "I see royal touches."

Gader al Zaman veiled her face and came in with a tray of grape nectar and offered it to the King and the Wazir.

The King was shocked when he was offered the grape nectar. "How did you know this is my favorite drink?"

Gader al Zaman smiled and said, "I was inspired by God."

When they sat down to eat and the King discovered that all the dishes were not only his favorites, but also that they were prepared just the way his late wife used to have them prepared. He said, "How could you possibly know these were my favorite dishes? No one knows this except..."

"...except your only daughter!" finished Gader al Zaman interrupting the King and unveiling her face.

The King was overjoyed! He embraced her, to the great astonishment of her husband Kareem and his family.

The King begged his daughter to forgive him, saying, "I tried to protect you, but instead caused you the loss of your mother and much misery."

Gader al Zaman cried joyfully, "Oh, Father, I love you so much!" Then she introduced him to her beloved husband Kareem and said, "You didn't cause me misery. Instead I have been blessed with a loving family."

The King told his daughter, her husband Kareem, and his family that they must all go back with him and his Wazir. They set sail the next day. The Princess took back her name and was again Princess Qamar al Zaman. When they reached the King's castle, the King welcomed them all there and said, "From now on, this is your home."

And there, in the King's castle, they all lived happily ever after.

Um Diyab

Kan ya ma kan, in an olden time, there was a man with a sharp-tongued wife named Um Diyab who took pleasure in fighting with people. No one dared go near anything that was hers in fear of her aggressive nature. The woman was forever fighting with people - sometimes with her neighbors, sometimes with her brothers and sisters, sometimes with her brothers-in-law. This would con-tinuously put her husband, Abu Diyab, in the awkward position of having to apologize to others on her behalf, until he hated his life. Finally, he decided to throw her into a dry, deserted well and be finished with her.

One day he said to her, "My friend has bought a house and you and I must go to congratulate him." They set off in what Abu Diyab said was the direction of the house. After a long time, they passed by a graveyard where a dry, deserted well stood by one of its gates. Um Diyab was tired after such a long walk, so Abu Diyab put a pillow on the well and told her to sit and rest. No sooner did she sit than she fell to the bottom of the well.

Abu Diyab said to himself, "Now I have gotten rid of her and her sharp tongue." He went home, but his conscience would not let him rest. He fretted day and night about how her blood would be on his hands. He began to regret what he had done and returned with a rope to pull Um Diyab out.

Abu Diyab dangled the rope down and then began to pull, but when he finally got it up, instead of Um Diyab he found that a black python - a disguised Jinni - was clinging to the rope with its fangs.

The python said, "Relieve me of Um Diyab and may God relieve you from the Hellfire! Since she came down this well she has been talking and fighting and I know not what to say. She hasn't stopped screaming since she fell down the well. Indeed, I know neither rest nor peace. Relieve me of her and you can have all my treasure and all that I own as your reward. Just leave me the King's daughter, my beloved Princess, because I love her so. I put a spell on her and her father has her locked up in a room in his castle."

So Abu Diyab took all the treasure of the Jinni and enjoyed its wealth. He now had his own castle and a better wife than Um Diyab. One day he thought of going to the King's castle to see the Princess mentioned by the Jinni. When he reached the castle, he approached the window of her locked room and saw the black python next to her window.

The python was in a rage when he saw Abu Diyab. "Didn't I warn you not to come near my Princess!" hissed the python.

"Yes," said Abu Diyab, but I am here to rescue you from Um Diyab, for she is following me!"

"Oh no, not Um Diyab again!" screamed the black python. When he heard Um Diyab was coming, he ran for his life and escaped before she could arrive. By this trickery, Abu Diyab gained the King's daughter as well as the Jinni's treasure.

Abu Diyab starts out as a victim, but in the end he betrays the Python/ Jinni who enriches him, and although he gains the King's daughter through trickery, he apparently lives happily ever after. And what becomes of Um Diyab? Not all folktales have a moral and good does not always triumph.

SEVEN POTS

Kan ya ma kan, a long time ago, there lived three orphaned sisters who spun flax into yarn for a living. The sisters spun all week long and then the eldest sister, Futune, would go to the market to sell the yarn and buy food and more flax.

One day, while Futune was in the market selling her yarn, a man approached her and said, "My name is Ahmad. I'm a stranger in this country. May I go home with you?"

"Why?" asked Futune.

"I want to ask for your hand from your father," said Ahmad.

Futune blushed and said, "My parents are dead. The matter is in my hand."

So Ahmad accompanied Futune back home and spent the day with her and her two sisters Ghusune and Maysune. Ahmad was very nice and polite and charmed Futune. When she accepted his marriage proposal, Ahmad brought a government-approved Sheikh to the house to write up the marriage in a big book which they both signed after they agreed upon the dowry.

In a few days, Futune kissed her two sisters goodbye and left with Ahmad. They walked on foot until they reached the outskirts of the city.

"I can no longer walk," said Futune.

So Ahmad knelt down and said, "Ride on my back," and then flew with her in the air and asked her, "What do you see?"

"Everything seems very small!" said Futune.

In an hour or so, he landed next to an old castle with a wooden door. He asked Futune to follow him as he knocked on the door. A maid named Kherazan opened the door and welcomed them.

Ahmad said:

Oh Kherazan, the mortar pound
So the neighbors hear the sound,
Pound the mortar, pound with zeal
And quickly, bring your Lady's meal.

Kherazan went to the kitchen and came back with a small loaf of bread and an onion. Futune couldn't believe her eyes when she saw her meal.

"Is that all I'm going to eat?" she asked, angrily.

"Yes!" said Ahmad, coldly.

"I can't live with you if I have practically nothing to eat!" complained Futune.

All of a sudden, Ahmad yanked her by the hair and said, "It doesn't seem you will live with me at all!" Then, he dragged her down to the basement and threw her on the ground, and locked the door. Futune found herself with three other women who had all had the same experience as hers. They told her their story and said that Ahmad was the stingiest man in the world.

After a few months, Ahmad went back to visit Futune's sisters. When they asked him about Futune, he pretended to be very sad and said, "I deeply regret to announce the death of your sister." Then he asked for the hand of the second sister, Ghusune, and she accepted to be his wife. They were wed and they said goodbye to the youngest sister, Maysoun.

They walked on foot until they reached the outskirts of the city. When Ghusune could no longer walk, Ahmad knelt down and said, "Ride on my back." Then he flew with her in the air until he reached his old castle with the wooden door. Ahmad knocked on the door and Kherazan welcomed them.

Ahmad said:

Oh Kherazan, the mortar pound
So the neighbors hear the sound,
Pound the mortar, pound with zeal
And quickly, bring your Lady's meal.

Kherazan went to the kitchen and came back with a small loaf of bread and an onion. Like her sister, Ghusune couldn't believe her eyes when she saw her meal.

"Is that all I'm going to eat?" she asked in a shocked tone of voice.

"Yes!" said Ahmad coldly.

"I can't live with you if I have practically nothing to eat!" complained Ghusune.

Ahmad yanked Ghusune by the hair and said, "It doesn't seem you will live with me at all!" Then, as he had done with her sister, he dragged her down to the basement and threw her on the ground along with Futune and the other women.

A year passed until one day Ahmad went back to visit Maysune, the youngest sister. He told her that her sister Ghusune had died in childbirth and pretended to be very sad. Maysune felt very sorry for him, and when he asked for her hand, she accepted without hesitation. They were wed and left the next day after saying farewell to all the neighbors who had become like Maysune's own family.

They walked on foot until they reached the outskirts of the city. When Maysune could no longer walk, Ahmad knelt down and said, "Ride on my back." Then he flew with her in the air until he reached his old castle with the wooden door. Ahmad knocked on the door and Kherazan welcomed them.

Ahmad said:

Oh Kerazan, the mortar pound
So the neighbors hear the sound,
Pound the mortar, pound with zeal
And quickly bring your Lady's meal.

Kherazan went to the kitchen and came back with a small loaf of bread and an onion.

Unlike her two sisters, Maysune thanked Kherazan for the meal and scraped a small piece of the onion with the knife, and ate it with a small piece of bread. Then she scolded Kherazan for giving her too much food.

Ahmad's face brightened when he heard Maysune's words, "May God bless you," said Ahmad "You are the wife I have been looking for."

The next day, when Ahmad left the old castle, Maysune called upon Kherazan and asked her, "Do you really live on a piece of bread and an onion?"

Kherazan smiled and said, "Ahmad is a very rich man but, unfortunately, a stingy one, too!" Then she pointed at a storehouse in the yard and whispered, "We have a storehouse full of all kinds of food and he doesn't know I have a copy of the key."

Then Kherazan led Maysune down to the basement and opened the door. Maysune was shocked to see her two sisters and all the other women whom Ahmad had married before. Her two sisters recognized her and ran to her crying. She promised her two sisters and the other women that she would free them soon.

"They would have never stayed alive if I didn't cook for them," said Kherazan.

Maysune thanked Kherazan and said, "We must work together to help these poor women."

When they heard Ahmad returning, they left the storehouse, locked it, and hurried to meet him.

As time passed, Ahmad realized what a lucky man he was to have Maysune as his wife. She was even more careful than he was with money. In fact, she was so wise that he consulted her in all his business matters. All his friends noticed how happy he had become in his new marriage and insisted that he invite them for dinner.

But first he consulted Maysune and she assured him that the invitation wouldn't cost a lot of money. "Go hunting and shoot a bird for us and I'll divide it in half and cook a great meal for you and your friends!"

Ahmad loved her idea and went to shoot a bird in the forest. The next day, Ahmad invited his friends for dinner while Maysune called upon Kherazan and they took out whatever they needed from the storage room. Then they freed the two sisters, Futune and Ghusune and all the other women from the basement and asked them to help cook for the invitation.

When Ahmad came back, he saw seven big pots of food cooking on the fire. He went crazy at the sight, realizing that the seven pots could have never been filled by half a bird. He hysterically jumped up and down and cried out:

> Seven pots cooking and boiling
> All filled from half a bird?
> Seven pots bubbling and simmering
> It can't be true! It's just absurd!

Maysune innocently nodded her head and said, "O yes, my dear Husband, all from half a bird."

Still, Ahmad was not convinced. He violently hit his chest and stomped his feet in a rage, repeating the same thing over and over again. "Seven pots, seven pots, seven pots!" Until, all at once - he had a heart attack and died!

Maysune and her two sisters were very happy to see the end of Ahmad. They released the imprisoned women and then they divided Ahmad's treasure among themselves and the women. All of these women preferred to return to their countries. However, the three sisters stayed on in the castle with Kherazan and lived happily ever after.

❀ ❀

THREE RECIPES FROM ALEPPO

SAFERJALANIA — MEAT WITH QUINCE

Ingredients

1 kg. quince

1 kg. *mozat* with bones (lamb shanks)

1 kg. peeled and juiced pomegranates (about 3)

1 cup tomato paste

4 – 5 garlic cloves

1 tbsp mint

1 tsp salt

Juice of 3 lemons

1 tbsp sugar

Method

Cut quinces in fourths and don't peel (put them in water so as not to discolor)

Boil all ingredients with the meat except the quince

When the meat is tender, add the quince and cook another ½ hour

Serve with boiled kibbi or rice or burghol

MA'MUNIA — A PUDDING

Mamunia is a pudding which is garnished with cinnamon and nuts and served with cheese. It is served for breakfast or as a dessert. It is said that this pudding was named after the Abbasid Caliph al Ma'mun.

Ingredients

4 tbsp butter

1 cup coarse semolina

4 cups water

2 cups sugar

1 tsp vanilla

4 tbsp fresh curd (ricotta) cheese

1 tsp orange blossom flavoring (optional)

Nuts and cinnamon to garnish

Method

Melt butter in pot on low flame

Add semolina to butter and stir until it turns golden

Boil water and sugar in a large pot

Add semolina to water and stir for about 3 minutes

Let it cool, then add vanilla and orange blossom flavoring

Pour into small bowls and garnish with curd cheese, nuts, and cinnamon

It is served warm in winter and cold in summer

MEAT WITH CHERRIES

Ingredients

1 lb of black cherries

1 cup sugar

½ lb finely ground meat

1 tbsp tomato paste

Salt, cinnamon, and pepper to taste

2 Arabic loaves (pita) cut into bite-sized diamond shapes

Method

Wash cherries and cook in water and sugar just until tender

Remove pits when cooled, blend cherries in blender and return to pan Add salt, pepper, cinnamon, and pine nuts to meat

Make medium-sized meat balls and fry

Fry the diamond-shaped bread and place in a deep serving plate

Bring cherry sauce to a boil and add tomato paste

Add meat balls to sauce and cook 15 minutes

Pour sauce on fried bread, then place meat balls on top and serve

7

LATAKIA

The name "Latakia" is a corruption of the Greek name, Laodicea. Laodicea got its name when it was first founded in the fourth century BC under the rule of the Seleucid Empire. It was named by Seleucus I Nicator in honor of his mother Laodice.

The Muhafaza of Latakia embraces Syria's fertile Mediterranean coastal area. It is an important agricultural region, producing abundant crops of tobacco, cotton, cereals, and fruits.

The City of Latakia is the principal port of Syria. It is located on a good harbor with an extensive agricultural hinterland. Exports include bitumen, asphalt, cereals, cotton, fruit, and tobacco. Cotton ginning, vegetable-oil processing, tanning, and sponge fishing are local industries.

Compared to other Syrian cities, Latakia has been mostly spared the brutal civil war raging elsewhere in the country. As of 2015, many residents of Latakia continue life as usual.

As a personal note, my father-in-law is from Tell, but Itaf Mazloum, my late mother-in-law, was from Jebleh in the Muhafaza of Latakia.

Three Folktales from Latakia

Abu Qarnayn ou Qarn

When my husband and his sister were children, their Uncle Asaad Mazloum used to visit them during the long, dark nights of winter and tell them stories. One story my husband remembers well is 'Abu Qarnayn ou Qarn.' Although the story was scary, Khalo Asaad's funny gestures and narrating style made them laugh as he told the story. This folktale seems too dreadful for children to enjoy, but the truth is, they did.

The strange name, "Abu Qarnayn ou Qarn," literally means the Father of Two Horns and a Horn, in other words, a three-horned monster; whereas "Abu Qarnayn" is a monster with two horns.

Kan ya ma kan, many years ago, a woman had a beautiful daughter as pretty as the moon. One day, the mother's younger sister came to visit. As she was leaving, she said she wanted to take her niece home with her. "Please, dear Sister," she begged. "Let your daughter spend the night with me since my husband is away and I am alone."

The sister and her husband agreed reluctantly, but made her promise to keep an eye on their one and only daughter.

The little girl accompanied her Khaleh (Auntie) to her house on the other side of the forest. They both enjoyed themselves, eating and playing games until they fell asleep.

Suddenly, in the middle of the night, the Khaleh's husband came home unexpectedly and was furious to see the little girl sleeping on the sofa.

"You must get rid of her at once!" said the husband.

The Khaleh looked at her sleeping niece and asked her husband to let her stay just for the night. "Absolutely not," said the husband. "You must make her leave this minute!"

So the Khaleh reluctantly woke her niece and told her she must go back home. The poor little girl looked out the window into the total darkness and was scared to death.

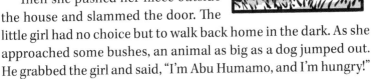

"Oh please, Khaleh, let me stay the night! I promise to leave in the morning."

"No," said the Khaleh roughly. "You must leave at once."

Then she pushed her niece outside the house and slammed the door. The little girl had no choice but to walk back home in the dark. As she approached some bushes, an animal as big as a dog jumped out. He grabbed the girl and said, "I'm Abu Humamo, and I'm hungry!"

The girl cried out, "Abu Humamo, please don't eat me!"

The heart of Abu Humamo softened and he let go of the girl and said, "Don't be afraid of me, dear Little Girl, but you should be scared of Abu Qarnayn."

The girl's heart was trembling by now, but she had no choice except to move on. In the middle of the road she suddenly saw two big eyes shining in the dark. Then an animal that looked like a hyena leaped on her and said, "I'm Abu Qarnayn, and I'm so hungry!"

The girl cried out, "Abu Qarnayn, oh, please let me go!"

The heart of Abu Qarnayn softened and he let go of the girl and warned her, "Don't be afraid of me, dear Little Girl, but you should be scared of Abu Qarnayn ou Qarn."

The girl's heart was about to fail her as she tried to imagine what kind of vicious animal Abu Qarnayn ou Qarn must be.

By now, the girl was very close to her house. All at once, a huge, hairy creature with three horns attacked her and growled, "I'm Abu Qarnayn ou Qarn, and I've been waiting for you all night!"

The little girl cried out, "Oh, please, Abu Qarnayn ou Qarn!"

Please don't eat me,
I'm as skinny as can be.
I'll give you raisins, dates,
    and bread
If you'll come home with me.

Abu Qarnayn ou Qarn agreed to give her a chance and accompanied her to her house, where he pounded on the door and shouted:

Abu Qarnayn ou Qarn is here at your door.
I've brought you your daughter and what's even more,
She's promised me raisins and dates and some bread,
And if you don't feed me, I'll eat her instead!

Unfortunately, the girl's parents were sound asleep and didn't hear Abu Qarnayn ou Qarn pounding on the door or his loud calls, so he leaped on the little girl and gobbled her up, and coughed out her bones and clothes.

In the morning, the girl's parents opened the door and were horrified to find the bones and clothes of their darling girl piled up near their front door. They cried brokenheartedly over their daughter and wished they had never sent her to her Khaleh. Not long after this, they died of sorrow.

Another folktale without a happy ending and without a moral.

SANASIL AND RABAB

Kan ya ma kan, a long time ago, there lived a Mother Goat with two little kids named Sanasil and Rabab. Every day before she left the house to collect some fresh grass, she would call them and say, "I must go and fetch some fresh grass for you. While I'm gone, watch out for the Dubaa (Hyena). For if she ever gets hold of you, she will swallow you up! Open the door only when you hear me sing these words:

Oh, Sanasil and Rabab,
Open for me the door,
I carry fresh grass with my horns -
The grass you are waiting for.

One day, the Dubaa overheard the Mother Goat, so she decided to find her way into their house. She made two horns from dough, baked them, and glued them on her head. Then she put some grass on the horns and headed to the goats' house. The Dubaa knocked on the door and sang the Mother Goat's song.

"Oh, Sanasil and Rabab,
Open for me the door,
I carry fresh grass with my horns -,
The grass you are waiting for."

The kids thought their mother's voice sounded strange, but when they looked through the keyhole they saw horns covered with grass. The kids opened the door, but instead of their mother, in rushed the Dubaa and swallowed them both in a single gulp.

When the Mother Goat came back home, she found the door open and her two kids missing. The Mother Goat knew it was the evil doing of the *Dubaa* and rushed to its cave. She stood on the roof of the cave and pounded with one of her hooves.

The Dubaa got annoyed and snarled.

"Someone is stamping up on my roof
And knocking mud in my pot with their hoof."

The Mother Goat proudly answered.

I'm the Mother Goat of the kids you ate
Come out, come out, don't hesitate
Come out of your cave, into the light.
Come meet me in the field to fight.

Again, the Dubaa made herself horns of dough, baked them, and glued them on her head. Then she came out to fight the Mother Goat. She fiercely flew at the Dubaa with all her might and knocked her down. The two dough horns broke into small pieces. Then the Mother Goat stabbed the Dubaa's stomach with her horns and cut it open. Out popped one kid, and it was soon followed by the other. They were not hurt at all, for the Dubaa had swallowed them whole.

The Mother Goat welcomed her kids with joy, then scolded them for opening the door to the *Dubaa*. They both promised their mother they would be more careful from now on and then they all trotted home happily together.

THE SHREWD WAZIR

Kan ya ma kan, in a bygone time, there lived a King who grew a very long beard. One day he looked at himself in the mirror, held his beard with his hand, and shook his head, saying, "Fine beards are short!" Then he struck a match and set fire to his beard. The fire burned his entire beard. After this impulsive act, the King was terribly embarrassed and depressed. He covered his face with a bandage and retired to his bed. He pretended to be sick and refused to meet anyone, especially his Wazir.

"I'm not a sane person," he said to himself. "I don't deserve to rule!"

His faithful Wazir kept lingering at the door of the King's room until he was given permission to enter. The King confessed to his Wazir what he had done to himself and said, "I must be insane! I will abdicate my throne to the Grand Judge."

The Wazir totally rejected the King's decision and tried to convince him that he was saner than anyone else in his Kingdom, including the Grand Judge. "I will prove this to you tomorrow," said the Wazir.

The next day, the Wazir brought eggs and made a pile of them in the King's antechamber. When the Grand Judge passed by, he was shocked to see the pile of eggs.

The Wazir explained that he intended to hatch the eggs in a matter of hours. Then he changed into a colored costume, carried a bell, and circled around the pile of eggs, saying, "Cluck, cluck, cluck."

The King's Chamberlain entered the room and announced that the King wanted to see the Wazir immediately. The Wazir pretended to be annoyed and said, "Oh my God, the eggs will never hatch if I stop walking around them!"

Then he turned to the Grand Judge and begged him to wear the costume and circle around the pile of eggs. The Grand Judge very reluctantly agreed to do this so the eggs would not be spoiled.

After a while, the King and the Wazir returned to find the Grand Judge dressed in the colorful suit, ringing the bell and clucking as he danced around the pile of eggs. The King laughed out loud to see his Grand Judge making such a fool of himself.

The Wazir whispered to the King, "I tricked him! He really believes that the eggs will hatch if he continues to dance and cackle."

This convinced the King that he was far saner than his own Grand Judge, and he stopped all talk of abdicating his throne, thanks to his shrewd Wazir.

A Superstition

The word for "thunder" in Arabic is raed. In Latakia, thunder is known as "Um Raeyda" and has become a Ghouleh in the local folklore. Mothers would threaten naughty children with Um Raeyda.

Two Recipes from Latakia
Jazarieh — A Carrot Sweet

Jazarieh is a very well-known traditional sweet in Latakia. It used to be made from small red pumpkin, but since farmers started growing white pumpkin, which has neither the sweet taste nor the color required, sweet carrots are used.

Ingredients
- 2 cups water
- 1 cup sugar
- 4 big, grated carrots
- 1 tbsp butter
- Crushed pistachios and coconut according to taste

Method
- Mix sugar in water and bring to a boil
- Add carrots and cook until well done
- Mash carrots with a fork and strain them
- Add the butter and mix until you get a solid mixture
- Make round balls and coat them with pistachio nuts and coconut

SAYADIEH — FISH WITH SPICY RICE AND TAJEH SAUCE

Sayadieh is the most famous recipe of the coastal area of Syria. There is another version of it in the Muhafaza of Tartous. This recipe came from my husband's aunt, Khaleh Malak, who lives in Latakia.

Ingredients (12 servings)
2 kg any large white fish (marlin is used in Latakia)

3 cups short grain rice

4 ½ cups water

3 large onions

3 tbsp olive oil

¾ cup vegetable oil

½ cup pine nuts

½ cup almonds

2 tsp mixed spices

1 tsp cinnamon

2 tsp salt

Method
Note: the pan used to fry the fish should be large enough to cook the rice

Wash fish, fry in olive oil until tender – remove from pan and save oil to fry onions

Remove and discard bones, skin, head, and tail

Cut fish into big serving pieces - set aside - leave some small pieces for sauce

Cut onions and fry in same pan until crispy – set aside half for garnish

Add the spices and 4 ½ cups of hot water to the fried onions in the pan

Bring to a boil and add rice; cover the pan

Cook rice over low heat until done

Put the rice in a serving plate. Place the fried fish pieces on top

Sprinkle with fried onions

Fry pine nuts and almonds and pour on top of the rice and fish

Tajeh Sauce for *Sayadieh*

Ingredients

1 onion

1 tbsp veg oil

½ cup lemon juice

½ cup tahini

¾ cup water

Salt

Reserved small fish pieces

Method

Mince onion and fry in oil

Add ¾ cup water and boil onion until done

Mix lemon juice, tahini, and ¼ cup water

Add lemon juice and tahini mixture to onion and water

Add small fried fish pieces

Boil on low fire until creamy

Serve with sayadieh

8

TARTOUS

On the shores of the Mediterranean Sea, 90 kilometers south of Latakia, lies the city of Tartous. It is a very old town, and human occupation of this site dates back more than 6,000 years. The Muhafaza of Tartous, like so many other muhafazat in Syria, takes its name from its most important city.

Tartous is an important trade center in Syria and is the second port of Syria. It is also home to the only Russian naval base located outside of Russia. Because of its sandy beaches and several resorts, it is a popular destination for summer vacations. Tartous has remained largely unaffected by the Syrian civil war; however, it has had a few suicide bombings claimed by ISIS.

Two Folktales from Tartous

The Story of Pomegranate

During my seventeen years of teaching, I grew fond of many of my students. A special bond held us together. The younger students felt so comfortable in my classes that they would sometimes unconsciously call me 'Mama;' then, as I grew older, it became 'Tete.' As for the older students, they enthusiastically helped me research folktales and traditional recipes.

Raya Khowanda was one of my special students, and her memory is imprinted on my heart. She contributed these two folktales from her aunt in Tartous.

Kan ya ma kan, a long time ago, there lived a woman who had no children. One day, while she was going to the spring to fetch some water, she passed a pomegranate tree and picked a big pomegranate to eat. The seeds of the pomegranate were so red and sweet that the woman prayed to God, "Ya Allah, bless me with a sweet girl, as sweet as the taste of this pomegranate." Then she smacked her lips and said, "If my prayer is answered, I will call her Pomegranate."

Soon after, the woman became pregnant and had a girl, whom she named Pomegranate. In answer to her mother's prayer, she grew up to be a sweet and beautiful girl.

Unfortunately, the mother died and the father married a wicked woman who hated Pomegranate and was very jealous of her beauty. She put her to work all the time and forced her to scrub floors and wash dishes, but that only made her look more beautiful.

One day, the stepmother decided to get rid of Pomegranate and asked the father to take her out to the woods and leave her there.

"Please let us keep her with us, for she is a big help in the house."

"No," said the stepmother. "She must leave this house. You must choose between me and your daughter."

Pomegranate was lying in bed and overheard what her stepmother said. She was determined that if she were left in the woods she would find her way back home in spite of her stepmother. She slipped out of bed and filled a bag with the ashes of the wood stove in the kitchen and then went back to bed.

The next morning, the father woke Pomegranate and said, "Get up. We are going to the forest to gather some wood." Then he gave her a stale loaf of bread for lunch.

Pomegranate took the loaf of bread and put the bag of ashes in her pocket before they left the house. As they walked along the path in the forest, she dropped the ashes behind her. When they were deep in the forest, her father asked Pomegranate to collect wood while he sat in the shade of a large tree. While she was gathering wood, her father crept away, leaving her alone.

When Pomegranate returned carrying a big stack of wood, her father had disappeared. She called for him, but only heard the echo of her own voice. So she carried the stack of wood on her head and followed the ashes she had scattered on the ground until she reached her house.

When her stepmother saw her, she was furious and turned to the father. "Didn't you say that you left her in the forest?"

The father swore to death that he had left Pomegranate in the forest, but the stepmother didn't believe him.

After a few days, Pomegranate asked her father for permission to go to visit her aunt. Her stepmother enthusiastically said, "Yes, you may go, but you have to wait until I bake your aunt some cheese pies and cake."

The next day, the stepmother made cake and cheese pies and secretly slipped poison into them. Then she put them in a big basket and gave them to Pomegranate.

On the way to her aunt's house, Pomegranate was followed by a hungry cat. Pomegranate threw a cheese pie to it, which it ate. To her great surprise, the cat rolled on the ground and died.

As Pomegranate walked along, a dog ran towards her and barked at her so she threw a piece of cake in the air. The dog jumped up, caught the piece of cake, and ate it. At once the dog started to madly bite itself, and then it also dropped dead.

When Pomegranate reached her aunt's house, she told her what had happened. Her aunt grabbed the basket from Pomegranate and threw the pies and cake away.

The next day, Pomegranate took the water jug and went to the river to fetch some fresh water for her aunt. While she was kneeling down to fill the jug, she lost her balance and fell into the river. She was carried far away by the current to an island where she turned into a large tree.

One day while the Prince was walking, he saw this same tree and admired it. "This tree is large enough to make a beautiful bedroom for me," said the Prince. He ordered his guards to cut it down and send the wood to the carpenter. When the guards started to saw it, though, they suddenly heard a sweet voice singing.

Gently saw the tree apart

For Pomegranate lies in the heart.

The guards were greatly surprised at first, but gently sawed the tree, and inside it they found the most beautiful girl they had ever seen.

Pomegranate was scared to death of the guards and climbed a tree. "Come down!" called the guards, but Pomegranate was too frightened. The guards told the Prince about Pomegranate and he ordered them to bring her to him at once. As the guards were trying their best to persuade Pomegranate to climb down from the tree, an old woman passed by and said she would help them.

"Bring me a pan, oil, and some eggs!" said the old lady.

The guards brought the old woman what she asked for and hid behind the trees.

The old woman set a fire next to the tree and turned the frying pan upside down. She poured the oil over it.

Pomegranate was shocked and called out, "Oh no, my dear Grandmother, this is not how you fry eggs!"

"Oh, please, my dear, then come down and teach me how to fry the eggs, for the Prince will punish me if it is not done right!"

Pomegranate felt sorry for the old woman and climbed down the tree. Once she was on the ground, the guards captured her and took her to the castle of the Prince.

"Don't be frightened!" said the Prince. "Who are you?"

Pomegranate told the Prince her story, and he was taken by her beauty and character. He said, "You are a wonderful girl, and I'd like to spend the rest of my life with you! Will you marry me?"

Pomegranate willingly accepted the Prince's proposal. They held wedding celebrations for seven days, and everyone in the Kingdom was invited. Pomegranate's father and stepmother came to visit her, but the guards wouldn't let them in. The father pleaded to see his daughter and was finally brought with the stepmother to the Prince.

In the presence of the Prince and Pomegranate, the father and stepmother asked for forgiveness for their cruel treatment of her.

The Prince turned to Pomegranate and asked her, "Will you forgive them, my dear Wife?"

Pomegranate cried and then wiped away her tears and kissed her father's hand. Pomegranate and the Prince had many girls and boys and lived happily ever after in their beautiful castle.

FOWERA, THE NAUGHTY MOUSE

Kan ya ma kan, in a bygone time, there was a childless woman who longed for children. One day while she was cleaning her house, she caught sight of a mouse and prayed to God to send her children, even if they were a handful of mice.

Time passed and her prayer was answered. She gave birth to a handful of mice.

One day, while she was baking bread in the *tannour*, the mice ran everywhere and played with the dough and nibbled on the bread. The woman went crazy and caught them one by one and threw them into the fire – all except one, who hid in her pocket.

When the woman finished baking the bread and her anger cooled down, she wished she hadn't gotten rid of all the mice.

"Oh, I wish I had kept one mouse to help me take the food to my husband in the fields," said the woman.

Suddenly, Fowera jumped out of her pocket and said, "Don't worry, Mother, here I am! Give me the food to take to my father.

"The mother gave Fowera the food, and she carried it to the field where her father was plowing.

"Come eat lunch," called Fowera.

"Go to the river," said her father. "Fill the jug with cold, fresh water."

So Fowera went and filled the jug with cold, fresh water. Then she sat down with her father under the apricot tree to eat. Fowera felt her father was very tired, so she tried to plow the field for him.

When her father finished eating he called, "Fowera, Fowera where are you?"

"Here I am, Father," called out Fowera. "Under the earth!"

Fowera's father plowed the earth but didn't find her. "Fowera, Fowera," called her father again. "Where are you?"

"In the mud wall," called out Fowera.

Fowera's father broke down the mud wall, but didn't find Fowera. "Fowera, Fowera," called her father. "Where are you?"

"Inside the sheep!" said Fowera. Fowera's father frantically killed the sheep but didn't find her.

"Fowera, Fowera," called her father. "Where are you?"

"In the rose bush," said Fowera.

So her father took his ax and cut down the rose bush, but he didn't find her. By that time, Fowera's father was exhausted and lay down under the apricot tree. All of a sudden, Fowera crawled out of his *sherwal* and laughed. Fowera's father didn't think it was funny and carried Fowera back home.

Back home, Fowera's father told his wife what she had done to him and swore he would marry her off. But every time someone would propose to her, she would reject him, until one day a handsome rat came along and she fell in love with him at first sight. They got married and had a handful of naughty mice and rats who filled the life of Fowera's parents with happiness, and her mother never felt lonely again.

MEMORIES OF BYGONE DAYS

'Tete Mazloum' was the name my husband and his brother and sisters called their grandmother. She was born Hindia Mousa, in the coastal city of Banias in the muhafaza of Tartous. I met her when she was in her eighties, and was impressed by her strong personality and entertained by her family stories. One of the interesting stories she told was how she changed her name at the age of nine. I tried very hard to recollect the story, but my memory failed me. My husband's cousins, Rabab Mazloum and Hind Mazloum, got the story for me from their fathers.

The Girl Who Changed Her Name

Nine-year old Hindia hated her name and, for as long as she could remember, she had longed to change it. All her friends seemed to have nice names, but her name meant "the Indian," and she was teased about this.

One day, on her way home, she passed by the government department of Civil Records where names, births, marriages and such are recorded. She went in and asked to see the official responsible for the department.

The official, who had recognized her at first glance as the daughter of the distinguished Agha Mousa, assumed that she had been sent by her father. He received her and patiently listened to her complaint.

"I was named 'Hindia' without being consulted," she said.

"What name do you want?" he asked, laughing.

"All I ask you to do is to cross out two letters. I want the name Hind."

The man was taken aback by her cleverness and did as she asked, changing her name from Hindia to Hind. Hind thanked the man and returned home with a new name.

That same day, her father, the Agha, happened to pass by the place and was shocked to hear of the story of the little girl who had changed her name. In disbelief, he kept asking the man to describe the nine-year old who had asked to change her name.

When her father arrived home, he hit his daughter. When her mother tried to stop, he said, "If my daughter changes her name at the age of nine, she may change the government when she grows up!"

Although she was allowed to keep her new name, she was taken out of school for punishment. Nevertheless, Hind was determined to learn, even though she was kept home. She listened to the private tutors who were hired to teach her brothers and managed to learn to read on her own.

When she grew up, she married a Merchant called Musbah Mazloum and had seven sons and one daughter, my future mother-in-law. Although Hind had many domestic responsibilities, she helped her husband in his business of selling fine fabric. She became a good businesswoman, even inventing a cream that removed freckles and successfully selling it. After awhile, the family moved to Damascus.

In her later life, Hind Mousa, who was called "Tete Mazloum" by her grandchildren and me, asked one of her grandsons,* who was in primary school, to teach her arithmetic and accounting – and he did. This was a big help to her in the business venture she started soon after with her son, Abdul Fattah. This son, who was living in Germany, exported used trucks to his mother and she sold them in Damascus. It became a very successful business. She was a capable, intelligent woman who succeeded in the "man's world" of business in Syria.

THE KIDNAPPED BOY

Tete Mazloum was good at many things, including telling family stories. One of her stories was about the kidnapping of her son Khaled, who later became a poet. At the time of the kidnapping,

---

* This clever and helpful grandson was Nizar Zarka, my future husband.

Tete Mazloum had five sons, and Khaled was the youngest. Again, my husband's cousins Rabab and Hind helped me with this story.

One hot summer day, while Tete Mazloum's boys were playing soccer out in the street with their friends, an old gypsy woman was lurking behind the palm trees observing the boys. The gypsy's eyes followed the boys and carefully examined each one. Her eyes lit up when she caught sight of the light-haired, blue-eyed two-year old sitting on the steps of his house watching his brothers play.

When his brothers and their friends ran up the street to fetch the ball, the gypsy took out a large cloth bag, snatched the little boy, put him in the bag, and carried him away.

After a while, Tete came out to see what her boys were up to and found her son Khaled missing. When Tete and her neighbors had searched every house and every street corner in vain, the family went to the police station to file a claim.

In the meantime, the gypsy was heading back to her village carrying Khaled, while the police convoy, headed by Tete's cousin, was searching everywhere. By now the entire town had heard about the kidnapping, so when a crowd of children saw an old woman with a large sack that seemed to wiggle every now and then, they stared suspiciously at her sack. The gypsy noticed the children looking at her and, holding tight to the sack, she tried to hide in the shadow of a tree. All of a sudden, Khaled poked his head from the sack and the children screamed, "The gypsy stole the boy – the gypsy stole the boy!" They surrounded the gypsy and then yanked and dragged her toward the police station. She was arrested on the spot, and Khaled was returned to his mother.

After that day, whenever Khaled was naughty or gave trouble to Tete Mazloum, she would jokingly say, "I should have let the gypsy keep you!"

TWO RECIPES FROM TARTOUS

LOOF OR PALESTINIAN ARUM (SOLOMON'S LILY) —
AN APPETIZER

This is a strange recipe made from the toxic leaves of a wild plant. Gloves should be worn when handling the leaves since they will cause itching, and the leaves should be cooked for hours before even tasting, to prevent your tongue from itching. Loof is thought to be a remedy for cancer.

Ingredients

1 ½ to 2 kilos loof

1 ¼ cup chick peas

1 ½ cup lemon juice strained through cheese cloth

1 large onion, chopped

2 ½ cups olive oil

2 ½ cups water to start

Salt

Method

Mince loof - wear gloves to avoid itchy hands

Wash loof well, then put in a strainer and pour boiling water over it

Put water in a big pot and, when it boils, add loof, lemon juice, onion, chick peas, and salt

Return to a boil and when it boils again, skim off the yellow foam

Add olive oil and boil 4 to 5 hours (replace water as necessary)

Don't taste before it has boiled at least 3 hours

It is served cold with bread or mujadara – and is delicious!

ANOTHER *SAYADIEH* RECIPE — FISH WITH SPICY RICE

This recipe came from a dear friend who wishes to remain anonymous.

Ingredients

    2 cups rice

    3 cups water or fish broth as below

    5 pieces fish fillet

    2 large onions, sliced

    Flour seasoned with salt, black pepper, cinnamon, and
        allspice

    Salt, black pepper, and cinnamon for rice broth

    Oil or ghee for frying fish and browning onions

Method for fish

    The traditional method is to season the head, fins and
        tail of the fish to make a broth, which is used to cook
        the rice

    Cover the fillets with seasoned flour, then fry them
        and put aside

    Brown the onions in oil or ghee in a pot big enough
        to cook the rice

    Put fillets on browned onions; add salt, black pepper,
        and cinnamon

    Add 3 cups fish broth or water

    When broth boils, add rice and cook tightly covered
        on low flame

    Once it's done, remove the lid, cover pot with a big
        plate, and turn it upside down

    The onions and fish will be sitting on top of the rice

9

DARA'A

Dara'a is a city in southwestern Syria, located about 13 kilometers north of the Jordanian border. It is the capital of the Muhafaza of Dara'a, which is historically part of the ancient Hauran region. The city is located about 90 kilometers south of Damascus on the Damascus-Amman highway, and was used as a stopping station for travelers before the war.

Dara'a is called the cradle of the revolution because this is where the civil war began in March 2011. Several clashes have occurred within the muhafaza throughout the civil war. Dara'a is now largely under government control.

Three Folktales from Dara'a

The Greedy Snake

Kan ya ma kan, a long time ago, a woman dreamed that a relative of hers was bitten by a snake and died immediately. This dream frightened her terribly, so the next morning she went to her relative's house and told him the dream and expressed her fear for his life. She told him to pay attention and to be careful. The man vowed to sacrifice two rams to God in thanks for his safety from this nightmare.

Sure enough, he did as he vowed, and that night he invited his relatives and neighbors for dinner and distributed the remainder of the meat to the poor, leaving nothing but a leg. The owner of the house was so anxious that all his guests should eat that he ate nothing. After they had all finished dinner, the man wrapped the leftover leg in a piece of bread and was about to bite into it when he remembered an old woman who was one of his neighbors. She couldn't come to the dinner because she was too frail. He reproached himself for forgetting her and decided that the leftover leg would be her share. So he took it to her and apologized to her for being late.

The old woman was pleased to receive the meat. She ate it and threw the bone out the window. Late that night, a snake came searching for food and was lured by the smell of the meat. The snake began to greedily lick the meat and fat off the bone. Eventually, the hooked part of the bone got caught in its throat and the snake couldn't loosen it and began to choke. In an attempt to rid itself of the bone, the snake kept raising its head and banging the bone on the ground over and over again.

In the early hours of the morning, the man's children heard a racket from behind their house, so they told their father and he went out to see what it was. He found the snake and killed it and thanked God for his safety.

People spoke for some time about this, and they repeated the following phrase until it became a saying, "Feeding many mouths can prevent disaster."

THE CLEVER BEDOUIN GIRL

Kan ya ma kan, in a bygone time, an old man decided to get married after his wife's death. The children were surprised at their father's insistence, but they gave in. It took them some time before they found a young girl who was willing to marry their old father. The wedding took place and the young girl joined them in their tent. The next day, the man did not leave his tent so his children entered and found him dead.

They buried him and the bride returned to her family after this short marriage.

A relative asked for her hand in marriage, and her family married her to him before the legal waiting period of four months and ten days had passed. Her firstborn was a son and he used to help his father at work, but the father gave him no love or tenderness, although he was very loving with his other children. He would beat this son and treat him harshly. The son grew older and continued to help his father, and the father continued to mistreat him.

One day, while they were working together, he began to hit his son violently for little or no reason. The son ran away from him until he reached a tent in which lived a number of brothers with their flocks and livestock. He asked them for protection against his father and said, "Save me from my father, for he has beaten me almost to death."

The youth sat down with them to tell them his story and his host felt a strong closeness to him. He asked the boy, "Who is your father?"

The boy said, "I am so and so's son."

He asked him, "Who is your mother?"

He said, "My mother is so and so, daughter of so and so."

The host said, "You are not that man's son, but rather my brother."

The bewildered boy asked, "How can I be your brother and I have never seen you before?"

The man said, "I will tell you when the time is right."

In an hour's time, the father came to get his son, but the man refused to let him take him and told him he is not your son. The boy's father protested, but the man said we will let the wisest man of the tribe be the Judge. Tomorrow we will meet at the tent of the Sheikh, and he will decide who is the father of the boy. The next day the brothers and the father went to the Sheikh and each side told his story.

The Sheikh said, "I will not Judge between you until I do my duty by you as guests, but I need this boy to help me." He asked the boy to go to the nearby valley where his daughter took care of their flock of sheep and to catch her unawares and steal a sheep from her. The boy did as he was told and the sheep was prepared for dinner. The daughter came home sad because of the lost sheep.

Her father asked her, "Was it eaten by a wolf?"

"No, it was stolen," she replied.

"Did you see who stole it?" asked her father.

"No," she answered, "but I know he is young from his foot tracks. Also, his mother is young and his father is old."

"And how do you know he is young?" asked the father.

The daughter said, "His footprints are small, like those of one who hasn't reached puberty yet."

"What about his parents? Why do you think one was young and one old?"

"Well his tracks are sometimes close to each other and other times distant. I figured when his strength came from his mother, he would run and his footprints would be far from one another, and when his strength came from his father, his footsteps would be close together. So I knew that his mother was young and his father was a very old man."

The Sheikh said, "Go, my daughter. We will search for the sheep later."

The Sheikh looked at his guests then he said, "The case is solved. You are not this boy's father. As for you, my boy, go join your bothers and return to your family.

And so the clever Bedouin girl solved the case, and the young boy was saved from the oppression of his alleged father. He was returned to his brothers and family and they were overjoyed to have him.

THE SEVEN BROTHERS

Kan ya ma kan, in an olden time, there was a man who had seven sons and a large piece of land. Six of his boys were lazy and did nothing all day long, but the seventh son was very hardworking. His brothers did not like him, but his father loved him because he always helped him in the field. The father continuously fought with his other sons because they refused to do anything, while the youngest son worked side by side with his father every day.

One afternoon, they saw a turtle on their land and took it home with them. The next day, they found a hen and a rooster and brought them home, too. The father became very attached to these three animals and took good care of them. He said to his children, "If I die, be sure to look after these three - the turtle, the hen, and the rooster." But behind their father's back, the six older sons laughed and said we shall kill them as soon as our father dies.

When the father died, the six brothers divided the land amongst themselves and denied their youngest brother his fair share. Instead, they gave him the turtle, the hen and the rooster.

They said, "You will get nothing else from us."

He said, "Just give me a small piece of land."

But they refused, so the seventh son went to work as a laborer until he had saved enough to buy a small piece of land, on which he built himself a one-room hut. He lived there contentedly with his animals, caring for them and tending his land. He planted a tree in front of his home, and soon an owl came to live in the tree. All night long it would screech, preventing him from sleeping and frightening his animals. After a while, he decided to kill the owl, especially since his turtle, hen, and rooster were afraid of it. He collected rocks and small stones, and every day he would try to hit the owl but would miss. At last, one day he struck the owl with a pointed rock that entered its throat, and it died.

He shouted, "I killed it, I killed it!" and it fell from the tree.

But as soon as he touched the owl, it turned into a dead Ghouleh. He was so frightened of it that he dragged the corpse to the river and threw it in. When he returned home, he found a man, a woman, and a young girl in his home.

They told him, "We were the turtle, the hen, and the rooster you and your father took such good care of. The Ghouleh put a spell on us and turned us into animals because her son wanted to marry our daughter and we refused."

Furthermore, the man said, "I was a King and this was my Queen and our little Princess. We lost our Kingdom to the Ghouleh and her son, the Ghoul, who is now ruling it. The Ghouleh kept an eye on us wherever we went, which is why she turned herself into an owl to watch us from the tree."

The King and Queen then asked the seventh son to go to their Kingdom to see how it was faring under the Ghoul. When the seventh son came back, he said he had found the Kingdom in very bad shape. The King and the Queen asked for his help in regaining their Kingdom from the Ghoul and restoring it to its former glory, and he agreed to try.

They arrived at the palace dressed as beggars, and when the Ghoul saw the pretty face of the disguised Princess, he was very quick to ask them in. As soon as they were inside, the seventh son killed the Ghoul and rushed to throw him in the river. The King and Queen reclaimed their rightful place in their palace and once again ruled their Kingdom. The grateful King rewarded the seventh son by naming him a Prince, and not long afterwards he and the Princess were married.

In the meantime, the six brothers had become poor because of their laziness, and when they heard of their brother's good fortune, they lost their minds. They traveled to the Kingdom where their brother now was a Prince, and at the palace they asked to see him. When their brother agreed to meet them, they begged his forgiveness and he forgave them on the condition that they change their lazy ways. They promised, but no one remembers whether they kept that promise or not.

FOLKLORE

THE FORTY DAYS OF WINTER

One day I saw an old woman peddler from Houran selling vegetables by the side of the road. We began talking, and when I asked her about traditions of Houran, she told me about the Forty Days of Winter. The winter season, she explained, is divided and named according to climate changes and people's experience throughout many generations. It turns out that some Damascenes also speak of the Forty Days of Winter, although growing up in Damascus, I never heard of it. Furthermore, my sister, who lives in Amman, says that Jordanians and Palestinians are familiar with this division of winter. According to this tradition, winter has four periods:

Saad the Slayer - a very cold period - from 1 February to 13 February

Saad the Swallower – a period when it rains a lot and the earth swallows the rain – from 13 February to 25 February

Saad the Lucky – a period when life flows in plants and people get warmer - from 26 February to 10 March

Saad the Concealed – a period when snakes and scorpions

come out - from 10 March to 22 March

The woman peddler pointed out that there was a story behind the name "Saad the Slayer" - in Arabic Saad al Dabeh - and I took out my pen and pad as she began to tell me the tale.

SAAD THE SLAYER

Kan ya ma kan, a long time ago, lived a great Merchant who owned a large caravan of camels. One very cold day in the middle of January, the Merchant got very sick and couldn't leave on his long winter voyage. His older son, Saad, decided to save his father's business and go instead of him. His father tried to persuade him not to travel in bad weather, but Saad had made up his mind.

After he loaded the caravan of camels with goods, he went to bid goodbye to his father. Feeble and sick, the father held his son's hand and said, "My dear son, if it snows, slaughter the largest camel, open up its stomach, remove its intestines and sit inside, and you will be saved."

Saad was shocked and said, "What about the caravan and the goods?"

"Your survival is more important than anything," said the father. "Just forget about everything and don't get out of the camel until the snow melts away."

Saad led the caravan through endless deserted roads until it started to snow. When he was no longer able to move forward, he did as his father had said and slaughtered the largest camel, sheltering inside it for thirteen days.

During this time Saad didn't feel the outside cold. So, from 1 February to 13 February is called "Saad the Slayer." Next, Saad began to eat the camel's liver and this period, from 13 February to 25 February, is named "Saad the Swallower." When the snow finally melted, Saad got out of the camel alive on 26 February and this period from then to 10 March is called "Saad the Lucky." Finally, Saad turned the camel's hide into a cloak and strolled around wearing it. This period is known as "Saad the Concealed."

Now that the weather had cleared up with the arrival of spring, Saad returned safely to his family and his father thanked God for his safe return.

PROVERBS

- Every night is followed by a morning.
- The wicked man is always punished.
- The stone that you look down upon is capable of injuring you.
- Just like a loaf of pita bread, he is turned on both sides - said of one who often changes his opinion.
- Trust men like you trust water to stay in a strainer – said by cynical women.
- Once you have your eye on something, everyone has their eyes on it.
- He went to Hajj when the people were returning - that is, he went on Pilgrimage when the time for Pilgrimage had ended.

Dara'a

❀ ❀

THREE RECIPES FROM DARA'A

ASADIA — CORN PORRIDGE

Ingredients

4 cups jareesh – half ground white corn

Water

Salt

Semnay (ghee)

Method

Add the jareesh and salt to hot water

Stir with a wooden spoon until corn is tender and water has been absorbed

Pour onto a tray; make a hole in the middle

Pour very hot semnay in the hole and let it cool

Say bismillah (in the name of God) and scoop it up with your fingers

When finished eating, don't forget to lick your fingers and say alhamdulillah – thanks be to God!

MANSAF MLAYHEE — A MAIN DISH OF MEAT, YOGURT, JAMEED, AND BREAD

Ingredients

- 2 kg lamb chunks
- 32 oz yogurt
- ½ ball of jameed (dehydrated and fermented ball of goat's yogurt)
- 8 tbsp semnay (ghee)
- 4 cups short grain rice
- Shirak bread (or pita bread)
- Salt and pepper to taste
- 1 cup pine nuts or almonds for garnish

Method

Crush jameed into small pieces and soak in 2 cups of warm water for an hour

Boil lamb meat in 10 cups of water

Blend jameed, 4 tbsp semnay, and yogurt in a second pot, stirring constantly

When it boils, lower heat

Add meat and 2-3 cups of meat broth to the yogurt and let it simmer

Sauté rice in 2 tbsp semnay, then cook it in the meat broth, adding enough water to make 6 cups

Line a large tray with shirak bread and drizzle some yogurt broth on it

When rice is done, pile it on the shirak bread, drizzle some yogurt broth on it, and place the meat chunks on top

Fry pine nuts or almonds in 2 tbsp semnay and pour nuts and semnay over all

Dara'a

HABEET — Meat cooked with dried fruit and vermicelli

No amounts for the dates, raisins, or vermicelli were given.

Ingredients

1 kg. lamb chunks

Dates

Raisins

Vermicelli

Method

Cook meat until done

Add dates, raisins and vermicelli

Cook until vermicelli is done

10

SWEIDA

Sweida is the southernmost of Syria's fourteen muhafazat and is on the border of Jordan. Along with Dara'a, it is historically part of the ancient Hauran region. The capital and largest city is also named Sweida, and a large majority of the population is Druze. It has largely stayed out of the Civil war in Syria.

Two Folktales from Sweida

The Woodcutter

Kan ya ma kan, a long time ago, a poor Woodcutter found himself growing old and tired. He had been a hardworking man all his life, and his many children added to his burdens and worry so that one day he said to his wife, "I can no longer go on working in the forest."

"Oh, but what will become of us?" she exclaimed. "If the children do not go hungry today, they will tomorrow."

The Woodcutter answered, "My dear Wife, I can no longer do this difficult work." Nevertheless, to please her, he took his axe and went out. Just before he reached the forest, he saw a strange, blind bird standing between two jars; one was filled with water and the other with seeds. The bird would peck a seed from one jar and then search for the other jar for a drink.

The Woodcutter stood for a long time observing this scene, and then he went home and described it to his wife and said, "My Wife, if Allah did not forget the blind bird and sent it its provision, then no doubt He will not forget us after spending our lives working hard and never shirking."

A day or two passed and the Woodcutter sat daydreaming. On the third day, a rich Merchant came and asked the Woodcutter to dig him a well in his garden. The Woodcutter agreed and immediately went to the Merchant's house to begin working. After a few days of digging, the Woodcutter came upon a sealed clay pot. When he opened, it he found it full of gold coins, so he finished digging the well, resealed the pot, and took it to the Merchant, saying, "I found this treasure in the garden of your home. It must belong to you." The Merchant took it inside, opened it, took out a few gold coins and then returned the gold coins to the jar. He went back to the Woodcutter and paid him for his work and told him to never return.

The Woodcutter returned home, not sorry at all for what he did, because he knew that he did what would please Allah and satisfy his conscience.

As for the Merchant, he went back home and told his wife the story. She asked, "And did you give the Woodcutter anything in return for his trustworthiness?"

Sweida

The Merchant answered, "I gave him the sum we had agreed upon for digging the well; as for this treasure, it belongs to us for it was found on our property."

Then he opened the pot, but to his surprise it was now crawling with red-winged wasps ready to take flight. He quickly covered the pot and began to curse the woodcutter, calling him a cheat and a liar. He vowed to take his revenge on him.

That evening, he made his way to the woodcutter's home and climbed up on the roof. There, he opened the pot and poured its contents down the chimney upon the Woodcutter and his family.

The next morning, the Woodcutter and his wife and children woke up to find the floor of their home covered with gold coins.

A FOOLISH MAN

Kan ya ma kan, in days gone by, there lived a man who always failed in everything he planned to do or started to do. One day, in desperation, he decided to travel to a very distant place to pray to Allah and describe his problem to Him. Perhaps Allah might feel sorry for him and turn failure away from him. The man walked and walked, until one evening he came across a frightful looking hyena. The hyena asked him, "Where are you going, O Man?"

The man explained his problem to the hyena, who answered sadly, "Look at me, my good man. My fur is falling out day after day, and winter is about to start with its cold storms and blizzards. Would you please ask Allah for a cure for my case?" The man said he would and continued on his way.

Soon he came across a peasant who greeted him, so he sat down to rest and talk to him a bit. When the peasant heard the man's story he said, "My brother, will you do me a favor?"

"Yes," said the man.

The peasant said, "For the longest time, I have worked on this land that I inherited. I have been plowing it, sowing it, and harvesting it, and yet I grow poorer day after day. I fear the day will come when my family and I find ourselves without food or drink. Would you please tell Allah about my situation and ask when I might find some relief?" The man reassured him that he would.

After a short walk, he came upon a thin horse in a lush valley. The mare looked at him with beautiful, sad eyes and asked him where he was going. The man told his story and the mare asked, "Will you do me a favor?"

"Yes, indeed," he replied.

"Please ask why, although I eat my fill and roam in this rich valley as I please, I remain tired and frail. Ask about my problem and what might cure me." The man reassured the horse that he would and he continued on his way.

By evening, he reached a magnificent castle with a high wall around it. When he asked the guards about the owner, they told him that it was the castle of their king. They also said that the King didn't like anyone to pass through his Kingdom unless he visited him and explained his story. They also said that the King was the most just of kings and the most merciful to his subjects.

The man entered the castle and asked to see the king, and immediately he was granted permission. The King was extremely good looking and was dressed in very elegant clothes. The man told his story and all that had happened to him on his way. He told the King that the place he was heading for was just beyond his Kingdom, and that was why he had to pass through. The King said, "Can I ask you a favor?"

"Certainly, Your Majesty," answered the man.

The King said, "I have been ruling this Kingdom for ten years now, since my father's death, as I was his only child. I have been the kindest and most just King to my subjects, but my problem is that some of the generals of the army and some high officials do not obey me. Please pray that God shows you the reason for the predicament that I am in."

The King saw to it that the man was well fed and was shown to a fancy room to sleep. The next morning, the man took off on his journey.

After a two-day walk, he reached the place he was searching for. He began his program of worship, praying to God and pleading with Him to be merciful to him and to point out to him the reason for his failure in all matters. Finally, he had a dream in which a voice that either came from above or from within the depths of the mountain and said, "What is it you want, oh Visitor?"

The man told his story and then asked, "What shall I tell the hyena?"

The Voice answered, "Tell the hyena that its disease will be cured once it eats a foolish person." Then it told him to tell the peasant that he should continue to work hard and that soon his land would give him wealth enough for him and his children after his death. And as for the mare, she should submit to a human who would know how to cure her and give her the right food and drink, in the right amounts, to make her strong and healthy. Then, the Voice explained that the King was actually a woman in man's clothing, and that although she was disguised as a man, her heart remained that of a woman. Finally, the Voice said, "Concerning you, O

Man, know that your providence is before you. You only need to pay attention and think."

The man started back happily, glad to have all the answers. First he stopped at the King's castle, and when he was granted an audience with the King he said, "You are a woman disguised as a man, and this is the reason for your problem, since your heart is the heart of a woman despite your appearance."

The King shouted, "Be silent or I will kill you! The guards may hear what you said to me just now, which is something no one knows but me, you, and God. Were people to find out the truth, they would attack me with their swords. But can I suggest something?"

"Yes, I'm listening."

The disguised woman paused uncertainly, then she said, "I offer you my hand in marriage and you can become my Wazir and help me rule this great Kingdom of mine." The man declined, explaining that the voice had told him his providence was before him and at the moment he was not interested in getting married.

The man continued on his way and soon he reached the thin mare. He said to her, "You need to hand over your affairs to a human who would take the best care of you."

The mare nodded its head and said, "Very well then, I grant that you may be my guide, and I will carry you on my back wherever you wish."

The man said, "No, no. I have much to do ahead. My providence awaits me; I cannot stay."

The man passed by the farmer and told him the message of the Voice and then continued on his way. He had only walked a short distance when the farmer began to call him back, saying, "Come back, good brother, for my plow has pulled up a treasure box, and I will divide the fortune between us."

The man turned around and answered, saying, "No, no. The Voice said to me that my providence would be before me." And he went on.

Finally, the hyena intercepted his path and asked him, "Tell me, O Man, how did things go for you?"

The man told the hyena all that had happened and ended his story saying, "And you will not be cured until you eat a foolish man." The hyena bared her teeth saying, "In truth, I will never meet anyone more foolish than you!"

Two Recipes from Sweida

Baksama — Snow Ice Cream

There is a rhyme in Sweida:

The first snowfall is sem (poison),
The second snowfall is dem (blood),
The third snowfall: Kol wa la teh tem!
(Eat as much as you like!)

The third snowfall is thought to be very clean snow,
  clean enough to eat.

Dibbis (pomegranate molasses) and semnay (ghee) are
  added to the snow for a sweet treat.

MABSALEEYA — FRIED ONIONS WITH MOLASSES

Cut onions and/or green onions in rings and fry until
golden brown and tender in semnay, then add dibbis.
Eat with bread.

ANOTHER VERSION OF MABSALEEYA — ONION OMELET

Fry four bunches of green onions that are cut in one
centimeter pieces

Add cumin, black pepper, and salt

Add five beaten eggs - cook on one side and then flip

When done, add a little lemon juice.

11

QUNEITRA

Quneitra is in southern Syria and borders Jordan, Israel, and Lebanon. It is overlooked by snow-covered Mount Hermon, the highest mountain in Syria, and cut by the deep canyons of the Yarmouk River which descend almost to sea level. The Golan Heights in Quneitra are at an elevation of 1,000 meters above sea level and lie 70 kilometers south of Damascus. The Golan has green fields, meadows, and orchards. Most of the muhafaza has been occupied by Israel since 1967.

Since the civil war began, there have been severe clashes between the Syrian Army and the rebels in Quneitra.

A Folktale from Quneitra

Fish in the Watermelon

This story was given to me by Kherieh, the daughter of Sheha, who used to work for my Tete a long time ago. Sheha was brought to Tete by her father as a young girl. Her family fled from Quneitra during the 1967 war and she helped support it from a young age. Although she left us when she was fourteen, she is now considered part of our family and we keep in touch. She gave me the two recipes from this muhafaza. Her daughter, my friend Kherieh, is a widow who lost her husband when she was pregnant with her first child. She collected this folktale from her old relatives in Quneitra. She also helped me buy a traditional dress from the Golan and one from and Dara'a, and taught me how to wear the headdresses for both.

Kan ya ma kan, not so long ago, there was a man who was harsh and mean to his wife. Not only did he expect her to do all the household chores without help, but he also tried to confine her at home for no reason, turning the home from a haven of peace and love into a prison. Each time she tried to argue with him or discuss the matter in order to convince him how harmful this was for their family life, the man would increase his irrational restraints upon her. He not only kept the door locked, but began to shutter the windows until all she had left was one narrow window to connect her to the outside world.

At this point, she decided to seek the advice of her relatives and friends and, in the end, she chose to resort to trickery to free herself from her husband's imprisonment.

One day her husband brought her a watermelon and she thought of a wonderful plan. As soon as the fishmonger passed under her window, she let down her basket and bought some small fish. Next, she cut a small hole in the watermelon and poked the fish into it; then she pasted back the piece she had cut out with a mixture of flour and water. After her husband came home, she prepared lunch and then asked him to cut the watermelon.

The husband brought the watermelon to the table, placed it in a large tray, and was shocked to see fish slithering out of it as soon as he cut it. "This would make a fine dinner," he said. "Let me go invite our families while you fry the fish." As soon as he was gone, the wife packed all the fish into the basket and dangled it down from the window with a rope, telling one of the passersby to take the fish.

The husband returned with his family and hers. When they were all seated and his wife had placed the food on the table, the man called out angrily, "Where is the fried fish?"

The wife answered innocently, "What fried fish are you talking about, my Husband?"

"I'm talking about the fish we found in the watermelon!" he retorted.

At that point she looked meaningfully at her parents and his and said, "Have you ever heard of fish coming out of a watermelon? My husband seems to have lost his mind or is about to lose it."

When he insisted that they had found fish in the watermelon and that he had asked her to fry them while he invited their families to dinner, the woman pleaded with her family to save her from her crazy husband.

The wife's family took her home with them and, after a few days, they went to the Judge asking for a divorce on the grounds of his insanity. In the court, the husband stood to defend himself before the Judge. He made sense until he got to the part about the fish coming out of the watermelon. The Judge said, "This is where the insanity begins. My Son, there is no sane person who would claim they found fish in a watermelon." The Judge decided to separate the couple, but the wife pleaded with him to allow her to have a private moment with her husband.

When they were alone, the wife confessed to what she had done and told her husband to either stop holding her prisoner in her home and mistreating her, or she would allow the Judge to go through with the divorce. She knew that her husband loved her and suffered from a severe case of jealousy, but now he had to stop treating her this way or he would spend the rest of his days in an insane asylum.

The husband asked his wife's forgiveness and she cancelled her charges against him. On their way home she said to him, "No more fish in the watermelon." And he answered, "Only love and trust."

PROVERBS

- Warmth is good for you, even in summer.
- The camel limped because of its hurt lip – said when someone gives a very weak excuse.
- He who says a word will be remembered for it.
- When he knew I was a widow, he came running.
- Once he became somebody, he left,

- The milk he nursed will bring him back [to his mother].
- Either drink from the spring or remain thirsty all your life - meaning, do not accept anything less than the source.
- As long as this counts as a meal, you might as well eat your fill.

THE WHITE STORK – ABU SAAD

The white stork is a transient migratory bird and is one of the first to herald the arrival of the migratory season in Syria. It used to be seen in great numbers over Quneitra and is called Abu Saad by the local people. In the past, it used to nest and breed in farmlands and meadows close to rivers or on buildings, trees, and pillars. It is a very large, white bird with black flying feathers and a long neck that is outstretched during flight. It has red legs and a long, pointed, red beak. Although it is considered beneficial to farmers, it has been over-hunted and now fewer are seen in Syria.

A SONG FOR THE WHITE STORK

When children in Quneitra used to see the white stork migrating, they would sing:

> *Abu Saad, turn around, turn around,*
> *Dead in the grave your mother was found.*
> *Abu Saad, over here, over here,*
> *Locusts have pulled out her eyeballs, I fear.*
> *Three doves; one prays, one fasts,*
> *And one praises God and the Prophet.*

Children's Eid Song

Children would sing this song to their grandmothers in the Eid (holiday):

I put on new clothes, ya Tete
And today is Eid, ya Tete
Give me a coin, ya Tete
From under your mattress, ya Tete.

Two Recipes from Quneitra

Kibbi Kathabeeya: "False" or Meatless *Kibbi*

This recipe from Quneitra is from Sheha; however, I was given a very similar recipe called Kheleh or Vegetarian Kibbi by my friend Fadia Shabarak from Aleppo. She said this recipe does not use meat because the woman who invented it was very poor. With it, she pleased her children who wished to eat kibbi when there was no money for meat. Later on, Fadia said, many Syrian Christians began to serve it during Lent, when the faithful abstain from eating meat, poultry, and their products.

Ingredients for Kibbi shell

2 cups fine burghol

2 cups flour

Salt, pepper, and enough water to make a dough

1 medium onion

A little sweet red pepper for color

1 tsp each of pepper and cumin

Ingredients for stuffing

3 onions, coarsely chopped

½ cup walnuts and pistachios, coarsely chopped

¼ cup pine nuts

A pinch of sumac and salt to taste

½ tsp dibbis (pomegranate molasses)

Method for Kibbi shell

Soak burghol in water until it softens, then squeeze the water out

Mix burghol, spices, red pepper, and onion in blender

You may need to add a little water to hold it together like dough

Form hollow balls with the dough and fill with stuffing

Method for stuffing

Fry onions, walnuts, pistachios, and pine nuts in olive oil

Add sumac, dibbis and salt to taste and mix together

When kibbi balls are stuffed, fry them in olive oil

Kibbi Kathabeeya can also be made with boiled potatoes instead of burghol

TARATOUR IS OFTEN SERVED WITH KIBBI KATHABEEYA

Ingredients

½ cup tahini

1 clove garlic

¼ to ½ cup water

½ cup lemon juice

Method

Crush garlic with ¼ tsp salt

Add tahini and beat well

Add water and lemon alternately and beat together

Kibbi Kathabeeya made with potatoes can be served raw as an appetizer

RIQAQA — LAYERED CHICKEN

Riqaqa means thin layers and it was so named because the dish consists of thin layers of dough brushed with oil, with chicken and onions sandwiched in between.

It is a popular traditional dish served on happy social occasions. It suits all seasons, yet most people prefer to eat it in cold weather. It is easy to prepare and serving it is considered a sign of generosity. This is another recipe from Sheha.

Pastry Ingredients

1 ½ cups white flour

1 ½ cups brown flour

2 cups lukewarm water

Fennel and black cumin (black seed or hebet baraka) –
no quantities given

1 tsp salt

Filling Ingredients

10 medium onions, minced

2 cups olive oil

2 bouillon cubes

1 chicken cut into small pieces and rubbed with salt
and vinegar

1 tsp allspice

1 tsp ginger

1 stick cinnamon

2 bay leaves

5 pods of cardamom

5 cloves

Salt and pepper to taste

Filling Method

Boil cut chicken with bouillon cubes

Fry the chicken pieces in the olive oil until lightly brown or done

Add the onions and spices to chicken and sauté on low flame

Remove from fire and let cool off

Divide the chicken filling into three portions

Pastry Method

Combine the white and brown flour, water, fennel, black cumin, and salt

Mix well until it becomes a consistent dough

Divide the dough into four balls

Flatten each ball and brush one with oil and spread it on a round, buttered oven pan

Cover it with ⅓ of chicken filling

Flatten second dough ball and place over the first, brush with oil and cover with ⅓ of filling

Repeat with third ball and cover with last of filling

With fourth ball, flatten, brush with oil and place it on top

Bake in oven at 350 F until light brown

Turn it over on a large serving plate and serve with a bowl of yogurt

12

DEIR EZ ZOR

The city of Deir ez Zor, like Raqqa, stands on the shores of the Euphrates River. It is called the pearl of the Euphrates and has interesting historic quarters, forts, palaces, temples, churches, and mosques. The muhafaza is full of archeological sites on the river banks of the Euphrates and Khabour rivers. The ancient town of Mari, for example, dates back to the beginning of the third millennium BC.

In this fifth year of the war in Syria, Deir ez Zor has been wracked by battles and is now under ISIS control.

THREE FOLKTALES FROM DEIR EZ ZOR

THE SENTENCE OF THE JUDGE - (JUDGE QARAQOSH AGAIN)

Kan ya ma kan, a long time ago, a thief planned to rob a house in the city by climbing to the roof and dropping into the courtyard below. However, there was a lantern hanging from a metal rod in the courtyard which he did not see, and when he jumped down, the metal rod of the lantern poked his eye out. The thief screamed for help crying, "My eye, oh my eye!" The members of the household rushed to his aid and tried to save his eye, but failed.

The next day, the thief decided to go to the Judge and complain about the family that had failed to save his eye. The Judge ruled that just as the thief lost an eye, the owner of the house should lose his eye. The owner of the house was shocked by this unfair sentence, so he tried to convince the Judge to change his sentence.

"Your Honor, this thief came to our house to rob us, and even so we cared for him and tried to save his eye. Is this what we get in return for our good deed?"

The Judge would not accept this argument and said that the sentence had been proclaimed and that the man should accept it whether he liked it or not. So the owner of the house asked the Judge to postpone executing the sentence until the next day so he would have a chance to spend some time with his wife and children before this terrible sentence was carried out.

The Judge agreed, but the owner of the house came back the next morning saying, "I have thought about the matter and I have a suggestion. What if you put out the eye of my neighbor, the Hunter, since he only needs one eye for his work as a Hunter?"

The Judge thought deeply and then said, "It is a good idea. Summon the Hunter for me."

When the Hunter was brought before the Judge and informed of the sentence against him, he was shocked, "My house was not robbed. I did not put out anyone's eye, and I have nothing to do with this matter. Why have you proclaimed this sentence against me?"

The Judge was adamant, "The sentence has been proclaimed and your eye will be put out."

The Hunter thought deeply and then he said, "May I have fifteen days to enjoy the beauty of spring before I return to receive my sentence?" The Judge agreed. During this time, the Hunter was thinking of a way out of such an  unfair sentence. When the fifteen days were over, the Hunter returned to the Judge and said to him, "You know that I have been a Hunter for many years, so that now I understand the language of all types of birds. Before you put out my eye, it would please me to take you on a trip to the forest to show you that I speak the language of the birds."

The Judge agreed, and they decided to meet a week later. During this week, the Hunter planned the trip and figured out where each type of bird would be. Then he bought a sheep, slaughtered it, and cooked it in a lot of salt. Next, he filled a jug with water. He dug a hole on the right side of the path he planned to take – just at the end of the path - and placed the cooked sheep in it. On the left side of the path he dug another hole and placed the jug inside.

The next day, the Judge and the Hunter started out. They crossed meadows and hills and valleys until the Judge felt weak with exhaustion and hunger. He said to the Hunter, "You claim you know the language of the birds. Ask them where we can find some food."

The Hunter raised his head and began to speak to a bird and then he turned to the Judge and said, "The bird says there is food to the right of this road."

The Hunter uncovered the sheep and the Judge ate his fill. Then, because it was salty, the Judge told the Hunter to ask the birds if there was anything to drink close by. Again, the Hunter pretended to speak to a bird and then brought the Judge the jug of water and the Judge drank until his thirst was quenched. Afterwards, he lay down under a shady tree. Two owls on the tree were hooting at each other, so he asked the Hunter what they were saying.

The Hunter said, "The first owl has a son who wants to marry the second owl's daughter."

The Judge asked in wonder, "And have they agreed upon the marriage?"

The Hunter said, "No, because the dowry the daughter's mother wants is too high."

Curious to know what kind of a dowry an owl would ask for and how it could be too high, the Judge asked again, "What is the dowry she asks for?"

The Hunter answered, "Ten thousand destroyed cities for her to hoot in."[*]

The Judge said, "Indeed, a difficult request to fulfill."

---

[*] Superstitious Arabs associate owls with death and believe they live in abandoned and destroyed cities and graveyards.

The Hunter said, "But the bride's mother says it shouldn't be difficult to get that dowry at all, as long as there are the likes of this unjust Judge lying down under the tree. It will not be long before many cities are destroyed."

The Judge took these words to heart and realized how unfair he had been acting. He cancelled the Hunter's sentence and he was spared the loss of his eye due to his wise plan.

QARAQOSH AND THE FAINTING MISER

Kan ya ma kan, in days gone by, a certain old miser was subject to fainting fits, which tantalized his two nephews who were his heirs and who desired his death. Although he was constantly falling down lifeless, he always got up again. Unable to bear the strain any longer, they took him in one of his fits and prepared him for burial.

They called in a professional to prepare their uncle for burial and he took off the miser's clothes, which by custom were his perquisite, bound up his jaws, performed the usual ablutions upon the body, stuffed the nostrils, ears, and other apertures with cotton wool against the entrance of insects, and sprinkled the wool with a mixture of rose-water, pounded camphor, and dried and pounded leaves of the lotus tree. He then bound the feet together at the ankles and disposed the hands upon the breast.

All this took time, and before the process had quite finished, the miser revived, but he was so frightened at what was going on that he fainted again and his nephews were able to get the funeral procession under way.

They were halfway to the cemetery when the miser was again brought to life by the jolting of the bier, which was caused by the constant change of the bearers. They kept pressing forward to relieve one another in the meritorious act of carrying a true believer to the grave. Lifting the loose lid of the coffin, the miser sat up and roared for help. To his relief he saw Qaraqosh, the impartial Judge, coming down the path, and he appealed to him by name. The Judge at once stopped the procession and, confronting the nephews, asked, "Is your uncle dead or alive?"

"Quite dead, my lord," said the nephews. Qaraqosh then turned to the hired mourners and said, "Is this corpse dead or alive?"

"Quite dead, my lord," came from a hundred throats.

"But you can see for yourself that I am alive!" cried the miser wildly.

Qaraqosh looked him sternly in the eyes. "Allah forbid," said he, "that I should allow the evidence of my poor senses and your bare word to weigh against this crowd of witnesses. Am I not the impartial Judge? Proceed with the funeral!"

At this, the old man once more fainted away, and in that state was peacefully buried.

Qaraqosh was a real historical figure, not a fictitious one. It is unfortunate that "the rulings of Qaraqosh" have come to signify oppressive and bizarre rulings, since the historical Qaraqosh, Prince Bahaideen Qaraqosh al Asady, was a scholar in jurisprudence who dedicated his life to government and military service. He was appointed a Wazir in Egypt by Saladin (Saladin al Ayoubi) and was known for being stern but just. His closeness to Saladin caused him to be envied by Muslims and hated by the enemy. He was wise and firm in his attempt to remove the Fatimids from power, and they found no way to counter him except by spreading rumors about him and tearing down his reputation. They wrote a book called "Al Fafoush (the nonsense) in the Rulings of Qaraqosh" which was filled with lies. These anecdotes have been repeated down through the ages until they have become folktales.

ADVICE IN EXCHANGE FOR THREE CAMELS

Kan ya ma kan, in a bygone time, there lived a poor man named Khaled who couldn't find a job to support his newly wedded wife. When he finally lost hope, he decided to seek his fortune abroad.

He bid farewell to his wife Amina and traveled to another country, looking for work. He searched very hard until he reached the home of a wise Sheikh who agreed to employ him for three years in return for his food, drink, and three camels.

Days, months, and years passed during which Khaled proved to be a hardworking employee. At the end of the third year, he asked the Sheikh's permission to leave and to receive his three camels. As Khaled prepared his bags and the three camels to leave, the wise Sheikh called him back and said, "I will give you some advice in exchange for your three camels!"

Khaled was surprised at the Sheikh's suggestion, but he knew how wise he was and how all his tribe sought his advice. Therefore, he agreed to give up his first camel for the Sheikh's advice.

"My first piece of advice for you is - do not sleep between two strangers."

"Good advice," said Khaled. "Thank you, my dear, wise Sheikh." Then he gave the Sheikh one of his camels.

"My second piece of advice for you is," said the wise Sheikh, "be careful not to sleep in a valley. Sleep in a high place rather than a low place."

Khaled thanked the wise Sheikh again, although he thought the advice rather strange. Now Khaled was very worried about losing his third and last camel, so he bade the Sheikh farewell and started to leave. But the Sheikh called him back and said, "You didn't hear my third piece of advice!"

Khaled hesitated, but then worried he would regret not hearing the third piece of advice from this wise Sheikh, from whom everyone sought advice. So he turned back and said, "Yes, dear Sheikh, I would love to hear your third piece of advice."

The wise Sheikh said, "It is better to be upset than to be regretful."

So Khaled gave him his last camel and thanked him for his valuable advice, but deep inside he was very sad about losing all three camels and having to walk back home on foot. After walking in the desert for miles, he sat down to rest and to have something to eat. As he did, two men passed by riding on a camel. Khaled invited them to share his food and drink. They gladly accepted and sat down and ate with him. After they ate and drank, they thanked Khaled for his generosity.

In the evening, Khaled spread his blanket and all three lay down to sleep. The two strangers slept on the sides and Khaled slept in the middle. After the strangers went to sleep, Khaled suddenly remembered the Sheikh's first piece of advice: *do not sleep between two strangers.* So he got up and put his pillow under his abaya so it looked like he was still sleeping between the strangers. Then he stood far away in the dark, watching to see what would happen.

To his great surprise, the two men woke up at midnight, drew their daggers, and accidentally stabbed each other to death, each thinking the other was their host.

Khaled thanked God and thought to himself, *this advice from the Sheikh was worth not one camel, but a hundred camels!*

Then he collected his things, loaded them on the strangers' camel, and set out again. He traveled until he reached a huge valley. There he met a caravan and decided to camp with them.

When it got dark, they invited him to share their tent. He was just about to accept their invitation when he remembered the wise Sheikh's second piece of advice: *do not sleep in a valley; sleep in a high place rather than a low place.* So he apologized and climbed up the hill and slept there.

In the morning, he woke up and saw that a flood had swept away the whole caravan. Only the herds of camels and sheep, which had been on the hill, survived.

Khaled thanked God and happily collected the herds of camels and sheep and continued his journey until he reached the door of his house.

Khaled froze when he heard a man laughing out loud inside his house. He peered in the window and saw his wife sitting next to a young man.

At once, he drew his sword and was about to burst into the house and kill the man, when he remembered the Sheikh's last piece of advice: *it is better to be upset than to be regretful.* So he controlled himself and knocked on the door.

His wife opened the door and warmly welcomed him and then introduced the man as her younger brother who had been living abroad when they got married.

Khaled thanked God for remembering the Sheikh's advice and not losing his temper. He told his wife and brother-in-law about his adventure, and how he'd won his fortune, and they were amazed at what they heard.

Later on, Khaled and his wife Amina had many children and they lived happily ever after, thanks to the advice of the wise Sheikh.

There is a saying, "A piece of advice used to be worth a camel." This story explains the meaning and origin of this saying.

A Song

I'm in a country and my dear ones are in another.
From separation, my heart became a blacksmith's coal
Oh you Woodworkers, stop making tent stakes.
On the day people are happy, my misery increases.
Four waterwheels turn in the western wind
And the four wheels cannot wash the rust from my heart.
I'll climb a high peak and call, "My Lord!
I am poor and lost; who will guide me to the Path?"

Three Recipes from Deir ez Zor

Baitinjan Mishwee — Grilled eggplant

Ingredients

Eggplant

Semnay (ghee)

Garlic

Salt to taste

Method

Grill the eggplant over charcoal

Remove the skin of the eggplant under cold running
water

Lb the flesh with semnay and a little salt and garlic

Eat with bread

Deir ez Zor

MALDOUM — AN EGGPLANT DISH

Ingredients

- 3 medium-large eggplants
- 1 ½ lbs ground lamb with salt, allspice, and pepper to taste
- 2 large sliced tomatoes
- 2 large sliced onions

Method

Peel eggplant

Cut the eggplant horizontally, each cut about an inch apart, but don't cut all the way through

Arrange the eggplants in the pot you will cook them in

Between each slice put alternately: meat, a slice of tomato, and a slice of onion

When all the spaces between the eggplants are filled, add some water and salt and pepper to taste, cover and cook on medium heat until done. Serve with rice or pita bread

Tharud — Okra and Meat

This is the most famous dish of Deir ez Zor. My father said that whenever he visited Deir ez Zor, tharud would invariably be served as the dish of honor. A dear friend kindly gave me this recipe.

Ingredients

  1 kg large chunks of lamb meat on the bone

  1 ½ kg okra (bamiyeh)

  2 large tannour bread rounds cut in small pieces

  5 tbsp tomato paste

  6 crushed garlic cloves

  3 garlic cloves, coarsly chopped

  Meat spices: allspice, ground cardamom, black pepper, salt

  Ghee (or butter and olive oil) to sauté the meat

  A few cardamom pods

  ½ tsp sugar

Method for Meat

  Season meat with above spices

  Saute meat in ghee (or butter and olive oil) until it browns

  Pour boiling water on the meat, add a few cardamom pods and salt

  Simmer until tender

Method for bamiyeh

Brown okra in ghee (or butter and olive oil) with 3 chopped garlic cloves

Add tomato paste, meat broth, salt, 6 crushed garlic cloves and ½ tsp sugar

Simmer on low heat around 40 minutes, adding more water as needed

There should be enough sauce to cover the okra

Preparing the Tharud

Put bread pieces in a large dish; pour some sauce on bread to moisten

Cover the bread with the bamiyeh

Spread the meat on the top of the bamiyeh

Serve with raw green peppers

13

RAQQA

The city of Raqqa is 110 meters above sea level and is 140 kilometers east of Aleppo and 105 kilometers west of Deir ez Zor. It stands on the shores of the mighty Euphrates River where many ancient civilizations arose. In the 2004 census, Raqqa was the 6th largest city in Syria. It is located 40 kilometers (25 miles) east of the Tabqa Dam, Syria's largest dam. The Tabqa Dam, built in the sixties, is a huge rockfill dam which creates the 80 kilometers long Lake Assad. The most important crop in the Muhafaza of Raqqa is cotton.

In 2013 the city was captured by ISIS, who declared it their capital in 2014.

Three Folktales from Raqqa

Lababeed

This story has hints of the Cinderella story. I found another version in which the heroine goes to a carpenter and he makes her a dress of grass. It is possible the story came to Syria from Iraq.

Kan ya ma kan, a long time ago, there lived a beautiful young girl who only had one relative, a cousin, who wanted to marry her. He said to her one day, "You have no one but me in the whole world, oh Cousin, so marry me."

The young girl answered, "I will marry you if you break your tooth and poke your eye out." And because he loved her, he did. But the young girl then ran away.

She passed by a carpenter and asked him to make her a dress of felt. The carpenter did, and the girl put on the felt dress over her own clothes, went to the King's castle, and asked there, "Do you need a servant?" They asked her her name and she answered, Lababeed (meaning felt).

Lababeed became a servant in the castle and after some time passed, a wedding was held and she was asked, "Will you go to the wedding?"

She answered, "My appearance is not the appearance of one who attends weddings."

So everyone went and they left Lababeed. But when she was alone, she cast off her felt dress, put on her former clothes, and went to the wedding. The Prince was astounded by her beauty and asked his sister about the beautiful young girl. She told him this was the first time she had ever seen her. He asked his sister to ask for her hand in marriage for him.

The Princess asked Lababeed if she would marry the Prince and Lababeed answered, "And who would decline such an offer from the Prince?" So the sister went back and informed the Prince that the beautiful girl had agreed. The Prince offered her his ring as a gift, and she gave him hers.

When it got late, she said, "I must leave or my family will worry."

He asked her, "Where do you live?"

"When we meet again, I will tell you," she replied.

The Prince followed her footsteps in the winding lanes until her saw her enter his own castle. He went in after her and looked in all the rooms and halls, but found no trace of the beautiful woman. He only found Lababeed, sitting alone. He asked her about the young girl who had just entered the castle, but she told him that she had not left the castle nor seen anyone enter, and that surely the young girl must not exist.

The Prince was disappointed to lose the young girl and angry at Lababeed for making fun of him, so he struck her. But the blow did not hurt her for the felt protected her although she pretended to feel pain.

One day, the Queen decided to go to the hammam (public bath) and she called Lababeed to go with her. Lababeed made fun of herself, "I go to a hammam? I am not suitable for the hammam."

All the Princesses, servants and handmaidens went, and Lababeed was left alone. Quickly, she cast off her felt clothing, put on her former clothes, and followed them to the hammam. There again, everyone was taken by her beauty. The Prince was watching the hammam, so when he saw her leave, he followed her footsteps. Again they led to his castle, and once again he found no one inside but Lababeed. When he asked her about the young girl, she said that she had seen no one and that he must be dreaming. The Prince was so angry he beat the servant girl soundly.

One day, a big party took place and, as usual, Lababeed did not go with those invited but followed them on her own later on. When the Prince saw her, he asked her, "Where do you disappear to?"

She said, "I am not a ghost who disappears." He gave her his handkerchief and, when she left, he followed her to the castle but found no one there. Even Lababeed's room was closed. He knocked on the door but no one answered. He returned to the party, hoping that his beautiful girl had come back to see him, but she had not returned. He sadly went back to the castle, and at the door he found his handkerchief. Picking it up, he went in and knocked on Lababeed's door, and she opened for him.

"When did you come back?" he asked.

"I did not leave in order to come back." She answered.

"I knocked so hard that I almost broke down the door," he said.

"I must have been asleep," she answered. In a rage, the Prince beat her viciously and she screamed with pain.

One day, the Prince fell ill. He asked his mother to make him *kibbi darawish* because he was craving it. He warned her not to let Lababeed touch it, for he wanted it from his mother's hand. The Queen prepared the ingredients and Lababeed asked her, "What does Your Majesty want to cook?"

The Queen answered that her son was craving *kibbi darawish*.

Lababeed said, "Away, I shall prepare it." The Queen objected, telling her that her son wanted it from her own hand and that he had specifically warned her that Lababeed was not to touch it.

Lababeed answered, "Don't tell him I made it, for indeed no one can cook it better than I."

Lababeed prepared the food and put it on the fire to cook, and when it was done she placed it on a platter and dropped the Prince's ring inside. His mother served him the dish, and he ate with delight. Suddenly, his spoon rang against the ring. He called his mother and said, "You did not cook this kibbi. Who did?"

She said, "If I tell you, will you promise not to get angry?"

He said, "I promise."

She said, "Lababeed insisted on making it for you."

He said, "Ask her to bring me water to drink with her."

The Queen called her and ordered her to carry water up to the Prince, but Lababeed refused, claiming the Prince beat her each time he saw her. The Queen assured her that he would not touch her if she took the water up to him, so Lababeed carried the water to him, entering his room taking one step forward and two steps back. He asked her to hurry and she said, "You will beat me."

He said, "No, I will not." When she drew closer, he took her hand and said to her, "I know who you are. Take off this felt dress."

She said, "Have you gone mad?"

He said, "Enough hiding. You are the beauty I've been looking for, and if you don't take off the felt dress on your own I will do it myself."

The girl took off her felt clothing and lo, she was the same stunningly beautiful young girl the Prince guessed her to be. The Prince called his mother, saying, "Bring me someone who can write up my wedding contract immediately to this beautiful woman."

THE GIRL WITH THE GOLDEN HAIR

Kan ya ma kan, in an olden time, a young girl whose parents were dead lived with her stepmother and stepsister. The stepmother treated her very badly and would send her each day to collect dry cow dung for fuel and would give her a jug to fill with water.

One day, the young girl met an old woman who asked her for a drink. When the old woman had drunk her fill, she led the young girl to a well where she called out:

> O Well, O Well,
> The best of deciders,
> What will you give this fair and virtuous daughter of the fair and virtuous?

The young girl's cheeks became as pink as roses and her hair turned as gold as the sun and flowed down to her waist, but more extraordinary was the fact that with each word she spoke, pearls and gems fell out of her mouth.

The young girl went home and the stepmother was shocked to see the change in her. "What happened to your hair and your cheeks?" she asked. The young girl told her the story of the old woman, and pearls and gems fell from her mouth as she spoke.

The next morning, the stepmother sent her to collect cow dung, but sent her own daughter to fill the water jug. The old woman crossed her path and asked her for a drink, but the girl said, "I brought the water for myself, not for a stranger." The old woman led her to the same well and addressed it, saying:

> O Well, O Well,
> The best of deciders,

What will you give this unkind daughter of the unkind?

The girl became dirty and grimy, and with every word she spoke, frogs and snakes fell out of her mouth. She returned to her mother in the worst of conditions. Both mother and daughter then increased their mistreatment of Golden Hair, as she now was known.

It happened that each person that met Golden Hair would say she was fit to be a royal wife. She couldn't escape her stepmother, but she thought that if she produced enough gems and jewels for her to become rich, perhaps she would allow her to leave. If she were able to leave, she decided to go to the palace and see if the Prince might marry her.

She said to her stepmother, "If you allow me to leave, I will give you a large amount of gems and pearls."

The stepmother said, "Give me what you have promised and we shall see." The young girl spoke and spoke until there was a small pile of jewels. She handed the jewels to the stepmother, who said, "You were born in this house, and in it you shall die." Golden Hair pleaded and pleaded with her to no avail.

Finally, the stepmother said, "I will let you leave if you pluck out your eye." The young girl did, but the stepmother was not satisfied. She said, "I will let you leave if you pluck out your other eye." The girl did, but still the step mother had another demand, "Cut off your hair." The girl did, but still the stepmother and her daughter were not satisfied. They took Golden Hair to the forest and threw her into such a deep pit that they were sure she would never be able to escape.

The Prince had heard of the golden-haired girl from whose mouth pearls and gems issued as she spoke, and he set off to seek her and ask for her hand in marriage. So the stepmother took Golden Hair's locks, glued them on her daughter's head, and married her off to the King's son. As for our poor orphan girl, Golden Hair, she remained thrashing and flailing about in the pit.

One day, two birds alighted on a tree next to the pit and saw the young girl inside. The first bird said to his brother, "If the blind girl were to rub her eyes with the leaves of this tree three times, they would be cured." So the girl felt around until she touched the leaves on a branch that was within reach. She rubbed her eyes thrice and lo, she was able to see. Still, she was unable to climb out of the pit.

A shepherd passed by with his flock and saw her. She said to him, "If you help me out of this pit, I will make you rich." The shepherd helped her out and she gave him enough jewels that he was able to build a palace. But Golden Hair suddenly died, so the shepherd put her in a casket and built a dome over it.

One day, the Prince was out hunting and he saw the dome. He entered and found the coffin, which he opened. Inside lay the body of the most beautiful young girl whose pink cheeks belied her death. He saw a scarf wound around her neck and pulled it off. Immediately, she took a deep breath and came back to life.

He asked her about herself and she told him the whole story. As she spoke, pearls and jewels fell from her mouth. The Prince took her back to his castle, where he told his wife to put a huge pot to boil on the fire since he was planning a big dinner.

When the water boiled, the Prince threw his wife and her mother into the pot and then he married Golden Hair.

Hudedan

The Sa'lawa is a female demon similar to the Ghouleh. Some say the Sa'lawa is a sorcerer jinni that can change shape and appear as a nice old woman to trick young children and kidnap them to eat them, or appear as a beautiful young woman who kidnaps solitary travelers to amuse herself with them and then eat them. Mothers in Raqqa and Hasaka scare their children with the Sa'lawa as mothers do with the Ghouleh in other areas.

Of course this folktale will bring to mind the story of "The Three Little Pigs," but whereas the wolf "huffs and puffs," the Sa'lawa has a ruder method of blowing don a house.

Kan ya ma kan, in an olden time, lived an old man who had three sons, "Quseban" (meaning reed), "Khusheban" (meaning wood), and "Hudedan" (meaning iron). One day, the father told his sons that he would build a small house for each of them, using for each house the material for which they were named.

When the houses were finally built and each son moved into his own house, the Sa'lawa came along and knocked at the door of Quseban and said, "Quseban, Quseban, open the door and let me in!"

Quseban answered, "Who told you I was so foolish?"

"Will you be foolish if you open the door for your aunt?" asked the Sa'lawa.

"You will eat me if I open the door!" said Quseban.

"If you don't open the door for me, I'll fart and I'll fart and I'll blow your house down!"

"Fart if you can!" said Quseban, defying the Sa'lawa.

So the Sa'lawa farted, and farted, and blew his house down. The reeds flew in the air and Quseban hid under a stack of reeds. The Sa'lawa wildly searched for him among the reeds, found him, and ate him up.

Days passed and the Sa'lawa got hungry again, so she went to the second brother Khusheban and said, "Khusheban, Khusheban, open the door and let me in so we can enjoy ourselves on this moonlit night!"

Khusheban answered, "Do you think I am so foolish? You will eat me like you ate my brother Quseban!"

"If you don't open the door I'll fart, and I'll fart, and I'll blow your house down!"

"Fart if you can!" said Khusheban, defying the Sa'lawa.

So the Sa'lawa farted, and farted, and she destroyed his house. The planks of wood flew in the air and Khusheban hid under a stack of wood. The Sa'lawa wildly searched for him among the planks of wood, found him, and ate him up.

Days passed and the Sa'lawa got hungry again, so she went one evening to the third brother Hudedan and said, "Hudedan, Hudedan, open the door and let me in so we can chat with one another!"

Hudedan answered, "Do you think I am so foolish? You will eat me like you ate my two brothers Quseban and Khusheban. I am sure now you think it is my turn!"

"If you don't open the door, I'll fart, and I'll fart, and I'll blow your house down!"

"Fart if you can!" said Hudedan, defying the Sa'lawa.

So the Sa'lawa farted and farted, but couldn't blow the house down. When she found that she could not blow it down with all her farting, she threatened, "Your day will come! I promise I'll come back again and eat you!"

In a few days, the Sa'lawa returned to Hudedan and said from behind the door, "The son of the King has pulled down the wall of his fig orchard for the public. Let us go and take our share!"

"I don't like figs!" said Hudedan.

Once the Sa'lawa left, Hudedan sneaked out of his house and reached the fig orchard before the Sa'lawa came. He climbed up the trees, picked a lot of figs, filled his big basket, and ran back home.

When the Sa'lawa passed by Hudedan's house, she showed off her big basket full of figs and said, "Look what you missed!" Hudedan laughed and held up his full basket to the window. The Sa'lawa was furious and threw her basket on the ground, saying, "Eat as much as you can, for sooner or later, you and the figs will be in my stomach!"

Days passed and the Sa'lawa returned to Hudedan, knocked on his door and said, "The son of the King has pulled down the wall of his watermelon field for the public to harvest. Let's go and get our share!"

"I don't like watermelon!" said Hudedan.

Once the Sa'lawa left, Hudedan sneaked out of his house and reached the field of watermelon before the Sa'lawa came and ate all the watermelon he could. Then he chose one of the biggest watermelons, cored it out, and hid inside.

When the Sa'lawa reached the field, she approached the large watermelon and tested it by tapping on it with her finger. When she didn't hear an echo, she assumed it was not ripe and left it, not knowing it was hollow. While the Sa'lawa was searching for ripe watermelons, Hudedan got out of the large watermelon and sneaked off, carrying some watermelons on his head.

When the Sa'lawa passed by Hudedan's house, she showed off her ripe watermelons and said, "Look what you missed!"

Hudedan lifted up his large watermelons to the window and said, "I got there before you and chose the largest and ripest ones!"

The Sa'lawa was furious and went home muttering, "Eat as much as you can, for sooner or later, you and the watermelons will be in my stomach!"

Days passed and the Sa'lawa returned to Hudedan, knocked on his door and said, "The son of the King has pulled down the wall of his vineyard for the public. Let us go and take our share."

"I don't like grapes!" said Hudedan.

Once the Sa'lawa left, Hudedan sneaked out of his house and reached the vineyard before the she came. He picked a lot of fine grapes and filled his saddlebag.

When the Sa'lawa reached the vineyard, Hudedan hid behind a large tree. The Sa'lawa was taken by the grapes and didn't notice when Hudedan put his saddlebag on her donkey and galloped off towards his house. Unfortunately, when Hudedan tried to get off the donkey, he was stuck by the tar that the Sa'lawa had put on its back. The donkey brayed out loud and the Sa'lawa ran towards them, shouting, "At last you are mine!" Then she dragged him to her house and imprisoned him in her well.

The Sa'lawa called her daughter and said, "Bake the *tannour* bread while I go invite your aunts for a big feast!"

Hudedan felt bored down in the well and started to sing. His voice reached the ears of the Sa'lawa's daughter, who looked down the well and said, "Oh Hudedan, you have a very nice voice indeed!"

"You haven't heard anything yet!" said Hudedan. "You should hear me sing while I dance!"

"Then dance for me!" said the Sa'lawa's daughter.

"Dance!" said Hudedan. "How can I dance down in the bottom of the well? Pull me out of the well and I'll dance for you until your mother returns!"

The Sa'lawa's daughter pulled Hudedan out of the well and he sang and danced for her until he saw the *tannour*. He leaned over it, pointed at the fire, and said, "Oh! Look at those golden chickens!"

The Sa'lawa's daughter took off her scarf and coat because it was too hot and leaned over to see the golden chickens. Hudedan pushed her into the *tannour*, where she died at once.

Then Hudedan pulled her body out and put her in the large pot boiling on the stove, which was actually awaiting him. Then he put on the coat and scarf of the Sa'lawa's daughter and baked some bread in the *tannour*.

When the Sa'lawa returned with her sisters, she assumed Hudedan was her daughter because he was dressed in her clothes.

"Where is Hudedan?" asked the Sa'lawa.

"He is already in the large pot!" said Hudedan.

"You are wonderful!" said the Sa'lawa as she looked at the boiling water in the pot.

When the meat was cooked, the Sa'lawa sat down with her sisters and they ate every bit of the meat and sucked on the bones, not knowing they were actually eating the Sa'lawa's daughter.

Once they finished eating, Hudedan took off the coat and the scarf and said, "I hope you enjoyed eating your own daughter!"

The Sa'lawa went crazy and realized that she was had been fooled by Hudedan again. She and her sisters chased Hudedan, who ran as fast as he could back to his house and locked himself in.

The Sa'lawa decided to burn Hudedan alive and gathered wood and tried to set his house on fire. Most of the house was made of iron and only the roof would burn. Fortunately, Hudedan sat in a barrel of ice-cold water and was untouched by the fire. The Sa'lawa jumped on the roof and let out happy squeals, but the flames shot out suddenly and her behind was badly burned. She jumped down and barked like a dog from the pain.

When the fire calmed down, Hudedan escaped from his house and found the Sa'lawa barking from pain. When she saw Hudedan, she swore she would never live in the same country as he did and ran away as fast as she could. No one ever saw the Sa'lawa again, and Hudedan rebuilt his house and lived happily ever after.

A RECIPE FROM RAQQA: *THAREED* — A KIND OF *FITTEH*

Ingredients

1 kg meat

1 loaf of pita bread, cut into pieces

1½ cups burghol or rice

½ kilo yogurt

2 tbsp tahini

2 garlic cloves, mashed

1 tbsp lemon juice

Semnay (ghee)

Method

Sauté the meat well in semnay, then boil until tender

Cook 1 ½ cups rice or burghol

Stir tahini, mashed garlic cloves, and lemon juice into yogurt

Place cooked rice or burghol on top of the bread

Pour stock of boiled meat over the rice or burghol

Pour yogurt over all

Arrange meat on top and pour boiling hot semnay over the dish and serve

14

HASAKEH

This muhafaza lies in the extreme northeast corner of Syria. It mainly occupies the Khabour river basin, but extends also up to the Tigris River at the borders of Turkey and Iraq. It is thus part of the Fertile Crescent and has witnessed numerous ancient civilizations: the Akkadians, the Amorites, the Assyrians, and the Arameans. It is distinguished by its fertile lands, plentiful water, picturesque nature and more than one hundred archaeological sites.

Since the civil war, violence has caused the displacement of large numbers of people. Many battles have been fought and currently the city of Hasakeh and much of the muhafaza is under the de facto control of a Kurdish federation.

TWO FOLKTALES FROM HASAKEH

I was told these two stories by a pleasant old lady from Hasakeh named Um Mohammed, whom I met on a bus in Damascus.

Straw Hut

What is very strange, indeed astonishing, about the following story is that when I was a child in primary school there was a story called "The Hobyahs" in one of the British primers we read in our English class. The plot of "The Hobyahs" is uncannily similar to this Arab story, "The Straw Hut," and I would love to know how this folktale traveled from Syria to England – or did it possibly travel in the other direction? In the British tale, a faithful dog takes the place of the faithful cow and the little old man and the little old woman survive the attack of the Hobyahs.

Kan ya ma kan, a long time ago, there lived a little old woman and a little old man in a hut made of straw. They had a cow that was very faithful and protective of the little old woman and the little old man. The cow would moo and shake her sharp horns whenever anyone approached their hut.

One night, while the little old woman and the little old man were asleep, a Sa'lawa - a Ghouleh - quietly sneaked up from behind the high palm trees, knocked on their door, and said:

> Straw Hut, Straw Hut,
> I shall tear you down,
> Drag out and eat up
> The little old woman
> And the little old man.

Then the cow wildly waved her sharp horns and loudly mooed and said:

> My eyes can burn,
> My tail can whip,

240

My horns can tear and rip!

The Sa'lawa was afraid and ran away as fast as she could.

The little old woman woke up and cried, "That cow keeps mooing all night! I can't sleep. We must slaughter it."

"Oh no," said the little old man. "It feeds us and keeps us company."

Day after day, the little old woman kept insisting on killing the cow until the little old man slaughtered it and threw its hide on the ground in front of the hut. That night, along came the Sa'lawa, creeping from behind the high palm trees.

She cried out:

Straw hut, straw hut,
I shall tear you down,
Drag out and eat up
The little old woman
And the little old man.

To her great surprise, the cow's hide answered her:

My eyes can burn,
My tail can whip,
My horns can tear and rip!

The Sa'lawa was even more afraid to hear the cow's hide threaten her and ran away as fast as she could.

The little old woman woke up and shook her head and said, "We should have gotten rid of the cow's hide!"

The little old man covered his head and whispered, "I'll sell it first thing in the morning."

So the next morning, the little old man sold the hide to a shoemaker.

That night, along came the Sa'lawa, creeping from behind the high palm trees.

She cried out:

Straw Hut, Straw Hut,
I shall tear you down,
Drag out and eat up
The little old woman
And the little old man.

To her great surprise, the Sa'lawa heard the cow's blood on the sand answer her:

My eyes can burn,
My tail can whip,
My horns can tear and rip!

The Sa'lawa was horrified to hear the cow's blood threaten her and ran away as fast as she could.

The little old woman woke up and shook her head and said, "We should have gotten rid of that bloodstained sand!"

The little old man covered his head and whispered, "I'll get rid of it first thing in the morning."

So the next morning, the little old man scooped up the blood-stained sand and threw it in the river.

That very night, along came the Sa'lawa, creeping from behind the high palm trees.

She cried out:

Straw Hut, Straw Hut,
I shall tear you down,
Drag out and eat up
The little old woman

And the little old man.

To the Sa'lawa's great joy, there was no cow, no hide, and no blood-stained sand to stop her from creeping towards the hut. She pulled down the straw hut and caught the little old woman and said as she poked her with her nails, "Where shall I start to eat you, my little old woman?"

The little old woman cried and said, "Start with my tongue for asking my husband to kill our faithful friend the cow!"

So the Sa'lawa started eating the little old woman's tongue and soon gobbled her all up.

As soon as she had finished from the little old woman, the Sa'lawa heard the little old man burp from under the bed. So she pulled him out and cried: "Oh little old man, tell me where shall I start to eat you?"

The old little old man cried out, "Start with my two ears for listening to my wife's advice. Then go on to both my hands for slaughtering my dear faithful friend, the cow!"

So the Sa'lawa started eating the little old man's ears and then his hands and so on until nothing was left of him.

It may be that the Sa'lawa is borrowed from the myths and folktales of other nations that would pass through our land. Arab traders would see frightening pictures of creatures that combined human and animal traits on the walls of Babylonian and Pharaonic temples and perhaps they would remember such images as they walked alone in the dark through the desert.

THE TALKING STICK

Kan ya ma kan, in a bygone time, a simple muallim (a teacher of small children) passed by an unguarded field where large bags packed with lentils stood side by side. He poked his head in one of the bags and was tempted to steal some lentils, but decided it would be better to return at night.

When it became dark, the muallim took a big bag and sneaked back to the field. He stood next to the bags of lentils and was about to grasp a handful, when he suddenly felt terribly guilty. So he decided to ask permission.

> Lentils, oh Lentils,
> Picked and packed,
> Muallim has come to you hesitantly,
> Eating you is permitted or forbidden?

The muallim waited for the lentils to answer him. When silence prevailed, he considered it was a sign of consent. So he filled his big bag with lentils and carried it home on his back.

The next morning, the owner of the field was shocked to find that a large quantity of lentils was missing. He decided to hide behind a large tree at night to discover who was stealing them.

Sure enough, the Muallim turned up in the middle of the night carrying an empty bag and, as he had done before, he stood next to the bags full of lentils and said:

> Lentils, oh Lentils,
> Picked and packed,
> Muallim has come to you hesitantly,
> Eating you is permitted or forbidden?

The muallim, as before, waited for the lentils to answer him.

To his great shock, the owner rushed out from behind a tree waving his stick and crying out:

Stick, oh Stick,
Long and stiff,
Muallim has come in a state of stupidity,
Beating him is permitted or forbidden?

Then the owner of the field answered himself and shouted out loudly, "Permitted, permitted, and permitted!" as he beat the muallim with his stick. Afterwards, he made the muallim lead him to his house where he retrieved the large bag of stolen lentils.

SUPERSTITIONS

Superstitions are handed down orally from generation to generation. There are many superstitions in Hasakeh about what should not be done at night. As a psychologist in Hasakeh explained, many of these superstitions arose from people's fear of the dark and fear of the future. As education and scientific information became widespread, people began to lose their belief in these superstitions. Still, many superstitions persist, even though people may realize they are unreasonable.

Maha, a young woman from Hasakeh whom I met in a park in Damascus, told me she still remembers how her mother used to warn her not to count the stars or point at the moon so she wouldn't get warts on her fingers. Her mother also warned her not to cut her fingernails at night, and her mother never threw out the trash at night so the blessings would not leave the house.

Some other superstitions include:

- Do not leave scissors open at night because it will cause friction between a husband and wife. Another belief is that open scissors are like an open mouth and will cause the neighbors to gossip about you.

- Do not take a bath at night or the moon will harm you.

- Do not throw hot water on the floor at night because the jinn and their families live under the floor and hot water will harm them.

- Do not make a fire or play with fire at night or you will wet your bed.

- When there is an eclipse of the moon, people are afraid a whale has swallowed the moon, and they go into the streets beating pots to make the moon return. In the early sixties, there was an eclipse of the moon in Damascus while my parents were sitting with some neighbors on the balcony, and my mother later told me they heard people beating pots in the streets when the moon vanished. They kept beating until a sliver of the moon reappeared. I am sure people were just having fun with an old custom and not really worried that the moon would disappear.

THREE RECIPES FROM HASAKEH

The following two recipes were given to me by Atika, my daughter's friend, a master's candidate at Damascus University. Atika is from Hasakeh and spent most of her life there. She only came to Damascus when she and her brothers and sisters registered in Damascus University. During her college years, she always returned to Hasakeh by bus for the holidays.

Unfortunately, the civil war forced her parents to move to Damascus, and almost all her aunts and uncles have left the country. Atika's family had to leave everything behind them when they left Hasakeh; their beautiful house, personal souvenirs, and photo albums - their entire past was left behind. It has now been two years since Atika last visited Hasakeh, and she still has a picture of the last dinner her mother prepared for her there.

KLEJEH — A FESTIVE PASTRY

Atika remembers her mother and aunts preparing klejeh to celebrate the Eid holidays when she was a child. Today, preparing these meals with her mother, reminds her of her hometown, her relatives and all the good old days she had in Hasakeh.

Although klejeh is associated with the Eid in Hasakeh, it is also considered a Ramadan dessert, as it is made and served in that holy month.

Ingredients

3 cups whole wheat flour

1 cup white flour

1 cup sugar

1 tbsp hebet baraka (black seed or black cumin)

Warm water as needed

½ cup fine semolina

¾ cup ghee or vegetable shortening

¼ cup corn oil

1 cup milk

1 tbsp yeast

1 tbsp klejeh spices – 2 tsp ground caraway, 2 tsp mahlab,* 1 tsp cloves, 2 tsp cinnamon, 1 tsp nutmeg

Method

Prepare the klejeh spices and add them to the dry ingredients

Mix dry ingredients well

Form a well in the middle, pour in oil and add shortening, then mix and knead

Form a well again and gradually add the milk and enough warm water (kneading

as you go along) to form a dough that can be rolled

Cover and let it rest half an hour

Roll out the dough and cut into shapes (usually diamond shapes)

Brush with beaten egg

Bake in moderately low oven for about half an hour until lightly browned

---

* *Mahlab* is a Syrian spice from the kernel of the black cherry stone. The spice is always sold whole and is a small seed, smaller than a coriander seed. Pound in a mortar before using to flavor *klejeh*.

KABEYBIAT — BABY KIBBI

Atika had a nice photo of this dish as made by her mother. Unfortunately, we cannot find it.

Ingredients

- 1 cup dashayshay (coarsely ground unboiled wheat, similar to semolina) or use 1 cup semolina
- 1 cup of fine burghol
- 1 kilo ground meat
- 4 medium onions, minced
- ½ bunch parsley, cleaned and chopped
- 1 tsp each of salt, pepper, and dried mint

Method

- Soak burghol in water with a pinch of salt for one hour
- Saute the meat with the minced onion and salt, pepper, and spices until well done
- Remove from heat, add finely chopped parsley and dried mint and set aside
- Squeeze out water from the burghol and mix with the dashayshay or semolina
- Knead dough thoroughly
- Shape the dough into small balls. Flatten each ball, place filling inside, and close it into an oblong, boat shaped kabeybi (meaning baby kibbi)
- Drop carefully into boiling water and let cook for 5 to 7 minutes, then serve

DANUK — WHEAT AND CHICKPEAS WITH LAMB

This is one of the oldest traditional recipes in Kamishli in the muhafaza of Hasakeh. Usually the Tete, the oldest member of the family, prepares danuk and invites the whole family to share the meal. It is considered a winter dish and is often served at the beginning of the winter season.

Ingredients

    2 cups wheat, soaked overnight

    2 cups chickpeas, soaked overnight

    ½ lb lamb cubes

    Salt and butter to taste

Method

    Boil lamb cubes until tender

    Drain water from meat and add to it enough water to make 6 cups

    Add wheat and chickpeas to meat and cook for half an hour

    Add butter and salt to taste, then cook 10 more minutes

    Serve hot

Part II
FOLKTALES FROM ETHNIC GROUPS IN SYRIA

THE PATCHWORK QUILT OF SYRIA

Muna researched the different ethnic groups to understand why they ended up in Syria. She believed strongly that they all made a positive contribution to the country and felt that this should be remembered and commemorated, now that civil war and sectarian strife are tearing the country apart. (E. Imady and S. Imady)

In the nineteenth century and the beginning of the twentieth century, several waves of immigrants sought refuge in Syria, and Syria opened her heart to these people. There were the Armenians, the Circassians, the Chechens, the Dagestanis, and the Kumyks, who all originated in the Caucasus region, although their languages are different and they are not related groups. In addition to these immigrants from the Caucasus, Syria also took in Assyrians, Uzbeks, Turkmens, Kurds, and Albanians. Expulsion from their homelands, persecution, and the threat of genocide were the main reasons that drove these diverse ethnic groups to Syria, where they were warmly received. Among them were workers, artisans, farmers, doctors, teachers, lawyers, and Merchants who brought their talents and skills with them. They became part of what I call "the patchwork quilt" of Syria and helped in building the country. Furthermore, they shared with us their folktales and recipes.

1

ARMENIANS

The Armenians are descendants of a people who have existed continuously in Transcaucasia since about the sixth century B.C. Armenians are proud that in 301, the Kingdom of Armenia became the first country in the world to adopt Christianity as its official religion. Another unusual fact about Armenians is that their language has its very own unique alphabet.

Throughout its history, Armenia has been invaded and conquered many times. By the 20th century, historic Armenia was partly within the Ottoman Empire and partly within the Russian Empire. When the Russian and the Ottoman Empires went to war in 1914, the Ottoman Armenian citizens living along the border were viewed with suspicion by their government, who feared their sympathies might lie with the Christian Russians. The Armenians were no longer welcome in Turkey.

Starting in the spring of 1915, thousands of Armenians were forced to leave their homes on foot and were marched under guard out of their towns and cities to Syria. Many died on the journey and only 150 women and children reached Aleppo out of 180,000.

A far greater number of Armenians reached their final destination in the deserts of Deir ez Zor, where those who survived the death march were herded into open air concentration camps and left to die of starvation or were killed. While the exact numbers will never be known, it is estimated that at least 600,000 Armenians had lost their lives by 1925.

Syrians in general didn't hesitate to shelter and support the Armenians. By 1925, Aleppo had become home to around 60,000 Armenians. Roughly 75 percent chose to stay in Aleppo, where they became a large and commercially important element of the city. However, there are also Armenian communities in Damascus, Hasakeh, Deir-Ez-Zor, Homs and the small village of Kasab on the Turkish border.

Armenians in Syria are city or town dwellers. They work chiefly in trade, the professions, small industry, or crafts, and a few are found in government service. Jewelers, shoemakers and photographers are some of the trades Armenians became noted for. Many of the technical and skilled workers of Damascus and Aleppo are Armenian; in the smaller towns they are generally small traders or craftsmen. They have helped to enrich the country and the economy of Syria.

Armenians are the largest unassimilated group in Syria. Most Syrian Armenians still speak Armenian and have preserved their identity and traditions. They retain many of their own customs, maintain their own schools, and publish and read newspapers in their own language. The majority of them belong to the Armenian Apostolic Church.

As Arab nationalism and socialism became more important in Syrian political life, Armenians began to feel left out. As a result, many Armenians emigrated from Syria in the 1960s and early 1970s. Before the present civil war there were about 150,000 Armenians in Syria, but their number has decreased. Many Syrian Armenians have returned to Armenia which gained its independence from Russia in 1991. One hundred years ago, Syria became a refuge for Armenians. Now the tables have turned and Armenia is welcoming

Syrian Armenian refugees from the civil war. However, many of these Syrian Armenians are homesick for Syria, the country they still consider home.

Memories of Bygone Days

The Story of Marina's Grandmother

Some years ago, my cousin Usama married a beautiful blond woman from Deir-ez Zor named Marina al Showa. Everyone was happy to welcome Marina into the family. She is an architect and a warm and friendly person, and I became very fond of her. I knew she was named for her Armenian grandmother and asked if I could include her grandmother's story in my book and she kindly agreed and gave me two family stories, not one. Here they are as she wrote them.

Many years ago, a baby girl was born into a farming family in a small Armenian village. One day when she was four years old, Turkish soldiers attacked the village and killed almost all its inhabitants. From her hiding place inside the *tannour*, the little girl witnessed her entire family – her father, mother, little brother, grandfather, and grandmother - being killed.

When the massacre ended, she heard some of her neighbors returning to the village from their distant fields. She recognized their familiar voices and ran to them. They took her with them as they headed south, trying to escape the Turkish militia. However, the children and the elderly who joined this convoy slowed them down, and it was not long before the soldiers reappeared. They showed no mercy and brutally aimed to kill them all. In order not to waste time killing children, they simply threw them into big ditches into which they had set fires.

It was mere luck that saved the little girl. Just as she was thrown into the ditch and before being harmed, a hand pulled her out of the fire! It was the hand of a servant of the Turkish "al Taweel" family. This family had only one son, who was fighting with the

Turkish army in the Balkans. The family had decided beforehand to adopt an Armenian child so that God might protect their only son on the battlefield. So it was that the al Taweel family sent their servant to bring them a child from the burning ditches, and by this act of mercy, the rescued child was destined to become my grandmother.

Around the same time my future grandmother was saved by the al Taweel family, a group of exhausted Armenians arrived near the home of my maternal great-grandfather, Mohammed Hattab in Deir ez Zor. My great-grandfather was one of the biggest land-lords in Deir ez Zor and Raqqa and had excellent relations with the Ottoman government. He was known for his noble character and was always willing to help anyone in need.

Mohammed Hattab realized the Turkish army was on its way to finish off the Armenians, so he gathered his men and had them dig deep trenches to hide the Armenians. Grass and shrubs were placed on these trenches to disguise them. The Turkish soldiers arrived and my great-grandfather welcomed them and said, "Look around, there are no Armenians here."

He then had a lavish dinner invitation for the Turkish soldiers. The Turks enjoyed their meal and then got on their horses and rode away. In this way, my great-grandfather saved a large number of Armenians from certain death.

To return to the story of my grandmother, she was brought to the al Taweel family where at first she was thought to be a boy, but when she was cleaned up from the soot of the fire, they found she was a girl. The husband really wished the child was a boy, but his wife was delighted to have a daughter. They kept the child and raised her as their own. She said her name was "Marina," but her new parents changed her name to "Maryam" so she wouldn't have a foreign name.

At the age of six, Maryam moved with her new family to the city of Deir ez Zor. The al Taweel family's happiness was complete when their son came back safely from the war. The young man soon got married and had his own family, but always had time for his new sister. They became very fond of each other.

At the age of eight, Maryam met her cousin by chance. He was a bit older than her and was working in a nearby bakery. It happened that one day he was sent to deliver bread to the al Taweel family. When Maryam opened the door, the two cousins immediately recognized one another and started to speak Armenian. While they were talking, Maryam's father overheard them and angrily came to the door. He expelled the boy and told him not to return. He told Maryam that she must never open the door again. That was the last time Maryam ever saw one of her family or spoke Armenian. In time she forgot her language, but she learned to read and write in Turkish and to speak Arabic.

Years passed and at the age of nineteen –a very late age for women to be single at that time – a young Arab named Mohammed Aref al Showa asked for Maryam's hand in marriage. At first her father rejected him because he was poor, but when the Imam of the mosque intervened and vouched for the young man's character, he finally approved of the marriage. However, when Maryam's mother found he had consented to her daughter's marriage to an Arab – not a Turk – she was very upset. Nevertheless, Maryam did marry Mohammed Aref al Showa and her mother went back to Turkey the day after the wedding ceremony.

Mohammed Aref was a loving and caring husband who not only respected Maryam but also consulted her about even the minute details of his private and business affairs.

After a while, the financial situation of her step-brother became difficult. Without hesitation, Maryam bought a sewing machine and started a small business for neighbors and friends, offering all her income to help support her brother.

As time passed, the business ventures of Mohammed Aref and Maryam flourished due to his seriousness and hard work as well as Maryam's ideas and suggestions. Mohammed Aref became one of the wealthiest merchants of Deir ez Zor. Maryam played a decisive role in his business, registering all goods bought and sold in Turkish. Although this was a language her husband did not know, he fully trusted Maryam to keep his accounting books.

Maryam and Mohammed Aref had two daughters and three sons, all of whom achieved an outstanding education. Their second son is Abdel Fatah, my father. Maryam was a good wife and a caring mother. She was greatly appreciated by her husband's family since she was always kind to them and would offer them financial support when they were in need. In fact, her compassion extended to the family of her step-brother, her neighbors, her friends, and to all the Armenian women in Deir ez Zor, many of whom had similar stories to her own. These women trusted Maryam and often asked her advice.

One day, a Lebanese lawyer knocked on Maryam's door. He was sent by a very rich Armenian widow in the United States who had no children and was looking for her sister who had been lost during the massacres. The lawyer told Maryam that she was thought to be the lost sister and offered her the inheritance of this aging "sister." Maryam thanked the lawyer but refused to take the money as she said she had no sister; she only remembered a little brother.

At the age of sixty-three, Maryam travelled to Aleppo for medical treatment on her pancreas with her two sisters-in-law. She needed a blood transfusion, but despite their love for Maryam, Mohammed Aref's sisters refused to have their blood types checked to see if it would be possible for them to give her their blood. At that time, blood transfusion was a weird and mysterious matter to the ordinary Syrian. By chance, her doctor happened to be Armenian and had her blood type, so he donated his blood. A few months later, in the winter of 1972, Maryam passed away. All who knew her were genuinely sad for the loss of this woman, my remarkable grandmother.

Three Armenian Folktales

The Snake and the Fish

Once upon a time, a snake became friends with a fish. "My younger sister," said the snake to the fish, "Carry me on your back and take me for a ride on the sea."

"Oh, with pleasure," answered the fish. "Sit on my back and I will carry you, so that you may see what our sea is like."

The snake curled around the fish, and they went to swim in the sea. They had hardly gone far when the snake bit the fish's back.

"Oh, my elder sister, why do you bite me?" asked the fish.

"Sorry, it was just by mistake," answered the snake.

They continued swimming for a while and then, again, the snake bit the fish's back.

"My elder sister, why do you keep biting me?" asked the fish.

"Oh, the sunlight was shining on my forehead," answered the snake.

Again, they swam for a while and, yet again, the snake bit the fish.

"My elder sister, why do you continue to bite me?" asked the fish.

"Well, this is my nature," answered the snake.

"Well then! I also have a nature," answered the fish, and it went down deep into the sea with the snake.

The snake couldn't breathe and it drowned.

"Sorry," said the fish, "this is *my* nature!"

THE KING AND THE SERPENT

Once upon a time, there lived a King who had a serpent that he loved very much. Every day he played with the serpent, throwing it toward his little son and watching them play together.

One day, when the King's son became a young man, he cut the serpent's tail with his sword while they were playing together. The serpent was furious and bit the Prince, who died on the spot. The serpent left the castle and traveled to a faraway land. When the King found his son lying dead on the ground next to the serpent's tail, he realized what his son had done and was very sad.

As time passed, the King missed the serpent very much and decided to send his soldiers to search for it. When they finally found it, they told the serpent, "His Majesty, the King, certainly knows that you only killed his son after he cut off your tail. Therefore, the King asks you to let bygones be bygones and to come back and live in the castle again."

The Serpent said, "The matter is not as simple as you say. Tell the King this: every time I look at my cut tail and you look at your son's grave, you will remember and I will remember, and our hate for each other will grow. Therefore, it is better that we stay away from each other so that hate will not grow between us."

Kikos in the Well

Once upon a time, there lived a poor peasant and his wife and their three daughters. One day, the man returned from a long, hot day working in the fields. He was thirsty, so he sent his eldest daughter to the well to fetch him a bucket of water.

Off she set, and when she reached the well, she looked up at the tree that towered beside the well. She began to daydream.

"Someday I'll marry," she said aloud. "And my husband and I shall have a son, and we'll name him Kikos after his grandfather. And one day, Kikos will walk to the well and climb this tree, and he will lose his balance, fall, and tumble into the well. Poor little Kikos will drown!"

And with this thought, she collapsed in grief beside the well. "My son Kikos," she wept, "Kikos with his hair of chestnut brown. Poor Kikos, my son, one day will drown ..."

The distraught girl could not stop crying, and she was so upset that she could not move. Back home the peasant waited, but when his eldest daughter did not return with the water, he sent his second daughter to find her.

When the second daughter saw her sister weeping by the well, she ran to her side. "What's wrong, Sister?" she asked.

The eldest daughter spoke through her tears. "Auntie of my child," she wailed. "Your sweet nephew Kikos one day will be born, but poor Kikos, with his hair of chestnut brown, will climb this tree and fall into the well and drown, and from that day on we shall mourn."

Now when the second daughter understood that the nephew she might one day have, a boy named Kikos, could fall from the tall tree and drown in this very well, leaving her an aunt mourning his death, she, too, began to sob.

Time passed, and when the two daughters had not come home, the peasant sent his youngest daughter to find out what the trouble was.

She ran to the well, and there she saw her sisters crying bitterly. "What's happened? What's wrong?" she asked.

The second daughter hiccupped through her sobs, "One day, our sister here is bound to marry, and our sister shall have a son, and this will be our nephew, a boy of beauty and fun."

The third sister smiled delightedly.

"Oh no, you mustn't smile," said the second sister. "For our nephew Kikos, with his hair of chestnut brown, will climb this tree one day and fall in the well and drown!"

"No!" cried the third sister, and when she did not return home, her mother ran to look for all three girls. She found them sitting by the well, their eyes swollen from crying.

"My beautiful girls," she said. "What has happened to you?"

"Mother, Mother, your own grandson, the child of your child, a boy named Kikos, will one day climb up this tree. Imagine his smile, his laughter, his glee. Imagine that hair, that rich chestnut brown, and imagine poor Kikos falling out of the tree, falling into the well and drowning!"

"Woe is me!" the mother wept. "My favorite grandchild! Kikos, my only boy!"

Now it was getting late, and the peasant could not imagine what could be taking his wife and daughters such a long time. So he pulled on his boots and trudged all the way to the well. There he saw all four women, tears pouring down their faces and noses so red they seemed to be on fire.

"Grandfather! Poor man!" they cried when they saw the peasant.

"Good heavens, what is this all about?" he asked. "And who is Grandfather?"

"You, my sweet," said the peasant's wife. "Your poor grandson, your namesake Kikos, will one day climb this tree ..."

"Oh, Grandfather, imagine Kikos, the boy of such wit and such glee ..."

"Like his grandfather Kikos, with thick hair, chestnut brown ..."

"But Father, your grandson will fall ..."

"And he'll drown!" they wailed together.

Now the peasant began to understand, and he shook his head and wondered what to do with his foolish women. But he loved them well, and so he said, "There, there, you'll never bring our boy Kikos back with your tears."

"Ahh, what shall we do, Father?" asked the eldest daughter, whose heart was nearly broken by the thought of losing her one and only future son.

"Come home with me," the peasant said, "And we shall invite the neighbors to a feast in memory of our little Kikos. In this way, our son and grandson will live forever in everyone's memory."

And so the women became calm again, and all went home happily.

Proverbs

- A woman is like the moon; sometimes she seems like silver, sometimes like gold.
- Choose your wife with the eye of an old man, your horse with the eye of a young man.
- He who runs a lot doesn't always arrive first.
- Give a horse to the one who tells the truth. He will need it to run away.
- He wants to buy a needle and inquires about the price of iron.

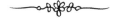

Two Armenian Recipes

Eech —Burghol Side Dish

Ingredients

- ¼ cup olive oil
- 1 large onion, chopped (saute half in oil, save other half for topping)
- ½ green pepper, chopped
- ½ bunch parsley, chopped (use ¾ in mixture, save ¼ for topping)
- 1 8 oz can tomato sauce
- ¾ cup water
- ¼ cup lemon juice
- 1½ tsp crushed dried mint
- 1 tsp crushed dried basil
- Pepper to taste
- 1 cup fine burghol

Method

Sauté onion and pepper in olive oil until soft

Add tomato sauce, water, lemon juice, and seasonings

Stir well, bring to a boil, and simmer 10 minutes. Remove from heat

Add burghol, stirring well. Stir in ¾ of parsley

When cool, shape into oval rolls (or use a ⅓ cup measuring cup for a uniform shape and look when inverted)

Sprinkle the top with reserved onion and parsley mixture

Makes 10 (⅓) cup servings

HARISSA — A PORRIDGE

Harissa is an ancient Armenian dish from the Ararat plain. It is a thick porridge made from korkot (dried or roasted cracked wheat) and fat-rich meat, usually chicken or lamb. Herbs are substituted for meat in harissa on Armenian religious fasting days. The extremely long cooking process is an essential part of the harissa tradition. Like other ritual dishes, the time taken for preparation is part of its cherished value.

According to Armenian lore, once when the patron saint of Armenia, Gregory the Illuminator, was offering a meal to the poor, he realized there weren't enough sheep to feed the crowd, so wheat was added to the cooking pots. When the wheat began sticking to the bottom of the cauldrons, Saint Gregory advised, "Harekh! Stir it!" Thus, the name harissa came from the saint's own words. Harissa has been offered as a charity meal ever since. The dish is traditionally served on Easter Day and is considered the national dish of Armenia.

Ingredients

- 3 lbs chicken
- 8 cups water
- 2 cups whole wheat kernels (korkot), rinsed in cold water and drained
- 2 tsp salt, or to taste
- cumin (optional)
- paprika (optional)
- butter

Method

Wash chicken and then bring it to boil in 8 cups water and salt

Lower heat to medium, cook with half-closed lid for around 1 hour or until done

Remove skin, bones, and fat and cut into small pieces

Strain broth and add water to make 8 cups

Place broth in a large pot with wheat, chicken and salt if needed

Bring to a boil then reduce heat to low

Skim foam from surface

Simmer covered on very low heat for about 4 hours, without stirring, until almost all liquid is absorbed

Beat vigorously with a long-handled wooden spoon, mashing wheat and chicken until it resembles thick oatmeal, and adjust salt

Serve in bowls with a pat of butter and sprinkle with a dash of cumin or paprika

2

CIRCASSIANS

Many of the people who entered Syria as refugees came from the Caucasus, a region between the Black Sea and the Caspian Sea, that is dominated by a very long mountain range, the Caucasus Mountains. Among these people were the Circassians. Circassia is located on the northwest bulge of the Caucasus Mountains.

The term 'Circassian' does not refer to a tribe, but is a name used by westerners to refer to the people in this region of the Caucasus. In fact, Circassians descend from different tribes, of which the main ones are the Adyghe, the Kabardian, the Cherkess, and the Shapsug. They converted to Islam about 400 years ago and are mostly Sunni Muslims today.

Due to the enormous natural resources and the key strategic location of the Caucasus, this area, like historic Armenia, has been invaded many times. In the 18th century, the Russian Empire invaded Circassia. The Circassians fought against the Russians for around one hundred years and finally were defeated in 1864. Following their conquest of the region, the Russians enacted a policy of ethnic cleansing. They forced Circassians from their ancestral homelands and gave them the choice of either living in

Russia, far from their homeland, or immigrating to the Ottoman Empire. Almost all rejected the idea of living on Russian land. One of my Circassian friends quoted her grandmother as saying, "We had no choice but to immigrate to the Ottoman Empire. The Russians would have treated us like slaves!"

Thus began the diaspora of the Circassians. Hundreds of thousands were transported to the ports of the Black Sea, where they waited for ships to carry them to the Ottoman Empire. While waiting, many died of disease and exposure. The ships were overcrowded and not very seaworthy, and not all the ships reached Turkey safely. The moment of departure was so painful for the Circassians that the memory of their devastating expulsion has been passed down for many generations. Folk songs were composed describing the sadness that filled their hearts as they said a last farewell to their country.

> Let us look back at our great mountains,
> They don't know where we are going.
> Let us leave a beautiful song
> To echo forever in the air.

> "Why are you leaving, my children?"
> Cries Mother Earth
> "Oh, please forgive us, we are really miserable
> We can't stay here,
> Yet our souls forever will stay,
> Will remain here until our contry decays."

During the passage by ship, many died of disease, starvation, and drowning. Here is another folk song about this tragedy:

> Once they start weeping,
> Stop talking.

Open your ears and listen,
Memorize what you hear in your hearts.

We are leaving our country,
Yet it will remain in our hearts.
God knows that we would never have left
If we hadn't been struck by evil powers.

Even though we are leaving,
We can't leave our hopes.
Our mothers will keep looking
Constantly towards our country.

The young travelers on the ship,
Forever watering its deck with their tears -
You can't pluck out
Their country from their hearts.

Many of them got lost in the great sea,
Fighting giant waves.
They will soon return to the Caucasus
And the fighters will resume their battle."

By 1914, perhaps three million Circassians had been evicted from Circassia. After their exile, Circassians first settled in European countries under Ottoman occupation. However, after the Ottoman defeat in the Balkan War of 1877-78, these mostly Christian countries won independence from the Ottoman Empire, and that prompted the Circassians to immigrate to the Empire's Syrian provinces in large numbers. About half of these Circassians settled in the Golan Heights, which they found similar to their homeland with its heavy rainfalls and snow. There they established their own villages. They were fine farmers and helped to develop the areas they settled. They built mills and stone houses and began planting new grains like oats and millet.

Other Circassian immigrants established a number of villages north of Homs and along the borders of the Syrian Desert, as well as in Marj al Sultan to the east of Damascus.

This stream of immigration continued until the year 1900. Approximately 100,000 of the Circassians who were expelled from Russia settled in Syria. Many of the Circassian immigrants left with only the clothes on their backs. The lucky ones carried their daggers, swords and traditional clothes. The wealthy ones were able to take their gold and jewelry with them.

The Circassians felt welcome in Syria and became full Syrian citizens. They fought in the Six-Day War of 1967, but when Israel took over the Golan Heights, the Circassians had to flee their villages, and many of them settled in the Rukn al Din district of Damascus. There also was a large settlement of Circassians in the village of Marj al Sultan to the east of Damascus, but again, they had to leave this village when it was totally destroyed in 2016 during the civil war.

Having resisted assimilation more successfully than other groups like the Turkomans, the Circassians retain many customs quite different from those of their Arab neighbors. Unfortunately, most of the fourth generation has lost its language, unlike the Armenians. However, they have preserved their traditional food, folk songs, and dances, as well as customs concerning weddings.

Music and dance are very important to Circassians. My Circassian friend, Nafen, sings and plays the accordion like many Circassians, and told me that Circassian songs are divided into two kinds: the *alganbara* (sad, tearful songs) which include songs about their homeland, wars, martyrs, and departing lovers; and the *alwerd* (dancing songs) which include love songs, songs of celebration, and children's songs.

Circassian folk dances are world-famous. The dancers wear traditional Circassian clothes, which consists of long, colorful gowns with flowing sleeves and headdresses for the women, while the men are outfitted in sheepskin hats, tunics and boots. The women dancers seem to glide – almost float – across the floor while the men leap energetically into the air and then loudly stamp their boots. It is an unforgettable experience to see a traditional Circassian dance.

My friend Nafen is a very proud Circassian who can trace her family tree back eight generations. Here is her story in her own words: "My name is Nafen Riad Kheraldeen Saleh Ismael Socar Somaf Louj Dodak. My great-great-great grandfather, Ismael, was born in the year 1825, and his wife, Hajj Nan, was born in 1830. In 1864, great-grandfather Ismael went on Pilgrimage to Mecca and died there. Unfortunately, 1864 was the year Russia expelled the Circassians, so my great-great-great grandmother was forced to flee Russia on her own when she received the sad news of the death of her husband and the death of her brother who was killed by the Russians. Grandmother Hajj Nan fled with her daughter Hanifa and three sons: Hajj Hassan, Saleh, and Andar. All these names have now become well-known last names of the Socars.

"Grandmother Hajj Nan was able to make the long trip from Russia on her own and bring her four children safely to Syria. Unlike most Circassians, my clever Grandmother was also able to smuggle out all her gold and jewelry in a cloth bag hung around her neck. Because of this, when she arrived in the Golan Heights, she was able to start a business with her children. They built mills, and eventually as many as 90% of the mills in the Golan Heights were owned by the Socar family.

"My family lived and prospered in the Golan Heights for one hundred years. However, in 1967 the region was seized by Israel and, for a second time, my family had to leave their homes, wealth, and land behind. For a second time, we had to emigrate. For a second time, we lost everything. And now we are living in Damascus," said Nafen.

Before March 2011, when the civil war began, the Circassian population in Syria was estimated at around 100,000. After 2011, many Circassians fled the conflict and returned to the Caucasus. This was possible because of a law Russia adopted which allowed thousands of Circassians whose ancestors had left their homes more than a hundred years ago to return to their homeland.

Some Circassians were overjoyed to return to their ancestral home, a place most knew only from stories and traditions passed down from generation to generation. The Syrian Circassians were made welcome in Russia, but unfortunately, many couldn't find jobs, especially doctors and engineers. They were given land in isolated places and the Syrian Circassians who were originally farmers were satisfied, but some city dwellers returned to Syria. In general, the Syrian Circassians patiently wait for the crisis to end so they can return to their second country, Syria.

As Nafen said to me, "I have two souls, one here and one in my ancestral land. Syria is my homeland and I have deep roots here. We never suffered any discrimination here; Syria embraced us all."

Three Circassian Folktales

The Story of Qasay (Adyghe Folktale)

Long, long ago, in the land of the Golan Heights, there lived a young man named Qasay and a beautiful girl named Satanai who were deeply in love and felt they couldn't live without each other. Yet when Qasay proposed to Satanai, her family rejected him because he was very poor. Qasay was brokenhearted and left to work in another village.

One evening, when Qasay returned to his village for a short visit, he suddenly heard the sound of accordions mixed with happy cheers breaking the silence of the night. As he approached, he saw his friends happily celebrating a wedding. When the young men and women saw Qasay, they warmly welcomed him and asked him to join them in a dance. Qasay was a great dancer and everyone enjoyed dancing with him.

Soon the young people enthusiastically filled the place with the sounds of stomping boots, slapping hands, accordion music and thundering shouts. Their happy cheers reached the bride, who was Satanai herself.

"Who is making all that noise?" Satanai wondered.

"Qasay has come back," whispered her friend.

At once, Satanai fainted, and all her friends realized she was still in love with Qasay. Therefore, they decided to give the lovers a chance to meet before the wedding ceremony took place. They set up a table and two chairs, and Qasay's friends brought him and Satanai's friends brought her so they could sit together and talk. However, when Satanai set her eyes on Qasay, her heart stopped beating and she fell lifeless to the ground.

Qasay was so terribly affected that he took out his dagger and killed himself at once.

The two lovers were buried next to each other, and two trees were planted over their graves whose branches later entwined in an embrace.

King Shkharpas and Dakhanef: A Shapsugh folktale

Once upon a time, there lived a King called King Shkharpas. One night, he came out of his palace and saw that in one of his villages a lamp burned.

He wondered, what do these people do so late at night? "Go and find out what they are doing in that cottage," he told his servant.

The servant obeyed and stole up to the window. There were three orphaned sisters living in this cottage, and the King's servant began to listen to the three girls as they spoke together.

The oldest sister said, "If I worked for King Shkharpas I would wash his clothes, cook his food, and never be hungry."

The second sister sighed and said, "If I washed and darned clothes, not for the king, but just for his servant, I would also never be hungry."

The youngest sister said nothing. "Why are you silent, Dakhanef?" her sisters asked her.

Then Dakhanef said, "What I say comes from the bottom of my heart. I not only don't want to wash clothes and cook for King Shkharpas, but even if he dressed me in gold and wanted me to become his wife, I wouldn't agree. Let him eat dung!"

The servant was very surprised by the sisters' conversation. He went to King Shkharpas and told him what he had heard.

The King was enraged when he heard what Dakhanef had said about him.

"Fetch all three sisters here immediately," he cried to his servant, and the girls were brought before him. "What did you just say about me?" he asked the oldest sister.

She answered, "I said that if I could wash your clothes and cook your food, I would never be hungry."

"Give her this job," King Shkharpas commanded his servants.

"And what did you say?" he asked the second sister.

"I said that if I could just wash and darn clothes for your servant, I would also never be hungry."

"Give her this job," King Shkharpas commanded his servants.

When it was Dakhanef's turn to answer, King Shkharpas looked at her fiercely.

"What did you say tonight?" he asked.

King Shkharpas thought that Dakhanef would be afraid of him and not tell the truth, but she looked at him with contempt and said, "I said that I wouldn't wash your clothes nor cook your food, and that even if you wanted to marry me and promised to dress me in gold, I would not marry you. I also said that you should eat dung. I would rather be hungry than work for you!"

King Shkharpas gritted his teeth. "Drive her out of my estate to the remotest forest!" he cried to his servants.

The girl was grasped, put on a cart, taken to the remotest forest, and left there.

It is frightening to remain alone in a forest, but Dakhanef was a courageous girl. She selected a sturdy stick and made her way in the direction of the sunrise. She walked for a long time until her clothes turned to rags. She had nothing to eat except wild pears and apples, and her strength began to leave her.

"Shall I really die here?" Dakhanef thought. She exerted herself and climbed up a high tree. Not far off, she saw smoke. Dakhanef happily descended and made her way in the direction of the smoke. Soon she saw an old man and an old woman plowing on the mountain slope.

"Salam aleykum," Dakhanef said.

"Aleykum salam, my beauty," they answered in a friendly manner. "Who are you, and where do you come from?"

"My name is Dakhanef and I am the daughter of a poor Shapsug, who died a long time ago. I have no relatives and I ask you to adopt me as your daughter," Dakhanef said gently.

The old people rejoiced at her words since they had no children. They brought her to their house and gave her the best bed.

The next morning, all three went to plow the land. The old woman guided the bulls and Dakhanef picked up sticks and stones. But it seemed to her that to guide the bulls was harder than to pick up sticks and stones.

"Mother," Dakhanef said, "let me guide the bulls for you."

The old woman gave the reins to her and began to pick up sticks and stones. However, Dakhanef quickly saw she was mistaken; to pick up stones was harder for the old woman than for her to guide the bulls. When Dakhanef noticed this, she immediately gave the reins back to the old woman and continued to throw stones away from the field.

Suddenly, Dakhanef turned over one stone and saw under it a hole with a jug at the bottom. The jug was filled with gold. "How wonderful!" Dakhanef thought. She put the stone back in its place and went on with her work. Dakhanef decided not to speak to the old people about her discovery for a while. They finished the plowing and in the evening, Dakhanef poured some gold into her pocket and left the rest of the gold in its place.

The next morning Dakhanaf came to the old man and said, "Father, soon we won't have anything to sit on. Look! The legs of this bench are broken and soon the table will fall as well. Let's go and buy everything new."

The old man laughed. "Alas, my daughter, if I had any money I would have bought new furniture long ago, but I am a poor man and can't afford it."

"I will find some money," said Dakhanef.

The old man didn't believe her, but he loved her very much and didn't want to upset her by refusing to go shopping with her. He harnessed the horse to the cart, and he and Dakhanef started out on a trip to buy what Dakhanef thought they needed.

The old woman also didn't believe her daughter, but she changed her mind when three days later, the cart was driven into the yard, loaded with expensive goods and clothes.

The old man and the old woman had never lived so comfortably before Dakhanef's arrival. However, up to now, nobody knew that the girl had found gold. Time passed and Dakhanef had a new request of the old man. "Father," she said, "Let me build a house at the place where seven roads converge."

The old man laughed again. "You amaze me, Dakhanef. In order to build a new house, you need a lot of money. And how can you build a house if you don't own the land? You must buy or rent the land from the landowner."

Dakhanef was a persistent girl. She went to a carpenter and he said, "If the landowner permits you, I will be only too glad to build you a house."

She obtained permission and had a house built at the place where seven roads meet. Dkhanef knew what a beautiful palace King Shkharpas lived in and tried to make her house even more beautiful. On all seven roads, she set sentinels and gave them the following order, "Everyone who passes along these seven roads must come into my house and be offered a meal as my guest. If anyone refuses my hospitality, he will not be allowed to continue on his way until he carries out the custom of my house."

Fame about the beauty and the strange custom of Dakhanef spread all over the world. King Shkharpas also heard this news, but he had no idea who this girl was. He changed into ordinary clothes, took two friends with him, and went to see who had dared to build a house that was more beautiful than his palace and introduce a custom that everyone liked so much. After ten days of traveling, they approached the place where seven roads converge.

"Stop!" a sentinel told them. "You must come into the house, refresh yourselves, and have a meal. It is the custom of Dakhanef, and you may not violate it."

"We have no time to spend on eating in this house," King Shkharpas said.

"In that case, you may not continue on your way."

There was nothing to do but comply. King Shkharapas and his friends dismounted their horses and started walking to the house.

Dakhanef saw King Shkharpas from the window and recognized him immediately. She told her friend, "When these three people come into my room, go out to the corridor and cry, "Dakhanef, come here, I see something very interesting!"

King Shkharpas came in the room where Dakhanef was. He had never met such a beautiful woman. He wanted to approach her, but at that moment her friend went out to the corridor and cried, "Dakhanef, come here, I see something very interesting!"

Dakhanef looked around for her shoes. King Shkharpas wanted to render a service to her so he picked up her golden shoes from under the bed and set them in front of her.

Dakhanef said, "You are King Shkharpas - I knew it was you at once. You forgot that you banned me from your estate and now you give me my shoes!"

Shkharapas was embarrassed in front of his friends. He left Dakhanef's house and returned to his palace. He had never been so angry, and yet he wanted to marry Dakhanef very much.

King Shkharpas changed into his royal attire, took precious gifts for Dakhanef, and went to woo her.

Dakhanef told him, "You banished me, a poor girl, to the remotest forest. I cannot forgive you and I refuse to become your wife. You had better leave now."

King Shkharapas had nothing to do but go home. On the other hand, Dakhanef and the old man and the old woman remained happily in her beautiful house where the seven roads converge, and perhaps they live there yet.

THE THREE BROTHERS AND THE GIANT

Long ago, there lived three poor brothers in a very small cottage. One day, the oldest brother decided to travel and seek his fortune.

On his way, he met a giant who needed help on his farm.

"I am not easy to work for," said the giant. "I am a very short-tempered giant, but I pay well!"

The oldest brother said, "Don't worry. I am a short-tempered person as well!"

"I will employ you for a year," said the giant. "Whoever loses his temper first will be branded on his back in three places and if it is you, you will lose your wages!"

The oldest brother started working for the giant and was a faithful worker. Moreover, he did a good job without complaining. But the giant was conspiring against him and kept thinking of a way to trap him so he would lose the contract. Finally, he thought of his bull, Barqoun. One day, the giant called his bull and told him, "Barqoun, don't obey the worker when you are out in the field."

The bull answered, "All right, master. I won't do what he orders me to do."

That day, the oldest brother and the bull went to the field, but when they began to polow, the bull didin't listen to the man and left the field. The man was angry and hit the bull very hard.

The man returned home at sunset, and the bull went to the giant, complaining about what the man had done. The giant called the man and told him, "You lost your temper and hit the bull."

The man replied, "Yes, but he…"

The giant said, "And that means you broke your word."

The man said, "But the bull…"

The giant interrupted him and said, "That means it's my right now to brand your back in three places."

The man said, "Please listen to me."

The giant said, "You lost your wages, too."

The giant branded the man's back and he went home with his back hunched in pain. The second brother's wife was very happy to see that he had failed and said to her husband, "Look, your brother came back from his job empty-handed. Why don't you go look for a job and come back loaded with goods?"

The husband replied, "All right, dear wife."

The next day the second brother decided to look for a job without asking his older brother about what had happened to him. The second brother met the same giant and worked for him, but he also wasn't patient enough and ended up branded like his older brother.

When the second brother arrived home, the youngest brother's wife told her husband, "Your brothers came back with nothing to show for their trouble. Why don't you go and look for a job? How long are we going to be poor?"

Her husband said, "All right my dear, I will do my best."

Like his brothers, the youngest brother left the house to seek his fortune and didn't trouble himself to ask his brothers why they had failed.

The youngest brother met the same giant and agreed to work for him until the day the crow caws to welcome the morning, and on that day the one who loses his temper first will be punished.

The youngest brother started working, but the giant, whose eyes shone with evil, was conspiring against him. The giant continuously thought of ways to trap this young man.

The first day, when the youngest brother went out to the field and started to plow, the bull refused to walk a straight line and zig zagged all over the field. The youngest brother said to the bull, "Watch out, Barqoun! You are not keeping a straight line."

The bull kept on refusing to obey, so the youngest brother told him in a calm voice, "Fine, Barqoun. Do whatever you want. We will finish fast if you keep on doing what you are doing."

The bull reached the end of the field and the youngest brother told him, "Don't go outside of the field." However, the bull continued on his way and went outside the field.

The youngest brother said to him, "All right, Barqoun. No matter what you do, we are going to spend the day plowing the field." The bull tried several times to anger the man and make him lose his temper, but he didn't succeed, so he came back to the field and obeyed the man.

The giant was very upset when he learned that the youngest brother hadn't lost his temper. Then the giant got a new idea. He would send the man and the bull to the forest to fetch some wood the following day. The giant told the bull, "When the man puts the wood in the wagon and orders you to return home, listen to him, but when you reach the valley, stand still and don't move at all."

The next morning, the youngest brother went to the forest, filled the wagon with wood, and the bull started to pull it till they reached the valley, where the bull stopped. The man wasn't upset; he got in the wagon and lay down to have a rest. The bull continued to stand still, and the man continued to rest until an eagle flew over their heads. Then the youngest brother spoke to the eagle and said, "You there! Tell the giant that Barqoun wasn't able to pull the wagon, so send us another bull to help him - and no need to hurry. We can wait."

The bull heard what the man said and got scared and said to himself, "I will die of hunger if I stay here." He gathered himself together and pulled the wagon through the valley.

The giant was furious when the bull told him what had happened. The giant said, "Barqoun, think with me, help me. What can I do to make this young man lose his temper?" The giant spent all night thinking until he started to lose his temper.

The next day, the giant climbed up a tree and cawed like a crow. The youngest brother, thinking it was a crow, took out his bow and arrow and shot the giant. The furious giant yelled in pain and jumped out of the tree, and he was very angry.

The youngest brother said to the giant, "I am sorry, but I thought I was shooting a crow. Are you angry?"

The giant replied, "Yes, and I will..."

The youngest brother smiled and said, "You forgot our deal."

The giant gave up and the youngest brother branded the giant's back in three places and got his wages - and his brothers' wages, too! He went back home happy and wealthy.

Sayings and Proverbs

- This man is so fine that his weight is as gold.
- After the wolf is captured, it is blamed for what it did and didn't do.
- He who respects you is related to you.
- The house in which your mother doesn't live is to be rested in and then left.
- Think and then speak.
- Look around you and then sit.
- Don't hit a chained or a tied-up man.
- Look at her mother before you marry her.
- The wind that blows from the west is not always damp.
- Work a lot and talk a little.
- Life and hope are twins.
- With help you can move a mountain from its place.

THREE CIRCASSIAN RECIPES
CIRCASSIAN CHEESE —
CONSIDERED ONE OF THE OLDEST CIRCASSIAN RECIPES.

Ingredients

1 cup yogurt

8 lbs whole milk (14 ¾ cups of milk)

Salt to taste

Method

Heat milk in a pot and stir until lukewarm

Before the milk boils, gradually add yogurt, stirring it with a wooden spoon (wait 10 seconds after every yogurt addition)

Mix well and stir until it boils

Lower heat and stir slowly and regularly for half an hour, until the milk begins to curdle and show on the surface

Place in a round colander to shape the cheese

Place a plate on the cheese and then a heavy jar of water or some other weight to remove the excess liquid

Salt to taste – the moisture will draw the salt through the cheese

Let it cool for a whole day

HALIVA (SMALL TURNOVER STUFFED WITH CHEESE)

Ingredients for cheese filling

1 gallon of milk	1 tsp ground savory
1 cup white distilled vinegar	1 tsp salt

Method

Bring milk to a boil, stirring constantly to prevent scorching

When milk starts to foam, turn off heat and add vinegar

Let it curd for 8 to 10 minutes, then add seasoning

Line a colander with cheesecloth and pour cheese through. What is left in the colander is the cheese for haliva. Set it aside

Ingredients for dough

1 cup warm water (102° F)

1 tsp salt

1 large egg

3 ½ cups all purpose flour (white or whole wheat)

½ cup corn oil for frying

Method for Dough

Put salt in the water, add egg and mix until well combined

On a clean, dry surface, pile up the flour. Make a well and slowly pour in the water and egg mixture with one hand, stirring the dough with the other

Knead the dough until semi-soft and smooth; cover and let rest for about half an hour for gluten to set

Roll the dough in batches to 1/8″ thick and cut out circles 5 ½″ in diameter – try using the cover of a small sauce pan

To assemble halivas, put one tablespoon of cheese on the disk and brush the edges with water using your finger or a pastry brush. Turn it over and pinch edges with a fork. Large pinches make a crunchy edge

In a large skillet, heat oil and fry 3-4 haliva at a time, 2 minutes on each side. Do not let them brown; they should be golden or orange

Drain fried haliva on a platter lined with paper towels

This recipe yields about 50 5 ½ ″ halivas

HALG SHEFAG — CIRCASSIAN BREAD

Ingredients

3 cups white flour
¼ cup corn oil
Luke warm water as needed
A sprinkle of salt
1 tbsp yeast
1 cup brown flour
½ cup milk

Method

Mix ingredients together with a spoon and leave for half an hour

Knead with both hands, then leave to rise for two hours

Divide dough into four or five pieces and form small balls

Roll out each ball of dough until it is a thin, round layer of dough

Brush the surface with olive oil

Roll the dough together and cut it into pieces with a knife

Again, roll out every piece with the rolling pin

Put each piece into a hot oven and leave until it rises – about 10 minutes

3

CHECHENS

Chechens come from the small Federal Republic of Chechnya which is part of Russia and is situated on the northern slopes of the Great Caucasian mountain ridge and on the adjacent plains. Southeast of Chechnya is the Federal Republic of Dagestan, which is also part of Russia.

The geography of Chechnya covers a wide range, with both mountains and plains and many climate zones. In the north are arid plains and the Terek-Kuman semi-desert lowlands, while in the south are cold and icy mountains. Also, the mountain landscape is diverse. The gentle slopes are mild, covered with leaf-bearing forests. Neighboring Alpine meadows are covered with rocks and evergreen forests. The mountains are cut with deep canyons made by streams, and lakes have been created by ancient mountain landslides. The variety of the natural environment has helped to produce a Chechen personality which is notably adaptable.

There are an estimated 5,000 Chechens in Syria. They are mainly descendants of people who had to leave Chechnya in two waves - first during the Caucasian War, which led to the annexation of Chechnya by the Russian Empire in 1850, and second during the

1944 Stalinist deportation of the Chechens of the North Caucasus to Central Asia during World War II.

The first wave of Chechens escaped to the Ottoman Empire and, in time, some of them moved south to what today are the countries of Iraq, Jordan, and Syria. The Dagestanis and the Kumyks also participated in the Caucasian War against the Russian Empire, and small numbers of these two ethnic groups also immigrated to Syria. Many Chechens joined the Circassians in the Golan Heights, as did the Dagestanis, until they were all forced to leave when it came under Israel's control.

Some well-known Syrian Chechens have served in the Syrian army including General Ozdemir Jamaludin and Shishan Farid Abdel-Hamid, a military leader recognized as a hero of Syria and Jordan. In addition, Khasan-Bek was the governor of al-Jazeera province, and Baarshakho Khasan headed the personal guards of Syrian President Shukri Quwatli. Other distinguished Syrian Chechens include Vappi Anvar, an adviser at the Syrian Ministry of Foreign Affairs, Kharcho Shukri, a painter-calligrapher, and Nadya Khost, a writer.

THREE CHECHEN FOLKTALES

THE RUBLE

Once upon a time, long ago, there lived a young boy named Asander who did not like to work. The only thing Asander liked to do was have a good time all day.

One day, Asander's father called him and said, "Enough is enough! You must get out of the house, find a job, work hard like everyone else, and bring home a ruble every day!"

Asander was very unhappy with his father's decision. He groaned and went to tell his mother.

"Don't worry, dear Asander" said his mother "I will give you a ruble every day to present to your father at the end of the day."

Asander was very happy with his mother's soothing words. From that day on, she gave him a ruble every day and he presented it to his father at the end of the day. As before, during the day Asander whistled, hummed, lounged around, and slept whenever he wished, with no one to disturb him. Then, every evening when his father returned home, he would take Asander's ruble and throw it into the fireplace.

Asander would watch it burn into ashes and walk away.

This continued for over three months until, one morning, Asander's mother whispered in his ear, "Sorry, my son, I don't have any more rubles to give you. From now on you must work to earn your own!"

Asander was shocked and wondered how on earth he could actually work all day to earn his wages.

Asander walked around the village searching for someone to employ him until at last a farmer agreed to do so.

Asander worked hard from morning to evening hauling water, gathering eggs, tending the garden, milking the cows, and harnessing the horses. The farmer was satisfied with his work and payed him a ruble and said to come back the next day.

As Asander held the ruble tightly in his hand, it seemed to have a different feeling than any other ruble he had ever held.

When Asander arrived home, his father snatched the ruble out of his hand and threw it into the fire, as usual. This time, Asander couldn't just watch his precious ruble burn to ashes in the fire. He jumped into the fire and saved it.

The father grinned and said, "This is your first earned ruble!"

"How did you know?" asked Asander.

"I know a hardworking man can't bear to see his money burn in front of him!"

"I'll never be lazy again," said Asander, and from that day on he worked harder than anyone else on the farm.

The Deeds of Women

A poor man was riding on his mare with her foal following behind. After some time, the foal started to trudge behind a horseman who was on his gelding.

"That foal is mine, my gelding gave gave birth to it," said the horseman.

"No," said the poor man. "My mare gave birth to it."

"It is my foal," insisted the horseman.

"In order to clear up this disagreement, we must go to the Prince," said the poor man.

Once they arrived at the palace of the Prince, they asked the Princess, his wife, "Is the Prince at home?"

"No, he's not home. But on what business have you come?"

"We have come to settle a disagreement about who owns this foal," said the horseman.

The poor man on the mare said, "Of course it is my foal, but this man claims his gelding gave birth to the foal."

"Well, my master is not at home. He rode off to put out a fire at Kazbek's Tower," answered the Princess.

"How amazing! How can it be that Kazbek's Tower has burst into flames," said the horseman in surprise.

"There's nothing amazing or strange about Kazbek's Tower bursting into flames at all. What's amazing is that your gelding has given birth," answered the Princess.

After some time, the Prince returned and asked his wife if anyone had come to see him while he was away. His wife said that two men with a disagreement had been to see him, and she told her husband how she had settled it.

"How many times have I told you not to interfere in affairs that have nothing to do with you!" shouted the Prince. "Take whatever you want and get out of my palace. Though before you go, give me a drink and put me to sleep."

The Princess poured her husband a drink, and as soon as he fell asleep, she put him into her trunk and set off with him to her parents' palace.

After some time, the Prince woke up in his in-law's palace and asked his wife what was the meaning of this.

"Didn't you say I could take whatever I wanted from your palace? Well, I took what was most valuable to me."

"I can't argue with you," said the Prince with a sigh. "It's better if we go home."

And so they returned home together.

THE HUNTER

A long time ago, there lived a Hunter and his wife. Every morning, the husband stood his wife up against the door, put an egg on her head and shot it with his rifle. Of course, the man's wife was terrified lest a bullet should hit her, but she did not confess this to her husband. She tried to think of a way out of the difficult position she was in, and finally, she somehow managed to get the attention of an old wise woman and told her everything.

The old wise woman asked, "What does your husband say to you after he shoots?"

"He says, 'What a man I am, what a Hunter I am!'"

"When your husband says those words to you tomorrow, say this, 'There are better men and better Hunters than you, who go everywhere and don't just sit at home all the time.' This was the advice the wise old woman gave to the troubled wife.

The next day, as usual, the husband shot the egg on his wife's head and bragged, "What a man I am! What a Hunter I am!"

His wife said to him, "You should stop sitting home all the time. If you only traveled around the world for some time, you might find better men and better Hunters than yourself."

"Ha! I'll see if there are better men or better Hunters than me or not," said the Hunter, and he set off straight away.

Time passed, and eventually he came to a tower. In this tower lived seven Narts and their mother.

"Do you welcome guests?" shouted the Hunter as he approached the tower.

The mother was baking flat bread made from corn flour, and her sons weren't home. She answered, "Of course we welcome guests, how could one not? But if my sons find out you are here, they will kill you. Quick - hide in the hem of my dress!"

So she hid her guest in the hem of her dress and soon her seven children returned home.

"Nana, who has come to see you?" they asked.

"If you give your word not to kill him, I will tell you."

After they promised their mother not to kill him, she brought the Hunter out from the hem of her dress.

"This is our guest, Nana?" roared the seven Narts with laughter as they began to throw the visiting Hunter from one to another.

They amused themselves with their "toy" and, because they had promised their mother, they did not kill the Hunter in their home. Instead, they decided to kill him on the road once he started on his way.

The seven Narts left their house early in the morning and sat in a place where the Hunter was sure to pass by. Their mother fed the Hunter and pointed out to him the road to take, advising him to leave before her sons returned. The Hunter quickly saddled up his horse and sped on his way. Once the Narts spotted him, they started shooting at him.

The Hunter took to his heels and on the way he came across Nart Gonchu, who was plowing the earth with eight wild boars.

"There are seven Narts chasing me who want to kill me! Save me!" the Hunter pleaded with Gonchu.

"Get out of here and don't scare my wild boars. You are ruining my strip of field!" cried Gonchu.

"Can it be that your plowing is more precious to you than my life? Save me!" the Hunter begged once more.

So Gonchu put the Hunter and his horse into his mouth, into a huge cavity in his mouth where a tooth once stood.

The seven Narts rode up and said, "Give us our guest!"

"The guest who asked for my help, I will not surrender. Be on your way and don't walk all over my field."

"If you don't give us our guest, then we won't leave!" said the seven Narts, and they went to stop the plowing.

Gonchu yelled at his wild boars and they attacked the Narts, who suddenly became afraid for their lives and ran away. Meanwhile, the Hunter was whiling his time away in Gonchu's mouth and thought, "I must ask him how he lost such a large tooth."

As soon as the seven Narts had run away, Gonchu took the Hunter and his horse out of his mouth.

The Hunter asked him, "Would you please tell me how you lost your tooth?'

"I'm too busy plowing and can't stop now to tell you about it."

"I can wait till evening if you will tell me," said the Hunter.

"Very well, in the evening I will tell you about it. Until then, go to the hut and wait for me," said Gonchu.

Gonchu plowed until evening and then came to the hut where the Hunter was waiting for him. After they ate, Gonchu began his story. "In my family, there were seven brothers, and I was the weakest of us all. We had only one sister, and one unlucky day she was stolen by a one-eyed Nart by the name of Sargan. My seven brothers and I set out to recapture her. We climbed over seven mountains in order to reach Sargan's dwelling. Sargan welcomed us well enough, questioned us, and started a fire in the hearth. After that, he stuck a dirty old metal rod in the corner of the hearth. He put it there until it was red hot, and then grabbed each of us and impaled us one by one onto the hot metal rod. Then he put the rod back in the corner of the hearth and went to lie down and sleep.

I was the last to be impaled, at the edge of the metal rod, and its sharp edge did not pierce my heart. When Sargan had fallen asleep, I jumped free from the metal rod and then removed my brothers from it. Then I heated the metal rod again and stuck it into Sargan's only eye and started to run.

Waking from the pain, Sargan filled the air with a horrible scream. He grabbed a rock and threw it after me. The rock fell not very far from me but hit another rock. A few pieces from it hit me and knocked out my tooth.

I buried my brothers in one tomb and, not finding any trace of my sister, left the wailing Sargan and went home."

"But you live in the mountains and not in the plains," said Gonchu at the end of his story. "Return to your home and your life as a Hunter."

Proverbs

- A pear falls close to the pear tree.
- Even the smallest thorn pricks the skin.
- One kind word can move a mountain.
- As long as you keep silent, your word is your slave; as soon as you say it, you become its slave.
- An intelligent man feels at home wherever he goes.
- You cackle for me, but lay eggs for my neighbors.
- A man who has just become rich has lit a candle in the daytime.
- A rooster, too, is brave at the door of its hen-coop.

TWO CHECHEN RECIPES

DJEPLGESH — A PANCAKE STUFFED WITH A FILLING AND FRIED

Chechens cook this for both breakfast and lunch. They either stuff it with potato (kertol in the Chechen language) or with unsalted cheese (beerem) and butter. This recipe is for djeplgesh stuffed with potato.

Ingredients for filling

4 lbs potatoes

2 rounded tbsp butter

Red pepper, basil, and salt according to taste

2 medium onions

Method

Boil potatoes and peel

Slice potatoes and mash

Add red pepper, basil, and salt to mashed potatoes and blend

Dice onions into small pieces

Fry onion until slightly brown in two rounded tbsp butter

Add fried onions to mashed potatoes

Mix together and mash well

Chechens

Ingredients for dough

- 1 envelope dry yeast
- ½ cup warm water
- 1 rounded tsp salt
- 4 lbs flour
- 1 rounded tbsp salt
- 4 tbsp olive oil
- Water as required

Method

- Empty yeast envelope into water - stir until it dissolves and set aside for 3 minutes
- Add salt and stir again
- Pour water and olive oil into flour, then mix and knead
- Add water until dough is firm, smooth, and not sticking to your hands
- Form a ball and cover it with a cloth until it doubles in size – about 2 hours
- Slice the dough into pieces large enough to hold in your hand
- Form small balls and flatten them with a rolling pin
- Place potato filling in the middle of each piece of dough and firmly close it into a ball
- Flatten each ball by pressing it gently and patiently with your hands into a circle
- Don't let filling leak through the dough
- Djepelg should have a pancake shape and fill a frying pan around 7 inches across
- Fry one djepelg at a time, browning both sides
- Serve each djepelg topped with a pat of butte – it is good with tea

GULNESH — CHECHEN GNOCCI WITH LAMB

Ingredients

- 2 cups flour
- 1 egg
- 1 lb lamb meat
- 6 cloves garlic
- 1 cup water
- Salt and pepper to taste

Method

- Boil meat in a liter of water
- Salt and pepper to taste
- While it boils, skim surface of the stock
- Reduce heat and simmer for 60-90 minutes until meat is tender
- Set aside a small bowl of meat broth for the garlic sauce
- Save the rest of the stock to cook the gulnesh
- Lb garlic with salt in mortar and add to bowl of stock set aside for the sauce

Dough

- Mix flour, egg, 1 teaspoon salt, and ¾ cup of water together and knead
- Add more water as required
- Cover and set aside for half an hour
- Shape dough into finger-shaped pieces of dough
- Drop finger-shaped dough in boiling stock and cook for 20-25 minutes
- To serve: set bowl of garlic dip in the center of a large plate and arrange the gulnesh fingers and the pieces of meat around the bowl
- To eat, dip the meat and the gulnesh in the sauce

4

DAGESTANIS

Russia established the Republic of Dagestan in 1921 on the north slope of the Caucasus mountain range. Unlike the Chechens, who have a republic and are an ethnic group, the Dagestanis, while they have a republic, are not an ethnic group. "Dagestani" is an umbrella term for the peoples of Dagestan who include many unrelated ethnic groups such as the Avar, Dargin, Kumyk, and Lezgian. These diverse groups speak different languages and have their own legends and national particularities.

The word *Dagestan* is of Turkic and Persian origin. *Dağ* means "mountain" in Turkic and *-stan* is a Persian suffix meaning "land." The word *Dagestan*, therefore, means "the land of mountains"; and since ancient times that has been its name. It is also called the mountain of languages because of the more than thirty ethnic groups who live in it, each with their own mother tongue. There is a folkloric legend to explain this astonishing diversity.

A snowstorm was raging in Dagestan on the day that god was distributing languages. The storm was so fierce that it was impossible to see anything; not a house nor a path in the mountains and valleys, and when god's mustache froze from the cold, he got so angry that he dumped all the languages he had left on the mountains and valleys of Dagestan. The people came rushing out of their homes to receive this golden flood, took of its riches, and each group received a language.

However it happened, Dagestan is considered by many to be one of the most ethnically and linguistically diverse areas on earth.

The people of Dagestan are a good-hearted, hospitable people who make their visitors feel welcome. Dagestan is famous for its dances and folksongs. The landscape of Dagestan is very beautiful and very varied. Side by side are semi equatorial forests and deserts. High mountains covered in ice and snow rise above the valleys and strong mountain rivers rush toward the warm Caspian Sea that is surrounded by sandy beaches.

Like the Circassians, the people of Chechnya and Dagestan have a long history of war with the Russian Empire. Several Imams led this resistance, most famously Imam Shamil. The Caucasian War raged until 1864, when Imam Shamil was captured. Later, Dagestan and Chechnya fought together again against Russia during the Russo-Turkish War of 1877-78. Defeat led many Dagestanis and Chechens to immigrate to the Ottoman Empire.

Syria received many Chechen and Dagestani families at this time. Most of them were the families of fighters, solders, and high ranking army officers who joined the Ottoman army. Later on, after the fall of the Ottoman Empire, they chose to stay in Syria.

Three Dagestani Folktales

A Brave Boy

Once upon a time, there was a boy who lived in the Dagestani Mountains. One day he went for a walk in the woods and, after roaming through them for a long while, he lost his way. He stopped and made a walking stick from a branch and started looking for the way back. Time passed and he got tired so he decided to rest under a bush. Shortly after he lay down, he saw a huge snake creeping up a nearby tree toward a nest filled with chicks. The snake hissed and flicked its long tongue in and out as it crept nearer and nearer the nest. The chicks were crying and screeching for help, but nobody came to rescue them.

Although the boy was very scared, he felt sorry for the chicks. He took a swing with his stick and hit the snake with all his might. The snake turned around, coiled up, and darted at the boy. The snake was huge and strong, but the boy kept hitting it with his stick. They fought for a long time, but finally the boy won. He threw the dead snake into the tree for the chicks to eat.

As the boy was exhausted after his fight with the snake, he lay down again under the bush and soon was fast asleep.

Suddenly the leaves on the trees started rustling animals hid in their holes, heavy clouds covered the starry sky. It was Magic Bird flying home to her chicks. She saw the boy and started squawking raucously, "Here is a man! I will tear him apart!"

"Oh, Mother," screamed the chicks, "Don't kill him! He saved us and fed us while you were away."

When she heard her chicks tell how the boy fought and killed the snake that was threatening them, Magic Bird swooped down and stretched her wing over the boy so that neither wind nor rain could disturb him. When the boy woke up and saw the huge bird looming over him, he began to cry, but Magic Bird calmed him down as she spoke to him gently, "Don't be afraid. Because you saved my children, you can ask me for whatever you want."

"Please, take me home," said the boy.

"Mount my back and put your arms around my neck."

Magic Bird lifted the boy high in the sky, carried him far away from the forest and put him on the roof of his house.

GUGLAHAY

Once upon a time, there lived a bird named Guglahay. She found a tall hollowed tree in the forest and twisted a nest in that hollow and laid her eggs in it. Soon there were three little chicks. Guglahay looked at them and thought, "I have the most beautiful children in the world."

One day, a fox was passing by the tree and heard the chicks peeping. The fox stopped and asked, "Who has built a nest in this tree?"

"I have. I am Guglahay."

"Do you not know, Guglahay that all this forest is mine, this tree is mine, and the hollow in it is mine, too? Get out, Guglahay! I'm going to cut this tree down."

"Sweet Fox," said Guglahay, "Let me feed my chicks and bring them up."

"How many chicks do you have?"

"Three, Sweet Fox."

"Why three?" shouted the fox. "Don't you know that you can't have more than two chicks? You must get rid of one of them. Give one to me."

"I won't give you my child, sweet Fox!" Guglahay answered.

"Won't you?" shouted the Fox. "Then so much the worse for you. I will call the frightful Woodcutter Basi-Ada to cut down this tree with his sharp axe and kill your chicks!"

Guglahay was frightened and threw one of her chicks to the Fox. The Fox hid in the bush and ate it.

The next day, the Fox came again and sang, "All this forest is mine; this tree is mine, the hollow in it is mine, and the nest in it is mine, too! Guglahay, get out! I'm going to cut the tree down!"

Guglahay sobbed and begged the fox, "Oh, sweet Fox! Let me feed my two chicks and bring them up!"

"I won't let you raise them both," said the Fox. "They will fight, then start pecking and shake my tree! Give me one chick and I'll feed it and bring it up myself!"

"No," said Guglahay and shook her head. "I won't give you my chick!"

"Well," said the Fox, then shouted, "Come here, Basi-Ada, you frightful Woodcutter! Bring your sharp axe! Cut down this tree."

Guglahay got frightened and threw a second chick to the Fox and she ate it.

Guglahay sat on the branch next to the hollow and cried over her two chicks. The Magpie was flying by, and when she saw

Guglahay crying, she stopped and asked, "Why are you crying, Guglahay?"

"I can't help crying! The Fox has eaten two of my three chicks," replied Guglahay.

"You shouldn't have given them to her!"

"There was nothing I could do. She wanted cut down the tree. She was even calling the frightful Woodcutter Basi-Ada."

"Don't believe the cunning Fox. There is no Basi-Ada in the forest, and the Fox can't cut down the tree by herself, can she? What is she going to do it with? Her tail?

The Magpie flew away. The next morning the Fox came again and sang, "All this forest is mine; this tree is mine, the hollow in it is mine, and the nest is mine, too! Guglahay, get out! I'm going to cut this tree down!"

"Oh, sweet Fox! Let me feed my chick and bring it up!"

"No, I won't!" said the Fox. He'll be bored alone in the nest! Give him to me, I'll lull him and take care of him."

"This is my chick," said Guglahay, "and I will bring him up. You go to your cubs, cunning Fox!"

"Well, then, I'll call the frightful Woodcutter Basi-Ada now. He'll come with his sharp axe and cut the tree down."

"You can call him," said Guglahay, "and I'll watch him cut my tree down!"

The Fox started to call Basi-Ada, but he didn't come. She called him for a long time, until finally she got tired and sat under the tree.

"Tell me, Guglahay, who has been talking to you?"

Guglahay replied proudly, "It was a good Magpie who told me everything."

"Oh, that Magpie!" cried the fox. "I'll punish her!"

The Fox ran away to find the Magpie and found the bird hopping on the ground, pecking some seeds.

"Got you!" said the Fox triumphantly. "I won't spare you. I'll teach you a lesson for warning Guglahay!" And she clenched the Magpie with her sharp teeth.

Seeing that she was in great trouble, the Magpie decided to trick the Fox.

"Oh, sweet Fox," she squeaked pitifully. "You punish me for nothing! You can eat me if you want, but I beg you to first cry out, 'I've caught a good Magpie!' Let all the other birds hear you say that!"

The Fox unclenched her teeth and shouted, "I've caught a good Magpie!"

The Magpie didn't hesitate to use her chance. She flew away, sat on a branch and said, "Thank you, sweet Fox, for being fooled by me!"

"How silly it is to praise your game before eating it!" said the Fox, and went away to the neighboring forest, ashamed and defeated.

Meanwhile, happy Guglahay brought up her chick, fed him, and sang songs with him. You may hear them if you listen.

The Witty Old Man (Kumyk Folktale)

The Kumyks speak a Turkic language.

One day, a noble Bey and his viziers were inspecting his lands and saw an old man who was reaping wheat.

"Hey, old man!" shouted the Bey. "The peak of your mountain is topped with snow."

"You can say that," replied the old man, "but the snow is spreading out to the plain."

"And what about your food?"

"Well, thanks. I'm munching bread with meat."

"What are you up to?"

"I'm collecting the debts I lent before."

"If I sent you three fat drakes, what would you do with them?"

"I would pluck them!"

The Bey gave a smile, whipped up his horse, and rode away. His viziers followed him. They had made nothing of this talk and were now trying to figure it out.

Finally the Grand Vizier approached the Bey and asked, "Honorable Bey, can you explain to us what you were talking about to the old man?

"You didn't understand us, did you."

"No. To tell the truth, I made nothing of it."

The Bey turned to the other viziers and asked them if they had understood the conversation. He got really angry when he saw them all shake their heads no.

"You are supposed to be my advisors, and yet you can't understand plain speech? Either you tell me what the old man meant or I no longer need you!"

The viziers rode away. They laid heads together and decided to go back to the old man and ask him for an explanation.

When the viziers got to the field, the Grand Vizier cried out.

"Old man, the Honorable Bey doesn't want to see us anymore because we failed to understand your talk with him. Will you clarify it for us?"

"I'll do it only if you give me your horses and clothes." The viziers hesitated. They were unwilling to give their horses and expensive clothes to the old man, but the risk of being sent away was too high. They dismounted, undressed, and gave him their clothes and horses.

Only then did the old man explain.

"When the Bey shouted, *The peak of your mountain is topped with snow!* He meant your hair has turned gray, old man!

"And when I replied, *The snow is spreading out to the plain*, I meant my eyesight has also gotten worse.

"The Bey asked me *And what about your food?* I replied that I'm munching bread with meat, and I meant I'm chewing on food with my gums because I have no teeth.

"What are you up to?" asked the Bey, and I said *I'm collecting the debts I lent before.* I meant that when I planted the field with wheat in the spring, it was as if I was lending it to the land. When you saw me reaping the wheat, I was taking back my debt from the land.

"Finally, the Bey asked me what I would do with three fat drakes if I got them, and I replied that that I would pluck them. So here you are; three fat, plucked drakes standing in front of me – undressed and unhorsed!"

A Dagestani Recipe

Shepherd Cakes — small stuffed pancakes

Ingredients for dough

 3 cups flour

 1 egg

 1 cup water

 1 tsp salt

Filling

 500 grams cabbage, minced

 500 grams lamb, minced

 4 onions, minced

 3 tomatoes, minced

 2 carrots, minced

 Ghee for frying

 Black pepper and salt

Method

Fry onions with lamb until golden brown

Add cabbage, tomatoes and carrots to meat and onions

Add pepper and salt to taste

Simmer in covered pot until tender

Combine egg, flour, salt and water - knead the dough, then roll into a ball

Cover with a cloth and leave for half an hour

Divide the dough into 8-12 pieces; roll each piece into a pancake

Cook pancake on a griddle until golden brown

Spread filling on the pancakes and fold like tortillas or roll into tubes and serve

Or

Put filled pancakes on a baking sheet and pour melted butter on them

Heat for 5-7 mins in the oven and serve hot

5

KURDS

The Kurds are an ethnic group whose people are found in a continuous swath of land stretching from the broad mountainous regions of northwestern Iran, to northern Iraq and Syria, and finally to eastern Turkey. Altogether, there are from 25 to 35 million Kurds who are mostly Sunni Muslims. They are a cohesive people with intricate intertribal ties and, although they make up the fourth-largest ethnic group in the Middle East, they have never obtained a permanent nation-state of their own.

The earliest Kurdish settlement in Syria goes back to the time of Saladin, during his jihad against the crusaders and his establishment of the Ayyubid Dynasty (1171-1341) which was administered from Damascus. Saladin himself was a Kurd from Tikrit, and the Kurdish soldiers who accompanied him established self-ruled areas around Damascus. Eventually, these settlements developed into the Kurdish quarter and the Salhiyya district.

In modern times, when Mustapha Kemal attempted to force his programs against the Kurds in Turkey, a large number of Kurds moved to Syria. Between 1924 and 1938 many Kurds settled in Hasakeh in the extreme northeast of the county near the Turkish border. Generally speaking, "new generation" Kurds have retained their native language (Kirmanji), dress, and customs, while "old generation" Kurds have become much more Arabized. Tribal identification and pride is strong in both "old" and "new" generation Kurds. Syrian Kurds are known for honesty, affection for their elders, and hospitality.

Sherin Shexani, a sixteen-year-old Kurd who lives in Hasakeh, told me that the Kirmanji language is well-preserved in her province. She says, "We cook both Arabic and Kurdish food and we always speak Kurdish at home."

While Syria's Kurds are almost entirely settled, they retain much of their tribal organization. Although some groups in the Jazirah are semi-nomadic, most are village dwellers who cultivate wheat, barley, cotton, and rice. Urban Kurds engage in a number of occupations, but not generally in commerce. Many are manual laborers and some are employed as supervisors and foremen, a kind of work that has come to be considered their specialty. There are some Kurds in the civil service and the army, and a few have attained high rank. Most of the small number of wealthy Kurds derive their income from urban real estate.

The Syrian Kurds fought the Ottomans and the French together with their Syrian brothers in every Syrian province and city. Kurds are famous as warriors, and Syria has two celebrated Kurdish heroes. In ancient times, there was the peerless Saladin, and in modern times there was Ibrahim Hanano, who is regarded as one of the most important heroes of the Syrian resistance to the French Mandate. I told Hanano's story earlier in this book in the chapter on the Muhafaza of Idlib. Today, Kurdish fighters are waging war against ISIS with considerable success.

FOUR KURDISH FOLKTALES AND A LEGEND

THE STORY OF THE BASKET PEDDLER

It is said the events of this story really happened, and that there are many grave shrines set up for the basket peddler, Zambeel Faroush, to celebrate his piety.

This story reminds me of an English folksong called "Green Broom." In the song, a 'woman in bloom' sends her maid down to ask the handsome young peddler of green broom to come upstairs to her chamber. But there the stories diverge. In the English song, the woman says to the young peddler, "Oh can you fancy me, will you marry a lady in bloom?" And they do marry – a happier ending than this folktale has.

Once upon a time there lived a young man who made his living as a basket peddler. One day he walked in the blazing sun for hours, hoping to sell his baskets. He imagined his beautiful wife and children receiving him happily at the door with the money he had earned from selling the baskets. He imagined his little son carrying the hot loaves of bread he brought with him.

As he walked through the winding alleys, he called out, "Baskets...baskets for sale." His sweet voice attracted the attention of the Princess, who was very bored that hot, hot summer day.

She looked down from her balcony and was taken by the handsome young Peddler at first sight. She called her maid and asked her to bring him to her at once so she could purchase his baskets.

The maid ran down the stairs and asked the basket seller to come into the castle to display his baskets.

The poor Peddler was very happy and hurried up the stairs to show the Prince his baskets.

"Where is the Prince?" asked the peddler.

"Here in his room," said the Princess. The peddler followed the Princess, but to his horror he didn't find the Prince.

"Show me your baskets," said the Princess. "How much are you selling them for?" Then the Princess playfully approached the peddler and said, "Oh Peddler, I've been waiting for you for so long!"

"You are very beautiful, my Princess," said the peddler, "but I am a humble, pious Peddler, whose wife and hungry children are waiting for him."

The Princess became enraged and screamed in a loud voice, "Stop being stupid and enjoy my company. The Prince is on a long trip and might never return." The Princess then let her golden hair tumble down her shoulders and said, "You will become the Prince!"

"I am so sorry, my spoiled Princess. I don't want to become a Prince here in this castle. My dear wife already considers me her Prince."

But the Princess would not take no for an answer. The peddler was silent and feared there was no way to get out of this trap, but then he thought of a way out. "I need to pray first," said the peddler. "Give me just ten minutes by myself."

The Princess felt triumphant and asked her maids to bring him a Persian prayer rug and a jug of water to wash for prayer and led him to a lavish room.

"Oh, no, not here," said the peddler. "I can't feel near to God in this castle."

"Where do you want to pray then?" asked the Princess.

"Permit me to pray up on the roof. There I can feel close to God."

The Princess let the maid lead him up to the roof, but as soon as he disappeared she worried he planned to run away, so she followed.

When the peddler saw her coming, he looked down at the ground and realized that the only way to escape from the Princess was by throwing himself from the roof.

"Ya Allah, please forgive me! I just can't commit adultery," he said. "This is my only way out!"

The Princess realized that the peddler was about to jump from the roof and screamed, "No, don't leave me!" She grabbed his arm and they both fell down on the ground and died.

To this day, the basket peddler is considered a symbol of steadfast morality among the Kurds.

THE SECRET OF THE DAUGHTER-IN-LAW

Once upon a time, there lived an old man who suddenly felt he should fulfill his duty to go on Haj. He consulted the members of his family and they all encouraged him.

The old man slaughtered a sheep and distributed the meat to some poor people, packed his bags, and prepared himself to travel at the beginning of the next week.

That night, he dreamed a strange dream. In his dream, his daughter-in-law was racing him with long strides to the black stone of the Kaaba and arriving there before him.

The old man woke up, murmured a prayer, and then fell asleep again. Then the next night he dreamed the same dream.

"What is the meaning of this dream?" asked the old man.

The members of his family looked at one another, but none could interpret it.

Then the old man turned towards his daughter-in-law and asked her, "What good deed did you do to reach the Kaaba before me?"

The daughter-in-law felt a little awkward and embraced him and said, "My dear father-in-law, the day you slaughtered the sheep, my pregnant neighbor knocked on the door and asked for some coal to start her fire. Her eyes twinkled when they fell upon my share of the sheep, and I could see she was craving it, so I hid my piece of meat and without telling anyone, I went and gave it to her."

The old man's tears rolled down his face and wet his gray beard and said, "Oh my dear daughter-in-law, no wonder I dreamed you were reaching the Kaaba before me. Good deeds are always greatly rewarded by Allah.

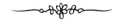

THE RESULTS OF GREED

Once upon a time, a long time ago, there was a poor shepherd. Every day, he took his flock of sheep to a meadow far from the village, and there he pastured them. One day, around midday, he took a sheep, milked it into a pot, and let it go. He put the pot next to a pile of rocks and sat down to have his lunch of bread and milk. All at once, he spied a snake coming out from the pile of rocks. It drank the milk in the pot and then went back into the rocks and came out with a coin in its mouth, which it put into the pot. When the snake left, the shepherd put the coin in his purse, and he was so happy his feet didn't touch the ground as he walked home.

In the evening he took his flock home, but that night he didn't sleep a wink. The next morning, he took his flock to the same place, and just as he had done the day before, he milked a sheep into the pot and put it near the pile of rocks. Once again, the snake came, swallowed the milk, and put a coin in the pot.

The shepherd continued doing this for many days, and in this way he became rich and decided to go on Pilgrimage. Before setting out on his journey, he called his son and disclosed his secret to him. After his father left, the boy led the flock out to the pile of rocks, milked a sheep into the pot, and stepped away to see what would happen. Just as before, the snake came out, drank the milk, and put a coin in the pot.

The son started thinking to himself, "By God, I have a silly father. Why should I sit around waiting for one coin a day? Why don't I just kill the snake and get the whole treasure for myself?"

The next day he took a sword, and when the snake came out, he attacked it and cut off its tail. The snake slithered back into the rocks. Then the son destroyed the pile of rocks, turning them upside down, but there was no snake and no treasure, either. There was nothing he could do but put the pile of stones back the way it had been, in hopes that the snake would come again and give him a coin.

The following day, the boy put the pot of milk next to the pile of rocks and went a little way off. The snake hissed and bit him on the top of his head, killing him on the spot.

Time passed and the shepherd returned from his Pilgrimage. One day, after the rejoicing was over, he went to the pile of rocks. To himself, he said, "One way or another, this son of mine must have done something to make the snake kill him."

While the man stood near the pile of rocks, the snake came out to him and said, "It would have been better for you, O Man, not to have told your secret to your son. You think I am a snake and that I take these coins from a treasure trove under this rock, but you should know that I am not a snake. I am the daughter of the King of the Fairies, and I have been turned into a snake by a magic spell. Recently, your son attacked me and cut off my tail. When the spell wears off, I will be marred. Now, as a punishment for not keeping this secret in your heart, I will have to kill you, too." And she bit the man on top of his head and killed him on the spot.

Hasan the Trapper

Once upon a time, there was a Hunter called Hasan the Trapper. He could understand the languages of all the animals and the birds. One day, he went out hunting. While in the wilderness, he saw an old snake attacking a beautiful young female snake. Hasan was highly displeased by this, so he pulled out his bow and arrow to kill the old snake, but unfortunately the arrow struck not the old snake, but the young one and wounded her. It so happened that the young snake was the daughter of the King of Snakes.

The young wounded snake went home and her father asked her, "Daughter, how did this happen? Who has wounded you?"

The daughter of the King of Snakes was too embarrassed to give all the details to her father, so all she said was, "Hasan the Trapper wounded me."

The King of Snakes glowered in anger and ordered all the snakes to gather. Then he said, "Hasan the Trapper has done me a great wrong. He is now in the village mosque. Whom shall I appoint to go into his shoe and bite him when he comes out and puts his shoe on?"

A very clever snake spoke up and said, "My lord, I'll go." The snake went to the mosque and curled up in Hasan's shoe and listened while Hasan was telling the people about his encounter with the snakes.

"People, listen to me. While I was in the forest, I saw an old snake attacking a young female snake, and since I understand all the animal languages, I realized the old snake had very bad intentions. The young snake was resisting him and refusing to give in to him. I couldn't stand for such injustice, so I pulled out my bow and arrow to kill him, but unfortunately I hit the young one and wounded her!"

When the snake heard this, he hurried back to the King of the Snakes and said, "My lord, Hasan the Trapper says it was otherwise."

The King summoned his daughter and asked, "Daughter, how can you blame Hasan? He says it was otherwise."

"Father," said the daughter, "He is right. I was too embarrassed to tell the truth."

"If this is so," said the King of Snakes, "Hasan the Trapper has done us a great favor and is worthy of thanks and reward." Then he told the snake to summon Hasan.

The snake went to Hasan and started hissing. Hasan understood and came to him. The snake said, "Actually, I came earlier to the mosque to bite your foot and kill you because we were told that you wounded the daughter of our King for no good reason. However, when I heard what you said in the mosque, I quickly took the news back to our King, and this is the reason he wants to see you – so he can reward you. You must say to him, 'I didn't do it to be rewarded, but if you insist on rewarding me, give me a drop of your venom.' Please don't mention my name in any of this, but if the King of Snakes puts a drop of his venom in your mouth, wherever you go, all the plants and trees will call out to you and tell you what ailment they are good for. In this way, you will become a famous physician and a very rich man."

When they came before the King of Snakes, he greeted Hasan warmly, thanked him for his courage, and said, "I want to reward you."

"I don't want anything," replied Hasan.

"But I want to give you something as a reward," said the King.

"If you insist on rewarding me," said Hasan, "Then give me a drop of your venom."

The King of the Snakes recoiled at these words and asked, "Who told you to say this?"

"Nobody," said Hasan. "If you are going to reward me, that is what I want."

The King of Snakes nodded his head and said, "Then I must agree because you have done me a favor, but if you ever disclose the secret to anyone, you will die on the spot."

After receiving the reward, wherever Hasan the Trapper went, the plants and trees called out to him and told him what illnesses they could cure. In this way, he became the most famous physician in the country, and everyone he treated was cured. It wasn't long before Hasan the Trapper became rich.

One day, his wife began to pester him, saying, "You have to tell me the secret of your success." No matter how often Hasan told her that he could not tell her, for if he did, he would die, it did no good. His wife paid no attention to anything he said and insisted she had to know his secret.

When she continued to pester him, he said to her, "All right. You don't mind seeing me die?"

"I don't know anything about all that," she replied. "I just want you to tell me the secret. Whatever happens then will happen."

"What can I do?" said the husband helplessly. "Go to the market and buy me a winding sheet for my burial. When you come back I will reveal the secret to you."

Now, Hasan the Trapper had a dog and a rooster at home. The dog was listening to this. Sensing that his master was going to die, he crept into a corner and tears began to stream from his eyes. It wasn't long before the rooster came home and saw the dog weeping. When he asked what going on, the dog said, "If tears are not good for such a situation, then what are they good for? Our master Hasan is going to die, and then I'll be put out into the streets, and they'll cut your head off and eat you."

The dog told the rooster the whole story. The rooster said, "Damn this master of mine! Here I am, a rooster who goes out every day with ten or twelve hens and then comes home all by himself. Is our master Hasan not man enough to get rid of his awful wife?"

Since Hasan understood the languages of all animals and birds, he listened carefully to the conversation between the dog and the rooster. In his heart, he reflected on the evil conduct of his wife, for whom it was so easy to see him die, while his dog was overcome with grief and weeping.

After some time passed, his wife came back in with a piece of untanned leather, thread, and soap.

"Wife," said Hasan, "What is all this?"

Coolly she replied, "It is for burying you."

"Is my death of so little importance to you?" asked Hasan. Thereupon, he quickly sent for two or three neighbors and divorced his wife in their presence. A short time later, he married another woman. In this way, the words of his dog and his rooster helped him to escape from his pitiless wife and start a new life.

The Legend of King Zahhak and Kawa the Blacksmith

In Syria, the Kurds put on their national dress and celebrate Newroz, the New Year, on the 21st of March of every year. The meaning of the word 'Newroz' is 'New day.' Newroz is considered the most important festival in Kurdish culture and is a time for games, dancing, family gatherings, preparation of special foods, and the reciting of poetry. On the eve of Newroz, bonfires are lit on the hills. These fires symbolize the passing of the dark season, winter, and the arrival of spring, the season of light.

The following ancient legend tells the story of the origin of the Kurd's celebration of Newroz.

Once upon a time, there lived an evil Assyrian King named Zahhak, who had a black serpent growing on each shoulder. He ruled for one thousand years, and during this time the sun refused to shine, the farmers' crops didn't grow, and spring no longer came to Kurdistan.

When the serpents were hungry King Zahhak was in terrible pain, and the only way to alleviate it was to sacrifice two young men and feed their brains to the serpents. Everyday King Zahhak gave the order for two young men to be sacrificed and their brains offered to the serpents on his shoulders to ease his pain. However, wirhout the King's knowledge, the man in charge of killing the two young men would only kill one and mix his brains with the brains of a sheep. In this way a large number of young men were saved.

As years passed, people grew very angry with the rule of King Zahhak, and Kawa, a blacksmith who had lost six sons to the King's serpents, planned a revolt against him. The young men who had been saved from the fate of being sacrificed were led to the mountains and trained by Kawa to be soldiers, and they soon formed an army.

On March 20th, Kawa led this army to Zahhak's castle where Kawa killed the evil King with his blacksmith's hammer. Then Kawa set bonfires on the hillsides to celebrate and announce his victory to the people. The next day, March 21st, spring returned to Kurdistan. The young men of Kawa's army who were saved from the serpents are regarded as the legendary ancestors of the Kurds.

Ever since then, the Kurds celebrate Newroz, the season of light, by setting bonfires on the hills and dancing and leaping through the fires. Newroz began in ancient times as a celebration to mark liberation from an evil king, and today it is still a very important holiday that reminds the Kurds of their strength. The lighting of fires on Newroz has become a symbol of the freedom to which they aspire.

PROVERBS

- If you burn a poor man, he won't even have a smell.
- The fire is burning my head and you want to cook your food on it.
- A pretty face with poison in its heart.
- One hand washes the other, and together they wash the face.
- Let the lion devour you and don't hide in the shadows of the forest.
- The lions went and left the owls behind.
- The camel shuts its eyes in the field, and thinks no one can see it.
- Man is sometimes a fox, other times a lion.
- Leave the annoying neighbor and pull out the painful tooth.

- Sometimes silence is better than talking.
- Mountain summits don't meet, but eyes do.

A Game: Boleh

In the winding streets of Hasakeh, children play this ball game in the long, hot summer days. The name 'boleh' has no meaning in Kurdish, so it must have been derived from the English word ball. Boleh is a game played in the streets of both the villages and the cities.

Rules of the Game:

All that is needed to play the game is one ball. Form two teams, for example five players for each team. One player from the first team starts the game by throwing the ball toward the other team, trying to hit one of the players. If a player gets hit by the ball, he or she will be out of the game and must stand to one side until the game is over. All the players should try to avoid getting hit by the ball to stay in the game. The teams take turns throwing the ball, and the last player to avoid being hit is the winner.

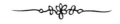

THREE KURDISH RECIPES

ALBALOIEH — A BURGHOL DISH

This simple dish was well known in Hasakeh during the time of famine, and both Arabs and Kurds make it. Many proverbs are said about it, such as, 'The hunger for Albalouieh shatters the ribs' and it rhymes in the Kurdish language.

Ingredients

1 cup of fine burghol soaked in water and drained

1 bunch finely cut parsley

1 finely cut green onion

1 tbsp tomato paste

¼ cup water

1 onion, finely chopped

1 cup oil

Salt and red pepper to taste

Method

Place drained burghol in a dish and add parsley, green onion, salt, and red pepper

Heat oil and fry the finely cut onion and set aside

Stir tomato paste into the water, then add to fried onions

Pour tomato sauce on burghol and mix together

Press the mixture together to form a ball

Taftafi — a thick stew

Ingredients

2 lbs of lamb or 1 whole chicken

2 cups drained chickpeas

2 cups drained wheat

2 medium onions, cut into small pieces

¼ cup oil

Salt and sumac to taste

Method

Boil chickpeas and wheat together in a pot

Fry the onions then add meat (or chicken) and stir

When chickpeas and wheat are done, add meat (or chicken) and onions to them

Cook until the meat is tender

Put the sumac in a small dish for people to sprinkle on their plates

AYRAN — A BEVERAGE

Ayran is a very refreshing drink which is served cold in the hot summer.

Ingredients

2 cups yogurt

1 cup water

Pinch of salt

Method

Put yogurt in blender or bowl and beat until smooth

Add water slowly while beating. If too thick, add more water

Beat in salt and serve chilled

6

TURKMEN

The ethnic origins of the Turkmens go back to the seventh and eighth centuries, to the Oghuz Turkic tribes in what is now Mongolia. By the twelfth century, Turkmen tribes had migrated into many parts of the Middle East.

Most Turkmen settled in Syria after 1516, when the Ottomans conquered Syria. The Ottoman government encouraged Turkmen nomad families from Anatolia to establish villages in Ottoman Syria. Migration of Turkmen from Anatolia to Syria continued until the dissolution of the Ottoman Empire in 1918. The Turkish settlement throughout the rural hinterlands of several Syrian cities was a state-organized population transfer that was used to counter the demographic weight and influence of other ethnic groups in the region. Furthermore, the Turkmen served as the local gendarmes to help assert Ottoman authority.

The Turkmens in Syria are divided ethnically and culturally into two groups. The largest group, the Turkmen of the cities, is of Turkish origin and makes up more than seventy percent of the Syrian Turkmen. The urban Turkmen have become arabized and no longer speak their mother tongue.

Rural Turkmen, also called Turkoman, are a much smaller group and have kept their mother tongue. They were originally nomads from Turkistan in Central Asia but now are semi-nomadic herdsmen and settled agriculturists in Syria. Although many Turkoman have assumed Arab dress and speak some Arabic, others, mostly in the villages, still speak only Turkic and retain some ethnic customs. Because they are Sunni Muslims, the Turkoman are likely to become further assimilated and may eventually disappear as a distinct group.

Syrian Turkmen choose Arab Islamic names like Mohammad and Ahmad. They rarely give their children Turkish names. Since the Syrian census does not ask about religion and ethnic background, there are different estimates of how many Turkmen are in Syria. Estimates range from a million and a half to as many as three million.

Today the Syrian Turkmen community shares common genealogical and linguistic ties with the Turkmen of Turkey. They share a closer kinship to the Turks of Turkey than to the Turkmen of Central Asia. They reside mostly near the Syrian-Turkish border, including in Ras al-Bassit and the Turkmen Mountain in the Muhafaza of Latakia. There are also Turkmen in the city of Homs and its vicinity, Damascus, and the southwestern muhafazas of Deraa and Quneitra. As for the rural Turkoman, they are semi-nomadic herdsmen in the Jazirah and along the lower reaches of the Euphrates River, and settled farmers in the Aleppo area.

During the present civil war, Syrian Turkmen have been involved in military actions against Syrian government forces and have looked to Turkey for support and protection.

Four Turkmen Folktales

"The Sultan's New Turban" is a Turkmen folktale that is exactly like Hans Christian Andersen's story "The Emperor's New Clothes," except a new non-existent turban is substituted for the new clothes. Andersen's tale is based on a story from a medieval Spanish collection of fifty-one cautionary tales with various sources such as Aesop and other classical writers, and Persian folktales. Perhaps "The Sultan's New Turban" is the original folktale. I have not included it because everyone knows the story.

The Slap

There are many folktales about Nasrettin Hoca in the Middle East. In Arabic he is called "Joha" and in Turkish, "Nasrettin Hoca."

Nasrettin Hoca was standing in the marketplace when a stranger stepped up to him and slapped him in the face, but then said, "I beg your pardon. I thought you were someone else."

This explanation did not satisfy the Hoca, so he brought the stranger before the Qadi and demanded compensation.

The Hoca soon perceived that the Qadi and the defendant were friends. The latter admitted his guilt, and the Judge pronounced the sentence, "The settlement for this offense is one piaster to be paid to the plaintiff. If you do not have a piaster with you, then you may bring it here to the plaintiff at your convenience."

Hearing this sentence, the defendant went on his way. The Hoca waited for him to return with the piaster. And he waited. And he waited.

Sometime later the Hoca said to the Qadi, "Do I understand correctly that one piaster is sufficient payment for a slap?"

"Yes," answered the Qadi.

Hearing this answer, the Hoca slapped the Qadi in the face and said, "You may keep my piaster when the defendant returns with it." And he stalked off.

THE BET

One day Nasrettin Hoca entered into a bet with a friend. The friend challenged the Hoca to spend a cold winter night outdoors wearing only minimal clothing. If the Hoca could stand the harsh conditions until daybreak without a fire, he would win. The loser would have to treat the winner to a feast. Nasrettin Hoca managed to survive, and he informed his friend that he had won the bet. But the friend was not willing to admit defeat.

"Nasrettin Hoca, were the stars out during the night?"

"Yes, the stars were out during the night."

"In that case, you were warmed by the light of the stars. That was against the conditions to which we agreed. Therefore, you must forfeit and provide the feast."

So the Hoca invited the other man to dinner and they began to make small talk. Nasrettin Hoca excused himself several times to supervise the kitchen preparations. Hours passed, but no food arrived. Finally, his friend could not stand it any longer, and he wanted to inspect the dinner that was taking so long to cook. To his amazement, he found a large kettle with a sheep in it and a solitary candle flickering underneath, where a hot fire is usually found.

In exasperation, the man shouted, "A candle to boil this kettle?"

Nasrettin responded, "If I can be warmed by the light of the stars, then why could not a candle provide the heat to boil a kettle?"

THE CLEVER BOY

Once upon a time, a Merchant caravan filled with servants arrived at a big river. The Merchants needed to cross the river, so they loaded their caravan and all their servants onto a large boat. Suddenly, a storm arose with very strong winds that blew the boat off course. It ran aground on a huge rock and sank.

All the people on the boat drowned except one of the young servants who fought the waves until he was carried to the shore. The servant boy woke up and began walking. He kept walking until he reached the large gates of a city. All at once, he was surrounded by crowds of people who picked him up and carried him away! The boy was terrified and said to himself, "What are they going to do with me?"

To his astonishment, the people carried him into a palace and sat him on the King's throne. The bewildered servant boy said, "Why did you bring me here? What does this mean?"

He kept on asking the people around him, but no one answered him until an old man with a white beard spoke up and said, "My son, this is the traditional custom of our city. Once our King's reign of one year finishes, our people carry him to a mountain full of snakes and scorpions and leave him there. After that, we choose the first man we see at the gates of our city to take his place."

The boy said, "Now that I am the king, does that mean that my wish is your command?"

The people said, "Yes, for a whole year."

The boy started ruling the city and one day he decided to visit the mountain of snakes and scorpions. Once there, he ordered his servants to get rid of all the snakes and scorpions and to establish parks and plant flowers and trees. When the boy's term finished, the people were pleased with him, so he was elected once more by his people and continued to do good deeds and govern the city well till the end of his days.

The Wicked Merchant (Turkoman folktale)

The old woman sitting next to me on the bus introduced herself as a Turkoman from Moudamieh, whose grandparents arrived in Damascus in the early twentieth century. I excitedly asked if she remembered a folktale told to her by her grandparents. She hesitated for a while, then nodded her head and gave me the following story. As she proceeded with her story-telling, I remembered that I had read the story somewhere as a child. To my great joy, I later found out the story I remembered was 'A Mountain of Gems,' an arabized version of this Turkoman folktale using Arabic names and a different title, but recounting the same events. I am continually fascinated by how folktales can survive through the years and travel from place to place.

Once upon a time, there lived a poor widow who had one son. His name was Suleman, and the widow was called "Um Suleman" - the mother of Suleman. The widow had to earn their daily bread by combing wool and knitting sweaters day and night.

When Suleman grew older, his mother said to him, "Listen to me, my son. I am growing old. I haven't the strength to work anymore, for my hands feel numb. You must find some work and earn your living."

"Very well, my dear Mother," said Suleman, and set off to look for work. He searched everywhere, but could not find anyone who would hire him.

On his way back home, he met a Merchant at the market. "Do you need a workman?" Suleman asked.

"Yes, I do!" replied the Merchant. "I need someone to accompany me on my long journeys."

The following day, the Merchant gave Suleman a knife and ordered him to slaughter a calf and skin it. Then he asked him to bring four large sacks and two camels for their journey.

When everything was ready, they set off on their journey. In an hour and a half, they arrived at the foot of a very high mountain. The Merchant ordered Suleman to unpack the sacks and the calf's skin, then said, "Spread the calf's skin on the ground and lie down on it." Suleman didn't know why the rich man wanted him to lie down on the calf's skin, but he didn't dare disobey.

Once Suleman lay down on the calf's skin, the Merchant rolled it up into a bundle with Suleman inside it. He then wrapped it tight and hid behind a large rock. Suddenly, two large hawks flew down and carried the bundle to the top of the mountain. The two birds pecked and gnawed at the skin until it finally unwrapped and Suleman rolled out. Frightened, the two birds flew away. Suleman got to his feet and looked around. To his great shock, the mountain was so steep that there was no way he could get down.

The Merchant saw him from below and cried out, "Throw down the precious stones lying at your feet!"

"But how will I get down?" asked Suleman.

"Don't worry!" answered the Merchant "I'll tell you how to get down from the mountain afterwards. Just throw the precious stones down to me!"

Suleman believed the Merchant and threw down as many of the precious stones as he could. The Merchant quickly picked them up, filled the four large sacks, and put them on the camels' backs.

"Don't leave me! Where are you going?" Suleman called out.

"You have done a great job!" said the Merchant, as he rode away.

Suleman looked around and there was no sign of life. All he saw were the scattered bones of human beings on the ground. "So that is the kind of work this Merchant gives his workmen!" he said to himself.

Suddenly, a great eagle flew towards him and was about to tear him to pieces. Fortunately, Suleman was able to tightly grasp the eagle's feet with both hands. The eagle let out a loud cry and began to fly around and around in circles. Then, exhausted, it flew down to the ground and Suleman landed with a thump.

Suleman couldn't believe how lucky he was to be saved from a ghastly death. Even though he was exhausted, he knew he had no time to waste. He wanted to get revenge on the wicked Merchant.

Suleman went straight back to the market, where he found the rich Merchant looking for more workmen. This time, Suleman introduced himself as 'Omar.' The Merchant didn't recognize him and hired him immediately.

Soon after, back at the Merchant's house, Suleman was ordered, just as before, to slaughter a calf, skin it, and to bring four sacks and two camels.

Then they made their way to the foot of the mountain. Again, the Merchant asked Suleman to wrap himself up in the calf's skin.

But this time, Suleman acted stupid and said, "I don't know what you mean, show me what to do!"

The Merchant stretched himself out on the skin and said, "This is the way it is done!"

At once, Suleman rolled the skin into a bundle, wrapped it tightly, and stepped away. "Wait!" cried the Merchant "What have you done to me!"

At that moment, two hawks swooped down and carried the bundle away to the top of the mountain and began to gnaw at it with their beaks, but when they saw the Merchant, they flew away.

Suleman whistled from below and cried out, "Don't waste time, throw the precious stones to me just as I did for you!"

Only then did it strike the Merchant that he had hired Suleman before. "How did you get down from here?" he shouted. "Answer me quickly."

"Don't worry, calm down!" said Suleman, "I'll tell you how to get down from the mountain afterwards. Just throw me the precious stones!" The Merchant threw the precious stones while Suleman picked them up as fast as he could.

When the sacks were filled to the top, Suleman piled them on the camels' backs and shouted back at the Merchant as he waved good bye, "I hope you enjoy the company of the ghosts of the workmen you sent to their death!"

The Merchant frantically gnashed his teeth and first shouted threats and then pleaded with Suleman on his knees, but all in vain. Suleman turned away and set off for his mother's house.

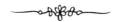

❊ ❊

A TURKMEN RECIPE

DOGRAMA — A MEAT AND BREAD DISH

This is the most traditional Turkmen recipe and is served on special occasions such as "Gurbanlyk," a three-day religious holiday that falls on the tenth day of the Islamic month of "Dhul-Hijja" In Syria, Gurbanlyk is the Eid al Kabir, which is also called Eid al Adha. The name of this dish comes from the word "dogramak" - to cut to pieces.

Ingredients for broth

1½ kg lamb or beef with fat and bones

5 litres water

2 tbsp salt

2 chopped tomatoes

Ingredients for bread

1 tbsp salt

600 ml warm water

1 tsp active dry yeast

1 kg flour

2 halved and sliced onions

Ground black pepper

Method for broth

Put meat and water in a pot and bring to a boil over high heat

Skim boiling broth and add salt

Reduce heat to medium and cover pot

After 20 minutes, add tomatoes.

Simmer in covered pot until the meat is tender

Taste and adjust the broth for salt

Method for bread

Mix all bread ingredients together in a large bowl and work into a dough

Divide dough in half and roll each piece between your palms into a ball

Preheat oven to 482°F

Roll out each ball of dough to a thickness of 1.5 cm

Prick with a fork and place on baking sheet lined with baking paper

Brush bread circles with water and bake on middle oven rack until golden brown, 15-18 minutes

Over a large kitchen cloth, tear bread into small pieces (leave ¼ of one bread circle for later) and toss in onion slices

Transfer meat from pot to cutting board, and then finely chop the meat and the remaining piece of bread

Return chopped meat and bread to the cloth and mix together with your hands

Drizzle 3-4 tablespoons of fatty broth over the mixture

At this point, dograma is ready but will taste better if left wrapped in the cloth for 20-30 minutes to let the bread absorb the flavor of the meat and onion

To serve, scoop some dograma into a bowl, add black pepper to taste, and ladle in enough hot broth to barely cover the dograma

Serves 8-10

7

ASSYRIANS

Assyrians are the indigenous descendants of the ancient Assyrian people, one of the earliest civilizations to emerge in the Middle East. The history of the Assyrians spans more than 6,000 years. Although the Assyrian Empire ended in 612 BC, history records the continuous presence of the Assyrian people until the present time. While they are classified as "Arab" by the Syrian government, they are actually a pre-Arab ethnic group. However, like Arabs, they are a Semitic people who write their Syriac language from right to left, like Arabic. The Assyrians are all Christians and have their own unique culture and heritage. They are mostly adherents of the Syriac Orthodox Church, with smaller numbers belonging to the Assyrian Church of the East, the Chaldean Catholic Church, and the Syriac Catholic Church.

The ancient homeland of the Assyrians was called in in their language "Bet Nahrain" or "the house of the two rivers," referring to the Tigris and the Euphrates. It included almost all of present-day Iraq, parts of southeastern Turkey, and northeastern Syria. Modern-day Assyrians live in the muhafaza of Hasakeh, as well as in the cities of Qamishli, Ras al Ayn, Qahtaniya and Tell Tamer. There are over 30 primarily agricultural Assyrian villages on the

343

Khabur River in Syria. There are about 700,000 Assyrians in Syria, and they make up around two percent of Syria's population.

The Assyrians in Hasakeh came to Syria as refugees fleeing from southern Turkey after World War I along with displaced Armenians. Both groups were survivors of killings and forced marches from Turkey. These Assyrians are known as the Western Assyrians. Given preferential treatment by the French Mandate which took power in 1920, they soon formed most of the new urban elite in the region. An additional influx of Assyrians from Iraq began to settle along the Khabur River in 1933. These refugees, known as the Eastern Assyrians, fled the killing of their people that broke out in newly-independent Iraq.

An Assyrian Legend

Hanno Karetho

This Assyrian legend goes back thousands of years in the far north-east region of Syria. It is considered one of the oldest Syrian legends.

Once upon a time, there lived an Assyrian King who, year after year, would lose in battles against his enemies. One year, he swore an oath that if he should defeat his enemies in battle this time, he would sacrifice to the gods the first person he met on his return home.

After he made this oath, the King's luck changed, and he won a battle against his enemies. He set out to return victoriously to his Kingdom and fulfill his oath.

To his great shock, his precious daughter Hanna, whom he loved more than anyone in the world, was the first one to greet him. A dark shadow passed over his face.

"What's the matter, dear father?" asked Hanna. "Did you lose the battle?"

"No, my dear Hanna," said the King with a tearful voice. "In fact, we have won for the first time!"

"Oh father," said Hanna. "I'm so happy!"

The King pressed his fists together and said, "This victory will make us pay highly! Before this battle, I swore an oath to myself that if I returned victorious, I would sacrifice to the gods the first person I met on my return!"

Hanna was shocked at the words of her father, but she courageously knelt down and kissed her father's hand and said, "Don't worry about me, father. You must fulfill your oath the the gods. But I ask you to give me forty days to celebrate your victory with my girlfriends before I die!"

The King wiped his tears and agreed to grant her this request.

Hanna called together all her girlfriends in the Kingdom and told them of her father's oath and her planned celebration. Her friends prepared large quantities of meat, vegetables, fruits, eggs, and other kinds of food and drinks and carried it all to the top of the mountain, where they celebrated for forty days and nights.

After forty days had passed, Hanna bid her friends farewell and asked them to remember her by celebrating in the same way every year. She then returned to her father, and he fulfilled his oath by cutting off her head.

Year after year, Hanna's girlfriends carried large quantities of food and drinks with them to the top of the mountain and celebrated there by feasting, dancing and singing for forty days and nights. Throughout the years, Hanna's girlfriends grew older and got married and spread out in the world. This celebration was transmitted down the centuries from one place to another.

As time passed and Christianity spread in the region, the legend underwent several changes. The story lost its pagan context and implications and was adopted by Christianity. Hanna now became the daughter of a priest, and a song was sung for Hanna which has been handed down orally from one generation to another. "Hanno Hanno Karetho barthat Kasho Metho."

People began to celebrate the feast of *Hanno Karetho* before the great Lenten fast. The inhabitants of the village of Jiser in Malkieh, situated in northeastern Syria, celebrate it every year before starting their Lenten fast by dancing and singing special songs.

Every year, the people of Jiser make a wooden statue of a girl and dress her in clothes. The young girls of the village walk around carrying this wooden doll as they sing, *"Hanno Hanno Karetho barthat Kasho Metho."* The girls knock on every door asking for eggs, meat, and burghol while the villagers sprinkle water on them and offer them the food they have requested. Then the women cook a big meal for the whole village to eat with the food the girls have collected - in celebration of the memory of Hanna. At the end the statuette, with Hanna's share of the food, is buried in the sand. Then the girls go around the church and sing *Istiskaa* songs (songs praying for rain). It seems that this celebration is also related to old rituals to bring the rain. The girls also sing an old song which has been transmitted orally from one generation to another which is about a shepherd who fell in love with a girl named Hanna and wanted to marry her:

HANNO KARETHO'S CELEBRATION:

Hanna, Hanna, oh Daughter of the Village,
Oh Daughter of the Dead Priest
Standing in the corner with her belt untied.
Your father, where has he gone?
To the barn to fetch a spindle for the evening.
Oh come, Hanna, you have filled my life with joy!
Our love for each other has become a love story.
The road in front of us is lit with candles,
People sing of the beauty of your eyes,
If you love me, you will marry me even if I'm poor
You will tell your parents that I can't give you a dowry.

Seven years I've been waiting, a shepherd I've become
To give your father the light, your mother to please.
Tomorrow we'll get married and have a wedding -
We'll dance in the fields of Albedar!
A house we will build, and children we will have;
We will eat a good meal made by your hands.
With an oil lantern, we will knock on every door
We will sing for Hanna and take what we can.
Tomorrow we will eat burghol for lunch,
We will keep some food aside for poor Hanna to eat.

I have my friend Marah Idou, who is an Assyrian Syrian, to thank
for all the information on the feast of Hanno Karetho. Marah stud-
ies engineering at the Higher Institute of Applied Science and
Technology in Damascus and was a student of my husband. She
participated in this celebration for many years and said the song
"Hanno Hanno Karetho barthat Kasho Metho" is sung in Syriac
and is accompanied by a special dance. Her translation of the
above song is, "Hanna, Hanna of Karetho, Daughter of the Dead

Priest." She told me that 'Hanno' is 'Hanna' in colloquial Syriac in the Jazira (the area she comes from) and 'Karetho' is the name of the village. She used to sing in the choir in her village and dance the traditional dances before the recent war erased everything.

The Assyrian lunar calendar is the most ancient calendar still in use today. In the Assyrian calendar, New Year's Day – which is called "Akitu" – falls on April 1st. On this day, the sun and the moon are in perfect balance with each other and the days and nights are equal in length. In the past, it was considered the most important religious celebration held in Bet Nahrain; a revival of nature after death. April 1, 2016 begins the 6766th year of the Assyrian calendar and, to this day, it is still a very important holiday for the Assyrians. Marah Idou remembers celebrating New Year's Day on the first day of April, when she and her family used to go on picnics with many of their friends. They would set up a barbecue and sing and dance the traditional songs and dances.

Early in the morning before the children wake up, Assyrians still pick a bunch of green grass which they call *Thaken Nissan,* or April's Beard, to hang in the entrance of their homes. Then people go out in the fields and celebrate the arrival of April, the good month. Assyrians usually get married during this month in an attempt to have nature be a part of their celebrations.

Now, says Marah Idou, it is all just a beautiful memory, and she has no photos left of those days because of the war. I also have Marah to thank for the following three Assyrian recipes.

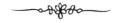

Three Assyrian Recipes
Burghol and *Kilyeh* (Meat)

"Kilyeh" is meat fried in fat and preserved for the winter. People used to make it in the old days, before refrigeration. It was usually cooked with burghol or fried with eggs. Nowadays, fresh meat is used.

Ingredients

1 lb lamb meat cut in pieces

2 cups coarse burghol

2 tbsp vegetable oil

Salt to taste

Method

Wash burghol and drain well

Cook meat for 40 minutes or until done

Remove meat and put broth aside

Fry burghol a little with vegetable oil

Add 4 cups of broth, cover and simmer on low flame 15 minutes.

Add the pieces of meat and salt to taste on top of the burghol and cook for five more minutes or until the burghol is done

Remove the pieces of meat and place the burghol on large serving plate

Garnish the burghol with pieces of meat

Serve hot with bowls of yogurt

Assyrian Cookies

Ingredients

½ cup butter

¼ cup shortening

½ cup sugar

2 beaten eggs

1 tsp vanilla

3 cups all-purpose flour

2 tsp baking powder

½ tsp baking soda

¼ tsp salt

¼ tsp cinnamon

¼ tsp nutmeg

½ cup whipping cream

½ cup sesame seeds

Method

In mixing bowl, cream butter, shortening, and sugar

Add one of the eggs and vanilla and beat well

Sift flour, baking powder, baking soda, salt, cinnamon, and nutmeg together

Add dry ingredients to creamed mixture, alternately with whipping cream

Beat well after each addition

Cover and chill 1 hour

On floured surface, use 1 tbsp dough for each cookie

Roll dough into 6-inch lengths

Shape into wreaths

Mix remaining egg and 1 tsp water to brush cookies, then top with sesame seeds

Bake at 325 degrees for 20 minutes

Makes 3 ½ to 4 dozen

Assyrian Traditional Salad

Ingredients

    3 cucumbers

    2 tomatoes

    1 green pepper

    1 small red onion

    1 tbsp vinegar

    2 tbsp olive oil

Method

    Peel cucumbers and cut them into cubes

    Dice tomatoes, red onion, and green pepper into small cubes

    Place vegetables into a large bowl

    Mix olive oil, vinegar, and salt to taste and toss with other ingredients

8

UZBEKS

Uzbeks speak a Turkic language and are descended from a mixture of Middle Eastern Caucasians, Central Asian Turks and Mongols, Iranians and other peoples. Uzbekistan is located in the heart of Central Asia, between two large rivers, Amu Darya and Syr Darya. Uzbekistan is one of only two countries in the world that is doubly landlocked – that is, it is completely surrounded by other landlocked countries. It is known for its fabled cities that were waystations on the ancient Silk Road: Samarkand, Bukhara, Khiva, Tashkent, and Fergana.

The Arabs brought Islam to Central Asia in the 8th century, and in this and the following century the area experienced a truly golden age. Bukhara became one of the leading centers of learning, culture, and art in the Muslim world. Some of the greatest historians, scientists, geographers, and scholars in the history of Islamic culture were natives of this region. An illustrious example is the religious scholar Imam Mohammad ibn Ismael al Bukhari. He is the compiler of the "Sahih Bukhari" (sahih meaning "sound" or "authentic"), a collection of traditions (*hadith*) that report the sayings and actions of the Prophet Mohammed (pbuh). It is one of the most important books after the Qur'an to Sunni Muslims.

After the Arabs, there followed a period of rule by Turkic tribes, followed by the rule of Ghengiz Khan and his descendants, and afterwards Timurlane and his descendants. However, by 1510, the Uzbeks completed their conquest of Central Asia, including the territory of the present-day Uzbekistan. In the centuries that followed, many different Uzbek khanates were established.

In the 18th and 19th centuries, the Russian Empire began to look greedily at Central Asia, and by the turn of the 20th century, all of Uzbekistan was under the Tsar's control. The Uzbeks were not happy with Russian rule, but things grew worse after the Bolshevik Revolution. Uzbeks fought the Soviets for independence, but the Red Army conquered them and viciously tore down their cities and villages, and some Uzbeks began to flee from the violence.

Uzbeks immigrated to Arab countries at different times and for different reasons. Statistics show that the first Uzbeks settled in Damascus in the 17th century. Some of them settled there on their way back from the Pilgrimage to Mecca. However, it was the Soviet Revolution that caused the greatest wave of Uzbek immigration. From 1917 to 1922, thousands of Uzbeks fled their country and entered Syria.

It is said that Uzbeks were called 'Bukharis' in Syria, either because they came from the same place as Imam Mohammad ibn Ismael al Bukhari or because they came from the Islamic Emirate of Bukhara.

When the Bukharis arrived in Damascus in the 1920s, they were well received by the Damascenes. They settled in the Azbakiyeh, Mohajareen, and Salhieh areas and the Nabaa neighborhood on the slope of Qasioun Mountain. In the Midan district, they established their own neighborhood in the fields. They also built mosques and founded schools which enrolled their own people and Damascenes as well. The last of these schools was in Shora and graduated some important people before it closed in the 1950s. The Uzbeks also established their own commercial trades in different neighborhoods of the city such as Mohajareen, Salhieh, Souk Sarouja, Midan, and part of the Hijaz.

Due to intermarriage, the Uzbek language was forgotten by the second generation. Nevertheless, the traditional Bukhari foods survived from one generation to another, especially Bukhari rice. Also, although more than seventy years have passed since their immigration and settlement in Syria, their distinctive Uzbek features haven't changed.

Most of the Uzbeks live in Damascus, although some settled in Aleppo. The Uzbek families in Syria are not related to each other, even though they share the same last name – "Bukhari." They came from different places in Uzbekistan and immigrated to Syria at different periods of time.

There are about 10,000 Syrian citizens of Uzbek origin living in Syria, including doctors, lawyers, teachers, Merchants, artisans, and government employees. One of the successful descendants of the Bukharis was Nasouh al Bukhari, who was born in Damascus 1888. He became Prime Minister of Syria in 1939. It can be said that the Uzbeks assimilated into Damascene society and helped wholeheartedly in building their adopted country. Of course, as with the other ethnic groups in Syria, the civil war has caused some Uzbeks to leave Syria and some to return to Uzbekistan.

I became acquainted with Dr. Mohammad al Bukhari, a professor of political science, on Facebook. Dr. al Bukhari was the son of a high-ranking general who sought refuge in Syria after the Red Army occupied Bukhara. Dr. al Bukhari's father formerly worked in the Palace of a Bukhari Emir. In the seventies, Dr. al Bukhari left Syria and returned to his homeland, where he has been living ever since. When I asked him for information about the Syrian Uzbeks, he very kindly referred me to a paper he wrote in 2014,

"The History of the Uzbekistani People in Syria." I am indebted to Dr. al Bukhari for much of the information in this chapter.

Four Uzbek Folktales

When I asked Dr. al Bukhari to give me the Bukhari rice recipe, he asked me if I lived in Damascus. "Yes," I said.

"Then all you have to do is to go to Souk Sarouja neighborhood, where most of the owners of the jewelry stores are Bukhari," he said. "Just ask one of them and they will give you the recipe."

I hesitated and explained that shells were randomly falling there and it was dangerous to leave the house, so he did agree to give me the recipe. However, in a matter of months, feeling desperate to find more Uzbek folktales, I chose a quiet day and took a bus to the Souk Sarouja neighborhood.*

A kind-looking old woman with her husband, both of whom had Uzbek features, happened to sit next to me on the bus. Exchanging conversation with them, it turned out to be my lucky day. They told me that their grandparents had immigrated to Damascus in the 1920s, and they introduced themselves as Abo and Um Muhammad, father and mother of Mohammed. Mohammed, their oldest son, had gone back to Uzbekistan five years earlier, at the beginning of the civil war, and now they were planning to join him, since he had found a good job.

I told Um Mohammad that I was collecting folktales and asked her if she could kindly tell me one. Um Mohammed looked surprised at my question, for she had never been asked to tell an Uzbek story by anyone other than her own grandchildren.

---

* Muna means a day in which there was no bombing or shelling

She cracked a big smile, collected her thoughts, and started spinning a story for me. As I listened, I was caught up in her words and forgot about the endless checkpoints. Suddenly, I realized to my shock that I was far out of my way! I thanked Um Mohammad, gave her a hug, left the bus, and ran to catch a taxi home.

Three Gold Watermelons

Once upon a time, a long time ago, there was a poor peasant who spent his days working constantly in his very small field. One fine spring day, the peasant began to plow his field. After he had plowed the field two times, he sat down to rest on the bank of a nearby river. Suddenly, a stork flying overhead fell out of the sky. The peasant got up to see why the stork had fallen and found that one of its wings was broken. He immediately brought the stork home and tied a splint to its wing, and for some time he took care of the stork. When the stork's wing was healed, it flew away.

Time passed. One day, when the peasant was planting cotton seed, the same stork passed over him, flying low. The peasant did not take any notice and continued planting his cotton seed. However, the stork flew over the field again, and this time it dropped three watermelon seeds. After several days, the watermelon seeds started to grow together with the cotton seeds. The peasant weeded, irrigated, and hoed his planted field in season.

Finally, it was time to harvest his field. One day, he picked three watermelons and brought them home. The watermelons were very big, so the peasant invited his close relatives and friends to share them with him. When he struck his knife into the first watermelon, his knife could not cut through it. He put the watermelon aside and took the second one, but his knife did not pass through it either, and the same thing happened with the third watermelon. The peasant was surprised and so were his guests. When they dropped one of the watermelons on the ground, it split open, and what did they see? The watermelon was full of gold coins! Then they dropped the remaining two melons on the ground and they, too, were full of gold coins. The poor man was very happy and he shared the gold with his guests and they happily went home.

When the peasant returned to his field, he found the three watermelon seeds had multiplied ten times. He harvested all the remaining watermelons and became very rich.

The peasant had a rich neighbor. One day the rich man asked the peasant, "How did you become so rich?"

The peasant told him this story, "Neighbor, you know my field. I started to plow the land in early spring. One day when I was tired and taking a rest on the river bank, a stork fell out of the sky. I saw that one of its wings was broken and felt sorry for it. I picked up the stork and carried it home. I tied a splint to its broken wing and took care of it. After some days, the stork was completely healed and flew away. Later on, when I had finished plowing and started to plant cotton seeds, the same stork flew over me as I was working. A while later, the stork came back and, when it was flying over me, it dropped three watermelon seeds. These seeds sprouted and grew, and I took care of them together with my cotton plants. When I cut the watermelons open, there was gold inside them. In this way, I became rich."

Upon hearing this, the rich farmer thought, "If I only could get hold of this gold myself," and he went to the bank of the nearby river, looking for a stork. When he saw one, he quietly crept closer, picked up a stone and threw it at the stork's leg, breaking it. Then he caught the stork, brought it home, and tied a splint to its leg.

As time passed, he took care of the stork and when its leg was healed, it flew away. The rich farmer went every day to the field and waited for the stork to appear. One day that same familiar stork flew above him, dropped two seeds and flew away.

The seeds started to grow and became watermelons. As soon as the watermelons ripened, the rich man invited all his relatives. He set one watermelon on the table and took out his knife, hoping for a shower of gold. However, when he cut the watermelon open, a swarm of large hornets flew out of the watermelon and started to sting the guests sitting at the table.

The rich man jumped up and tried to drive the hornets away, but the hornets attacked him and stung his head and face. In a short while the rich man's head, nose and lips started to swell and swell. He could not bear the pain and threw himself into the river and drowned.

Once again, as in the story of "The Woodcutter," the good men are rewarded with gold coins and the bad men get hornets or wasps.

Two Stubborn Goats

This folktale was told to me by an old woman whom I met at a bus stop. Although she spoke perfect Arabic, she had Asian features. When I repeated this story to Dr. al Bukhari, he thought that it didn't have the distinct features of Uzbek stories, but in my opinion, change is typical of folktales. As folktales travel, they are affected by the localities that embrace them. Also, every time a folkate is told, it may change. I remember hearing folktales originally told to me by my Tete being retold by my aunt to my own children in a different style, with modern touches added.

Once upon a time, there were two goats that lived in neighboring villages. One was white and the other was black, and both were very stubborn. Every day they crossed a very narrow bridge to graze on the grass of their opposite meadows.

One day, the two goats crossed the bridge at the same time and met in the middle of the narrow bridge. "Let me pass!" said the black goat.

"No!" said the white goat lowering his huge head so the curved horns were pointed at the black goat, "You get out of my way!"

"Back up," said the black goat. "I began to cross the bridge first!"

"You back up," said the white goat. "I am going to be the first to cross!"

The two goats quarreled with each other all day and neither could go forward and both refused to go backward. At last they pointed their horns at each other, locked horns, and pushed each other until they lost their balance and fell off the bridge into the river below.

Angry and wet, they both trampled out of the river. Then they both shook off the water and walked away, still hungry.

The Cauldron That Died

One day, Nasriddin Afandi needed a large cooking pot because he was having guests. He borrowed his neighbor's copper cauldron and then returned it in a timely manner.

"What is this?" asked his neighbor upon examining the returned cauldron. "There is a small pot inside my cauldron."

"Oh," responded the Afandi. "While it was in my care, your cauldron gave birth to a little one. Because you are the owner of the mother cauldron, it is only right that you should keep its baby.

And in any event, it would not be right to separate the child from its mother at such a young age."

The neighbor, thinking that the Afandi had gone quite mad, did not argue. Whatever had caused the crazy man to come up with this explanation, the neighbor had gained a nice little pot, and it had cost him nothing.

Some time later, the Afandi asked to borrow the cauldron again.

"Why not?" thought the neighbor to himself. "Perhaps there will be another little pot inside when he returns it."

But this time the Afandi did not return the cauldron. After many days had passed, the neighbor went to the Afandi and asked him to return the borrowed cauldron.

"My dear friend," replied the Afandi. "I have bad news. Your cauldron has died, and is now in her grave."

"What are you saying?" shouted the neighbor. "A cauldron does not live, and it cannot die. Return it to me at once!"

"One moment." answered the Afandi. "This is the same cauldron that only a short time ago gave birth to a child, a child that is still in your possession. If a cauldron can give birth to a child, then it can also die."

And the neighbor never saw his cauldron again.

THE THREE CLEVER BROTHERS

Once upon a time, there lived a poor man who had three clever sons. Although the father was not rich, he gave his sons something more valuable than gold and silver; he taught them how to use their minds.

Years passed and the father grew old and sick and felt that death was near. He called his three sons to his side and said, "My dear, clever boys, I feel that I'm dying. I have no gold or silver to leave for you, nor land, nor herds. But I raised you to be clever and to use your minds. Notice everything you see. Observe and learn. Your fine abilities will help you well." Then he turned his face away and died.

The three brothers mourned their father and, after a while, decided to leave their village to seek their fortunes and increase their knowledge.

They set out walking and, after many days, came to a road leading to a great city. The eldest brother said, "A large camel has passed this way."

"Yes," said the second brother, "And he was blind in one eye."

Farther down the road, the youngest brother said, "A woman and a small child were riding on that camel."

As they proceeded, they came upon a man on horseback who was clearly searching for someone or something. The eldest brother called out, "Are you looking for a large camel?"

"Yes," cried the man.

"And was the camel blind in one eye?" asked the second brother.

"Yes, yes."

"And was a woman with a child riding on it?" said the youngest brother.

"Yes! Where are they?"

"We have not seen them," said the second brother, "But if you ride to the east, you might catch up with them."

"Thieves!" cried the man. "What have you done with them? I demand you follow me to the Shah."

He led the men to the Palace of the Shah, and there he told the guards that the brothers were thieves, so the guards threw them into a dungeon. Finally, they were brought before the Shah in chains.

"How do you know these young men are thieves?" asked the Shah.

"I will tell you," said the horseman. "I was driving my herds to the mountains, and my wife and child were following. Somehow, they lagged behind and lost their way. When I came searching for them, these young men asked if I was looking for a large camel, blind in one eye, with a woman and child riding on it. Then they claimed they'd never seen them but that I would find them by traveling east."

The Shah turned to the prisoners. "Thieves!" he cried. "What have you done with them?"

"We are not thieves," replied the eldest brother. "We haven't seen his camel or his wife and child. From childhood on, our father taught us to observe and learn. We notice things that others miss."

The Shah thought for a time. Then he said, "I will put you to the test." He called his Vizier to him and whispered something in his ear.

The Vizier left the palace. He soon returned with two servants carrying a large chest. They set it down in front of the Shah.

"Now then," said the Shah, "Suppose you tell me what is in this chest."

The eldest brother said at once, "A small, round object."

"A pomegranate," said the second brother.

"A green pomegranate," added the youngest brother.

The Shah ordered the vizier to open the chest, and all were amazed to see that it indeed held one green pomegranate.

"Well done," the Shah laughed. "Tell us how you knew that."

The eldest brother spoke first. "I could tell from the way your servants carried the chest that it was not heavy, and when they lowered it, I heard something roll from one end to the other."

The middle brother said, "I saw the direction the servants entered from. I had seen pomegranate trees in your garden earlier."

"And at this time of year, pomegranates are not yet ripe," added the youngest brother.

"I am impressed," the Shah said, smiling. He turned to the horseman. "You should search for your camel by traveling east, as they told you."

The Shah then ordered food and drink for the brothers. "Tell me," he said, "how did you know so much about his camel?"

"I saw the tracks of a large camel as we were walking along," said the eldest brother.

"I knew it was blind in one eye because it nibbled grass only on one side of the road," said the middle brother.

The youngest added, "We came to a place where the camel knelt down. There in the sand I saw prints of a woman's boots and those of a child."

The Shah stood up. "I need men like you around me. You are rich in wisdom. If you are willing, you shall be my palace Counselors."

The brothers happily agreed and silently thanked their father for their good fortune.

Proverbs

- Your house is your house, even though it is small.
- The castle is not your castle, even though it is large.
- Even a piece of stone earned by your work is better than bread brought to you without work.
- When people gather together, they form a river.
- When they scatter, they become a stream.
- I'll burn my tongue if I speak, but I'll burn my heart if I keep silent.
- Be truthful and don't lie - even if the sword is over your head.
- Even if you find the door open, knock before you enter.
- A mouse doesn't approach a cat unless it has no hope in life.

Three Uzbek Recipes

Ruz Bukhari — Bukhari Rice

This recipe was given to me by Dr. Al Bukhari, as I mentioned earlier. It was brought to Syria by the Uzbek immigrants at the beginning of the twentieth century and is considered the pride of every Uzbek family. There are many versions of this recipe. It may be cooked with chicken, meat or vegetables. I was told that Uzbek men are very skillful in cooking this rice.

Ingredients for lamb/chicken broth

- 1 ginger stick
- 1 cinnamon stick
- 3 bay leaves
- 3 cardamom pods
- 1 tsp anise
- Salt and pepper to taste
- 3½ tbsp butter
- ½ cup of oil
- ¼ tsp clove powder
- ¼ tsp cinnamon powder
- 4 sliced onions
- 1 tbsp coriander powder
- 1 cut quince (small pieces)
- 5 carrots, cut into matchsticks
- 4 tomatoes, skinned and sliced
- 2 lbs chopped lamb (or 1 skinned and cut chicken)
- 6-8 whole cloves
- 10 garlic cloves
- 1 Maggi (bouillon) cube
- 3 tbsp tomato paste
- Water to cover
- Fresh cut coriander leaves

Method for lamb/chicken

Lb in mortar: ginger and cinnamon sticks, cardamom pods, anise, salt, and pepper and set aside

Heat oil and butter in pan; add clove powder, cinnamon powder

When aroma rises, add chopped onions and sauté until light brown

Add coriander powder and sauté

Add cut quince and sauté

Add carrots and sauté

Add sliced tomatoes and sauté

Add chopped meat or chicken and continue to sauté

Add bay leaves, cloves, garlic, tomato paste, Maggi cube, and water to cover

Cover and cook until meat is tender – add water as needed to just cover

Remove from heat, remove bay leaves, garnish with coriander leaves and set aside

Ingredients for rice

- 4 cups long grain rice
- 6 cups water
- 1 tbsp salt
- 1 cinnamon stick
- 3 cardamom pods
- 1 bay leaf
- 3 cloves
- 4 carrots, cut in matchsticks
- 2 tbsp oil
- 1 tbsp tomato paste
- ½ cup almonds
- ½ cup raisins

Method for Rice

Boil water, add salt, and set aside

Heat oil in pan and add cinnamon, cardamom, bay leaf, cloves and carrots

When the aroma of the spices is released, add rice and stir

When the color of the rice begins to turn light brown, add raisins and boiled water

Cover and simmer until rice is tender and water absorbed

Remove rice from heat

Add cooked meat and carrots and mix well, then cover tightly

When water is absorbed, uncover and let cool

Place the rice in a serving plate (remove bay leaf)

Garnish with fried almonds

HALEEM — WHEAT PORRIDGE WITH MEAT

Like the Kurds, the Uzbeks celebrate New Year's Day on the spring equinox, and while the Kurds call it "Newroz," the Uzbeks call the holiday "Navruz." Haleem is a special dish prepared the night before this holiday, and it is usually cooked by men. It is quite similar to the Armenian porridge Harissa. Both are porridges with meat that require a very long cooking time and constant stirring.

Ingredients

2 lbs of wheat grain

1 lb 5 ounces (600 grams) beef or lamb

1¾ cups vegetable oil

Salt, cinnamon, and ground pepper to taste

Method

Crush wheat grains with a mortar and pestle

Rinse in water to separate husks

Sift and soak in hot water for five hours

Cut meat into small cubes and simmer in hot oil

Add soaked wheat and water

Cook on low heat for 1 ½ hours, stirring constantly. This results in a brown porridge

Add salt to taste

Pour into bowls and season with ground black pepper and cinnamon

SUMALAK — NEW YEAR'S DAY PORRIDGE

This is a well-known dish among the first Uzbekistani generation that immigrated to Syria in 1920. It was cooked to celebrate the beginning of the New Year "Navruz," which brings happiness, luck, and joy to everyone. It is an ancient national dish which has been cooked for centuries only by women who sing, dance, and tell stories while they prepare the dish.

Ingredients

    2 lbs wheat grains

    8 lbs flour

    1 cup vegetable oil

    Water as needed

    Seven washed pebbles

Method

    Two weeks before Navruz, begin sprouting 2 lbs of wheat grains in a large container placed in a dark place

    When the wheat stems are about 10 centimeters high, cut them up, grind them, and squeeze out the juices

    Put them in a large pot with 8 lbs flour, ½ cup oil, and as much water as needed to cook it

    Add seven pebbles to the pot to keep the sumalak from scorching

    Stir constantly while cooking on low heat for a couple of hours until the porridge turns thick, brown, and sweet

    Serve immediately

Two Legends about the origin of Sumalak

An old Uzbek woman told me these legends, although Dr. Bukhari said he had never heard of them and that Sumalak is merely a dish prepared in the spring. Perhaps he is right; nevertheless, I think the reader will enjoy both legends.

Fatima's Porridge

Once upon a time, there lived a widow named Fatima who had two boys, Hasan and Husain. Fatima was very poor and had very little food to feed her sons, who were always crying from hunger. One evening, Fatima became so concerned about her sons that she decided to cook something for them although she had no food in the house. She asked her neighbor for some wheat, oil and flour and put it all in a large pot with some water. She also threw in a handful of pebbles so that they would make sounds and stop her sons' crying. As Fatima stirred the food in the pot, she sang and put herself to sleep.

When Fatima woke up in the early morning, she saw thirty angels standing around the pot, stirring. Fatima rubbed her eyes in disbelief. To her great surprise, a delicious porridge was bubbling in the pot. She ran to her sons and woke them up, and they excitedly filled their bowls with the porridge. From that day on, Hasan and Husain never went hungry.

People named the porridge *Sumalak,* which the old Uzbek woman told me means "thirty angels" in their language.

The Magic Porridge

A long time ago, there was a fortress town on the banks of the Djeikhan River that was under siege by nomads from the East. When the food in the fortress was all finished except for a few sacks of soggy, sprouted wheat, the general of the fortress ordered his soldiers to take those spoiled sacks to the cooks. Then he told the cooks to make some porridge from the wheat.

The cooks had nothing to add but a little flour and oil. They put it all in a pot with some water and stirred the mixture and hoped it would taste good.

When the soldiers were served the porridge, they felt a sudden burst of great energy. They picked up their arms and ran to drive off the enemy that held them under siege, and they fought until all the enemy soldiers retreated. The victorious soldiers cheered the end of the siege. Since that day, sumalak has become a special national dish that is believed to give people physical and spiritual power.

9

ALBANIANS (ARNAOUTS)

The first Albanians who arrived in Syria numbered about a thousand and were known as the "Arnaout," a name which refers to the people who came from the four states in the Western Balkans: Kosovo, Shkodra, Manastir, and Yanina. They came to Syria with Muhammad Ali Pasha, an Ottoman Albanian commander who led the Egyptian invasion of Syria in 1831. After the withdrawal of his army in 1840, these Albanians stayed on in Syria. Since the Ottoman Empire called Albania "luk" and its people "Arnaout," the common name for people from Albania in Syria became "Arnaout." Many of them use "Arnaout" as a family name to distinguish themselves as part of the ethnic Albanian minority.

In the 20th century, Albanians came to Syria from two places and during two eras. The first and largest wave of immigration came during the Balkan war of 1912-1913. Most of these Albanians came from Kosovo. When Kosovo was occupied by Serbia during the the Balkan wars and annexed to the Kingdom of Yugoslavia, Muslim Albanians were pressured to migrate to the east. As a result, thousands of Albanians immigrated to Damascus.

The second immigration wave took place in 1920, when Albania's Prime Minister, Ahmad Zogho, competed with Kemal

Ataturk in legislating secular reforms in his country. As a result, many unhappy religious Albanian families immigrated to Greater Syria, which at that time included Syria, Lebanon, Palestine, and Jordan.

When the Arnaouts first arrived in Syria, they worked in various trades and struggled under very hard circumstances. However, they all did remarkably well in different areas of society.

Some of the Arnaouts who made an important contribution to Syria include Marouf Arnaout (1892-1948), who is considered one of the pioneers of the novel and the theater in Syria, the famous actor Yasin Arnaout, as well as three great religious scholars who are experts in the science of Hadith and verifying the accuracy of Arab Islamic tradition: Nasiruddin Albani, Abdul Kader Arnaout, and Shoaib Arnaout. Their fame spread from Syria throughout the Muslim world.

In the last quarter of the 20th century, the community produced many doctors, engineers, and researchers. Also at this time, another small migration came to Syria of religious clerics who rejected the idea of Albania turning into a secular country.

There were about ten thousand Syrian Albanians before the war. Most of them lived in Damascus, while a few lived in Homs, Hama, Aleppo, and Latakia.

Those who settled in Damascus lived in the Diwaniya neighborhood, where there is still a mosque called the Mosque of Arnaout. In the second half of the 20th century, some of the Arnaouts moved to the south of Damascus to al Kadam, where they established their own district near the shrine built by Wali al-Sham Ahmad Arnaout in the seventeenth century.

The Albanians immigrated to Damascus with open hearts and considered the city sacred, referring to it as 'Sham Shareef' (Damascus the Noble) and their aim was to learn more about their religion and to learn to speak Arabic. In return, Damascenes received them very warmly, and they easily integrated into the local population. There is a Damascene saying that says, "Lucky is the one who has an Arnaout neighbor." Many of them intermarried with Damascene families, assimilated completely, and didn't preserve their Albanian traditions, culture, or language.

Two Arnaout Folktales

The few Albanians in Damascus who have retained their language are mostly of the old generation; in general, the young generation only speaks Arabic. This makes it much more difficult to find Albanian folktales and recipes.

One spring day in a park, I happened to sit down next to a sweet old lady with a radiant, peaceful face. She was crocheting a baby blanket which I admired. After some conversation, I found out that her grandfather had immigrated to Damascus in the beginning of the 20th century from Albania. As she knit the blanket, her words skillfully wove these two folktales that she had heard from her grandparents.

The Tale of Two Brothers

Once upon a time, there lived two brothers who were very different from one another. The older one was very wicked and greedy, while the younger one was kind-hearted and generous.

One day they decided to travel through the world and seek their fortune. On their way, they saw an old man in white with a long, gray beard carrying a bag. The old man asked the two brothers where they were going.

When he heard that they were seeking their fortune, he put his right hand in his pocket and said, "I want to help you, my dear boys," and he pulled out a handful of gold coins and asked "Who wants these?"

"I want them," called out the older brother.

The old man put his left hand in his other pocket and pulled out a precious gem and asked the two brothers, "Who wants this precious gem?"

"I want it!" shouted out the older brother. The old man smiled and gave him the golden coins and the gem.

Then he pointed at his heavy sack on the ground and asked the two brothers, "Who is going to help me carry this sack?"

The younger brother rushed to the old man and willingly carried the bag for the old man and asked him, "Where is your house?"

The old man smiled and said, "The bag is my gift to you for your kindness."

The younger brother opened the bag and found it was full of precious gems. He raised up his head to thank the old man, but to his great surprise, he had vanished.

THE MAGIC RING

Once upon a time, there was a poor woman who lived with her simple son, Ahmad. She was a widow and spun yarn day and night for a living.

One day, she gave some yarn to Ahmad to sell in the market and said, "Go sell the yarn and buy us a loaf of bread."

Ahmad sold the yarn and went to a bakery to buy a loaf of bread. When he reached the bakery, he heard some children crying because the baker was about to kill an old dog.

Ahmad was very affected and begged the baker to leave the dog alone, "Please don't kill the dog," said Ahmad.

The baker was very annoyed with Ahmad and pushed him away.

Ahmad asked him, "Will you sell the dog to me?"

The baker smiled happily and said, "I will, indeed!"

Ahmad paid the baker for the dog with most of his money, leaving only enough to buy food for the dog. When he returned home with the dog and told his mother what had happened, she scolded him, saying, "You are such a fool!" Then she returned to her spindle to spin more yarn.

The next day, she gave Ahmad the new yarn to sell. Ahmad sold the yarn, but he was startled at the sound of loud yowling. To his surprise, he saw a woman about to kill a big cat.

Without hesitating, Ahmad bought the cat from the woman and purchased some fish for the cat to eat.

When he got home, he let the cat into the house and said, "Mother, I bought you a beautiful cat to eat the mice!"

His mother flew into a rage and shook her head angrily. "You fool!" she said. "We have no mice in our house because there's nothing for them to eat here!"

Again, she returned to her spindle to spin more yarn.

The next day, after Ahmad had sold the yarn, he saw a farmer beating a donkey. Ahmad was horrified and said, "Don't kill the donkey. I'll buy it!"

So Ahmad bought the donkey and spent the rest of his money to buy him straw. When Ahmad arrived home, dragging the old donkey, his mother almost fainted. She was so furious that she locked herself in her room and spun more yarn, but this time, she sold it herself.

One day, when Ahmad rode his donkey to the forest to chop some wood, he saw a fire burning under a tree.

When he got near the fire, he saw a small snake trapped in the fire. "Save me," called out the snake.

"You will bite me!" said Ahmad.

"No, I promise you will be generously rewarded," said the snake.

Ahmad rescued the snake from the fire and the snake thanked him and asked Ahmad follow him to his cave so that his mother could reward him.

On their way to the cave, the snake said, "I advise you not to accept anything from my mother but the ring she keeps under her tongue."

When they arrived at the cave, the mother snake was about to bite Ahmad, but the small snake called out, "Please Mother, don't bite him! He saved me from a fire." The mother snake sprung away but the small snake called out again, "Please Mother, please give him a reward for saving my life!"

The mother snake asked Ahmad what he wanted as a reward.

"All I want is the ring under your tongue," said Ahmad.

The mother snake gave him the ring and said, "The ring will give you everything you desire. Be careful not to ever lose it!"

When Ahmad returned home, he called to his mother, "I'm hungry, Mother, let's have supper."

"I'm sorry, my dear Son," said the mother. "We have nothing in the house to eat."

Ahmad grinned widely and said, "Come over here and I'll fill the table with lots of delicious food."

As his mother approached the table, Ahmad rubbed the ring and said, "Ring, Ring, fill the the table with all kinds of delicious food!"

In the wink of an eye, his wish was granted and the table was full of delicious food. When they finished their meal, Ahmad asked his mother to go to the King and ask for the hand of the Princess.

His mother was shocked. She let out a deep sigh and said, "Have you lost your mind?"

Ahmad assured his mother that he knew exactly what he was doing, and said, "Please, Mother, go tell the King that your son wants to marry his daughter!"

So the mother went to the King and told him that her son wished to marry his daughter.

The King laughed at the poor woman's request and said, "Tell your son that if he can build a palace better than mine, he can marry my daughter!"

The mother returned home and told Ahmad what the King had said.

Ahmad took out the magic ring and rubbed it and asked for a palace better than the King's.

At once, a magnificent palace appeared next to the King's palace. So the mother returned to the King and and asked again for his daughter's hand.

The King was astonished to see Ahmad's palace next to his, but he said, "Tell your son he must pave a road of silver leading from my palace to his!"

The mother returned to her son and told him what the King had said.

Ahmad held the magic ring and rubbed it and asked it to pave a road of silver between the King's palace and his. At once, the silver road appeared.

The mother returned to the King to ask for his daughter's hand, but the King said, "I will consent to marry my daughter to your son on the condition that he fills his palace with grander furniture than mine!"

Again, Ahmad took out his magic ring and rubbed it and wished for his palace to be filled with the most elegant furniture in the world.

When his request was granted, Ahmad's mother accompanied the King to the palace to see the grand furniture. Everything was as the King had demanded, and the wedding date was set.

After the wedding was celebrated, the Princess decided that she didn't like her husband Ahmad and planned to get rid of him as soon as she gained possession of his magic ring.

One day, Ahmad forgot the magic ring on the table and the Princess happily picked it up and rubbed it and said, "Oh Magic Ring, take me to the other side of the Black Sea and send my husband Ahmad back to his old house!"

Immediately, the Princess was carried to the other side of the Black Sea and Ahmad and his mother were back in their old house.

Ahmad was very upset and searched for his magic ring everywhere but could not find it.

His dog licked his hand and his cat rubbed its head against his hand and then they both said, "Don't worry, we will go and search for the magic ring!"

So the dog and the cat set out together to search for the magic ring. When they arrived at the Black Sea, the cat climbed on the dog's back and they swam to the other side. It was dark by then, so they decided to spend the night in an old cottage.

In the middle of the night, they heard some sounds behind the wooden walls. They hid behind the curtains and suddenly, many mice appeared. The King of Mice was getting married and all the mice were celebrating.

As soon as the King and his bride entered the room, the cat leapt from behind the curtains and frightened them all to death. They scampered away in different directions.

The cat called the mice to come back, "Don't be afraid, dear Mice," he said. "I will not hurt you. I need your help to find a magic ring, but if you don't help me, I'll eat the bride!" So the mice agreed to help find the ring and they set out to find the Princess.

They reached the palace where the Princess was sleeping and the mice looked everywhere for the ring. The Princess was snoring loudly and heavily. The mice climbed up on the bed and looked into the Princess' nostrils and to their great delight found out that she had stuck the magic ring in one of them.

One of the mice stuck his tail into the Princess' nose and tickled her. She sneezed and the ring flew out and the mice caught it right away and gave it to the cat.

The cat and the dog hurried back to the Black Sea, where the cat again climbed on the dog's back and the dog started swimming across the sea. Once they were in the middle of the sea, the dog said, "Let me hold the ring for a while."

"No," said the cat. "I won't let you hold it!"

They began to fight until, suddenly, the ring fell into the sea. When they finally reached land, the dog and cat lay down on the shore, exhausted. All at once, a small fish appeared. The cat caught the fish and, to its great surprise, found the ring inside.

When the cat and the dog returned the magic ring to Ahmad, he rubbed it and said, "Ring, Ring, bring me back my palace with everything in it, and throw my wife into the sea!"

As soon as Ahmad uttered those words, he found himself back in his beautiful palace with his mother, his cat, his dog and his donkey. The next day, the body of his wife the Princess was found floating on the surface of the sea. The King and the Queen died of grief and Ahmad became the King.

A True Story: A Good Deed Returned

Mr. Muhanad Arnaout, a specialist in the history of the Albanian Syrians, gave me the following true story about World War I, which was handed down in his family. It should be pointed out that the Albanians fought on the side of the Germans in this war. Mr. Arnaout's grandfather was among the Albanians who immigrated from Kosovo to Syria during World War I. Mr. Arnaout told me that the immigrants from Kosovo preserved many folktales and songs.

During World War I, one of the bloodiest wars the world has ever seen, a Greek army officer was taken prisoner by the German army. His family appealed to the Albanian Commander in Chief, Ibrahim Daya, on his behalf. Ibrahim Daya was the uncle of Muhanad Arnaout's grandfather and had good relations with the Germans. After intensive talks carried out by both parties, Ibrahim Daya succeeded in freeing the Greek officer and even invited him to stay in his household until he was sent back to Greece.

Many years passed, and Ibrahim Daya's son, 'Ismail Gorani,' also became Commander-in-Chief in the Kosovan army like his father before him. During a fierce battle against the army of Serbia, his soldiers ran out of ammunition. They were trapped in the mountains and besieged by the Serbian army. Unfortunately, they had no option but to escape to Greece.

As soon as Ismail reached Greece, he was arrested by the border guards and handed over to the army, who put him behind bars. His name, along with the names of other prisoners, was submitted to the Greek Minister of Defense so that he could give a verdict on the prisoners' fate.

When the Minister of Defense looked through the list of names, his eyes watered as he read the name "Ismail Daya Gorani, son of Ibrahim Daya." He summoned his officers and explained to them that he intended to release Ismail because he was the son of the Albanian Commander-in-Chief who had saved his life during World War I by obtaining his release from German captivity.

Later on, the Minister of Defense had to defend his support for Ismail Gorani in the Greek Parliament several times until he won his case and Ismael was released from prison.

Once Ismail was freed, the Greek authorities got in touch with his cousin – the grandfather of Mohanad Arnaout - who lived in Damascus and arranged to send Ismail to Damascus. Ismail Gorani spent the rest of his life there and is buried in the Qadam cemetery in Damascus.

Unfortunately, Mr. Arnaout does not know the name of the Greek Defense Minister who played such an important role in this story. I also searched for his name on the internet, but in vain.

Proverbs

- Every pear has a stem.
- Drop after drop of water forms a brook.

Three Albanian Recipes

When I finally got this Pite recipe from a young woman named 'Reem Ramadan,' an acquaintance on Facebook, I was told that I had found the key that would open all doors of the Arnaout folklore heritage. Pite is a traditional Arnaout food known world-wide. It is a large pie prepared with different fillings such as spinach, meat, and cheese. It said that Alexander the Great, who was claimed by the Albanians as their own, would never have conquered half of the world if he had not eaten Pite every day!

Spinach *Pite* — Albanian Spinach Pie

Pastry Ingredients

 2 lbs flour

 ½ cup oil

 1 package yeast

 1 tbsp salt

 3 cups lukewarm water

Filling Ingredients

 1 lb spinach

 1 medium onion

 1 sliced garlic clove

 3 tbsp olive oil

 ½ tsp allspice

 1 tsp salt

 Lemon to taste

Filling Method

Wash and drain the spinach

Cut the spinach into small pieces

Combine spinach with other ingredients and sauté

Let it cool

Method

Combine the dough ingredients, mix well and knead

Cover and put aside for 2 hours until it rises

Divide the dough into two big balls

Cut each ball into 9 smaller balls

Flatten first ball with a rolling pin into a 3-4 inch oval – as thin as possible

Brush with butter

Flatten second ball as above, brush with butter and stack on first oval

Now repeat with the rest of the balls

When you flatten ball 9, place it on a buttered baking sheet

Stretch it to fit sheet

Put layer 8 on top and pinch edges together

Put the spinach mixture on the dough

Then put the other seven buttered layers on top of filling, pinch edges together

Brush top with butter and bake at 350 F until light brown

Serve with a bowl of yogurt and a glass of tea

The following two Albanian salads were given to me by Nada Ghnem, who has a PhD in Engineering. Her Albanian grandmother on her mother's side used to prepare them for lunch on Fridays.

Albanians (Arnaouts)

FRIED PEPPERS IN YOGURT

Ingredients

5 red peppers or 2 green peppers and 3 red peppers

2 cloves crushed garlic

1 cup yogurt

2 tbsp tahini

Salt to taste

Method

Wash the peppers, cut them in half, and remove the insides

Fry them and place them on a sheet to absorb the oil, then cut them into small pieces

Blend crushed garlic, salt, and tahini into yogurt

Put the cut pieces of pepper in a bowl and pour the yogurt over them

GRILLED PEPPER SALAD

Ingredients

- 3 green peppers and 3 red peppers
- 3 tomatoes
- 1 tbsp vinegar
- 3 tbsp olive oil
- 2 cloves crushed garlic
- Salt to taste

Method

- Wash peppers, cut them in half, and remove the insides
- Put peppers on a round, greased baking tray and place them in the oven
- Watch peppers and constantly turn them over until the skin turns almost black
- Take them out, cover them with a cloth, and allow them to cool
- Peel off the skin and cut the peppers into small pieces
- Dice tomatoes into small pieces and add them to the green peppers
- Mix vinegar, oil, and salt together
- Add to the peppers and tomatoes
- The salad is eaten by scooping it up with pita bread like a kind of dip

EPILOGUE

Kan ya ma kan, a long time ago, there lived a young woman who loved words and people and all that was good. She lived in a country called Syria, and this country had captured her mind and heart. She was a gifted listener, and she carried with her a jewel box of questions and exclamations that she administered to the people she met as she persuaded them to tell her a folktale. Through her, they relived their childhoods as they told her folktales they had heard from their grandparents.

The stories were stored carefully. Only the best words were selected to tell them. Each story was seen as a small scene in the panoramic picture she was painting of her country.

What you have been reading in this book is the collection of stories the young woman so painstakingly collected. We hope you will see through them, despite the despair of the times they were written in, all the vitality and originality of her beloved country.

If you have enjoyed reading these stories, we have achieved our fondest wish. How pleased our Muna would be to know her book is now traveling the world and finding new readers!

Elaine Imady
Susan Imady
Damascus, Syria
February 2017

389

GLOSSARY

Abayee: My abaya –abaya is an ankle-length open cloak with long sleeves

Affendi: A Turkish honorific, now a term of respect

Agha: Originally a Turkish honorific, now a term of respect

Al hamdulillah: Thanks be to God

Amo: Uncle (paternal)

Baraka seeds: Black seed or black cumin seeds

Bey: A Turkish honorific

Bismillah: In the name of God

Burghol: Cracked wheat – a staple of rural Syria and the base ingredient in kibbi

Dashayshay: Coarsely ground, unboiled wheat - similar to semolina

Dibbis: Pomegranate molasses

Dubaa: Hyena

Eid: A celebration or holiday, usually referring to one of the two major Islamic holidays – the celebration after the fasting month of Ramadan and the celebration at the culmination of the Hajj pilgrimage, which commemorates the story of Prophet Abraham

Fetti: Syrian dishes in which yogurt and bread are the basic ingredients – there are many kinds of fetti

Ghee: Clarified butter

Ghoul: A mythical male shape-changing monster that eats people

Ghouleh: The female version of the above male monster – more common in Arab folklore than the ghoul

Haffara: a long, thin, handled tool used to core vegetables

Hajj: Pilgrimage to Mecca – one of the five pillars of Islam

Hakawati: The traditional Damascene story teller

Hammam: The public bath

Hoca: A Turkish honorific

Ifreet: A kind of jinni

In sha' Allah: God willing

Jameed: Dehydrated and fermented ball of goat's yogurt

Jinni (jinn is plural): A supernatural being created by God from fire – they can be good or evil and appear to human beings in many disguises

Kabeybi: Small "baby" kibbi

Khaleh: Aunt (maternal)

Kibbi: Very famous Syrian dish with many varieties – fried kibbi is made from a shell of meat and burghol that is filled with meat, onions, and nuts. It is shaped like a small, egg-sized American football

Kibbi darawish: A kind of fried kibbi

Mahlab: A Syrian spice from the kernel of the black cherry stone. Sold as a whole, small seed, it is pounded in a mortar before using.

Muallim: A teacher of small children

Muezzin: The man who gives the Muslim call to prayer

Muhafaza (muhafazat is plural): Province – Syria is divided into 14 muhafazat

Naoura: Water wheel

Nargileh: "Hubble bubble," water pipe, or hookah

Nart: The Narts were mythical, hardworking giants who sometimes helped people, and they appear in many Chechen and Circassian legends, myths, and folktales

Qadi: Judge

Salam: A greeting meaning "peace be upon you"

Sa'lawa: Another word for ghouleh

Semnay: Clarified butter; a kind of ghee

Sherwal: The traditional baggy trousers of Syrian peasants

Shirak: A round, very thin, peasant bread of Syria and Jordan

Tahini: Sesame seed oil

Tanjara: A round cooking pot with no handle

Tannour: Mudbrick oven for baking bread in rural Syria – also *tannour* bread

Tete: Grandmother

Thobe: An ankle-length robe with long sleeves worn by some Arab men

Vizier/wazir: A high-ranking official in certain Muslim countries

Zalageet: The high-pitched trilling sound made by Arab women to express joy

DAYBREAK PRESS

D aybreak Press is the publishing arm of Rabata, an international organization dedicated to promoting positive cultural change through creative educational experiences. Daybreak is committed to publishing female scholars, activists, and authors in the genres of poetry, fiction and non-fiction. It sponsors the Muslim Women's Literary Conference in October of each year and recognizes the fantastic achievements of Muslim women writers through the annual Daybreak Awards. For more information please visit us online at: rabata.org/daybreakpress or Email: daybreakpress@rabata.org.

CPSIA information can be obtained
at www.ICGtesting.com
Printed in the USA
FFHW020951070119
50078383-54920FF